# A MILLION KISSES IN YOUR LIFETIME

# A MILLION KISSES IN YOUR LIFETIME

NEW YORK TIMES BESTSELLING AUTHOR

## MONICA MURPHY

Entangled Publishing, LLC
644 Shrewsbury Commons Ave., STE 181
Shrewsbury, PA 17361
rights@entangledpublishing.com

Amara is an imprint of Entangled Publishing, LLC.

Visit our website at www.entangledpublishing.com.

Edited by Rebecca Barney
Cover design by Emily Wittig
Cover images byElena777/ Depositphotos and
mario7/Depositphotos
Interior design by Toni Kerr

ISBN 978-1-64937-586-5

Manufactured in the United States of America

First Edition August 2023

10 9 8 7 6 5 4

*He was christmas morning,*
*crimson fireworks and*
*birthday wishes.*
Raquel Franco

At Entangled, we want our readers to be well-informed. If you would like to know if this book contains any elements that might be of concern for you, please check the back of the book for details.

# CHAPTER ONE

It's been three years, four months, two days and a handful of hours since the first moment I set eyes on *her*.

The most beautiful girl I've ever seen.

The absolute bane of my existence.

She arrived at Lancaster Prep boarding school the first day of our freshman year, and no one knew who she was. Fresh and untested, open and accepting with that damn smile that seems permanently etched across her face. Every girl in our class immediately fell under her spell. Followed her everywhere she went. Desperately wanted to be her friend, even fought for the coveted spot of *best* friend. They copied her effortless style, and she set the school abuzz every time she wore her hair a different way or put on a new pair of earrings, for Christ's sake.

Even the older girls, the upperclassmen, were drawn to her. Completely captivated by a seemingly innocent green-eyed girl who has barely spoken ten words to me in the entirety of her time here.

I've heard from more than one person that I scare her. Intimidate her. I am everything she fears, as well she should.

I'd eat her up. Swallow her whole—enjoy every second of it, too.

And she knows it.

We are opposites in every single way you can think of, yet we're also unspoken equals. It's the weirdest fucking thing.

She is a leader they all follow, and she quietly rules the school, just like me. Her crown is light though. Made of spun glass and airy effervescence and with zero expectations. While mine is heavy and cumbersome, reminding me of my duty to the family. To the name.

To the Lancasters.

We're one of the richest families in the country, if not the world. Our legacy goes back generations. I own this school—literally—and everyone in it. With the exception of one person.

She won't even look at me.

"Why you staring?"

I don't bother looking in my best friend, Ezra Cahill's direction when he asks me that stupid question. We're at the front entrance of the school Monday after Thanksgiving break, the crisp early morning air cold enough to penetrate through my thick wool jacket. I should've worn a heavier coat. And I sure as hell am not going inside. Not yet.

I do this almost every single morning: wait for the queen's arrival, for the day she actually acknowledges me.

Currently, I'm running at a zero percent rate of acknowledgement.

"I'm not staring," I finally tell Ez, my voice flat. Uncaring.

Outwardly, I act like I don't give a shit about anything or anyone. It's easier that way. Trust me, I'm perfectly aware I'm a complete cliché, but it works for me. To care is to admit vulnerability, and I'm the least vulnerable motherfucker at this entire school. Shit slides off my back. Expectations are never placed upon me. My older brothers think I'm the luckiest out of all of us, but I don't think so.

At least they're acknowledged on a consistent basis. Sometimes I think my father flat out forgets I exist.

"You're looking for her again."

My head snaps in Ezra's direction, my glare hard and cold, though he ignores me, his only admission he's aware being that smirk curving his lips. "When do I not?" The question is sharp. Like a slap to the face, not that he cares.

The fucker actually laughs at me. "Fuck all this waiting around. How long has it been? You should talk to her."

I shift my position against the cold pillar I'm leaning against, my entire body lax. Casual. Though deep inside, I'm coiled tight, my gaze going to her once more. Yet again.

Always.

Wren Beaumont.

She ambles up the walkway toward the school's entrance. Toward me. With a serene smile on her face, she radiates light, casting her unique beam on everyone she walks past, lulling them into a trance. She greets everyone—but me—in that high-pitched voice, offering them a pleasant good morning like she's Snow fucking White. Friendly and sweet, and so goddamned beautiful, it almost hurts to look at her for too long.

My gaze drops to her left hand, where the thin gold band fits snug around her ring finger, a single, tiny diamond resting atop it. A promise ring she received at one of those fucked-up ceremonies where a slew of prepubescent future debutantes are put on parade in a sea of pastel gowns cut in demure lines. Not an inch of scandalous skin visible.

Their dates are their daddies, important men among society, who like to own things, including women. Such as their daughters. Sometime during the evening, they are put through a painful ceremony where they turn to face their fathers and repeat a vow of chastity to them while the ring is slipped onto their fingers. Like it's a wedding.

Strange as hell, if you ask me. Glad my father didn't put my older sister Charlotte through that bullshit. Sounds like something he'd enjoy.

Our little Wren is a virgin and proud of it. Everyone on campus knows about the speeches she gives the other girls, about saving themselves for their future husbands.

It's fucking pitiful.

When we were younger, the girls in our class listened to Wren and agreed. They should save themselves. Value their bodies and not give them away to us disgusting, useless creatures. But then we all got a little older and fell into relationships or hookups. One by one, her friends lost their virginity.

Until she was the last virgin standing in the senior class.

"You waste your time with that one, Lancaster," says my other closest friend, Malcolm. The fucker is richer than God and from London, so all the girls on campus throw their panties at him, thanks to his British accent. He doesn't even have to ask. "She's a right prude and you know it."

"That's half the reason he wants her," Ezra cracks, knowing my truth. "He's dying to corrupt her. Steal all her firsts from that mythical future husband she'll have one day. The one who won't give a shit if she's a virgin or not."

My friend isn't wrong. That's exactly what I want to do. Just to say I can. Why save yourself for some fake man who will do nothing but disappoint you on your wedding night?

So damn foolish.

Malcolm contemplates Wren as she stops and talks to a cluster of girls, all of them younger than her. Each of them fluttering around her as if she's their mama bird and they're all her dependent babies, eager for a scrap of attention from her.

"Wouldn't mind having a go at her either," Malcolm murmurs, his gaze narrowing as he continues staring at her.

I send him a murderous look. "Touch her and you're fucking dead."

He throws back his head and laughs. "Please. I'm not interested in virgins. I prefer my women to have a little experience."

"Definitely don't like it when they're scared of a penis," Ezra adds, clutching his junk for emphasis.

Ignoring their laughter, I refocus on Wren, my gaze wandering the length of her. Navy jacket with the Lancaster crest on it, white button-up shirt beneath, her full tits straining against the fabric. Pleated plaid skirt that hits her just above the knee. Always modest, our Wren. The white socks with the little ruffle, the Doc Marten Mary Janes on her feet.

Her one sign of rebellion—albeit a minor one. Those shoes sent the girls of Lancaster Prep into an absolute tailspin when she showed up to school wearing them, the day we came back from winter break our freshman year. It threw the girls off. Everyone at Lancaster wore loafers. It was an unspoken rule.

Until Wren.

By the beginning of our sophomore year, almost every fucking girl in attendance at Lancaster had Mary Janes on their feet, Doc Marten and other brands too. Funny how not a one of them wearing those shoes affect me the way Wren does.

The seemingly innocent shoes and little girl socks. The plaid skirt and flushed cheeks and the way she's always walking around campus at lunch or after school with a fucking lollipop in her mouth, her lips juicy red from the candy. I see her with a Blow Pop between her lips and all I can imagine is Wren on her knees in front of me. Her hand wrapped around my cock as she guides it into her welcoming mouth, that bullshit ring, her precious daddy gave her, twinkling in the light.

That's what I want. Wren on her knees, begging for my dick. Crying for it when I reject her. Because I *will* reject her eventually. I don't do relationships. They're a vulnerability I don't need. I see the way my father has treated my older brothers when they've brought women home to meet the family. Grant and his girlfriend, who actually works for him—Father made a pass at her, of course. My other brother Finn doesn't even bother bringing a woman around the family.

Not that I can blame him.

And then there's my sister, Charlotte. Our father sold her to the highest bidder and now she's married to a man she doesn't even know. He's a decent guy, but shit.

No way am I going to let my father meddle in my relationships. Best way to avoid that?

Don't have one.

I think of my cousin, Whit. How he was embroiled in a minor scandal during his senior year at Lancaster Prep with a girl who he's now about to marry. They even have a child—out of wedlock, the ultimate scandal for a Lancaster. My own mother calls Whit's future wife absolute trash, but that's what happens to a family like us. Our reputation precedes us, and sometimes it ends up getting tarnished.

A lot of the time it does.

And Whit's fiancé isn't trash. She's in love with him, and no one tolerates his shit like Summer.

Wren draws closer and I stand up straighter, trying to meet her gaze, but as usual, she refuses to look at me. I almost laugh when she says good morning to Malcolm. To Ezra.

She doesn't say a damn word to me as she walks past, entering the building without a backward glance, followed by the younger girls who all shoot me a look, big doe eyes, every single one of them.

The moment the door slams shut, Ezra starts laughing once more, slapping his knee for emphasis.

"You've been trying to catch that girl's attention for how long, and she still ignores your ass? Give it up."

The challenge is what drives me on, don't they see? Don't they get it?

"She's having a party, you know," Malcolm says once Ezra's laughter has died.

"For what?" I ask irritably.

"Her birthday. Jesus." Malcolm shakes his head. "For someone who's supposedly obsessed with Wren Beaumont, you don't know much about her at all, do you?"

"I'm not obsessed." I push away from the pillar and go and

stand closer to my friends, needing every detail. "When is this party?"

We're three weeks from winter break, in the throes of working on projects and preparing for finals for our last fall semester as seniors, and we're already exhausted. I'm over busting my ass for grades that don't matter since I have zero plans on going to college once I graduate. I've come into the first of three trust funds when I turned eighteen in September. Plus, my brothers want me to work for them at their real estate firm. Why go to college when I can just work toward my real estate license and then conquer the world selling luxury homes or giant corporations? My brothers have both residential and commercial divisions.

What I'd really prefer is to travel the world for a year or two after I graduate. Never work at all. Soak up the culture and the food. The scenery and the history. Eventually I can return to New York City, start working toward my real estate license, and eventually join my brothers' business.

I have options, despite what the old man might think.

"Her birthday is actually on Christmas, but she mentioned she's having the party the day after. Boxing Day," Malcolm says. "Most underrated holiday, I might add."

"Made-up holiday for the Brits to get more time off if you ask me," I mutter.

"The British equivalent to Black Friday," Ez adds with a grin.

Malcolm flips us both the bird. "Well, if she has it, I'm definitely going."

"So am I," Ez chimes in.

I frown. "You assholes were invited?"

Malcolm scoffs. "Of course. I assume you weren't?"

I slowly shake my head, rubbing my chin. "She doesn't speak to me. She definitely won't invite me to her birthday party."

"Eighteen and never been kissed." Ezra pitches his voice higher, trying to sound like a girl yet failing miserably. "You should sneak into the party and lay one on her, Lancaster."

"If only she could be so lucky," I drawl, enjoying his idea.

Far too much.

"The Beaumonts are rich as fuck," Malcolm reminds us. "The security for that party will be top notch, with all that priceless art hanging on their walls. Besides, her daddy watches over her like a fucking hawk. Hence the promise ring on her finger."

Ezra mock shudders. "Creepy if you ask me. Promising yourself to Daddy? Makes me wonder what's going on with that family."

I hate where my thoughts lead me after Ezra's comments. I hope like hell there's nothing strange, or dare I think it—*incestuous* going on within the Beaumont household. I highly doubt it, but I don't know her or her family. I only know what I witness, and I don't see nearly as much as I'd like.

"There were a lot of girls at this school wearing promise rings that were given to them by their fathers," Malcolm says. "They all copied Wren. Remember? It was a bunch of girls in our class and the freshmen when we were sophomores."

Annoyance fills me. "That trend died a slow, painful death."

Pretty sure Wren is literally the only one still wearing the ring.

"Right," Malcolm drawls with a dirty grin. "Now they're all a bunch of sluts, begging for our cocks."

I chuckle, though I don't find what he said very amusing. Malcolm has this way of insulting women that I find extra annoying. Yes, we're all a bunch of misogynistic assholes when we hang out together, but none of us go around calling girls sluts like Malcolm does.

"Such a derogatory term," Ezra says, causing us both to glance over at him. "I like whore better. Slut is just so...mean."

"And whore isn't?" Malcolm laughs.

We're veering off track. I need to bring the conversation back to Wren.

The sweet little birdy who's scared of the mean and nasty cat with fangs.

That would be me.

"If she's actually having a birthday party, I want an invitation to it," I tell them, my voice firm.

"We can't work miracles," Ezra says with a nonchalant shrug. But what does he care? He's already been invited. "Maybe you should try a gentler approach with Wren. Be nice for once, instead of your glaring asshole self all the time."

Seeing her makes me automatically scowl. How can I be nice when all I want to do is fuck her up?

Fuck her up as in, fuck her senseless. I see her, and I'm immediately filled with lust. Watching her suck a lollipop between her lips makes me hard. She's sweet, gentle Wren for everyone else.

I see her differently. I want her...differently.

I don't know how else to explain it.

"He's glaring just thinking about her right now," Malcolm points out. "He's a lost cause. Give it up, mate. She's not for you."

What the hell does he know? I'm a Lancaster for God's sake.

I can make anything happen.

Like fucking a virgin.

## CHAPTER TWO

## WREN

The moment the double doors clang shut behind me, I'm glancing over my shoulder, trying to spot Crew Lancaster through the opaque glass. But all I can make out is his dark blond head, plus the heads of his other friends. Malcolm and Ezra.

They don't intimidate me like Crew does. Malcolm is a giant flirt with a distinctly wicked edge. Ezra is always looking for a laugh.

While Crew stands there and broods. It's his thing.

I don't like his thing.

I frown at my thoughts—that last one in particular seemed vaguely inappropriate, and I do not have thoughts like that—

"Wren, will you sit with us today at lunch?" one of the girls asks me.

Oh. I get to thinking about Crew and I forget what's going on around me. Like the fact that I have four freshmen currently following me everywhere I go.

Smiling faintly at the girl who asked me about lunch, I say, "I'm so sorry, but I have a meeting to attend today during lunch. Maybe another time?"

The disappointment they feel at my rejection is palpable, yet I smile through it. They all reluctantly nod their heads at the same time, before they send each other a look and slink away, never saying a word to me.

It's odd, having a fan club when I do nothing but simply... exist.

A shuddery exhale leaves me, and I head down the corridor. The pressure these girls unknowingly put on my shoulders to be perfect sometimes feels insurmountable. They have me up on such a high pedestal, it would take nothing to send me tumbling. I'd end up a disappointment to all, and that's the last thing I want. The last thing they'd want.

I have an image to uphold, and sometimes it feels...

Impossible.

It's a lot of responsibility, being a role model for so many females like me. Lost girls who come from rich families. Girls who just want to fit in and belong. To feel normal and have a typical high school experience.

Granted, we're at an exclusive private school that only the upper echelon of society attends so there's nothing normal about our life, but still. We try and make it as normal as we possibly can, because some of us suffer, just like everyone else. With self-esteem issues, our studies, the expectations put upon us by family and friends and teachers. We feel unseen, unknown.

I know I did.

Sometimes I still do.

That's my goal in life currently—to help others feel comfortable and maybe even find like themselves. When I was younger, I used to think I might want to be a nurse, but my father talked me out of that profession by ranting on and on how nurses do a lot of hard work for nominal pay.

Nominal according to him. Harvey Beaumont is rich—he took over his father's real estate business when he was barely thirty and made it thrive, and now he's a billionaire. His only daughter becoming a nurse would be so beneath him and the Beaumont name.

It's something I can't even consider. It doesn't matter what I want.

Whatever move I want to make, I need his permission first. I'm his only child, his only daughter, and I can't be trusted to always make the right decision.

I make my way toward my first period class, Honors English. Only twenty people are allowed in the class our senior year and, of course, Crew is in there. I've had a few classes with him since I started at Lancaster Prep, but I've never had to sit by him or talk directly to him, which I prefer.

As in, I've never had a conversation with him. I don't think he likes me much, considering the faint sneer that's always on his face when he watches me.

And he watches me a lot.

I don't understand why. I avoid eye contact with him as much as possible, but every once in a while, I stare into his icy blue eyes and I see nothing but disgust.

Nothing but hate.

Why? What did I ever do to him?

Crew Lancaster is too much. Too moody and too dark and too quiet. Too handsome and magnetic and smart. I don't like how I feel when his eyes are on me. All shivery and strange. The feeling is completely unfamiliar and only happens when I'm in his vicinity, and it doesn't make any sense.

I turn down the corridor that houses the English department, eager to get to class early, so I can secure my seat in the front row, direct center. When my friends come into class, I always make sure they sit by me, so no one unsavory can. Like Crew.

Knowing him, if he had the chance to sit close to me, he would. Just to rattle me.

I think he would enjoy that.

Our teacher, Mr. Figueroa, doesn't assign seats, and he has a very relaxed attitude in this class. Considering we're seniors and he handpicked each student to be in his advanced class before the school year started, he trusts us not to act out or cause trouble. He just wants to "mold young minds," as he says, without restrictions or boundaries. He's my favorite teacher, and he's asked me to be a teacher's aide for the spring semester.

Of course, I immediately said yes.

I enter the classroom, coming to a sudden stop when I spot Figueroa in an embrace with someone. A student, because she's wearing a plaid uniform skirt and blue blazer. Her hair is a deep auburn, a shade I recognize, and when he gives her a nudge, she springs out of his arms, turning to face me.

Maggie Gipson. My friend. Her face is streaked with drying tears, and she sniffs, blinking at me. "Oh hey, Wren."

"Maggie." I go to her, lowering my voice so Fig won't hear us. That's what he tells us to call him, though all the guys make fun of the nickname behind his back. I figure they're all just jealous of the relationships he has with us girls. "Are you all right?"

"I'm fine." She sniffs again, shaking her head. Which tells me she's not fine at all, but I can't press the situation. Not when we're in class. "Just...I got into another argument with Franklin last night."

"Oh no. I'm sorry." Franklin Moss is her on-again, off-again boyfriend, and he seems very demanding. Always pressuring her to do things with him sexually. She just needs more conviction within herself, so she can tell him no, and mean it.

But she never tells him no. She's already had sex with him multiple times, and it doesn't matter. He doesn't love her like she wants him to.

I think it's because she gave it up to him too soon, but she won't listen to me. Once we entered our junior year and sex became more and more rampant, one by one my friends sacrificed themselves to the boys who begged them for it. At least that's the word my father used for it—a sacrifice.

The majority of them got nothing but heartache to show for it, and the words *I told you so* are always on the tip of my tongue when they complain to me, which isn't too often. Not anymore.

They know how I feel. They know what I might say. They'd rather avoid me versus hear the truth.

"You'll be fine, Maggie. Keep your head up," Fig says, his voice soft, his eyes glowing as he takes her in.

I watch him, the hairs on the back of my neck rising as I glance between the two of them. The way he said that, how he's looking at her—it's very familiar.

Too familiar.

Other students come shuffling in, their voices loud as they chatter animatedly among one another. I settle into my desk, zipping open my backpack and pulling out my notebook and pencil, getting ready for class to start. Maggie does the same, her gaze on Fig the entire time as he rounds his desk and settles into his chair, a few girls from class coming to talk to him. They all giggle when he says something, the sound grating.

I watch Maggie watch him, wondering at the jealousy I see in her gaze. Hmm.

I don't like that either.

Just as the bell rings, Malcolm and Crew enter the classroom, as per their usual habits. Sometimes they're even late, though Fig never marks them tardy for it.

I look away at the last second, not wanting to make eye contact with Crew, but it's no use. He catches my gaze, his cold blue eyes seeming to penetrate mine, and I stare at him for a second too long, my mouth growing dry.

It's like being caught in a trap, staring at Crew. It's almost scary, how much power he seems to wield with just a glance.

His name is on the building. His family has owned Lancaster Prep for hundreds of years. He's the most privileged student at this school. Whatever he wants, he gets. The girls all want a piece of him. Every boy here wants to be his friend, yet he shuns most everyone. Even a lot of the girls.

I hate to admit this, but we're a tiny bit similar, Crew and me. We just move about our day in a different way. He's cruel and unyielding, whereas I'm kind to a fault. I try to be nice to everyone I encounter, and they want a piece of me. He's mean and snarly, and they always come back for more.

It's odd.

I finally manage to look away from Crew when Fig stands in front of the white board, his booming voice drawing my attention as he launches into a lecture about our upcoming read, *The Great Gatsby*. I've never read Fitzgerald before, and I'm looking forward to it.

"Wren, can you stay after class for a moment? I'll make sure to give you a pass," Mr. Figueroa says to me as he hands me a battered copy of our assigned book.

"Sure." I nod and smile.

He returns the smile. "Good. I have a few things I want to run by you."

I watch him walk away, curious. What does he want to talk to me about? We're still three weeks away from winter break, meaning we're over a month away from me becoming his teacher's aide for the spring semester.

Not too sure what else there is to talk about.

"What does he want anyway?"

I glance over at Maggie, who's watching me with narrowed eyes. "You mean Fig?"

"Yes, I mean Fig. Who else?" Her tone is nasty. Like she's mad.

I lean back a little in my chair, needing the distance. "He just asked me to stay after class. That he had a few things to run by me."

"Probably has to do with me and what you saw." Maggie's expression turns knowing. "He'll probably ask you to keep it quiet. He doesn't want anyone to know."

"Know what?" I mean, I sort of get what she's implying, but there's no way Maggie would get—*involved* with our teacher, would she? She's been with Franklin for over a year. They're pretty serious, though they've argued a lot lately. Maggie says their relationship is extremely passionate in all ways, and makes it seem like that's her preference.

But why would you want to be with a guy who you hate and love equally? That makes no sense to me.

"About our friendship, silly." She watches Fig head back to his desk, a faintly dreamy look on her face. One she usually only reserves for her boyfriend, not our teacher. "People wouldn't understand."

"I know I don't understand," I retort.

Maggie actually laughs. "Figures. You know Wren, you can be kind of judgey."

I'm offended. And is that even a word? "You think I'm judgmental?"

"Sometimes." Maggie shrugs. "You're so damn perfect in everything you do, and you hold everyone else to the same standards, which is impossible. You get good grades, and you *never* cause any trouble. The teachers and staff all adore you. You volunteer every chance you get and all the younger girls think you can do no wrong."

She lists every one of those things like it's a fault versus a good quality.

"What do you think of me?" I brace myself, sensing I'm not going to like what I hear.

A sigh leaves her as she contemplates me. "I think you're a very naïve girl who's been sheltered your entire life. And when the real world finally bites you in the ass, you're going to be in for a big shock."

The bell chooses that exact moment to ring, and Maggie doesn't hesitate. She leaps to her feet, grabs her backpack, and shoves the book into it before she makes her escape without another word. Not even a goodbye to me or Fig.

The rest of the students exit quickly, even Crew, who doesn't look in my direction. He's too busy smirking at Malcolm about something.

Something I don't care to know about, that's for sure.

I remain in my seat, suddenly nervous over why Mr. Figueroa might want to talk to me. I set my backpack on my desk, shoving the old copy of *The Great Gatsby* in the front pocket, briefly checking my phone to see I have a text from my father.

*Call me when you get a chance.*

My stomach bottoms out. When he texts me to call him, it usually isn't about anything good.

"I have a free period right now." Fig strides over to the open classroom door and pulls it shut, cutting off the noise coming from the hallway. It's eerily quiet. "So it's the perfect time for us to—chat."

I rest my hands on top of my backpack and offer him a faint smile, fighting the nerves bubbling up inside me. "Okay."

He walks over to the desk Maggie just vacated and settles in, his warm gaze landing on mine. I take a deep breath, reminding myself that Fig doesn't want anything from me beyond help. Despite the whispers and the rumors I've heard over the years about him and other female students, he'd never try something like that with me.

Fig knows better.

"What did you want to chat about?" I ask, when he still hasn't said anything, hating how breathless I sound. Like I'm trying to flirt with him, when that's the last thing I want to do.

He tilts his head, contemplating me. "You're turning eighteen next month, aren't you?"

I blink at him, surprised he'd know that fact. I'm sure he could look it up in my personal file, but why would he care? Do teachers even have access?

"I am. On December 25th." The words fall from my lips slowly, my gaze questioning.

Where is he going with this?

A pleasant smile curls his lips. "A Christmas baby. How sweet."

"It's actually the worst. People give you presents wrapped in bright red paper with Santas all over it." God, I sound ungrateful, but I'm only speaking the truth.

"Is that a cardinal sin?" His brows shoot up, his eyes sparkling. I'm sure he's teasing me, but he doesn't understand what it's really like.

No one does, unless they have a birthday on a major holiday like me.

"I wouldn't say it's that bad. It's just no fun having your birthday and Christmas at the same time. Your birthday is never as special as someone's who's in June or whatever," I explain.

"I'm sure." He nods, his tone grave. "Well, Wren, I'm excited to have you come on as my TA next semester."

I'm thankful for the change in subject. I don't want to talk about anything personal pertaining to me.

"I'm excited too." I'm just grateful for the free period next semester. I've heard it's pretty easy, being his TA. He doesn't ask you to do much.

"You'll be replacing Maggie. That's why she was crying earlier. I told her I didn't need her to be a TA for me any longer."

Alarm races through me, leaving me cold. "What do you mean? I thought you always had a couple of TAs each semester."

"I do. I still do. Maggie just wasn't—working out." He leans over the desk, his face drawing closer to mine. Close enough that I can't help but rear back. "She's a little clingy sometimes."

His voice is low, as if he's letting me in on a secret.

Unease slips down my spine. "Clingy how?"

When he hesitates, I regret asking. Maybe I don't want to know.

"I gave her my phone number. In case of an emergency, or if she needed to contact me. I didn't think it would be any big deal."

If he says so. I think it sounds like a terrible idea. A teacher giving a student his number? That's a line he probably shouldn't have crossed.

"And she won't stop texting me. It's become...an issue," he continues.

An issue he brought on himself, is what I want to tell him. But I keep my mouth shut.

"I hope if we happen to exchange numbers when you become my TA next semester that you won't react that way. I'm looking for someone a little less...excitable. If you know what I mean." His smile, his entire demeanor is giving off easygoing, no big deal vibes.

But there's a tension in him, lying just beneath the surface. He just doesn't want to reveal it.

I'm having a hard time agreeing with what he's trying to say. I don't plan on giving him my number ever. That's inappropriate. And I'm not interested in having a relationship with him beyond student/teacher.

It makes me wonder what exactly happened between Maggie and Franklin—and if Fig has anything to do with it.

"I should go." I rise to my feet, grabbing my backpack and slinging it over my shoulder. "I don't want to be too late to second period."

I'm almost to the door when Fig calls out my name. I freeze, my hand on the doorknob as I slowly glance over my shoulder to see Fig standing directly in front of me.

Terribly close.

"You forgot your pass." He hands out the familiar blue slip of paper. "Don't want you to be marked tardy."

I face him fully and take the note from his fingers, hating how he tightens his hold on it for a second too long, making me tug. Pulling me even closer to him. He eventually lets me take it, his lips curved, his gaze dark.

"Thank you," I say weakly, turning toward the door.

"Bye, Wren," he calls once I've pushed the door open.

I don't answer him as I flee.

# CHAPTER THREE

## WREN

The rest of my day goes by normally. I worried about spending lunch with Maggie at our Honors Society meeting, but she ended up spending it with Franklin, so I didn't have to deal with her asking me about my conversation with Fig.

A conversation that's left me unsettled. It's like he was trying to communicate with me with unspoken words. Implying one thing while saying something else. I didn't like his tone. His familiarity. He knows what I'm about.

He knows I'm not interested in boys or drinking or sex. That's not my scene. It never has been. I'm a good girl.

Those kinds of things...scare me.

When I walk into my seventh period class, the last one of the day, I'm excited. Psychology is my favorite class. I love learning how people act and think, and the motives behind our actions. It's so interesting. Today is when Ms. Skov announces our last project for the semester, and she usually has us work in groups. There are a couple of girls in this class that I've worked on group projects with before, and I know it'll be easy to work with them again. They'll at least carry the workload equally with me.

Crew is already there, the only other class I have with him, as well as Ezra and Malcolm. They're all three sitting together in the back of the classroom, surrounded by girls. Girls who roll their skirts up so high they practically flash their underwear, and they have so much makeup on their faces I'm surprised they can open their eyes all the way. There's too much mascara on their lashes weighing them down.

I really shouldn't be so mean in my thoughts. It's not kind. I blame it on it being a Monday. The tension between Maggie and me—and Maggie and Mr. Figueroa. The conversation with Fig.

It's all so unsettling.

"Okay, everyone, listen up!" Skov slams the door behind her once she's entered the room, striding toward her desk. She's fluid movement and rhythmic noise, the bangles on her wrists clanging as she moves her hands. And she likes to move her hands *a lot*.

We all settle down, sitting face forward and paying attention. Everyone respects Skov. She's fun and interesting and makes us excited to learn, which can be a rarity, even at a private school that pays a generous salary to have the best educators on staff.

"As you're all well aware of, it's time to begin our final project for the semester. I took the time over Thanksgiving break to really think it over and I came to the conclusion that after doing pretty much the same damn thing for the last eleven years...I'm bored." Ms. Skov glares when Crew and his clan hoot and holler from the back. "Settle down, boys."

They go quiet and I can't help but glance at them over my shoulder, a smirk already on my face. It disappears when I catch Crew glaring at me, those blue eyes freezing me in place.

I hurriedly turn back around, clutching my hands together on top of my desk.

"I decided to change it up. You're going to work on your project on a one-on-one basis. As in, you'll be paired up with someone." She pauses. "And I'm the one who assigns you your project partner."

A collective groan rings through the room, though I still remain quiet. And a little nervous. Hopefully Skov won't pair me with someone too horrible.

Nerves eat at me when she starts rattling off names. I realize quickly she's pairing us up with someone who is our polar opposite. There are more groans. A couple of curse words dropped.

My heart is in my throat when she finally says my name.

"Wren Beaumont, you're going to work with..."

The pause lasts all of two seconds, but it feels like a lifetime.

"...Crew Lancaster."

*What?*

The word actually flies from my lips. I said it out loud, when I didn't mean to.

Oh God.

"Lucky fucker," I hear Ezra say, and I close my eyes in shame at the word he just used. I hate it when the boys curse.

And they know it.

Ms. Skov finishes with her list of partners and clears her throat loudly, causing the voices to go quiet. She scans the room as she starts pacing in front of our rows of desks.

"I know this isn't what you envisioned, but let me tell you what your assignment is. It'll make more sense when you hear." She stops in front of my desk, because, of course, I sit in the front row. "I paired you with someone I knew would be the opposite of you. I want you all to interview each other. Study each other carefully, because you're going to take all of that information you learn and give a speech on why and what makes your project partner tick."

There are more groans. I sink in my seat, gnawing on my lower lip. There is no way I'm going to tell Crew a single thing about myself. He hates me. Whatever information I give him, he'll find some way to use it against me eventually.

He's never done anything like that to me before, so maybe my thoughts are just...extreme.

"Now, of course, you shouldn't share any intimate, long held secrets you don't want anyone else to know. I know everyone in this class is mature enough to respect each other's privacy, but you know how it is. Things will eventually get out," Skov explains.

Exactly. And there's no way I want Crew to find out anything about me.

Nothing.

"For some of you, this is going to be hard. But I did some research on this type of project, and many of those involved said they found it almost easier to confess their darkest fears or most secret dreams to someone they consider a complete stranger. Those who know us, tend to judge us."

I think of what Maggie said to me, and how she thinks I'm too "judgey" sometimes. That kind of hurt. I never mean to be judgmental...

"For the next three weeks, there will be no lectures, no tests and no side projects. From now until winter break, I want you to spend this period with your partner. Get to know them, interview them about their past, ask them questions about their future and what they hope for. What they aspire to be. Try your best to dig below the surface. Be real with each other, gang! Don't present your picture-perfect Instagram life to someone. We all know that's a figment of your imagination," Skov teases.

"No one's on Instagram much anymore, Ms. Skov," one of the guys shouts, causing a few chuckles to ripple through the classroom.

She smiles, dipping her head in acknowledgement. "I'm an old person, what can I say? I can't keep up with what social media you kids are on."

There's more joking and laughter, but I can't focus. I just want to disappear. Drop out of the class.

Maybe even drop out of Lancaster Prep.

God, see? I can't get away from him. Thinking about my school makes me think of him because of the name.

"All right everyone! Break up into your pairs. Do it quickly.

I don't want a lot of chatter going on, unless you're talking to your partner." She smiles, looking quite pleased with herself as she goes and settles in behind her desk.

I rise to my feet, ignoring everyone else as I make my way to her desk. I stop just in front of it, staring at her until she finally looks up, her expression calm. "Can I help you, Wren?"

I can see it in her eyes, that flicker of disappointment before I even open my mouth. She knows what I'm going to say. "I was wondering if you'd be open to me switching partners."

Skov sighs, resting her arms on top of her desk. "I knew I'd have at least one of you come to me and ask this. Didn't expect it to be you."

"I don't like him." Best to be open and honest, right?

She arches a brow at my bold statement. "You don't even know him."

"How do you know?" Oh, that sounded snotty, and that's the last thing I want to be toward a teacher.

"I've been at this school a long time. I know the students don't think we pay attention, but we do. I see a lot. And I know for a fact you and Crew don't speak. Ever. Which is funny because the two of you are actually quite similar."

What in the world is she talking about? We aren't similar. Not even close.

"No, we're really not," I tell her. "We have nothing in common, and he's always so...mean to me."

"How is he mean toward you?"

My mind draws a complete blank. I hate it when people ask for examples because most of the time, I can't provide them. "He gives me dirty looks."

"Are you so sure about that?"

Now she's making me doubt every horrible look Crew has ever given me. "I don't know."

Her smile is small. "That's what I thought. First, you have to get to know someone in order to understand how they feel about you. Don't you think?"

"I already know that he doesn't like me," I say with all the finality I can muster. "It would be a lot easier for all of us if I could do this project with someone else. Maybe Sam?"

Sam is sweet. I don't have a lot of guy friends, but he's one of them, and he's always been kind to me. We've had the same honors classes together since our freshman year, and he even took me to the prom last year, though just as friends. He knows where I stand when it comes to relationships and sex, and he's never tried to push himself on me.

He hasn't even tried to kiss me, and with Sam, I would've considered it. I still might.

I glance over to where he usually sits, one of the girls with a too short skirt on sitting next to him, a little scowl on her face as Sam tries to talk to her.

"I'm sure he'd want to switch to be partnered with me," I tell Skov as I watch Sam smile at that girl, hoping to warm her up. Her name is Natalie.

She's not very nice. I avoid her and her friend group at all costs.

"I'm sure he would." Ms. Skov sounds amused, which I find faintly annoying.

This isn't a laughing matter. This is the next three weeks of my life. The most intense time at school—nearing the most important finals week of my senior year. The one that counts the most. Daddy reassures me our family money can get me into any college I want, but I also prefer to get in to one of my dream schools on my own merit.

My family name makes that nearly impossible, but we'll see what happens.

"So you'll let us switch then? I bet Natalie would love to do this project with Crew." I think they were together at some point over the last couple of years. At the very least, they hooked up.

Ew.

"No, I'm not going to let you switch. The whole point of this project is to learn about someone who isn't like you, who is part of a different friend group. You and Sam went to prom together last year so that means he's out as a possible partner," Ms. Skov says.

Everything inside me withers and dies. "It'll just be easier. I'm comfortable with Sam, and Crew makes me...uneasy."

"In a threatening way?" The concern in her voice is very, very real.

Maybe this is the weak spot, where I can burrow my way into getting what I want. "Yes, he always has such a horrible look on his face."

"So he's never actually threatened you in any way?"

This is where my honesty gets me. "No. Not really."

His mere existence feels like a threat, but I can't tell her that. I sound like a horrible person for thinking such a thing, let alone managing to say it out loud.

"I think you need a challenge, Wren. You're always wanting to help people."

"Girls," I stress. "What do any of the boys have to worry about at this school?" I'm not condoning it, just stating facts. "They're all golden. Untouchable. They can do whatever they want, especially the one whose name is everywhere we look."

My skin grows prickly with awareness when I sense someone approaching. I can feel his warmth, smell his deliciously intoxicating scent, and I know.

I just know who it is.

"Is there a problem?" Crew asks, his deep, rumbly voice touching something foreign inside of me.

I brace myself for Skov to tell on me.

"Miss Beaumont had a few questions on the project. Right, Miss Beaumont?" Ms. Skov smiles broadly at the both of us.

I nod, keeping my head down. I can feel his gaze burning my skin as he watches me, and I'm worried if I look into his eyes, I'll turn to stone. Like he's freaking Medusa with a bunch of coiled snakes as hair.

"You two should go sit down and get started," Skov encourages.

"Okay," I croak, daring to look in Crew's direction.

To find him already watching me, the look on his handsome face so dark, my knees nearly buckle.

# CHAPTER FOUR

## CREW

Wren Beaumont is petrified of me.

I knew the moment she shot out of her seat and went to Ms. Skov's desk that she was trying to get out of working with me. I could tell. Everyone else in the class was shifting into position, pairing up with their project partners, while I sat there by myself and fumed.

She's making me look like a damn fool, and for what? Because she thinks I'm going to treat her like shit? Doesn't she realize she's only making things worse? She's just too wrapped up in her own worry to realize what she's done.

Typical behavior.

In tandem, we turn away from Skov's desk, and Wren goes to hers, about to settle in when I speak up.

"I don't want to sit in the front."

A frown mars her pretty face. Because there is no denying it. Wren Beaumont is beautiful. If sheltered little prudes are your thing—which, apparently, they are for me. "Why not?"

"I'd rather sit in the back." I indicate with a nod toward my desk that sits empty.

She turns her head, studying the empty desks surrounding mine and her shoulders sag in defeat. "Okay."

Triumph ripples through me as I watch her grab her notebook and her backpack, my gaze dropping to her legs. She wears the skirt at normal length, which is too long in my opinion, and she has white knee-high socks on today, so I don't get to see much actual flesh. Those stupid fucking Mary Janes are on her feet, but they're not her usual Docs. They're another brand and style, sleek and shiny.

Little Miss Virgin is changing it up. Nice.

I follow her to the back of the room, taking in the straight line of her shoulders, the glossy straight brown hair that falls down her back. She's got the front pieces pulled back in a white bow like a child, and I wonder, yet again, if she's ever been kissed.

Probably not. She's as sweet and innocent as they come, with a diamond on her finger, promising her father she will keep herself pure until marriage.

I have no idea why I find that so damn attractive, but I do. I want to mess her up. Fuck her up. Fuck with her, actually fuck her until she's completely addicted to me and forgets all about her virginal promises. Destroying this sweet, innocent girl feels like sport.

A challenge.

A game.

She daintily settles into the empty chair beside mine, dropping her notebook onto the desk with a loud slap. I sit next to her and lean back, sprawling my legs wide, my foot nudging against hers purely by accident.

Wren immediately jerks her foot away as if I scalded her.

"Are you going to get a notebook out?" she asks.

"For what?"

"To interview me. Ask questions. Take notes."

"Skov said we're getting to know each other. It's the first day of the project. We still have a long time to go." This chick needs to chill the fuck out.

"I want to do well on this," she stresses, her gaze fixated on the empty page in front of her. "I want to get a good grade."

"I do too. We will. Don't sweat it."

"Is that how you approach everything?" She lifts her head, mossy green eyes meeting mine. Don't think I've ever sat this close to Wren in the over three years we've gone to school together, and I'm taken aback at how gorgeous those eyes are. "No sweat. Don't worry about it?"

"Yes," I say without hesitation. "Have a problem with that?"

"That's not how I operate. I work hard to get good grades and maintain my 5.0 grade average."

She dropped that little tidbit on purpose. A total flex for the virgin, big deal.

"We have something in common," I tell her, making her frown.

"What?"

"I have a 5.0 grade average too." We've both been in advanced classes since freshman year.

The look of disbelief crossing her face is undeniable. "Really?"

"Don't sound so skeptical. It's true." I shrug.

"I never see you study."

"We don't exactly hang in the same areas. I never see you study either."

Wren says nothing to that because it's true. We definitely don't hang with the same crowd in the same places.

"I'm sure the only reason you get good grades is because of your last name," she retorts.

Whoa. Little Miss Virgin has some bite.

"You think I have a 5.0 grade average because I'm a Lancaster? And I go to Lancaster Prep?" I raise a brow when she dares to look at me.

She drops her gaze, her head bent. "Maybe."

"I'm offended." Her head lifts, her expression now full of remorse. "I'm not an idiot, little birdy."

"Little birdy?"

"Your name is a bird." My nickname isn't that original, but

that's what she reminds me of sometimes. A sweet little bird, flitting from branch to branch. Chirping at everyone, the sound light and melodic.

"And your name is a sport. Shall I call you that? What's up, old sport?" She rolls her eyes.

Huh. She also has a bit of a sense of humor. I didn't think that was possible. She's always marching around campus, advocating for her causes. The plight of young rich women, which is totally uninteresting, if you ask me. I don't care about a bunch of virginal freshmen girls. Not like she does.

"You can call me whatever you want," I drawl. "Asshole. Fuckhead. Whatever. It doesn't matter to me."

There's no hesitation in her reaction. She's glaring at me, those narrowed green eyes shooting sparks in my direction. "You're revolting."

"Oh, my bad. I forgot you don't say such foul language."

"Things can be said without having to sprinkle dirty words throughout. They're completely unnecessary."

Her prim voice saying the word dirty is a complete turn-on. Meaning something is really fucking wrong with me.

"Sometimes the word *fuck* is really satisfying to say." I pause, already knowing the answer to the question I'm about to ask. "Have you ever said it before?"

She quickly shakes her head. "No. It's the worst word of them all, if you ask me."

"I don't know about that. I can think of some even more vulgar words to say." They're all on the tip of my tongue too, but I restrain myself.

Barely.

She scowls, and it's adorable. "I'm not surprised. You and your friends are extremely vulgar."

"Such a judgmental little priss, aren't you?"

Wren blinks at me, a hurt expression on her face. "You're the second person to call me judgmental today."

"Hmm, you should probably take that as a sign." When she doesn't say anything, I continue, "Perhaps you are a little judgmental."

"You don't even know me," she retorts, clearly offended.

I don't say anything—just look at her. It's a pleasure, watching her squirm, and she's obviously squirming, though it's more internal than anything else.

The perfect little princess everyone supposedly adores is getting called out for her faults—multiple times. I'm sure she doesn't like that.

Who would?

"This isn't going to work." She rises to her feet, her entire body shaking. She clenches her hands into fists. "I can't be your partner."

I gaze up at her, surprised. "You're giving up already?"

"I don't like you. And you don't like me. What's the point of working together? I'll talk to Ms. Skov some more after school. She'll listen to me."

"Don't be so sure." Damn, it's fun rattling her. She makes it so easy.

"Wouldn't you rather work with Natalie?"

"Not at all." I grimace. "She's shallow. Rude. Doesn't give a shit about anyone but herself."

The pained look on Wren's voice at me saying the word shit is almost comical. This girl clearly has issues.

"Sounds familiar." Her tone is haughty and cool, though I can detect the faintest tremble. "You two should get along perfectly. Didn't you go out with her?"

"Fucked her a couple of times." I say that on purpose, and it has the effect I want. The offended look on Wren's face is so extreme, I'm concerned she might burst into tears. "Nothing serious."

"That's disgusting."

"No, little birdy, it's perfectly normal. We're hormonal

teenagers. We're supposed to fuck anything we can get our hands on. Something you don't have a clue about." I decide to ask the question that's been lingering in my mind since we started this absurd conversation. "Have you ever been kissed?"

She lifts her chin. Appears ready to bolt. I wait for her to run, but surprisingly, she stands her ground. "That's none of your business."

The obvious answer is no.

My gaze finds Sam Schmidt, who's currently being tortured by Natalie as she drones on about her meaningless life. Though he doesn't appear miserable over it. He's too busy staring at her glossy lips as they keep moving. He's the guy that took Wren to prom last year. Two boring people who most likely had a boring time together.

Jealousy flickers deep inside and I shove it away. How can I be jealous of Sam? Because he got to dance with her? Put his hands on her? Have her smile at him and want to actually talk to him for an entire evening?

"What about Sam?"

Wren flinches, as if I said something that hurt her. "What about him?"

"He didn't try to kiss you on prom night?" I'm sure that would've met her dreamy, romantic expectations, though I get the sense Sam isn't particularly romantic. The guy is too in his head for that.

That fucker is scary smart.

"How did you know Sam was my prom date?"

If she really wanted to leave me and this conversation, she would've done so already. She almost did.

"It's a small school, and we're a small class. Everyone knows everybody." I hesitate, my gaze drifting down the length of her. The blazer and button-up shirt completely contain her tits, and what I remember from seeing her in the fairly demure dress she wore to the dance, the girl is stacked. "Do you remember who

I went with?"

"Ariana Rhodes," she immediately says, biting her lower lip the moment the words are out.

"See?" I incline my head toward her. "We know what everyone else is doing at all times."

"I only knew because I was friends with Ariana," she says.

Poor Ariana. She left the country after our junior year, banished to England to a finishing school in the remote countryside out in the middle of bum fuck nowhere. She was a broken girl with a talented mouth, who had a minor drug problem that blew up into a big one last summer. Her parents got her the hell out of here before it became worse.

"Well, maybe now we could become friends," I suggest, sounding like a goddamn villain, even to my own ears.

"I don't think so. Like I said, I'm talking to Ms. Skov after class." She slings her backpack over her shoulder. "Be prepared. You'll most likely be partnered with Natalie tomorrow."

"I'll miss you, Birdy," I call after her as she walks away.

She doesn't bother saying anything. Doesn't even look back at me.

Whatever she thinks she's going to say to convince Skov we shouldn't be partners, isn't going to work. I know Skov—and deep down, so does Wren. Our teacher's mind has been made up. This is how it's going to be.

Whether Wren likes it or not.

# CHAPTER FIVE

## WREN

I wander through the empty halls of school, trying to hold back the tears that threaten, but it's no use.

They're streaking down my face, and I wipe them away as best as I can, irritated with myself. With my teacher. With the entire day.

Thank God no one is really around to see them, since school let out almost thirty minutes ago.

I stayed after class, just as I told Crew I would, and spoke again to Ms. Skov, trying to plead my case. She wouldn't budge. She wasn't mean about it, but she refused to listen to my reasoning as to why I couldn't work with Crew. It didn't matter to her that he was vulgar and said crude things to me to get a reaction. That he didn't care about the project and just assumed he'd get a good grade because he's a Lancaster.

He didn't necessarily say that, but when I asked him about it and he didn't deny it, I can only assume.

Something I hate doing, but I did anyway—and mentioned it to Skov too. Her skeptical look told me she wasn't falling for it, but whatever. I was trying to think up every reason imaginable why I didn't want to work with Crew.

And I'm still stuck with him.

Stuck with his hateful attitude and his mocking gaze. His disgusting vocabulary and the way he looks at me. Like he can see right through me.

I hate that most of all.

I dash away another streak of tears, sniffing loudly.

"Wren!"

Turning, I spot Mr. Figueroa standing in the open doorway of the faculty room.

"Oh." I come to a stop, hoping that I don't look too terribly upset. "Hi, Mr. Figueroa."

Slowly he approaches me, his brows lowered in concern. "Are you all right?"

"I'm fine." I smile, hating how my chin wobbles. Like I'm going to burst into sobs at any second. "I just—had a rough afternoon."

"Want to tell me about it?"

I shouldn't. He doesn't need to know about my problem with Crew, or with Ms. Skov. But the moment he asks, showing that he cares, I start talking.

And don't finish until I've told him everything that happened during seventh period, leaving out some of the more embarrassing parts. Like Crew asking if I've ever been kissed.

As if it's any of his business. Besides, the answer is no, and if I told him that, he'd laugh at me and then would go and tell all of his friends. It would spread like wildfire that it's been confirmed—Wren Beaumont has never kissed a boy. Has never kissed *anyone*.

Though everyone probably already thinks that. They know how I feel about sex and relationships. I wear my virgin badge proudly, because why not? Societal pressure is too strong on girls. It's downright crushing. And we need to take ownership of our bodies in any way that we can.

I don't like being made to feel stupid for doing what I believe is right for me. Crew Lancaster has no business looking down upon me for not having sex. Just because he so easily gives himself away to whoever wants him doesn't make him a better person than I am.

Of course, the idea of Crew "giving himself away" to another girl has my curious mind whirring. I've seen him with his shirt off—last spring, near the end of school, when all the boys were out on the field, running around and goofing off as boys do. I sat in the bleachers with my friends, my gaze snagging on him when he ripped off his shirt, revealing tanned, smoothed skin stretched taut over lean, rippling muscle.

My mouth had gone dry. My heart started to race. And he glanced over at me, our gazes locking, as if he knew what sort of effect he had on me.

I banish the thought, refocusing on my teacher, the concern etched on Fig's face as I spill my story, his gaze warm and comforting. About halfway through my story, he put his arm around my shoulders, his touch loose as he steered me into the faculty room, which was blessedly empty. He sat me down at one of the tables, sitting right next to me. And when I finished, he patted my arm in reassurance, exhaling loudly.

"You want me to talk to Anne?"

I blink at him, realizing he's referring to Ms. Skov. I never think of her first name. She's just Skov to me. "I'm not sure if you should."

"I could put in a good word for you. Anne and I are pretty close. She'll listen to me." He settles his hand on my forearm, where it rests on the table, giving me a reassuring squeeze. "You shouldn't have to be tormented by Lancaster these next few weeks. You're under enough pressure as it is."

The relief that floods me at his understanding words is so strong I almost want to start crying all over again. "I'm under *so* much pressure. There's a lot going on right now."

"Did you turn in your college applications already?"

I nod, appreciating that's the first thing he thought to ask me.

The college thing causes a lot of stress, for so many of us. Most of the teachers seem to forget, piling on the work like we can handle it when most of us are on the verge of a nervous breakdown.

"That's good. I'm sure you have a few final projects and tests, including mine." His smile is soft. "Which you'll do fine with. You always do."

"I'm excited to read the book."

"I'm sure you are." He removes his hand from my arm and leans back, glancing about the room. "I'll talk to Anne. And maybe I'll even talk to Crew as well."

"What? *No.*" I hurriedly shake my head, ignoring the surprised expression on his face. "I'm serious, please don't bring this up to him. I don't want you drawn into this mess."

"I'm already drawn in. I want to help you." His jaw hardens. It's the most ferocious I think I've ever seen Fig look. "Guys like him get away with everything. Like they're untouchable, never thinking of how they affect other people."

"It's fine—"

"No, Wren. It's not fine. I won't stand by and let him hurt you repeatedly."

I press my lips together, worry making my insides twist. I don't want him talking to Crew about me. I can only imagine what Crew would say to him. What he would eventually say to me. Something about me sending my watchdog teacher on him or something like that. He'd call Fig all kinds of names and make fun of me, that mocking gaze never looking away from mine.

That's the last thing I want.

"Please, Fig." It's my turn to reach out and touch him, and he drops his head, taking in my hand resting on his arm before he lifts his gaze to mine. "Please don't talk to him. I can handle Crew on my own. But if you could put in a good word to Ms. Skov about my switching partners, that would be wonderful."

His brown eyes are steady as he watches me, and I can tell from the stern look on his face that he's displeased with my request. "All right. I won't talk to Crew. But I will speak with Anne. I'm sure she'll listen to reason."

"Thank you." I smile at Fig, shock coursing through me when he reaches for me, pulling me into his arms and giving me a hug.

It's awkward and weird, since we're both sitting down, and he's my teacher, so I do my best to quickly disengage. A shaky breath leaves me and I tuck a strand of hair behind my ear, all the air leaving me when I hear a familiar female voice screech.

"What the *fuck*, Fig?"

We both glance toward the door to find Maggie standing there, her mouth hanging open, her pale face suffused with red. Her narrowed gaze finds mine, and she glares, her expression full of hatred.

"Maggie." His voice is steady as he rises to his feet. "Calm down. It's not what you think."

Maggie snorts, entering the faculty room as if she's been in here a million times before. "Oh sure. More like it's *exactly* what I think. This is how it starts, right, Fig? All sweet and kind and caring to that one student. Making her feel special. You ask her to be your TA, bring her in like the innocent lamb to slaughter, right before you go in for the kill."

I leap out of my seat, eager to make my escape. "I need to go—"

"No, stay. Though I'm sure what I have to say will blister your virgin ears, you deserve to hear it. To know what this man does." Her smile is brittle, her eyes shiny, as if she might cry at any second. "Because for once in his damn life, he's going down. How many years have you worked at Lancaster? And how many girls have you fucked? I'm sure the list is endless."

I flinch at her using that word, my gaze sliding to Mr. Figueroa's, but he's not even paying attention to me.

He's too focused on Maggie, his hands clenched into fists at his sides, though he's trying to keep a calm exterior. "Watch your mouth, Maggie."

"Oh yeah, I need to protect the untried ears of the biggest virgin on campus, right, Figgy? I'm sure you're just dying to get in her pants. There's probably a lock on that vagina, but with your persuasive ways, she'll end up handing you the key. No problem." Maggie marches farther into the room, until she's standing directly in front of Fig, and I can tell he wants to touch her. Grab her.

Hurt her even?

I'm not sure.

And I don't know why I have to be a witness to this any longer.

"I-I'll leave you two alone so you can talk privately." I head for the door, Maggie no longer paying attention to me.

Fig isn't watching me either as I exit the room. They're too wrapped up in each other.

Like lovers.

# CHAPTER SIX

## WREN

I make my way back to my private room, grateful for the reprieve. Though I don't have long to bask in the silence because my phone starts ringing, startling me.

Dad flashes across the screen and I realize with a sinking feeling that I never did call him after he sent that text.

"I'm so sorry, Daddy. The day got away from me," is how I answer.

His chuckle is rich and warm, making me smile despite how agitated I still am over that confrontation between Fig and Maggie. And me, I guess. I've never been involved in something like that before in my life, and it was disconcerting. "I've heard from the head of the Art History Department at Columbia."

My heart flies up and sinks, all at the same time. "Oh."

"Don't you want to know what he had to say?"

I already know. He's dying to have me attend. Thanks to my father calling in a favor. "What did he say?" I keep my voice light and bubbly, exactly how he wants me. His sweet and happy daughter, who would do anything for her daddy. He feels the exact same way.

When it suits him.

"They want you, darling. You're in," he says, bursting with pride.

"Oh. That's so great," I say, my voice weak. I settle into the chair at my desk, staring out the nearby window that overlooks the campus. There are a few students milling about, though I can't make out who's who. They all look the same, since they're still mostly in uniform.

"You don't sound happy, Pumpkin." I can hear the disappointment in his voice. "I thought Columbia is where you wanted to go the most."

I never said that. I just always agreed with him when he went on and on about how great the college is and that they have a solid art program. Not that I want to be an artist—more like I want to study art. Someday, I would love to work in a gallery or museum. Maybe even have my own art gallery, where I could discover up and coming artists and support them.

That's my dream, and my parents know it. They also encourage it, though I don't think they believe I could do anything on my own. I'm sure they're just indulging me. Daddy's motives are not for me, but for himself.

Columbia University is too close. New York City means no escape because that's where my family lives. Where I grew up.

I want something different. Far away.

It'll never happen if my father has anything to say about it.

"I'm thrilled. Really." I infuse my voice with excitement, hoping he can detect it. "Thank you so much for talking to him. I can't wait to see where else I get in."

"Does any other college matter? I thought Columbia was end game."

I'm not about to list the colleges where I applied, the ones I really want to go to. He'll call them up and get me in, or he'll flat out tell me I can't go to some of the locations. I can't risk it.

"It's smart to have options, Daddy."

"You're right. Options are always good to have. A backup plan." I can envision him nodding his agreement.

"Can I talk to Mom?"

"Oh, I'm not with her. I'm currently in Boston, on business. I'll head home Friday. You should call her. She probably misses you."

"I was just with you guys this weekend." I arrived on campus yesterday afternoon, after spending all of Thanksgiving break with my parents.

"We always miss you, darling. Especially your mother. You know how needy she gets." I do. And she doesn't necessarily need me—she needs him. Not that he notices. "How was school?"

I give him a brief rundown, careful not to mention anything about Crew or Fig and Maggie. This day has been unlike any other day I've had so far at Lancaster Prep.

And I've had a lot of days here. I didn't expect my senior year to take such a dramatic turn, and so quickly. It's all drama I'm not necessarily involved in too, which is odd.

I don't usually find myself in the middle of drama.

We talk for a few minutes more before I hear a soft feminine voice say, "Harvey, let's go."

"I'll talk to you later, darling. Just wanted to give you the good news. Make sure you tell all of your friends. Love you." He ends the call before I can say goodbye.

I set my phone on my desk, staring at it. Who told my father it was time to go? A business associate? His assistant? I know he has a new one, though I don't remember her name.

Or was it another woman?

He's been known to cheat. Men as powerful as my father always seem to, which is disappointing. Maybe that's why loyalty is so important to me. Maybe that's why I'm afraid to get involved with any boy.

The boys never seem to stick around. And most of them can't be faithful, like it's in their DNA or something. They become so easily bored, so quickly. It's as if once a girl gives it up to them, they're ready to move on.

Look at Figueroa and Maggie. It's obvious they've been involved for a while, which is almost too much for me to comprehend. He's taking such a risk, getting involved with a student. The rumors have been rampant about him for years— even before I started attending Lancaster, but it's never been officially confirmed.

That little confrontation I observed was definite confirmation. Maggie was furious. I wonder if she truly thought Fig was trying to make a move on me? I don't think he was. I just think he was being kind. He felt bad for me because he caught me crying in the hall, and I've heard plenty of times that men don't like tears. My father never has.

Men. I don't understand them.

Suddenly craving a snack, I pull open a desk drawer and pull out a Blow Pop, tearing off the wrapper and tossing it in the small wastebasket before I pop it into my mouth. I suck on the sweet cherry candy, the burst of sugar coating my mouth.

My one major indulgence that's not healthy for me. I watch what I eat and drink, but I have a sweet tooth. I love candy, especially lollipops.

There's a sudden knock on my door and a booming voice sounds from the other side. "Beaumont! You have a visitor!"

I lean back in my chair, surprise rippling through me. Who could want to visit me? We're allowed visitors in the common room of the dorm building, which is on the first floor and near the front desk where our RAs sit with their all-seeing eyes. Visitors are the occasional townie or boys. Boyfriends. Lots of couples hang out in the common room after school.

I don't have a clue what that's like. I've never hung out in the common room with Sam, and he's my closest male friend. If we do anything together, it's during lunch, or we go to the library.

"Thank you. I'll be right down!" I call to the person who's probably already taken off.

Rising to my feet, I go to the full-length mirror, holding the lollipop in between my fingers as I contemplate myself. Popping the sucker in my mouth, I tuck my shirt deeper into the waistband of my skirt before I run a hand across my hair to smooth it out. I ditched the jacket the moment I got in my room, and I was about to change into more comfortable clothes before my dad called.

This will have to do.

I skip down the stairs, since I'm only on the second floor, not bothering to take the old, iffy elevator. That thing breaks down more than it actually works.

When I enter the common room, I come to a stop when I see who's leaning against the back of one of the old couches. His long legs are crossed at his ankles, and he's still wearing his uniform, though he ditched the jacket just like I did.

Crew Lancaster.

He's got his head bent, staring at his phone, his golden-brown hair tumbling across his forehead. The tie is gone too, a few buttons undone at the top, revealing the strong column of his throat. Offering a glimpse of his chest. His sleeves are rolled up to his elbows and my gaze drops to his forearms. They're corded with muscle and dusted with golden hair and an unfamiliar, weird feeling starts to pulse low.

Between my legs.

I try to ignore the sensation as I watch Crew, sucking hard on the candy in my mouth. He's not even doing anything but standing there, and he still exudes an authoritative aura.

Like he owns the place.

Which he does.

I lightly clear my throat and his head jerks up, his blue eyes meeting mine and I just stare at him.

His gaze drops to my lips, noting the lollipop stick, and I grab it, pulling the sucker from my mouth. "What do you want?" I ask him, my tone haughty, trying to hide the nervousness currently twisting my insides.

He pushes away from the couch and pockets his phone as he slowly approaches me. "You have a minute?"

I glance over my shoulder at the two RAs sitting behind

the desk, neither of them paying any attention to us. It doesn't matter. I want him to know I know they're there, and they would come to my rescue if this guy so much as says one rude thing to me. "Sure."

I follow him across the room until we're both settling in overstuffed chairs that face each other, a low, round table in between us. There aren't many other people in the room, so we have some privacy, though I'm sure it'll go around campus by the morning that Crew and Wren were seen together, talking.

Crew and Wren. I never realized before how close our names are. That they share three letters. Hmm.

"What did you want to talk about?" I ask when he still hasn't said anything. He must use his silence to unnerve people, and it works.

Quite well.

He leans forward, resting his elbows on his knees as he studies me. "Just had an interesting chat with Skov."

My eyes fall briefly shut with humiliation, and I plop the sucker back into my mouth. Could this day get any worse?

"I'm pissed at you, Birdy. She asked me if I've ever done anything inappropriate that would upset you so much. What the hell are you telling her?"

"Look, you don't want to work with me—"

"You're damn right I don't, not if you're going to tell teachers that I'm sexually harassing you or what the fuck ever you said to her." His words are like bullets, piercing my skin.

"I never said that—"

"You implied it. That's what I got from Skov, and I had to defend myself, without making you look like a flat-out liar." He hesitates, his cold stare making me helplessly shiver. "Which you are."

"I didn't say you did anything inappropriate. I just told her you said vulgar and crude things."

"Curse words. That's it. I never said anything about wanting to fuck you."

I'm taken aback at his fierce tone, and the words he just said. The dark way he skims his gaze over me. As if he actually might want to do—exactly that to me.

My mind takes me to a place I don't want to be, like I can't help myself. But really…what would it be like, to have this boy's total attention? To have him look at me as if he actually cares, and not with so much hatred?

My gaze drops to his arms, the way his biceps strain against the white cotton fabric. What would it feel like, to have him hold me? Whisper sweet words in my ear—though he's probably incapable of that.

I stare at his mouth, his lips. How perfectly shaped they are, with a slightly fuller lower lip. How would he kiss—soft and sweet? Or hard and fierce? I think of the books I've read, the movies I've watched, and imagine that first moment, the slow slide of his tongue against mine—

*No. No, no, no. That is the very last thing I want.*

"You said it just now," I point out shakily.

He glares. "I didn't mean it. Trust me, you're the last girl I want to fuck."

And now I'm insulted, which is so stupid. "Good, because you're never going to be able to."

"I know. We *all* know." He leans back in the chair, the tension easing from him somewhat. Why, I'm not sure. "You can't go around saying shit like that. Teachers take those kinds of accusations seriously, no matter how thinly veiled they are. They have to follow up on everything."

I wasn't even thinking about the repercussions of my words when I pled my case to Skov earlier. I was just looking for a way out of the project. "I'm sorry. I didn't mean to get you into trouble."

"Jesus, you really are always so damn nice, aren't you?" He seems surprised by my quick apology, though he just ruined it by being rude to me. What else is new? "You didn't get me into trouble. I just had to deal with Skov and her endless questions. Just—watch what you say. We're stuck with each other. Deal with it."

"Is that all you came here to tell me?"

Crew nods.

"You could've just sent it in an email." We have access to the student email directory, as well as the staff.

"I wanted to tell it to your face, so you could see just how pissed off I am." He glares, though it's not as intense as when we first started talking. "Your actions have consequences, Birdy. You need to be careful."

I hold onto the lollipop stick, sucking hard on the candy, contemplating breaking it apart with my teeth when Crew says, "One more thing."

"What?" I pull the sucker out of my mouth.

"You really shouldn't eat those things in front of me." He nods toward the sucker in my hand.

"Why not?" I frown.

"Watching you play with that thing in your mouth, all I can think about is you sucking my dick," he says, his tone casual. As if he just didn't say what he said.

And with that, he gets out of the chair and strides away, not letting me say anything in response. Leaving me sitting there, my mind going over all the things I could've said to him.

He's unnecessarily rude toward me.

Says extremely vulgar things, just to get a reaction.

Calls me by a silly nickname that I don't particularly like.

But he didn't give me the chance.

Typical. I'm starting to realize that's how everyone treats me. It's as if they all talk at me, instead of with me. I'm never involved in the conversation. I'm only supposed to sit there and take it like a good little girl.

It's annoying.

Worse?

It hurts.

# CHAPTER SEVEN

## CREW

I'm minding my own damn business, striding through the hallways at school and heading for the dining hall, since it's lunch, when I hear my name being called.

Glancing over my shoulder, I see it's fucking Figueroa headed my way, his expression full of steely determination.

Great.

Since we came back from Thanksgiving break, it's been one thing after another, and it's only Tuesday. It frustrates the shit out of me. Most of it has to do with Wren too, which is interesting.

There's more to Wren Beaumont than just a pretty face. Which deep down, I always knew. She's smart, she's kind to everyone—maybe not me, but I asked for that—and she's influential. All things I can respect, though for whatever reason, the word respect and Wren never went together in my brain.

I'm attracted to her. When does respect ever come into that equation for me? Not like I degrade girls for sport, but they're just…there. To talk to and to kiss and to fuck.

That's it.

It threw me off when she apologized for what she said about me to Skov. I exaggerated a little bit, just like she did, acting like our teacher questioned me thoroughly regarding her allegations, which she sort of did, but it wasn't as bad as I made it out to be. I was trying to make Wren feel like shit, and it worked, though I guess I shouldn't have been surprised.

The girl is easily manipulated, and too nice. So damn nice, you get a toothache every time you talk to her.

She's just that sweet.

Wren has to know I say all that shit to get a rise out of her, and it's so easy. Her bird feathers get ruffled way too quick. It's almost fun, making her upset.

Harmless fun.

"Can I have a word with you for a minute?" Figueroa asks me, his tone friendly. Though I sense the dark undercurrent beneath his words. He's unhappy.

Guessing he's unhappy with me.

What the fuck did I do now? Oh, I know, I was born. With that supposed silver spoon in my mouth. He resents all of us rich kids, which is funny as fuck, considering he works at one of the most exclusive private schools in the entire country.

But he's in to the broken, damaged little rich girls with daddy complexes. He eats them up with our discarded silver spoons and then spits them out when he's done with them. On to the next one, and the next one after that. Like a damn shark swimming in the sea, a killing and eating machine.

Figueroa is more like a grooming and fucking machine among the halls of Lancaster Prep, the sick asshole.

"What's up?" I flick my chin at him, already bored.

"Let's talk somewhere more private? It'll just be a minute."

I follow him until we're outside, standing in front of the school's main entrance. Not many people are out here at the beginning of lunch, so this is probably the most private spot he could've found.

"What did you want to talk about?" I ask him, when the dick still hasn't said anything. He's too busy looking around, as if he's afraid someone's going to leap out of the bushes.

"Wren Beaumont," he says as he faces me fully. "Leave her alone."

His tone is threatening, his gaze hard.

What the actual fuck? Is this guy for real right now? "What are you talking about?"

"Stop giving her grief in class. She doesn't like it. And since she's stuck with you for the psychology project, she's not happy about it," Figueroa explains. "At all."

"Did she tell you that?" I'm floored. She actually went to this guy, trusted him and told him how much she hates working with me?

That's some fucked-up shit.

"Yes, she did. Yesterday. She was crying. Upset that she couldn't get out of being your partner on that project." His lips tighten into a thin, firm line. "I tried my best to console her, but she wouldn't stop crying."

"I bet you tried comforting her," I retort. This guy.

We all know he's been fucking Maggie in secret these last few months. Franklin dumped her ass when he found out. Rumor has it she's knocked up with Fig's kid, though I don't know if that's true.

I hate how all the girls call him Fig. It pisses me the hell off. He doesn't deserve their attention or affection. He's a complete creep.

"Tell Skov you want a new partner," Figueroa demands.

"No."

"She'll listen to you. They all do." That last sentence is said with total disdain.

He hates that I'm a Lancaster. That he can't do shit to me because it won't stick. I'm untouchable—for the most part. Hell, I'm the most powerful person on this campus and most of the staff and admin don't give a shit what I do. They're used to the Lancaster white glove treatment.

For whatever reason, this guy cares—he cares way too much

about me. And not in a good way.

"Maybe I actually want to work with Wren." I take a step closer, my voice dropping. "Maybe I want to get closer to her. Learn all of her secrets. What she likes. What she doesn't like. Maybe the more time she spends with me, she'll let down her guard and realize I'm not such a bad guy after all."

Figueroa snorts. "Please. You don't give a damn about her."

"And you do?" I raise my brows. "You're just mad because you know, no matter what, she'll never fall for your tricks. Not really. She's such a good girl, Fig. A sweet little virgin who wouldn't dare to *ever* think of having sex with a guy who's old enough that he could be her father. Her teacher. Someone she looks up to and admires."

Figueroa's expression tightens, but he doesn't say a word.

"Unfortunately for you, Wren is saving herself for her future husband, not some perverted asshole who's her English teacher," I tack on, just to make him angry.

It works. His jaw shifts and his lips part as if he's about to say something, but I cut him off.

"Wren might consider something with me though. I'm young— more age-appropriate than you, that's for damn sure. Really, we're just two horny teenagers, working together on a project, you know? We'll definitely need some library time. Private time. Just the two of us. I know she likes to study in there—it's her favorite place on campus. I'll make sure we're tucked away in a dark corner, and I'll eventually make my move there, among the stacks."

"She'll slap you in the face."

"Or, she might spread her legs wider and let me slip my hand in her panties. I'm willing to take the chance. I'm sure once she gets a taste of it, of me, she'll be willing—and eager—to experiment. With me." I grin when I see the anger flare in his eyes. I'm having way too much fun with this, but I probably need to back off. Knowing him, he'll run to my little birdy and tell her what I said about her. She'll probably believe him too.

Which I suppose she should.

Figueroa blows out a harsh breath, pointing at me. "You so much as touch a hair on her head and I'll—"

"You'll what?" I interrupt, my voice scarily calm. "You'll kick my ass? Bring it. I'm not scared of you. And I know for a fact I could destroy you, *Fig*. You're getting soft in your old age. Your only exercise currently is rolling around with Maggie in the back seat of your car. Don't you get sick of that shit?"

He stares at me, his breathing coming fast, his chest rising and falling rapidly, and I shove my hands in my pockets, already bored with our conversation.

"Leave Wren alone," he demands, but there's not as much power in his voice as there was before. "That's all I'm going to say. If you do anything to hurt her, there will be repercussions."

I watch him walk away, amused. His threats are meaningless. They just make me want to break down that steel wall Wren guards herself with and fuck with her head. Drive her out of her mind with wanting me.

I could do it. It wouldn't take much. The girl is starved for male attention. You can just tell. She keeps herself so tightly locked up. She's got to be harboring some secret fantasies deep inside.

Hopefully they're sick and twisted, and she'll let me reenact them with her.

This stupid project will help me get to know her. Learn what makes her tick. I'll figure her out, seduce her, and next thing I know, I'll be walking into Honors English with her under my arm, my lips on her forehead as I stare at that jealous dick we call our teacher, sitting behind his desk.

It'll be my fucking pleasure to put on that performance.

A smile curls my lips as I, once again, head for the dining hall.

I can't fucking wait.

· · ·

The moment I enter Skov's classroom, my gaze lands on Wren. She's sitting in my seat, Malcolm and Ezra flanking either side of her at their desks, the two of them competing with each other as they try to gain Wren's attention. Her head whips back and forth between them, a little smile curling her lips.

I suddenly understand what Figueroa must've been feeling when I said all of that shit about Wren to him. I'm feeling it now, no matter how much I want to deny it.

Full-blown jealousy consumes me, making my blood run hot and my head want to explode.

She doesn't notice me until I'm practically standing on top of her Mary Jane'd feet, her head lifting so her wide-eyed gaze meets mine. My friends go silent. Feels like the entire room goes quiet as we study each other.

"You're sitting at my desk, Birdy," I accuse, my voice low.

My friends share a look, no doubt noting my ominous tone.

Wren is seemingly unaffected by it. "I thought we were meeting back here."

I glance over at Ezra, who has a shit-eating grin on his stupid face. "You shouldn't talk to her."

The smile fades and now he's scowling like me. "You don't own her."

"You definitely don't," Wren retorts when I bring my attention back to her. "They're my friends. Unlike you."

Point taken. One for Birdy.

"Lay off, mate." This comes from Malcolm.

I ignore them both, focusing all of my attention on Wren. "Where am I supposed to sit then?"

"You can sit at my desk." She points at the empty seat in the very front of the room.

I grimace. "No thanks."

She rests her linked hands on top of my desk and the wildest idea comes to mind.

I decide to go with it.

Dropping my bag on the floor, I stop right next to Wren's—my—chair and sit down, nudging her over, which isn't too difficult.

She weighs nothing, and doesn't take up much room on the chair. Her scent is heady, like a burst of wildflowers in the middle of a spring meadow. She's warm and soft, and she fits perfectly by my side. I sling my arm around the back of the chair, half-tempted to pull her onto my lap.

"Crew!" She's squealing. "What are you doing?"

"What does it look like?" She angles her head toward mine, and our faces are so close, I can make out the faint freckles across her nose. Of course, she has freckles. She's sweetness personified. "I'm sitting at my desk."

"I told you to go sit at mine." For someone who looks ready to swallow her tongue, she's pretty damn calm. The only tell being her pulse fluttering rapidly at the base of her throat. Her lips part, soft puffs of breath leaving her, and I wonder what she'd do if I leaned in and pressed my mouth where her pulse throbs.

She'd probably freak the fuck out.

"I told you yesterday, I don't like sitting in the front." I draw a finger down the center of her back, and she jumps. "Guess we'll have to share."

The bell rings, Skov waltzing in at the last minute, doing a double take when she sees Wren and me sharing a seat. "Don't you two look cozy."

Nervous laughter sounds from the class, Ez included. Wren sits up straighter, her hands still on top of my desk, her attention for the teacher and no one else.

I don't bother looking at Skov. I'm too enraptured with the delicate curve of Wren's ear. The tiny pearl earring dotting the lobe. The smooth skin of her neck, how perfectly glossy and straight her dark hair is. She parts her lips, her gaze flitting to mine quickly before she looks away.

She can feel my eyes on her. Good. Do I make her uncomfortable?

Or does she like it?

My vote is uncomfortable. She's not used to male attention.

"Crew, sit somewhere else, please," Skov orders.

"Wren is sitting at my desk."

Skov is mildly amused, I can tell. She points at Wren's empty spot. "Then come sit at her desk."

"I don't like sitting in the front."

"I'm sure you don't." Skov crosses her arms. "Come on."

"I'll go," Wren says, sending me another one of those quick looks. She doesn't seem mad. More like she's afraid to go against authority. "I don't mind."

Ezra and Malcolm both groan their displeasure at losing their rapt audience of one, and I send them a murderous look.

It does nothing to shut them up, the assholes.

Wren slides off the chair we're sharing as Skov begins taking attendance, and I immediately miss her warmth. Her scent. She's rattled, if her shaking hands are any indication as she snatches her notebook from the top of my desk and clutches it in front of her chest.

"Can I leave my backpack here?"

Nodding, I sprawl in the chair, as if I don't have a care in the world, but damn, I'm a little rattled too.

Having her so close threw me.

And I don't like it.

# CHAPTER EIGHT

## WREN

I don't like being made a spectacle in front of the entire class, and that's exactly what Crew just did. Attention doesn't bother me, as long as it's not negative.

What he just made happen felt negative. Almost mocking. Shoving me to the side, so we could share his desk chair, even for those brief few minutes, had been annoyingly...

Pleasant.

He's solid. Hard muscle and hot skin. Broad shouldered with a wide chest and strong arms. Being so close to him, his arm slung behind me and across the back of the chair, I felt as if I was in a Crew Lancaster cocoon. And I liked it. I liked having him close. My heart started to race with having him so near.

It's still racing.

I settle into my seat, dropping my notebook on top of my desk, keeping my attention on Ms. Skov, who's wrapping up attendance. The hairs on the back of my neck slowly rise, and it takes everything inside me not to turn around and see who's staring.

I already know. I can feel his gaze on me, heavy and brooding. As subtly as I can, I glance over my shoulder, catching his eyes on me and no one else, and then he does the strangest thing.

He smiles.

It's small and quick, and if I told anyone else it happened, no one would believe me, but oh my God, Crew just smiled at me, and my stomach feels like a million butterflies just took flight, their fluttering wings making me tingle everywhere.

All from a brief smile.

What in the world is wrong with me?

"All right. Pair up with your partners. We're all set there, right?" Skov settles her gaze on me, her thin brows shooting up. I barely nod, embarrassed at being called out yet again. "Okay. Get to work."

I leave my desk and make my way back to Crew, who's sprawled in his seat rather insolently, his expression one of pure boredom, his body language telling me he'd rather be anywhere but here.

I step over his feet and plop myself into the empty desk next to Crew, which was just abandoned by Ezra. "Did you prepare anything for today?" I ask, knowing what his answer will be.

"No." He lifts his heavy-lidded gaze to mine. "Did you?"

Nodding, I flip open my notebook to the list of questions I jotted down earlier this morning, when I realized I had no choice, that whether I liked it or not, Crew would remain my psychology partner. "I came up with a few questions."

"For me?" He sits up straighter, rubbing his hands together. "Let me hear them."

I send him a strange look, surprised by his behavior. I don't understand this boy. I know I wouldn't be eager to hear any questions he might have for me.

"They're simple questions—" I start, but he shakes his head, cutting me off.

"Nothing is simple when it comes to you, Birdy. I get the feeling you're going to try and figure me out."

He's so right, not that I think I have a chance in doing so, not with the limited time we have to work on this project.

Figuring out Crew Lancaster and what motivates him will probably take months. Maybe even years.

"That's what we're supposed to do," I stress, leaning across the desk. His gaze drops, lingering on my chest, and I realize a second too late, my breasts are basically resting on top of the desk.

I pull away, my cheeks going hot, and when he returns his gaze to mine, he's smirking.

"I have an idea," he says, and I momentarily forget my embarrassment, just grateful he's willing to come up with something.

"What is it?"

"Let's make a list of our assumptions about each other." It's his turn to lean in closer, those glittering eyes of his never leaving mine. "I'd love to find out what you think you know about me."

I don't want to know what he thinks about me. I'm sure it's all terrible, more gossip than facts. Most of the guys at this school don't care for me, only because I won't succumb to their charms.

I sound like my mother with that term, but it's true. I don't fall for the coercion, or their lies. They flatter, they say what us girls want to hear, and next thing we know, we're on our knees for them. Or beneath them in a bed, or a car, or whatever dark, supposedly private place they can get us into. They ask for provocative photos, claiming they're private, and then they share them with their friends. Making them a mockery.

They don't respect women. And that's the problem. They're all a bunch of bros, who are eager to add girls' names to their sexual conquest list. That's it.

That's all we are.

Even Franklin and Maggie, who I thought were sort of solid, really aren't. Theirs is a volatile relationship that I wouldn't want.

None of the relationships at school are ones I long for. The boys are either too forward, or too immature. I'm not a particularly religious person, but I do value my body and my morals. My parents have always stressed how careful I should be when choosing who I eventually share my love and my body with.

They do their best to talk me out of being in any sort of relationship with someone right now, especially my father.

"Well?" Crew's deep voice pulls me from my thoughts, and I blink him back into focus. "What do you think?"

"You'll be nice?" My voice is cautious.

"You want real? Or do you want nice?"

I guess when it comes to Crew and his opinion of me, they don't go hand in hand.

Good to know.

"Real," I say, sounding a lot more confident than I feel.

"I want the same. Lay it all out, Birdy. Tell me all your secret thoughts about me."

His words make me bristle. How can he take something that sounds so innocent and make it seem dirty? "I don't have secret thoughts about you."

"I'm disappointed." He chuckles, the rich sound making me warm. "I have all sorts of secret thoughts about you."

Interest flares deep, and I mentally tell it to stop. I don't care about his secret thoughts of me. "I don't want to know them."

"You sure about that?" His brows knit together. He seems surprised.

I shake my head. "Absolutely. I'm sure every one of them is lewd."

"Lewd." He chuckles again. "Nice word choice."

"I'm sure it's accurate." I flip past the list of questions I created in my notebook, smoothing my hand across the fresh clean page. "Are you ready?"

"We're doing this?"

"Let's set a timer." I grab my phone and open up the clock app. "Ten minutes?"

He nods. "Tell me when to start."

I set my phone on the desk and grab my pencil, my finger

hovering above the start button as Crew grabs a pen, clicking it a couple of times, I'm sure only to bother me. "Ready?"

"Yeah."

"Let's go."

I start scribbling immediately all of the things I've heard about Crew over the years. A few of my own assumptions. Considering we've never really talked before, I have no clue if any of the things I'm listing are actually true or not.

Which makes me feel kind of bad, but I don't let the guilt linger for too long.

I'm too busy writing out my list.

Crew, on the other hand, takes his time, scribbling a few words here and there. Tapping his pen against his slightly pursed lips as he contemplates whatever he's thinking about.

Knowing that he's thinking about me throws me a little. Makes me hesitate, my pencil still poised upon the paper, my breath lodging in my throat when I glance up to find him watching me. We stare at each other for a beat until he points the pen at me and immediately starts putting something down on paper.

I do the same, writing blindly, not quite sure if I'm actually composing words but hoping for the best.

What did he just realize? Was it good or was it awful? Knowing Crew, it was most likely terrible.

When the timer finally sounds, it makes me jump, my pencil falling to the floor and rolling in Crew's direction. He stops it with his foot, bending down to pick it up while I attempt to shut off the alarm. I finally manage it at the same time he hands me my pencil, his hand covering almost the entire thing.

Forcing me to touch him when I take it from him.

His fingers slide over mine, electricity crackling between us at the connection, yet his expression is completely neutral. As if what just happened never happened at all.

Again, another figment of my imagination.

"Read me your list," he demands, his voice smooth as silk as it washes over me.

I shake my head, frowning at the scribbles across my paper. "I need to decipher what I wrote first."

He holds a single sheet of paper in front of him, his eyes narrowing in seeming concentration. "I'll go first then."

I lean back in my chair, my entire body stiff with worry. Pressing my lips together, I swallow hard and wait for the horrible words to come.

"My assumptions about Birdy." He glances at me over the top of the paper. "That's you."

I huff out a laugh, though there's really no sound. "Right."

"She's nice to everyone. She wants people to respect her. To listen to her. Though really most everyone just takes advantage of her."

I remain quiet, absorbing his words.

"She's a good student. Smart. She wants teachers to admire her. To think she's a hard worker. Some admire her too much." The pointed look he sends my way has me immediately thinking of Figueroa.

Doubtful. But whatever.

"She surrounds herself with a lot of people, but I never see her with actual friends. She's closed off. Thinks she's better than everyone else. Judgmental."

I wince at that particular word.

"...she's also a prude. A virgin. Not interested in sex. Probably scared of it. Scared of guys. Scared of everyone. Possible traumatic experience in her past?" He lifts his gaze from the paper, his eyes meeting mine. "And that's it."

My mind is awhirl with a mountain of things. None of them positive.

I'm not scared of guys. I'm not scared of anyone.

Well, this particular guy makes me feel a decent amount of fear, not that I'd ever admit it.

"That was plenty, don't you think?" I try to smile at him, but it comes out so twisted, I give up.

"You don't have an opinion about any of my thoughts?" He raises his brows in question.

"There was never a traumatic experience in my past."

"Are you sure about that?"

That he would even doubt me...

"Yes," I say firmly.

We're quiet for a moment, watching each other, his gaze finally dropping from mine to stare at the scribbles on his paper. All while my mind goes over what he said about me.

Take advantage of her.

Closed off.

Has no friends.

Judgmental.

A prude. A virgin.

Scared of sex.

None of that is true. I have friends. I don't let people take advantage of me, and I'm very open. I'm not afraid of sex. I'm just not interested.

The only thing that's true is I'm a virgin. And proud of it.

"Your turn," he says softly, yet again interrupting my thoughts.

I glance down at the paper in my notebook, squinting at some of the hurried words I wrote. I can't make out all of them, but here I go.

"Crew Lancaster believes he's untouchable, which he mostly is. He's arrogant. Demanding. Sometimes even a bully." I chance a quick look at him, but he's not even paying attention to me. He's tapping his pen against his pursed lips and I get caught up in the shape of his mouth yet again.

There is no reason for me to be so fascinated with his lips. He says horrible things. That's reason enough to hate that mouth. To hate him, and everything he stands for.

I force myself to keep reading.

"He's smart. Charming. Teachers do what he says because

his family owns the school."

"Facts," he adds.

I roll my eyes and continue.

"He's cold. Doesn't say much. Scowls at people a lot. Not very friendly at all, yet everyone wants to be his friend."

"It's the name," he says. "They only care because I'm a Lancaster. They want to get in good with me."

He interjects a lot, while I didn't say a thing.

"He's threatening. Cruel. He doesn't smile—like ever. Probably not happy with his life," I finish, deciding to add something at the last second. "Has poor little rich boy syndrome."

"What the fuck is that?"

I ignore his f-bomb, trying my best not to visibly react. "Come on, you know."

"I want to hear you explain it." His voice is deadly soft and the gleam in his eyes is so, so cold.

Taking a deep breath, I tell him, "It's when your family ignores you completely and money is the only source of love. They pay attention to you when they deem it necessary but otherwise, you're just a prop in their so-called family life. You're the baby, right? They're too busy getting involved in everyone else's lives, while they forget all about you."

His smile is not friendly. It's downright menacing. "Interesting description. I get the sense you're familiar with that sort of treatment."

I frown. "What do you mean?"

"Harvey Beaumont is your father. One of the largest commercial real estate brokers in all of New York City, correct?" When I just stare at him, he continues, "My brothers are in the business. They know all about him. He's a ruthless motherfucker who has an enormous collection of priceless art."

Hearing him call my father, a mother-bleeper, is a tad disconcerting.

"My mother is the collector," I admit, the words falling from my lips without thought. "It's the only thing she's got in her life that makes her truly happy."

Oh God. I hate that I just admitted that to him. He doesn't deserve to know anything about my private life. He could take any info I give him and twist it. Make me sound like a sad little girl.

Which according to him, I am. And maybe he's right. My mother doesn't particularly like me. My father uses me as a prop. They're both too controlling over my life, and use that to say they want to protect me. I thought I had friends, but I now I'm not so sure.

"The penthouse in Manhattan that showcases all of the art—you grew up there?"

I try to ignore the alarm rushing through my veins at his words. At his familiarity with my life. A life I don't really feel a part of anymore, since I've been at Lancaster Prep for most of the last three years, going on four.

Sitting up straighter, I push all thoughts of poor pitiful me out of my mind and smile politely at Crew.

"We moved to that apartment when I was thirteen," I confirm.

"And you're an only child."

My smile fades. "How do you know all of this?"

Crew ignores my question. "No other brothers or sisters, right?"

I am my father's pride and joy, and my mother's worst nightmare. She told me exactly that last summer, when we were on vacation on the Italian Riviera and my father bought an extravagantly priced piece of art by an up-and-coming artist he just discovered.

*We* just discovered. My father purchased the piece because *I* liked it, completely ignoring her opinion. Mother hated it. She prefers more modern pieces while this artist had works that harken back to the Impressionist period.

She was so angry with me when Daddy bought that painting

and paid an enormous amount of money to have it shipped home. She said he didn't listen to her anymore, only to me, which wasn't true.

Harvey Beaumont doesn't listen to anyone but himself.

"No siblings," I finally admit. "I'm an only child."

"That's why he's so overprotective of you, right? His precious daughter, promised to him thanks to a—weird purity ceremony."

His gaze lands on the diamond ring on my left hand, and I immediately drop it into my lap. "You all just love to make fun of me for that."

"Who's 'you all'?"

"Everyone in my class, at this entire school. It's not like I was alone at that ball. There were other girls there—some even currently attend this school. The ceremony wasn't creepy. It was special." I close my notebook and bend down, reaching for my backpack. I shove everything inside and zip it closed before I stand, slinging the backpack over my shoulder.

"Where are you going?" he asks incredulously.

"I don't have to tolerate your questioning any longer. I'm leaving." I turn away from Crew and head for the doorway, ignoring Ms. Skov calling my name as I exit her classroom.

I've never left class early before, but at this moment, I feel powerful.

And I didn't even apologize.

# CHAPTER NINE

## WREN

It's lunchtime the next day, after my fleeing seventh period moment, and I'm approaching a table filled with girls in my senior class. Girls I've gone to school with since the beginning of freshman year, but none of them I can really call my friends.

Not anymore.

Oh, we were close when we all first started. I was brand new and a complete novelty to them, though I didn't see it then. They thought I was cute and stylish, and I reveled in their attention and approval.

It's all I've ever wanted. Approval. To fit in.

Instead, I stood out. As time went on, they eventually became weary of me, and we all grew farther and farther apart. Until they eventually stopped wanting to spend time with me. They're all still perfectly polite toward me, as I am to them. The only one who truly tolerates me is Maggie, but not as much since the start of our senior year, especially after I saw what happened between her and Fig.

Something that's never been brought up again, which is fine by me. Maggie hasn't confirmed it, but I heard recently that she and Franklin are done for good.

That's probably best. I hope our teacher had nothing to do

with their breakup, though deep down, I have a feeling he did.

If only I had actual proof—then I would say something. But I can't go to anyone with only a suspicion. What if I was wrong?

I startle the girls when I plop down at their table uninvited, but not a one of them actually says anything to me. Instead, they all smile in my direction before resuming their conversations.

I start eating the salad I purchased in the lunch line, eavesdropping on their nonstop chatter. Hoping to hear a tidbit about Crew I could take back to him during psychology class today.

After walking out on him yesterday, he completely ignored me in Honors English earlier. He wasn't even waiting in his usual spot at the front entrance like he does every day. I actually missed my morning scowl courtesy of Crew Lancaster.

Not that I think he's always waiting for *me,* but it sort of feels that way most of the time...

I quietly eat my salad, not really engaging in any of the conversations around me until Lara asks me a direct question.

"What's up with you and Crew Lancaster?"

I pause in my chewing, the lettuce turning to mush on my tongue. I choke it down, take a sip of water and clear my throat before I answer, "Nothing."

"Oh. Well, he's been asking about you." This comes from Brooke, who is Lara's best friend.

My fork drops with a clatter into my nearly empty salad bowl. "What do you mean?"

The best friends share a look before Brooke continues.

"He was asking questions about you. About your family. Your past." She shrugs.

I hate that he was digging for information. Why didn't he just come to me and ask? "What did you tell him?"

"What could we tell him? We don't know a lot about you, Wren." Lara's tone is a little snotty. She's always acted like she has an issue with me.

This is why I don't bother arguing with her.

"Why is he asking about you anyway?" Lara stares me down.

"I don't know. We're working on a project together," I admit. "In psychology. He's my partner. Skov assigned us."

"Ahh. I didn't take that class this year." Lara actually sounds disappointed.

"Me either. We should've, just for the chance to possibly work with Crew," Brooke says, right before they both start giggling.

I wish I could tell them how God-awful it is working with Crew, but neither of them would believe me, so I keep my mouth shut.

"He is so incredibly sexy," Brooke says when the giggling has mostly stopped. Lara nods her agreement. "Last summer, I heard he was seeing that one girl who's TikTok famous, with like a trillion followers. The one who made a movie?"

"Ugh, I remember. She played all coy and never confirmed it, but I swear I saw photos of them together. She's disgustingly gorgeous. Of course, he dated her." Lara rolls her eyes before glancing down at herself. "I could be so lucky to be as thin as she is."

I take in Lara's figure as discreetly as I can. She's very fit. I don't know why she's complaining.

"I hear he likes older women," Brooke says, but I assume she's only heard gossip about Crew and his supposed preference for older women. I mean really—how does she know? "I can't remember the last time he was dating a girl who goes here."

"Freshman year maybe?" Lara nods her agreement.

"What about Ariana?" I say.

They both study me, eerily quiet.

"He went to prom with her last year," I remind them. "Weren't they a thing?"

"Oh please. She was a total drug addict. She went to rehab over the summer." Brooke wrinkles her nose. "He was probably with her to get in good with her dealer."

Lara laughs, slapping her best friend's arm. "Brooke!"

"What? It's true. I know Crew Lancaster likes to partake on occasion."

How she knows this, I'm not sure, but whatever.

"And like I said, he prefers older women. He definitely doesn't like girls who go to Lancaster, that's for sure. Not anymore. Maybe it's the uniforms?"

I tune them out, glancing down at my uniform skirt, how it drapes over my knees, covering them completely. I hear my father's voice in my head, always so old-fashioned with his remarks about my appearance. Reminding me I need to keep my skirts at a modest length. No need to show off excess flesh. I've been sheltered my entire life, especially after that one painful incident when I was twelve.

When I was young and gullible, and believed everything I was told.

My gaze drops to the stupid shoes on my feet. I remember feeling like they made me seem so stylish, and for a while, I was. The girls here at school considered me a total trendsetter for wearing these shoes.

Now I look at the Mary Jane's and realize that I look like a child. A little girl with white socks, my bare legs exposed to the chilly air because of "fashion."

What sort of fashion is this? I look ridiculous.

I *am* ridiculous. No boy will ever notice me when I look like this.

Certainly not Crew Lancaster.

And since when do I want that particular boy to notice me? He's horrible.

Yet attractive.

Rude.

Somehow charming.

He doesn't like me. He basically said that to me, more than once. I don't like him either. Yet...

I'm drawn to him.

Frustrated, I kick the leg of the table so hard, the entire thing rattles, making the girls' laughter come to a complete stop.

"Did you just kick the table?" Lara asks me after a moment of uncomfortable silence.

"Sorry." I shrug, not sorry at all. The word just automatically leaves me every time someone calls me out on something. "I didn't mean to."

"You know, Wren, you're actually really lucky, working with Crew on that project," Brooke says, and I wonder if she's suddenly being extra nice to me because of my mini temper tantrum.

"How's that?"

"Well, it's psychology, right? Does he have to reveal his innermost secrets or fantasies to you? That could be juicy." Brooke's eyes are sparkling with excitement at the idea of learning Crew's secrets.

I don't want to know them. He's mean and horrible, and he calls me judgmental? He's just as bad as I am.

Maybe even worse.

"I doubt he'll reveal anything to me," I admit.

They both stare at the diamond ring on my finger, sharing another one of those looks that communicate so much without ever saying a word.

"True," Lara says, shifting in her seat.

Normal Wren would pretend she didn't hear that, or see the shared look, like they know something I don't. She'd try to change the subject or leap from the table and go find someone else to talk to, but I'm not feeling very 'normal' right now.

"What do you mean by that?" I ask.

"Well, that ring you're wearing, for one," Brooke says, clearly the braver one of the two. She just comes straight out with it, no hesitation.

"What's wrong with my ring?" I grip my hands together, turning the ring so the diamond doesn't show.

"It's kind of a stigma, you know? Crew probably won't talk to you since he believes you're nothing but a scared little virgin promised to her daddy."

Brooke smirks.

So does Lara.

"I'm sure all of the boys think that," Brooke adds.

I leap to my feet, purposely nudging the table with my thighs, so I shove it in their direction, making them both yell out their displeasure.

"Oops. Sorry," I tell them before I turn and leave the dining hall, ignoring all the curious looks aimed in my direction as I flee.

God, I'm so stupid. So…I don't even know how to describe myself. Pitiful?

Pathetic?

I want to smack myself in the face. Only I would think I'm being strong by shoving a table in their direction after they said something so rude, only for me to go and apologize to them before I run away.

No wonder Crew thinks so little of me. I'm a sheltered little girl pretending to be an almost adult. About to turn eighteen and I haven't done anything.

Nothing.

It never bothered me before, so why does it bother me now?

For the second time this week, I can feel tears flowing down my face as I walk the empty corridors of school, speeding up my pace as I go past the faculty room.

No way do I want Fig to come out and catch me again. He'd probably offer me more comfort and try to feel me up.

A shiver steals over me at the thought. The first horrible thought I've had about Figueroa since I started at Lancaster.

Maybe I shouldn't be his TA.

I head for the side doors that lead to the quad and push through them, the icy cold air is like a slap to the face. I suck in a sharp breath, tucking my jacket around me, wishing I'd brought my coat, but I left it in my locker, not planning on needing it until school was finished.

Rounding the corner of the building, I come to a stop when I spot three male heads bent together. A puff of smoke rising from the center of the circle they make. I know every single one of them, and I come to a complete stop, frozen.

Not just from the chilly air, but from the straight panic zipping through me at seeing these particular three boys.

Ezra, Malcolm, and Crew.

It's Malcolm who spots me first, holding a strange looking cigarette to his lips before he wraps them around it and takes a long, hard pull. His gaze finds mine, surprise clearly on his face as he removes the cigarette from his lips and drops his hand to his side. "Oh fuck, look who's joining us."

He elbows Crew, Ezra glancing over his shoulder, his eyes going wide when he spots me. "Great," Ezra moans, "you going to tell on us, Beaumont?"

Tell on them for what? My nose wrinkles when the scent hits me. Like skunk. Oh…

They're smoking weed.

Crew watches me with those all-seeing blue eyes, never saying a word, and my heart starts to beat faster.

"I'm sorry." I *really* need to stop apologizing all the time. "Didn't mean to interrupt. I was just leaving…" I start to walk backward slowly, one step at a time, keeping my eyes on them. At the last second, I turn.

And run.

# CHAPTER TEN

## CREW

I chase after her, Malcolm and Ezra right behind me, both of them shouting, "Get her!"

Fuck, could they be any more obvious? We don't need to call attention to ourselves. Don't need to startle her either.

Too late for that. She's broken out into a full-on run, her dark hair streaming behind her, that annoyingly childish yet sexy white ribbon at the back of her head bouncing with her every step. Her skirt flares, offering us a glimpse of slender bare thighs and I pick up speed.

I'm going to catch her first. Fuck these guys.

Ezra gives me a run for my money, keeping the same pace as me while Malcolm gives up, falling into a spasm of constant coughing. Too much weed does that to a person.

And Malcolm really loves his weed.

Determination filling me, I pump my arms and legs, pulling past Ezra, ignoring his "hey!" as I take the lead over him once again. I'm drawing closer to Wren, her steps slowing as her head turns left, then right.

Trying to figure out where to go next.

*Don't worry, little bird, I've almost got you figured out.*

I'm within reaching distance when she darts to her left,

dodging me at the last second.

"Birdy!" I yell her hated nickname at her, and she glances over her shoulder, her frightened gaze meeting mine.

It's wrong that I feel joy at seeing the fear in her eyes, isn't it? Yet a small part of me does. Knowing she's scared gives me a sense of power, a heady rush straight to my head.

And my groin.

Looking back at me is where she made her mistake. It slows her step, throws her off when she realizes just how close I am. Her hesitation gives me the advantage, and I grab hold of her, sliding my arms around her waist from behind and yanking her off her feet.

She howls, her curled fists coming back and nearly connecting with my balls, smacking me in the thigh instead. "Put me down!"

"Sshh," I whisper near her ear, tightening my hold on her as she thrashes about. She's so damn angry, I can feel the vibration just beneath her skin. "Calm the fuck down."

"Let me go!" She pushes against my hold and I shift my right arm upwards, readjusting my grip. Her tits press against my forearm, lush and full, and I wonder what she looks like naked.

She stomps her foot on top of mine, making me curse. Of course she chooses today to wear the damn Doc Martens.

Those things should be labeled as weapons.

I loosen my grip and she makes her move, trying to lunge out of my arms. I slip my hand beneath her uniform jacket, cupping her right tit.

Wren goes completely still, her breathing ragged, her chest rising and falling. I don't let go of her.

It's like I can't.

"Wh-what do you want from me?" Her voice trembles. Her entire body is shaking.

And it's all my fault.

"What do you think?" My tone is dark. Suggestive. From the way I'm touching her, she can figure it out.

Though that's not what I want.

Not right now.

"Crew!"

I glance over my shoulder to find Ezra approaching, his brows lowered in question. I shake my head once, glaring at him, and he takes the hint, turning on his heel and heading back toward where Malcolm stands. Far enough away from us that they can't hear.

But they can watch.

"Let me go, Crew. Please," Wren pleads, her voice full of agony. I see it written all over her pretty face as it nearly crumples with pain.

Fear.

"Afraid I'm gonna have to keep tabs on you, Birdy, after what you just saw."

"I won't say anything," is her immediate response.

"Better not. We can't afford to get in trouble this late in the game. It's zero tolerance here, baby." I give her breast a gentle squeeze and a whimper escapes her. "Even with Lancasters. They find out I'm smoking a blunt on campus, I'm out."

Wren remains quiet, her body convulsing with shivers.

"There's a lot of power in your hands right now." I dip my head closer to her ear, my lips practically brushing her flesh. "You could ruin me."

She shakes her head, her silky hair brushing my face. "I-I won't ruin you. Or your friends. I didn't even really see what you were doing."

"Liar." I drop my other arm so it bands across her hips, directly across the front of her skirt. It would take nothing for me to slip my fingers beneath it and touch her. "You saw us."

"You were smoking—something."

Come the fuck on. She had to know exactly what we were smoking. "You're going to have to forget what you saw."

"O-okay."

"You have to promise, Birdy." My hand slides down, toying with the hem of her skirt.

Wren whimpers. "Please don't hurt me."

Oh Jesus. She thinks I want to *hurt* her? In the middle of campus at lunch? "I'm not going to do anything to you that you don't want." I let my lips tickle her earlobe, making her shiver. "I'm pretty persuasive when I want to be."

"You're disgusting," she spits out.

"You're telling me if I reach beneath your panties right now, you won't be wet for me?" I don't believe it. She might be scared of me, but she's also aroused. I swear I can smell it on her. Sharp and fragrant.

Intoxicating.

A low, frustrated moan leaves her. "Stop saying things like that."

"Why? Because it goes against everything you believe in? Or because you like it too damn much?" I streak my thumb across the front of her tit, wishing she didn't have on such a heavy bra, so I could tell if that nipple was hard or not.

"Both," she admits.

So softly, I almost didn't hear her.

It's my turn to be surprised. "Really, Birdy?"

She doesn't respond. Her breathing is still rapid, and tremors wrack her body, but she doesn't seem as scared as she was only a few minutes ago.

I decide to push my luck.

"I would never hurt you." I nuzzle her hair, breathing deep the sweetly floral scent of her shampoo. Damn this girl smells good. "Unless you like it that way."

She whimpers. I'm probably confusing the shit out of her. She truly is such an innocent.

It would be fun, toying with her.

"I don't like you," she bites out, sounding nothing like our usual sweet little Wren.

"Good." I breathe into her ear, smiling when I feel her shiver. "I don't like you either. Though I can't deny I like the way you feel in my arms."

"Is this how you operate then? You have to force girls to get what you want from them?"

A chuckle leaves me. She is a vicious little thing when she wants to be. Didn't believe she had it in her. "I don't have to force girls to do shit. Including you."

"Let me go then. See if I'll stick around," she taunts.

"Nope." I make a popping sound with the word, tightening my hold on her. "You'll go running to Headmaster Matthews' office and tell him everything. I can't risk it."

"I told you I wouldn't tell. Come on, Crew. Please. Let me go." I like the pleading. I'd enjoy some begging too, but not here.

"We need to make a deal, Birdy."

"What do you mean?" She stiffens in my hold, wariness tingeing her voice.

"I don't trust that you're not going to tell on us. At the very least, you'll go to Figueroa, and I don't want to deal with his shit. Which means I'm going to have to trail you everywhere you go."

An irritated sound leaves her. "That's ridiculous. And impossible. Besides, I already promised."

"I don't trust you."

"I won't say anything!" she practically wails. "What would I gain by doing something like that?"

"Getting rid of me and my friends from school so you don't have to deal with us ever again. Sounds perfect, right? Don't bother denying it. I can feel your hatred for me emanating from your body."

The bill rings, the sound faint since we're so far from the building, and she jerks against my hold. "Let me go. We have class."

"We can be late."

"No." She shakes her head, her soft hair brushing against my chin. "I'm never late. I don't even skip."

"Yes, actually, you do. We all witnessed you leaving Skov's class early yesterday," I remind her.

An irritated sound leaves her. "That was different. And all your fault, I might add."

"I'm not responsible for your actions." I caress her tit, my touch extra gentle, noting how she slowly melts against me. "Like I said, we need to strike a deal, little birdy."

"I'm not striking anything with you. Let me go." She stomps on my foot again, surprising me. A yelp escapes and she breaks free, running away from me, never once looking back.

I watch her go, ignoring the pain throbbing in my toes, focusing on the erection I'm sporting thanks to having Wren's sexy little body rubbing against mine for the last five minutes.

Hearing her confess that she both hated and liked what I said shocked me.

That's something I'm definitely going to explore further.

# CHAPTER ELEVEN

## CREW

By the time I'm walking into seventh period, I spot Wren sitting in her usual spot, front and center, her head bent, her long hair covering most of her face. I pause in the open doorway, studying her. Everyone is talking. Laughing. Except Wren. She just looks...sad.

Defeated.

Alone.

Her obvious pain is a heavy weight on my shoulders and it annoys the shit out of me. I'm responsible for it, and normally that sort of thing wouldn't bother me, but come on. What the hell did Wren Beaumont ever do to me?

Not a damn thing. Her mere existence annoys me, but that's not reason enough to torture her.

Or is it?

Jesus. I am seriously fucked up.

I walk past her, not saying a word, making my way to the back of the classroom and plopping my ass in my usual seat. Ezra is already at his desk, Natalie perched on his knee, eating him up with her sultry gaze while he sits there like a dumbass and basks in it.

Knowing how Natalie operates, I don't trust her motives. She wants something from Ez. That's the only reason she's paying attention to him.

"Crew, oh my God," she says when she spots me, rolling her eyes as she turns on Ezra's knee to face me more fully. "Are you bored yet?"

With this conversation? Hell yes. "What exactly are you referring to?"

"Working with the virgin. I'm sure you're hating every second." She points at Wren's back. "I cannot stand having Sam as my partner. He's *so* boring. He drones on and on. Talks about stuff I don't even understand."

That's because Sam is brilliant and Natalie is an idiot. Not that I can actually say that to her. "Sam is a smart guy. He'll ensure your grade is an A for the project."

"Ugh." Natalie leans her head back, her gaze meeting Ezra's, the two of them smiling. "I'd much rather work with you, Crew."

"What about me?" Ezra wraps his arm around her, resting his hand on her stomach, the bold motherfucker. "Wouldn't you rather be my partner, Nat?"

She wrinkles her nose. "Not even." She shoves his hand away from her and rises to her feet, coming to stand in front of me.

This is what I don't like about Natalie. She's a tease. When I wasn't around, she's perching her ass on Ezra's knee and probably giving the poor fucker a boner. The moment he tries to be a little forward with her—and she was giving him all the signs that he had permission—she acts like he's a disgusting perv and pushes him away.

I believe every woman has the right to say no—even Wren. I was just fucking with her at lunch, not that she'd even know the difference.

Natalie is constantly testing that line, trying to cross it and then running back on the other side when shit doesn't go her way. It's exhausting. And dangerous.

A weary sigh leaves me when I realize she's not done with the conversation, and I tilt my head back, meeting her gaze. "What do you want, Nat?"

"Come with me and talk to Skov. I know you're miserable with her as your partner." She tips her head in Wren's direction. "I bet if the both of us went up there and pled our case, Skov would listen."

Probably not, but it could be worth a try. I know Wren would breathe a sigh of relief, not having to deal with me anymore. Getting away from her would also probably ease my frustration level.

And my new urgent need to jerk off every night in the shower to thoughts of Wren on her knees with those pink lips of hers wrapped around the head of my cock.

Fuck, I could give myself a semi just thinking about it right now.

"I'm not switching partners." My voice is firm.

Natalie's mouth hangs open. "Oh, come on. Don't tell me you enjoy working with the virgin."

"Quit calling her that," I say irritably.

"What? It's the truth! Isn't she a virgin?"

"Yes. I am."

Oh shit. Looks like Wren came over to join the conversation.

Natalie just stares at her, a faint sneer curling her upper lip. "What are you doing here?"

"If you're going to talk about me, then maybe I should be in on the conversation." Wren crosses her arms in front of her chest, plumping up her tits and giving me plenty to stare at.

"You weren't included in this conversation in the first place," Natalie mutters.

Wren stands up taller. "Then I'd suggest you stop constantly putting my name in your mouth."

"Whoaaaa." Ezra draws out the word, practically bouncing in his seat with excitement over the potential girl fight.

Natalie's gaze flicks to mine. "Aren't you going to tell her to go sit back down or whatever?"

"No." I barely look at Wren as I lean back in my seat, my arms up, hands behind my head, clutching the back of my neck, as if I have all the time in the world. "I think she's got a handle on this."

Natalie shoots me a dirty look before returning her attention to Wren. "Are you telling me that *Virgin* is your name? Because that's all I ever said."

Wren's expression turns dark. She's mad. And I don't blame her. Natalie is being a total cunt. "Quit talking about me, Natalie."

"Oh yeah? And what are you going to do about it if I don't stop?" Natalie taunts.

"I wouldn't go there if I were you," I murmur. Both girls glance over at me, Natalie's eyes flashing with annoyance. "I have a few—things on you, Nat."

Naked photos she sent to me in the past—that she's practically sent to every guy on campus. A video of her puffing away on a vape at a party last year. Another one of her getting thoroughly fucked by Malcolm, though I never watched it.

Malcolm made sure we all got a copy, of course—though I'm not too sure if she knows he made it. He got the idea from another guy in our class who does the same thing. So fucking sleazy.

"Are you serious right now? You're actually taking her side?" She waves a hand in Wren's direction.

"You put her on blast, I'll help her do the same thing to you." I shrug. "It's as easy as that."

Natalie doesn't say anything, but she's visibly trembling. With fear. With anger. Maybe a combination of both. "You're an asshole."

"That's old news, babe. Tell me something I don't know."

With a huff, she turns and walks away, plopping into her chair a couple of rows over with an extra loud, "Humph."

Malcolm chooses that moment to enter the classroom, his gaze zeroing in on Wren standing by my desk, his eyes narrowing.

He doesn't look pleased.

The one who has the most to lose out of all of us getting ratted out by Wren is Malcolm. He'd be sent back to England—the last place he wants to go. He has a volatile relationship with his parents, especially his mother. Everything he does is not good enough for the woman. If he were to get kicked out of school and sent back to the UK?

Forget it. She'd be furious and probably cut him off financially.

Malcolm heads for his desk, which is on the other side of me, closest to where Wren is standing. He bumps right into her, not even bothering to say *excuse me* or *sorry*, which is unusual because he's British and polite as fuck, before he settles into his desk, glaring at her.

"Do you mind?"

Wren rubs her arm where he ran into her, blinking rapidly.

What the hell? The motherfucker *hurt* her.

If she starts crying, I'm going to lose my shit.

"Watch it, Mal." When he glances over at me, I give him a look, one that says, *lay the fuck off.*

He shrugs. "She was blocking my way."

"She's a girl. You ran into her like you're a linebacker or some shit."

"You say it like it's a bad thing," Wren adds.

I turn my attention to her. "Say what like it's a bad thing?"

"That I'm a girl. Like it's a curse, or I'm subhuman or whatever."

"Well…" Malcolm drawls. "You're the one who said it."

Ezra laughs.

I remain quiet, my anger simmering just below the surface.

"Women are only good for one thing, don't you think, Crew? That's what you've said before." Malcolm hesitates for not even a second. "Fucking. That's it. Oh, and cooking. Guess that makes two things."

"You're disgusting," Wren whispers, her gaze shifting to mine. "And you're no better, considering you're sitting there letting him say such awful things."

My anger rises at Wren being her typical judgmental self. "What do you want me to say? That I think Malcolm is right? That women aren't good for anything else but a quick lay? He might be on to something."

"You're such a dick, Lancaster!" Natalie screams from her seat, laughing her head off.

She's only getting away with saying it because Skov still hasn't waltzed into the classroom. It's like a free-for-all in here right now.

"She's right," Wren says, her voice eerily calm. "You are a complete—*dick*."

My mouth drops open. Ezra is in near hysterics, he's laughing so hard. Even Malcolm is chuckling.

Wren turns on her heel and rapidly walks up the aisle, snatching her backpack from the floor before she jogs out of the classroom. Running right past Skov, who watches Wren leave before she pulls the classroom door shut.

"Why does that girl keep running out of my classroom when she's never ditched before a day in her life?" Skov asks no one in particular as she heads for her desk, shaking her head.

"What the hell was that all about?" I ask my friend. "Did you purposely run into her to hurt her?"

Malcolm glares at me. "I don't trust her. You shouldn't either. That little goody-goody will eventually tell on us, and then we'll be fucked."

"Calling her out and making her look stupid in front of the entire class is your way of trying to keep her quiet then?"

He has the decency to appear contrite. "If she's afraid of us, maybe she won't say anything."

"Scaring the shit out of her might drive her to confess what she saw, too." Shit, I don't know what's going to keep Wren quiet. Maybe I should be nice to her for once. "Don't forget she could ruin everything for you—for us—with a single visit to the headmaster's office. Great plan you've put into place, my friend. Really solid."

Though who am I to talk? I did nothing but threaten her earlier. I'm just as bad as Malcolm.

Probably worse, considering all I want to do is fuck her.

The realization smacks me in the middle of my chest, reminding me that I'm mortal after all. I like to act as if nothing touches me, but currently there is only one thing—one person who has the power to touch me. Fuck with my head.

Completely ruin me.

And that's Wren.

"Maybe someone needs to threaten her in order to get her to keep her mouth shut, since you're the one who can only think about de-virginizing her," he retorts.

My glare burns into Malcolm. I hate how he knew what I was thinking. It's my own damn fault though. I've been lusting after Wren since our senior year started. Hell, even longer than that.

Why should I give a damn about a sheltered little virgin, who would probably slap my face if I tried to hold her hand? She's probably never seen a dick in her life. Never been kissed. Never been touched.

She's pure. Pristine.

Not my type at all.

So why am I dying to dirty her up?

I glance over to find Natalie listening to our conversation with interest. Fucking great. "That's not true."

"Bullshit. You want her so damn bad. I can see it in your eyes. Which means you won't really do anything to threaten her pretty ass." Malcolm shakes his head. "She's going to take us down, and you're going to let her."

"Keep your voice down," I practically hiss, glaring in Natalie's direction. She quickly glances away. "I won't let Wren ruin anything, okay? I'll make sure she stays quiet."

"Uh huh," Ezra says, a shit-eating grin on his face. "The only thing you want to use to keep her quiet is your dick shoved deep in her mouth."

"Shut the fuck up," I snap, loud enough that my voice catches Skov's attention.

A sigh leaves her, and she rests her hands on her hips. "Mr. Lancaster, I really don't appreciate that kind of language in my classroom."

"Sorry." I don't sound that sorry though, and she knows it.

"Oh, I'm sure you are. Since you can't seem to settle down just yet, you get to go in search of your psychology partner. Bring her back to the classroom, okay? I'd hate to have to mark her absent." When I just sit there and gape at her, Skov waves her hands toward the closed door. "Go on. Go. Find Wren, and drag her back in here."

I grab my bag, so no one rifles through it—I trust not one single jackass in this room—and leave the class, unsure where a scared little virgin might go after getting into a fight with a mean girl and then calling me a dick.

I still can't believe she said that. Those types of words are not part of her vocabulary. That's what makes her saying such a thing so shocking.

She's been doing a lot of things this week that are un-Wren-like.

I meander down the hall, killing time. I check my phone, but nothing's going on. When I spot a girls' bathroom, I hesitate, thinking that must be where she is.

Without hesitation, I go to the door and push my way inside, stopping short when I see Wren standing in front of the sink, staring at the mirror. She lifts her gaze to mine in the reflection, her wounded expression trying to tear down the wall encased around my heart.

"What do you want?"

Her voice drips with tears. Any other guy would hate the sound, and I try to convince myself I'm not any other guy. I can look past it. So she's hurt and she's been crying.

So what?

But the longer she stares at me with those sad eyes, the guiltier I start to feel.

"Skov sent me to bring you back to class," I finally say.

She glares. "Tell her I'm not coming."

"I don't think you have a choice, Birdy—"

"Don't call me that!" she screams, whirling around to face me. Her cheeks are damp with fresh tears, and her eyes bloodshot. "Just—go away. You got what you wanted, okay? My self-esteem is in the toilet. I've realized I don't have any *real* friends. None that actually know me. They don't ask me how I'm doing, or check in on me to see if I'm okay. No one cares. My life is a complete mess. I hope you're happy with yourself."

I frown. "Why would I be happy that you're a mess?"

"Because you *hate* me. I think you're trying to drive me out of this school. I know it's your territory. Eventually you'll convince everyone I'm not worthy, and I'll have no choice but to never come back."

"Oh, come the fuck on, Wren. You're being melodramatic."

"Because of you! You make me feel this way." She throws her arms out. "This is just Crew Lancaster's world and we're all merely living in it, right?"

No. It feels like I share my world with Wren, even when I don't want to. She's unlike any girl I've ever known: an independent thinker, yet a snobby little prude. Despite that snobby exterior, I can tell she cares. She wants people to like her, and she wants to guide girls into what she thinks are the right choices—such as being a prude like her.

She is in search of constant approval.

Attention.

She gets it from all kinds of people.

But not the kind of attention she needs.

The kind only I can give to her.

# CHAPTER TWELVE

## WREN

I reluctantly follow Crew back to psychology class, quiet the entire walk. He doesn't say a word either, though his body practically vibrates with some unrecognizable emotion.

I don't know and I don't care what's bothering him. If it's me?

Good. I hope I drive him out of his mind. He does the same to me, so it's only fair.

We enter the classroom and I immediately go to Ms. Skov's desk, my expression contrite when her gaze meets mine.

"I'm sorry I just left," I say, my voice quiet. "Sorry about yesterday too. I've been—moody, though that's no excuse."

A sigh leaves her and she rests her hands on top of her desk. "It's okay, Wren."

I'm about to turn away from her when she keeps talking.

"I want you to know, I've been giving it some thought, and if you want to switch your partner to Sam for this project, you have my permission," Skov says.

I turn and blink at her, shocked by her offer. "Really?"

She nods. "I can tell being with Crew makes you very uncomfortable."

He does. He literally just chased after me, groped me and threatened me. I should tell Skov right now what he did. How badly it rattled me.

In more ways than I can describe.

But then I'd have to tell her why he chased after me, and what I saw. Which means they'd eventually get expelled, and it would be all my fault.

I don't want the responsibility. Or their hatred.

"Did you talk to Sam about making the switch?" I ask her.

"Well, no. Not yet. But Natalie has come to me as well, requesting a new partner, and she mentioned she wants to work with Crew. Even though that goes against my views of the entire project, I don't like seeing you so miserable." Her gaze is knowing as it settles on me. "You look like you've been crying."

"I'm fine." I shrug, then glance over my shoulder to see Natalie trying to talk to Crew, and he's doing his best to ignore her while Ezra watches her with puppy-dog eyes. I turn to face my teacher once more. "I don't want to switch partners."

Skov's eyebrows shoot up almost to her hairline. "Are you sure?"

"Yes." My nod is firm, as is my resolve. Besides…

I don't want Crew to work with Natalie. That'll make her feel like she won, and I don't want her to.

She doesn't deserve it. Or him.

"If you're going to work with Crew, I can't have these daily emotional outbursts. Do you understand?"

"Yes, ma'am." I bend my head, embarrassed. I don't let things get to me like this usually. Though no one really ever tries to mess with me. I have my followers who respect what I say, and anyone who doesn't agree with my values usually leaves me alone.

Until Crew. It's like he can't stop messing with me, and I hate it.

There's the smallest part of me that doesn't hate it, though. It's buried deep. A small, dark kernel of pleasure unfurls in my chest every time he touches me. Earlier when he tried to hold me back, when he had his hand on my breast, I should've been disgusted. Frightened.

And I was. At first. But there was something else going on. It was almost thrilling, knowing he might want me. I could hear it in his voice. Feel it in the way he touched me.

In that moment, he *did* want me. Even if it was only for a second.

"Okay then. Go on, get to work," Ms. Skov urges, and I leave her desk, making my way to the back of the classroom where Crew sits, Natalie in the desk next to his.

"Are we switching partners?" Natalie chirps, her gaze sliding to Crew.

He's not even watching her. His focus is one hundred percent on me.

"No," I say, shaking my head, my gaze stuck on Crew's. "We're still partners."

"God, Skov is such a bitch," Natalie mutters under her breath as she slides out of the seat and heads over to the empty desk next to Sam.

I settle into the chair Natalie just vacated, tamping down the wave of triumph trying to consume me. I drop my backpack on the floor and zip it open, pulling out my notebook and pencil, settling them both on the desk.

"Skov is sticking to her guns, huh?" Crew's deep voice washes over me, leaving me warm.

I send him a secret smile, unable to help myself. "Guess so."

• • •

School is pretty monotonous for the rest of the week. Not much is happening and we're all preparing for finals and projects as winter break draws closer. I try my best to ignore Fig and never allow myself to be alone with him in class. I even show up late, though my seat is always empty and waiting for me. No one else wants to sit in the front and center seat.

Maggie has been distant toward me, spending her time chasing after Franklin, I guess, and never hanging out with me anymore.

It's fine. Whatever.

I observe the way people talk to me at school, specifically everyone in my grade, and realize I exist on the fringe of every friend group among the seniors. No one truly pulls me in or seeks me out.

It's depressing. Before Crew pointed it out, I was completely oblivious, and sometimes I think I want to go back to that state of mind. When I believed everyone liked me and they were all my friends. When I thought I was a positive influence who made a difference.

Oh, the younger girls still want to spend time with me, and I hang out with them during lunch because I have no one else, but they look to me to make themselves feel better for the choices they've made so far in life. The majority of them will succumb eventually. They'll get a boyfriend. They'll fall in love. They'll have sex.

And then they'll leave me behind.

Psychology class and the project is the only thing that fills me with faint apprehension. Having to face down a smirking Crew every afternoon is starting to take a toll on me, but I try my best to smile through it all. To keep our conversation as impersonal as possible, which is tough since we're both supposed to be digging under each other's skin, trying to figure the other person out.

I've already given up. I cannot figure him out, no matter how I try. He's mean yet levels me with that fiery gaze, as if he's envisioning me naked or whatever. He makes me uncomfortable.

And not always in a bad way either.

I wasn't about to back down from Natalie, though. I know she's still angry that Crew is my partner and not hers. Too bad. She's just going to have to deal with it.

He's mine.

When it's finally Friday, I feel as if I can breathe a sigh of relief. I'm going to see my parents this weekend, and I can't wait. Not because I'm dying to see them—I was with them only a week ago for Thanksgiving—but my father and I are going to an art exhibit Saturday that features an up-and-coming artist whose work I strongly admire. Plus, I'm eager to get away from campus. I'm tired of being here already, and I still have two weeks until winter break.

And my birthday—that big bash I planned on hosting for my supposed friends? I don't know why I'm even bothering.

I'm going to cancel it. Who would come anyway? It's not like there will be drugs or alcohol. I'd be surprised if anyone showed.

After that depressing thought, I shove it from my mind before I allow it to completely crush me.

I'm walking down the hall, heading for my last class of the day when I hear someone from behind me clear their throat.

"Wren, hey."

I turn to find Larsen Von Weller standing in front of me, a smile curling his lips.

He's a senior like me. Quiet. Smart. Athletic but not a complete jerk like some of the jocks that go to this stupid school. Attractive with brown hair and brown eyes. A lean yet muscular build.

"Hi," I say with a faint smile, wondering why he's talking to me.

We were closer our freshman and sophomore years, when we had more classes together, and saw each other throughout the day. We sort of went on separate paths junior year because of our class choices, and now we never really speak.

"How are you?" he asks.

"I'm good." I nod, glancing around the hall, watching people walk past us, their gazes curious when they see who I'm talking to. "How are you?"

"I can't complain." His smile is easy. "I heard a rumor."

"Oh?" God, what does he know?

"Yeah. That you're going home this weekend." He smiles.

I frown. "Where did you hear that?"

His expression turns sheepish and he shoves his hands in his front pockets. "My mom mentioned it to me because I'm going home too. My parents invited yours over for dinner Saturday night, and your mom mentioned to mine that you would be coming."

"Oh. Yes, I guess I am." I didn't realize his parents were friends with mine, but my father never turns down a friendship. He views almost everyone in his life as potential business since he's in real estate. Someone is always looking to buy or sell something in his eyes.

"It'll be good to catch up, don't you think?" he asks, keeping pace with me, as I start walking.

"Definitely." I offer him a quick smile, stopping near my classroom door. "Guess I'll see you tomorrow then."

"Something to look forward to." He flashes me a brilliant smile. "See you tomorrow, Wren."

Larsen walks away quickly, getting swallowed up in the crowd, and I watch him go, leaning against the wall to stay out of the way of the people rushing to their last class.

"What the hell was that about?"

I turn to find Crew standing there, a glower on his face, staring in the direction Larsen just left.

"What exactly are you referring to?"

"Larsen. Why is he sniffing around you?"

I wrinkle my nose, disgusted by his chosen terminology. "It's really none of your business."

I stride into the classroom with Crew on my heels. "It's my business when I know the guy is a fucking perv."

"You two must be great friends then." I smirk at him from over my shoulder, settling into the chair right next to his.

We've been merely coexisting the last couple of days, but in this moment, I'm fired up. Ready to give him a piece of my mind.

"I'm not friends with that asshole. He's a smug prick," Crew spits out as he sits down.

"Sounds familiar." I drop my backpack on the floor beside me, turning to glare at him. "Stay out of it, Crew. It doesn't concern you."

"If he messes with your mental state, it'll definitely concern me. We have a project to work on."

"My mental state is precarious only because of you." It's pure habit when I pull out my notebook and pencil. Crew isn't going to talk to me or give me anything. He never does. I could ask him an endless list of questions and he'd still remain mum. It's so frustrating.

*He's* frustrating. Claiming that Larsen is a pervert when they aren't even friends. How would he know?

"He'll make it worse," he retorts.

"How?" I'm genuinely curious. "What could he do to me that would be so awful?"

"God, you really are that innocent, aren't you?"

I flinch at his words. I hate that he makes me feel terrible for being a nice person. I can't help it if I'm not completely corrupted like he is. "I'd rather be innocent than hard and jaded like you."

Crew ignores my insult. "You really want to know what Larsen is up to?"

"Please!"

"He puts on this—sweet act for the girls. Like he wouldn't harm a fly. Very *aw shucks* of him, you know? He works his wholesome act on an unsuspecting girl, and the next thing she knows, she finds herself on her knees with his dick in her mouth while he secretly records the entire transaction," Crew explains.

I physically recoil at his words. That sounds absolutely awful. And Crew makes it sound so clinical with his use of the word 'transaction.'

Is that all sex is to him? A transaction? An exchange of bodily fluids?

Gross.

"He records it?" I ask, my voice hushed. I don't want anyone else to hear me say that. Too many people pay attention to me and Crew when we talk already, and I have no clue why.

Crew nods, his expression grim. "Then he sells it to his friends."

A gasp leaves me. "What? Why?"

"For beat-off material? Come on, Birdy. You don't think every guy in this place would love to see you on your knees for someone?" The look he gives me makes me think he might want to see me in such a—vulnerable position as well. "If Larsen was able to capture that, he'd be the hero of Lancaster Prep."

"That is so—disgusting." I stare down at my desk. Crew's words are on repeat in my brain. I don't know if I believe him. He thinks the worst of everyone. I've never heard of Larsen doing anything like that before. While I make sure I'm not involved in any scandalous gossip, I do occasionally hear tidbits, and that is one story I've never come across.

Ever.

"Watch out for him," Crew says, his tone ominous. "I've warned you."

Skov comes into class, just before the bell rings, launching straight into taking attendance. I sit there lost in thought, hating how Crew ruined my upcoming Saturday night dinner with a few choice words.

He has a way of doing that. Ruining my life.

Dramatic but true.

When Skov releases us to continue working on our project with our partners, I watch as Crew scoots his desk and chair closer to mine, which surprises me. Why is he coming closer?

I don't want him to. I'd rather he keeps his distance. Having him so close makes me uncomfortable—and not in a bad way.

Which isn't good.

Not at all.

"I've been thinking about what you said," I start.

"And?"

"I don't believe it."

An exasperated sigh leaves him. "Why am I not surprised."

"He doesn't seem like that kind of guy."

"Isn't that how it always starts? 'Oh, he was the nicest guy. I can't believe he's a serial killer.'" The look Crew sends me almost makes me laugh. "Get real, Birdy."

"I just think I would've heard about this from other girls. Ones who've been—recorded by him, you know?" I make a disgusted face at the thought of it happening—and what I would do if it actually happened to me.

Talk about humiliating. I'd never recover from it.

"You really think any of them actually talk about it? They'd rather forget the moment ever existed. And if they were to say something to you, you'd probably give them a nice little speech about their bad choices," Crew says.

My heart aches, only because what he says is, unfortunately, true.

I've given plenty of lectures in my time to girls who've made bad decisions. No wonder people think I'm judgmental.

"I probably should stop doing that," I admit, my voice soft.

Crew leans in closer, his shoulder brushing mine, making me tingle. "Stop doing what?"

"Being so judgmental all the time." I lift my gaze to his. "You were right. So was everyone else who told me that."

"Aw, little birdy is learning something from the project." He reaches out, tucking a stray strand of hair behind my ear. "I'm proud of you."

My skin warms from his touch and I try to push past the foreign feeling. He shouldn't say words like that either.

I might end up liking them too much.

"Have you learned anything about yourself yet?" I ask hopefully, trying to ignore the swarm of butterflies taking flight in my stomach from him touching me.

"I learned that you think I'm an asshole."

I frown. "I never said that."

"You don't have to. I can just tell."

I've been told I wear all of my emotions plainly on my face...

"You also think I act like I own the school."

"Um, you literally do."

"My family does," he corrects.

I roll my eyes. "Whatever."

"You're sassy today, Bird."

"When you push yourself into my personal business, it makes me sassy." I tap my pencil against my notebook. "Are we going to actually *work* on this project today?"

"Yeah. Let's do it." He leans back in his chair, his gaze still on me. "I want to interview you."

Unease sweeps over me, setting me immediately on edge. "How about I interview you instead?"

"No." He shakes his head. "I came up with a few questions last night. Things I'd love to know about you."

Why do his words sound more like a threat? "Trust me. I'm not going to reveal everything about myself to you."

"I thought that was the point of this project."

"You're supposed to be analyzing me. Trying to figure me out versus me just giving you all the information you want," I remind him.

"You always have a way of making everything extra difficult, don't you." He doesn't phrase it as a question.

His words sting and I hate that. "Fine. Ask your questions."

Crew grabs his phone and opens it to the notes section, scanning whatever he wrote there, his brows drawn together. I take the opportunity to stare at him, taking in his chiseled features. The sharp jawline and soft lips. The strong nose and angled cheekbones. The thick brows and icy blue eyes. His face is like a work of art, something you'd find in a painting from hundreds of years ago. A callous aristocrat, clad in tights that showed off his muscular legs, a heavy velvet coat to show off his opulent wealth.

He would've fit in then as he fits in now. What's that like, knowing your place? Being so confident in it?

I thought I knew, but ever since this project started, I've been thrown off. Feeling out of sorts.

"Okay." Crew's deep voice pulls me from my thoughts and I refocus on him. "Do you have any hobbies?"

"Such a general question." Wait, am I teasing him?

"It's a solid way to find out what you like."

He's got a point.

"I like to travel."

"Where have you been?"

"Lots of places. All over Europe. Japan. I went to Russia a few years ago."

"And how was that?" I notice he's not taking notes.

Hmm.

"I went with my parents for an art exhibition there."

"Right. They're massive collectors."

"Yes. My mother has become an expert in the art world. She'll travel anywhere just to get a piece she's had her eye on. We went to Russia in February a couple of years ago. It was freezing. We got stuck there for days because they kept canceling the flights due to weather," I explain.

"Did you like Russia?"

"It was beautiful, but so terribly cold. The sky was this steely gray and it never changed. Maybe during a different season, I would appreciate it more."

He actually types something in his notes and I wish I knew what he wrote. "What else do you like to do?"

"I like to read."

His gaze flickers to mine. "Boring."

"You can't have the kind of grade point average *we* have without doing a lot of reading too," I point out.

"True. I don't read much for pleasure though."

It's how he uses the word 'pleasure,' and the way he says it, that makes me think of…

Things.

Wicked things.

What does *he* do for pleasure?

"What else, Birdy?" he asks, his voice quiet. Probing.

"I like art," I admit.

"What kind?"

"All kinds. When you're dragged to various art galleries your entire life, you start to appreciate what you see. Pieces eventually start speaking to you. Suddenly you have a growing list of artists you admire." A sigh leaves me. "I resisted at first. I never wanted to go to museums or art galleries. I thought they were boring."

"When you're little, that's what they are. Extremely boring," he says.

"Exactly. I started appreciating it more when I was thirteen. There are pieces I fell in love with." A smile teases the corner of my lips. "There's one in particular I discovered a couple of years ago that's my absolute favorite."

His eyes light with curiosity. "What is it?"

"Oh, it's nothing." I should've never admitted that. He wouldn't care. Not really. "Just a piece I found myself drawn to."

"Tell me about it," he urges, and I hurriedly shake my head.

"It's boring."

"Come on, Wren."

Even though he sounds completely exasperated with me, it's his use of my actual name that prompts me to keep talking. "It's a piece that was created in 2007 by an artist who explores a lot of mediums and uses a variety of materials. When he created my favorite piece, I read that he was still a drug addict."

"A drug addict? That sounds against your moral code, Birdy."

"He's clean now. People misstep sometimes. None of us are perfect," I say with a shrug.

"Except for you." He smirks at me. "You're the most perfect girl on this campus."

"Please. I'm definitely not perfect," I stress, hating that he would think I am. It's hard living up to everyone's standards. My parents. My teachers. The girls at school who look up at me. Even the people who think I'm ridiculous.

He completely ignores what I said. "What does this piece look like?"

I sit up straighter, excited to explain it. "It's a giant canvas covered in kisses."

"Kisses?"

"Yes. He had the same woman kiss the canvas in varying shades of Chanel lipstick." I smile when Crew frowns. "She'd kiss the canvas in a different way every single time. Harder. Softer. Her lips open wider, or pursed close together."

"Okay."

"It's originally untitled, but it's known in the art world as 'A Million Kisses in Your Lifetime.' My father tried to buy it for me as a surprise for my birthday last year, but whoever owns it now won't part with it. And there's another piece that's similar, but you can't find that one either."

"How much is the one you want worth?"

"A lot."

"Define a lot. That could mean a variety of amounts."

"When it went to auction, it sold to a private collector for over five hundred thousand dollars."

He makes a scoffing noise. "Easily bought."

"Not when the owner won't sell. To them, it's priceless." I grab my phone. "Do you want to see it?"

"Sure."

I open Google, and in less than a minute, I have the piece

brought up on my screen. Just seeing it makes my heart ache in a good way. In that visceral sense, where something calls to you, touching a part of you buried deep.

I've never been kissed, but I can only imagine what it would be like, to kiss a man and leave your lipstick on his mouth when you're done. That seems so...

Romantic.

"Here it is." I hold my phone out to Crew and he takes it, studying the piece for long, quiet seconds. "What do you think? Can you see how it almost undulates? The artist had the woman press her lips to the canvas in precise spots to create the illusion."

"I see it," he says as he squints at my phone screen.

"Isn't it beautiful?" My voice is wistful, as it tends to get when I talk about my favorite piece of art. It's still such a disappointment that the work isn't mine. My father tried so hard to make it the starter piece for my own collection.

When he couldn't get that one, he purchased another piece by the same artist. It's lovely, but not the one I wanted the most.

"I think you could recreate that on your own, no problem." He hands my phone back to me.

"But I don't want to recreate it." I stare at my screen, at the lipstick-covered canvas that I adore. "I want this one."

"How many Chanel lipsticks do you own?"

"None. I don't really wear lipstick much." Just lip balm and mascara. That's about as far as my cosmetics regimen goes.

"With a mouth like that, you should invest in some lipstick," Crew says.

An unfamiliar sensation trickles through my blood, making me aware of how he's currently studying my lips. "What do you mean?"

"No one's ever told you?"

"Told me what?"

He reaches out, his thumb pressing at the corner of my lips, lingering. A barely-there touch that has me tingling all over. "You have a sexy mouth."

# CHAPTER THIRTEEN

## CREW

Her lips are soft. The way she's looking at me? Sexy as hell.

I'm tempted. Tempted to do a lot of things. Trace her full bottom lip with my thumb. Test her limits, see how she would react to me touching her. What would she do if I slipped my thumb into her mouth? Would she freak out? Bite me? Or would she close her lips around it, holding me there. Maybe even nibble on it? Suck it?

Yeah, zero fucking chance of any of that ever happening.

I reluctantly remove my thumb from her mouth and drop my hand on my desk. She stares at me, her green eyes wide and unblinking. "Wh-what do you mean?"

"I mean what I said, Birdy. You have a fuckin' sexy mouth."

She reaches up, brushing shaky fingers against the corner of her lips where I just touched her. "I never really thought of it like that before."

"I'm guessing you don't think anything about yourself is sexy."

"No." She shakes her head. "I really don't."

"You've never thought of recreating your favorite piece? Buy a bunch of lipsticks and kiss a blank canvas over and over again?" If I had to watch her do that I might jizz in my pants, as if I have no control of myself, which is something I haven't done in a while.

Something about this girl makes me want to lose all control.

A soft laugh leaves her. "No, I've never thought of doing that. Can you imagine?"

I can. I'd love to see that sexy lip print of hers all over a canvas in various colors.

"You should consider it," I say, purposely keeping my tone even. Casual. "Might be a project for you to work on later."

"I have enough projects to work on. Including this one." She taps her pencil on my arm. "Did you have any other questions for me? Class is almost over."

Damn, time goes way too fast when I'm with her. "I do have another question."

"What is it?"

"Though I've asked you this before."

Her expression turns wary and a sigh leaves her. "Go ahead. I'll probably give you the same answer as I did before too."

"Actually, you never answered me."

"Oh. Well that was rude of me."

This girl. I'm surprised she didn't apologize for her lack of an answer.

"Promise you'll answer this time?" I raise a brow.

"Maybe." Her tone is cautious.

Smart move.

"All right." I lean forward, my gaze locking with hers. "Have you ever been kissed? Be honest, Birdy. Tell me the truth. I'm dying to know."

She drops her head, staring at her desk. "That's really none of your business."

"Only a girl who's never been kissed would answer that way." She doesn't react. "Come on. Tell me. You've never felt the press of another mouth on yours?"

Wren stays quiet.

"Warm lips connecting again and again?"

Still nothing.

"That first touch of someone's tongue, sliding inside your mouth? Circling. Searching. Hands start wandering..." My voice drifts and still no reaction. She's gone completely still, her head still bent, long dark hair obscuring her face. "Next thing you know, hands are sliding under your clothes, touching you—"

"Stop," she whispers, lifting her head, revealing her pink cheeks.

"What's your answer then, Wren?"

"No. Okay? Are you happy? I've never been kissed. But please...keep that to yourself."

I'm filled with the urge to kiss her right now, but I tamp it down. "Do you want to be kissed?"

"Of course. I just—it hasn't happened for me yet."

"Why not?" I glance down at her hand, that damn diamond winking up at me. "Because you promised yourself to your father?"

"It's not like that." She shakes her head. "You wouldn't understand."

"Please explain. I'd love to understand."

"Look, no one's been interested in me enough to even want to kiss me. And no one has really interested me either."

"What if I told you I was interested." The words leave me as if I have no control of my thoughts or feelings. I should've never said that. The entire moment feels too real, too raw.

I should be threatening this girl to keep her mouth shut after what she saw, but I don't even bring it up. Not anymore. Even stranger? I'm not worried about her telling on us. She won't.

I can sense it.

She rolls her eyes. Tries to laugh off what I said. "Please. You definitely don't want to kiss me."

"How do you know?" I lean in closer, her intoxicating scent wrapping around me. "You going to let Larsen kiss you then?"

"What? No." More nervous laughter leaves her. "Not after

what you told me."

"Good girl," I murmur, noting how her eyes shine at my approval. "You need to stay far away from that asshole."

"Might be kind of difficult since I'm going to his house for dinner tomorrow night."

"Don't let him get you alone." I'm fucking jealous that she's going to spend Saturday with that prick Larsen. "Promise me, Birdy. I won't be there to watch over you."

"Like I need you as my guard dog. Don't forget you're the guy who just chased after me a few days ago and tried to assault me," she says.

"Assault?" I'm grateful her tone is quiet so no one else heard her say that. "I think you liked it too much to call it assault."

Her entire face reddens. "You're awful."

"But you like it."

"Not really."

"A little bit? Come on, you can admit it."

"Not enough to give you the satisfaction of saying so." Her smile is serene. "Quit digging, Crew. It's not a good look for you."

We're smiling at each other and it feels...weird. In a good way. In a *I might like this girl more than I want to admit* way.

The bell rings, knocking us from our trance, and Wren jolts in her chair, immediately reaching for her backpack. I watch her as she puts her stuff away, zipping it up and slinging it over her shoulder before she stands. "Bye, Crew."

She walks away before I can say anything, her hair swaying. My gaze drops to her skirt, lingering there, wishing I could see more of her.

Wishing I could protect her.

The foreign feeling settles over me and I rub my chest, frowning. Why do I want to protect her? Why do I care so damn much? I don't get it.

I don't understand my feelings for her.

I leave the classroom and exit the building, heading for the junior and senior dorm building. I don't have a room there. As a Lancaster, I automatically get one of the private suites in another building that once housed staff when they lived on campus. But I hang out here sometimes, usually in the common room.

Where I'm headed right now.

I find a chair and settle in, waiting while I scroll on my phone, my gaze going to the door, knowing eventually I'll see him appear. He's so damn predictable. His favorite place to hang out after school is in this very room. All of his followers surrounding him, waiting for another story about yet another innocent girl who gave it up to his douchey ass.

The problem with the girls not talking about what he does is they don't warn the others who follow after them. It's like this weird secret that grows and grows. Everyone knows it's happening, but no one admits it's actually happened to them.

It's kind of fucked. Someone needs to call Larsen out for his shit.

Maybe that someone should be me.

What does it really matter, what Larsen does with other girls? We've let it happen for the last couple of years, so what's the difference now?

Wren.

She's the difference. I can't stand the thought of him even *looking* at her, let alone touching her. He's a piece of shit creep who doesn't deserve even an ounce of her attention. Wren is so damn sweet and pure and good.

*I* barely deserve her attention, and I'm ten times the man that Larsen the fuckhead is. And if he were to do something that would devastate her completely, like film her while he took advantage of her after slipping a drug in her drink? Holy shit.

I'd probably kill him if given the chance.

It takes him a solid twenty minutes, but he finally shows up. Larsen enters the common room with a smile on his face, high fiving a couple of dudes who greet him like he's their long- lost leader.

Such a bunch of shit. That they even look up to this supreme asshole says a lot about them.

He spots me, surprise on his face since I'm sitting in the chair he usually occupies. See, I know what he's up to. I know how he operates. And I can tell by his grim expression that he doesn't like me sitting in his chair.

My family owns this place. Technically it's my mother fuckin' chair. I can sit wherever the fuck I want.

"Hey, Crew," Larsen says, stopping directly in front of me.

"Hey." I indicate the empty chair across from me. "Have a seat."

He reluctantly sits down on the edge of the chair, looking ready to bolt at any second. "What's up?"

"Nothing much. How are you?" I could give a shit how he's doing, but I'm not going to be an idiot and attack him at first sight.

I need a quiet approach. Lull him into thinking everything is fine before I lay down my threat.

"I'm good. Ready for the weekend."

Damn, he walked right into it.

"Got plans?"

He nods, relaxing slightly. "Headed to the city. Not till the morning though."

Good to know. I've already done a little research. Figured out exactly where this exhibit is happening that Wren is planning on attending.

"What are you doing while you're there?"

"Staying with the family. They're having company for dinner, and my mom wanted me there."

"Oh yeah? Who's coming over?"

"The Beaumonts."

"As in Wren Beaumont?"

He nods. Grins. "Hoping to spend a little one on one time with her, you know? She's the ungettable girl."

Is that even a word? Ungettable? "You really think she'll go for a disgusting pervert like you?"

His grin fades, replaced by a scowl. "What the fuck, Lancaster?"

I lean forward, resting my elbows on my knees as I glare him. "You're a scum sucking piece of shit who makes videos of girls you fuck. The only reason you fuck them is for the videos, so you can share them. Make money off them. You don't give a shit about the fact that those girls are devastated by what you do. Some of them have even left school over it. They never come back. And you keep doing it because not a one of them tell anyone what's going on. They're too embarrassed. They believe their lives are over. I'm surprised you haven't received a therapy bill from one of them yet."

"I bet you've watched a few of those videos," Larsen says, his expression surly. I'm sure it never feels good to have your dirty shit explained to you.

"One." It's the truth. "I watched one, and I was immediately disgusted and stopped."

"So high and mighty," he spits out. "You think you're the lord of the manor around here, and it fucking sucks. Not all of us have to do your biding, dickwad. If you have such a problem with me, tell on me. I mother fuckin' dare you."

"I have no proof. And I'm not about to put a bunch of girls, who don't want to talk about it, in the spotlight." I hesitate for only a second. "Is that your plan for Wren? You want to make a fun little video of her? Maybe of her sucking your pencil dick? Or of you fucking her from behind, so we can't quite make out her face?"

That's one of his tricks. He never actually shows their faces. Not all the way. But we can figure out who it is. Every time.

"You're just jealous," Larsen snaps. "You want her too. Don't think we haven't noticed you following Wren around lately. Hell, you've been watching her walk into the building every morning for the past two fucking years, staring at her like some sort of stalker. It's not my fault you've waited too long and now you've missed your chance."

"You actually believe you have a chance with her?" My voice is flat.

"A better one than you do, you stupid fuck. At least I have Mommy and Daddy's approval. And that's the hardest thing to get when it comes to the Beaumonts. Her daddy keeps her locked up tight. Not quite sure why. Maybe she secretly has a bad reputation? Baby prostitute at thirteen? I wouldn't doubt it. Look at her, with those giant tits and dick-sucking lips."

I'm on him in seconds, pulling him out of his chair. Grabbing hold of his tie so fucking tight he makes a choking sound, his eyes practically bulging out of his head when I thrust my face in his. "Shut the fuck up."

Larsen exhales raggedly, smiling despite the fact that I'm about to choke the shit out of him. "Or what? You going to beat my ass? Bring it, Lancaster. You don't scare me. Besides, you'll get kicked outta here so fast your head will spin."

His grin is back, and I want to slap it off his smug-ass face.

"Touch a hair on her head and I'll tell everyone about your recordings. I'll expose your ass for everything you've done the past two years. Forget the girls and protecting their privacy. In the end, they'll probably thank me when it comes out and I expose what a piece of shit you are."

Larsen's eyes fill with a mixture of anger and fear. "What's the big deal, huh? Why do you care whether I fuck her or not?"

"First, she'd never let your sleazy ass touch her. Next, I care because I actually like the girl, which is more than I can say about you." I go still the second the words leave me, shock coursing through my blood.

I like her.

I do.

*What the fuck?*

"Crew, come the fuck on. Leave him alone."

I turn to find Ezra standing there, slowly shaking his head. I ignore him, returning my attention back to Larsen. "Like I said—touch her and I'll break every bone in your body. Record her doing anything, even smiling at you, and I'll kill you." I shove him away from me, and he stumbles into the chair behind him, falling to the ground.

We glare at each other as I stand over him, my hands clenched into fists. I'm fucking panting, I'm so pissed.

I hate this fucker. So damn much.

Turning away, I leave the common room, Ezra hot on my heels.

"What the hell, dude? Why you fucking with Larsen? We always would leave him alone, you know."

Because we were a bunch of idiots who thought we were doing the right thing by protecting one of our own.

Well fuck that.

"He's a piece of shit." I wipe the back of my hand across my mouth. "He deserves to be called out."

"Why? What's the big deal now?"

I turn on my friend. "He's having dinner with the Beaumonts tomorrow night."

Realization dawns across Ezra's face. "And what? You think he's going to get with Wren? Give me a break. She's too scared to even look at him."

"I saw them talking in the hall earlier. I think she trusts that asshole."

"She shouldn't. Doesn't she know?"

"Probably not." She didn't. I don't know if she believed what I told her, either.

My mind won't stop imagining her with Larsen. Laughing with him as he slowly but surely earns her trust. Honing in on that needy side of her, the one she doesn't really show anyone. She wants attention. She's starved for it. And he'll give it to her.

He might even try to drug her.

Next thing she knows, she's getting fucked by that asshole. And I can see it. I can see it all in my head, and there's no way I can let that happen.

I can't.

I won't.

# CHAPTER FOURTEEN

## WREN

"I'm so sorry, Pumpkin, but I won't be able to make it tomorrow for the exhibit."

"Wait, what? Are you serious?" I clutch the phone closer to my ear, my fingers cramping, I'm holding it so tightly. "I only came home so we could go together."

"I know, and I wish I had a different answer for you, but something else came up," my father says.

I flop onto the blue velvet couch in the living room, hating how hard it is. How stiff. Like everything else in this cold, sterile apartment my parents live in. "What suddenly came up?"

"I'm meeting with some clients this evening for dinner," he says, his voice smooth. "You know how it is."

How it always is. For some reason though, it feels like he's lying. "On a Friday night?"

"I work seven days a week. You know this." He sounds irritated, and I immediately feel terrible for even doubting him.

"I know, you're right. I'm just—disappointed." I close my eyes, letting the emotion wash over me. The entire week hasn't gone well and I was so looking forward to seeing this exhibit tomorrow.

For once, I just wanted something to work in my favor.

"I'm disappointed too, Pumpkin. Maybe we can go another

time. I'd love to see her exhibit."

"It's over at the end of the year," I remind him. "And this weekend was the best time for me. I have finals to prepare for, and then it's Christmas. My birthday."

"Maybe we could go the week between Christmas and New Year's?" he suggests.

"But that's my birthday week. I might have plans."

With who, I'm not even sure anymore.

He chuckles. "Right. My little girl loves to string out her birthday for as long as possible."

Only my father would make me feel bad for something he started in the first place. When I turned ten, he made such a big deal about my birthday, trying to make it special considering I share the day with the one of the most major holidays of the year. He kept my tenth birthday celebration going for days, much to my mother's not-so-secret annoyance. It's been a tradition ever since.

"What sort of plans do you have?" he asks when I still haven't said anything.

"I wanted to go out of town," I admit, realizing there really isn't anyone I want to go with me anymore. I was thinking about asking Maggie, but she's still not talking to me after the Fig incident, so what would be the point? She probably hates me, and she was my last real friend.

"Where were you thinking of going? Somewhere warm?"

"Actually, I was looking at somewhere in the mountains with lots of snow. It sounds cozy, staying in a log cabin and drinking hot chocolate by the fire." Saying the words out loud, I'm sure I sound like a foolish little girl.

"You don't want to go somewhere tropical? Most people want to go to the beach during the winter. What about Aruba?"

A tropical vacation means bikinis and lots of skin. Guys leering at me and my chest. I hate having them on display. They're just so...big.

"I don't want to go to Aruba, Daddy," I say, my voice small.

"Okay. That's fine. How about I have Veronica look up some locations for you? She can do a little research, find a couple of options for you to look over," he suggests.

"Who's Veronica?"

"My assistant. She started a few months ago. I know I told you about her."

"Oh. Okay. Yes, sure. That would be nice."

"Just trying to help you, Pumpkin. I know you're busy with school with finals and all of your end-of-the-semester projects. Veronica is really great at making travel arrangements. She handles mine all the time."

"Thank you. That would be great." I really wanted to plan this trip on my own, but it's like no one can let me do anything by myself. And I allow it to happen. "I'm thinking I might go to the exhibit tomorrow."

"With your mother?"

"No. She probably wouldn't want to go with me." I tried talking to her about this particular artist a few weeks ago, when I first heard about the showing, but she wasn't interested.

She's rarely interested in anything I do lately.

His voice turns stern. "I don't want you going alone."

"Why not? I've gone to showings around there before. I'm familiar with the area." It's in Tribeca, and not in a terrible neighborhood or anything, but for my father, every neighborhood is bad when it comes to me.

"Never by yourself. I'll arrange for a car for you. You just call the office tomorrow whenever you're ready to be picked up and they'll come get you."

"Daddy. I can just take an Uber—" I start, but he cuts me off.

"Absolutely not. You'll use my car service." By the tone of his voice, I know he won't allow me to do anything else.

"All right." My voice is soft, and I close my eyes for a moment, wishing I was brave enough to tell him I'll do whatever I want.

But I don't. I never do.

"Is your mother home?" he asks.

"No. She's having dinner with friends."

He makes a harumphing noise. "Friends. I'm sure. Well, I'll see you sometime tomorrow afternoon. I get in around two."

"Wait a minute, you're not even here?"

"I'm in Florida. I'll be back tomorrow." A lilting, feminine voice says something in the background, and I can hear my father muffle the phone, so he can speak to her. "I've got to go, Wren. See you tomorrow. Love you."

He ends the call before I can respond.

I toss the phone onto the couch and tilt my head back, staring at the ceiling. At the elaborate and very expensive light fixture that shines above my head. Everything in this house is expensive. Some items are even priceless.

It's like I can't touch any of it. Too scared I might break something that's irreplaceable. Art. Objects. Things are more important to my mother, my father.

Me? Their daughter? Sometimes I wonder if I matter. If I've become nothing but another object they like to show off.

A piece of art that still needs plenty of molding.

I push myself off the couch and wander through the house. Down the hall, past the giant paintings that hang on the walls. The ones with the lights shining upon them, illuminating them perfectly so everyone on the street can see them as they walk past. Those who appreciate fine art would die to enter this house. To catch even a brief glimpse of the paintings and sculptures and pieces that fill our apartment.

I don't even see them anymore. They're meaningless.

Like me.

I lock myself away in my room and try to examine it with a critical eye. There's no color. My mother did that on purpose, so it wouldn't clash with any of the art she might choose to show in here. Because yes, even my bedroom is a potential showcase for her art. The piece my father bought me last year for my birthday hangs on the wall. It's a canvas with lipstick prints, though not nearly as many as the coveted piece I truly want, along with vibrantly colored already chewed gum stuck on it in random spots. It's kind of gross.

I had to pretend I loved it when he gave it to me.

Turning away from the piece, I stare at the white duvet cover on my bed. The black and steel gray pillows stacked against the silver metal headboard. The white furniture. The black and white photos on the walls, all of them from a different time. When I was younger and had real friends. Before we all changed and grew up and grew apart.

Now we talk on Instagram via comments and the occasional DM. They've all moved while I feel stuck.

I catch my gaze in the reflection of the full-length mirror hanging on the wall and I go to it, staring at myself. I changed into jeans and a black sweatshirt before I left campus, and if my mother saw me right now, she'd say I looked sloppy.

Maybe I do. But at least I'm comfortable.

I tear off the sweatshirt first, my gaze dropping to my breasts and I can't help but frown. I hate the way they strain against my plain white cotton T-shirt. My mother is constantly on me to go on a diet, but I don't think it's going to help. In the end, I'll still have my breasts, which are nothing like hers. She's flat. Her body is almost boyish, and she works hard to keep it that way.

While I'm over here fighting my curves and trying to restrain my breasts with the most restrictive bras I can find to please her.

It's exhausting, pretending to be something I'm not.

I whip the T-shirt off and drop it on the floor, kicking it out of the way. I step out of my shoes. Peel off my socks. Then I take off my jeans, flinging them so they hit the wall with a loud thwap.

Until I'm standing in the middle of my bedroom in nothing but my underwear.

Girls my age wear thongs or lacy, sexy panties. See-through bras or bralettes, or sometimes no bra at all. They wear these items for themselves, to give them confidence. To feel sexy. To turn on the boys or girls or whoever they're with. Whoever they allow to peel back the layers and see what's beneath their clothes.

I don't look at underwear that way at all. They're just daily items I've worn for what feels like forever. I started developing at a young age, like in the fifth grade, and it was so embarrassing, having to get fitted for my first bra, the salesperson exclaiming over my large cup size at such a young age. The way my mother viewed me, undeniable disgust flickering in her gaze.

My breasts have always felt like a burden.

Reaching behind me, I undo the snap, the garment sliding away from my body, and I let it drop to the floor. My breasts are free, my nipples growing hard the longer I stare at them. They're pink, the areolas large and nothing like what I've seen on social media, where all the girls have small breasts and pretty nipples.

Not that I check out nipples but...I'm curious. I've been curious about a lot of things lately.

I curl my hands around them, cupping them in my palms. Bringing them together so I can make deeper cleavage. I turn to the side, staring at myself. My stomach. The flare of my hips. My legs. I'm so pale. Almost translucent, with faint blue veins showing just beneath my skin.

I think of Natalie with her perfect body and her tiny breasts. Her long legs and obvious confidence when she sat on Ezra's lap a few days ago, like she belonged there. All while eyeing Crew as if he was a tasty steak and she was craving red meat. What would it be like, to act like Natalie?

I have no clue.

Facing the mirror once more, I drop my hands from my breasts and reach for the waistband of my underwear, yanking them down before I have second thoughts. Until I'm standing completely naked, staring at my reflection. My body on complete and total display, for my eyes only.

I fixate on my dark pubic hair, and what it hides just beneath.

I mean, I'm not an idiot. I know what a vagina is good for. I have periods every month. Sometimes I have cramps. When I was younger, I suffered from them all the time, and my period was so irregular, my mother secretly put me on the pill, never telling my father.

"Just because you're on birth control doesn't mean you get to have sex with whoever you want," she lectured me. I was fourteen at the time, and the last thing I thought about was having sex with anyone.

Someday I'll marry a nice man and we'll have plenty of sex that I might or might not enjoy and eventually make babies. That's how my mother explained it to me. That's what I have to look forward to.

God, it all sounds so clinical. Awful.

Boring.

I think of Crew. How he touched my breast when he caught me. His firm grip, his muscular body pressed against mine, his fingers streaking across my chest in a featherlight caress. I felt it.

I can feel it right now. When he touched my lips in class this afternoon.

*You have a sexy mouth.*

His deep voice washes over me and I cup my breasts. Brush my thumbs over my nipples. Making myself tingle.

I go to my bed and lie on top of it, quickly realizing when I prop myself up on my elbows, I can still see my reflection in the mirror. Slowly, I part my knees. My thighs. Until I can see everything. I'm pink.

Everywhere.

I've never done anything like this before, examined myself so thoroughly. I stare at the spot between my legs, really looking at myself, and wonder what it would be like, to have someone touch me there.

Oh, I've tried masturbating before—more than a few times. Lots of times. But I can never manage to actually make myself come. My mind would start to wander and I'd think of dumb things, like stuff that worried me. Or the guilt would creep in and I'd feel that hint of shame I'm so familiar with. Like I was doing something bad. Plus, I'd never allowed myself to crush on a boy before. Not really.

Until Crew. I think about him constantly. And he makes me feel all of these…things. Feelings I've never experienced before and am slowly becoming addicted to.

The way he watches me with that penetrating gaze. His flirtatious tone when he calls me Birdy. I act like I hate it, but secretly I enjoy the nickname.

It makes me feel like we share something special.

*He* makes me feel special.

Collapsing on the bed, I close my eyes and reach between my legs, skimming past my pubic hair, until I'm cupping myself. Teasing myself. I stroke the seam of my lower lips back and forth, slowly. Shivery sensations shimmering just beneath my skin, making my breath catch.

It feels good.

I carefully part myself, dipping my finger inside. Encountering nothing but slippery wet heat. My mind fixates on Crew. His face. His voice. His hands.

With tentative fingers, I search, sliding through my folds, tentatively circling my entrance before I slip a finger inside, wincing. Then pull it out.

Push it back in.

*Oh*. That felt good too.

What it would be like, to have Crew kiss me? He has a nice mouth. Full lips. He smells good too. He's strong. Muscular. I already know how it feels to be in his arms, but what would be like if he really hugged me? Held me close and ran his fingers through my hair? Pressed his mouth against my temple in the softest, sweetest kiss?

I tremble just thinking about it.

When my fingers brush against a distended piece of flesh at the top, I realize it's my clitoris. I brush it again, a soft sigh falling from my lips when I do so. I keep doing it, circling it. Rubbing it. My breath comes faster, and when I squeeze my thighs together around my hand, that feels even better. The pressure. The intensity.

I roll over onto my stomach, my hand still between my thighs, my fingers busy as I basically dry hump the bed. The heel of my hand. I rock against the mattress, my eyes flying open to catch my reflection yet again.

I'm a mess. My hair is in my eyes, my skin damp with sweat, my breasts swinging, my nipples hard. I arch my back and press my hips to the bed, grinding my palm against my clit and a choked sound leaves me.

*Have you ever been kissed?*

He whispers it in my ear in my imagination, his mouth brushing my skin. I shiver and shake my head, wishing he was the one who would kiss me first. His lips are soft and warm and that first glide of his tongue against mine...

He pushes my hand away and replaces it with his own, stroking me. He's so confident. So in command of my body and I let him take control. Just like I always do with everyone and everything in my life.

With Crew, I don't resent it though.

I want it.

I'm on my back once more, my fingers frantic, my breathing harsh as I seek out the unfamiliar sensation that I can feel growing inside me. It's almost scary, how big it seems, how mysterious. Almost as if I don't know what it is, yet I do.

But I'm not afraid. I chase after it, all the air sticking in my throat, my limbs straining, my legs shaking as I stroke and stroke, faster and faster. A gasp leaves me when I go completely still.

*So fucking sexy, Birdy.*

And then I'm quaking, my entire body consumed, a keening

cry leaving my lips as the orgasm slams into me. It's as if I have no control of my body and the climax stretches on for long, endless seconds. Just as fast as it hits, it's gone, and I'm left a shaking, sweaty mess. Barely able to catch my breath, my heart beating so hard I swear I'm going into cardiac arrest.

That's what all the fuss is about. Imagine what would happen if someone else gave me an orgasm? Like Crew?

I squeeze my eyes closed, imagining him in this bed with me, his mouth finding mine, his fingers between my thighs, working their magic.

"Oh God," I whisper out loud, staring blindly at the ceiling.

Maybe there's nothing wrong with wanting a boy like Crew. Maybe I deserve to fall in love and go out on dates and kiss a boy for hours and let him touch me wherever he wants. What's wrong with that?

Nothing. Nothing at all. Like Crew said, we're just normal horny teenagers looking to get off.

I mean, that's not something I would ever say, but he has a point.

Glancing around my room, I realize I'm not satisfied. I'm still restless. Even a little frustrated. I want to experience this feeling again.

I want it all.

With Crew.

# *CHAPTER FIFTEEN*

## WREN

I climb out of the car, wincing when the bitterly cold air hits my cheeks. It's abnormally brisk, despite the bright sunshine overhead, and I probably didn't dress right for the weather. I smooth my hands over the fitted leather skirt my mother bought me a few months ago that I immediately shoved into the back of my closet. I've never worn anything like this, so I don't know what possessed her to think I'd wear it.

But I woke up this morning with a new resolve. I'm branching out. Doing new and different things. I don't know exactly what those things are yet, but seeking independence is one of them. Hence the leather skirt, which really reveals nothing but still feels daring, along with the cream-colored cashmere turtleneck sweater, which emphasizes the size of my breasts. Normally I'd shy away from an outfit like this because I don't want to draw attention to myself.

There's nothing about this morning—or myself—that feels normal.

Like last night, when I skipped dinner completely and stayed locked away in my bedroom. I opened up my laptop and searched for porn sites, glancing around like I'd find someone watching me do something so forbidden before I watched a twenty-minute clip of a couple doing all sorts of things in a variety of sexual positions.

It was eye-opening. Undeniably arousing. When I watched the man go down on the woman, his lips and tongue and fingers everywhere, her hands in his hair clutching him close, I lost all control and masturbated again. Imagining someone was doing the same thing to me the entire time.

A certain someone with icy blue eyes and a shitty smile on his face as he watched me practically beg for him to do it. Just before he leaned down and dragged his tongue across my clit.

God, I'm a mess. Seriously. Why would I fantasize about him?

He's the worst.

"Call or text me when you're ready to be picked up, miss." The driver hands me a business card with his phone number on it. "I'll come right over when you're ready."

"Thank you." I offer him a smile and take the card from him, watching as he shuts the door. "I appreciate it."

I turn away and head for the gallery entrance, making my way inside. I'm greeted by a friendly gallery assistant, a woman who looks only a few years older than I am, her eyes flaring with interest the longer she studies me.

"Hello. Welcome. May I take your coat?"

"Good morning," I tell her as I let her help me out of my camel-colored coat. "Thank you."

She studies my face, her delicate brows drawing together. "Aren't you Cecily Beaumont's daughter?"

Of course, she'd recognize me. My mother is very well-known in certain art world circles, especially in Manhattan. "Yes, I am."

"Oh, it's such an honor to meet you," she gushes. "I'm Kirstin."

"Hi, Kirstin." I shake her offered hand. "I'm Wren."

"Will your mother be joining you this morning?" Kirstin asks hopefully.

"Unfortunately, no. She had other plans." I didn't even invite her. I haven't seen her since I came home yesterday, though I know she's been around.

The disappointment on Kirstin's face is obvious. "That's too bad. I'm so glad you're here though. Are you a fan of Hannah's?"

Hannah Walsh is the artist whose work is showing at the gallery. Her latest collection borrows heavily from Picasso, but she puts her own spin on it. Her work is fresh yet familiar, with a hint of a feminine edge to it.

"I am," I say as I glance around the narrow gallery. There aren't very many people here this morning, but I'm early, showing up just after the gallery opened. "I'm really hoping to find a piece to purchase."

Kirstin smiles. "That's fantastic. She's already sold a few paintings, but there are still plenty to choose from."

"I wish I could've been here for the opening, but I'm in school during the week, so it didn't work out," I admit.

"Oh, the opening was such a success. It helped that she brought her handsome fiancé, the professional football player. He was so proud of her." Kirstin smiles. "They were so sweet to see together."

"I'm sure," I murmur, knowing all about Hannah's backstory. What would that be like, to have such a successful, handsome man in your corner? Supporting you and your career? There's a lot written about him, but not as much about her, and I find her so intriguing.

I think that's why I'm also drawn to her work.

"Would you like me to walk you around the exhibit, or would you rather explore on your own?"

"If you don't mind, I'll walk around by myself for a bit. I'll call you if I need you though," I tell her with a faint smile.

"Okay, sounds perfect." I'm about to walk away when she continues, "Can I just mention how much I admire your mother and what she's done for the art world? She's so generous, and has such a smart eye. You're lucky to have learned so much from her."

I hear this a lot, but rarely does anyone include me in the

equation like she just did.

I stand a little taller, feeling proud.

"Thank you. I'll let her know you said that," I tell her before I walk away.

Kirstin's words stick with me as I stop in front of the first painting, staring at it blindly. It doesn't feel like I've learned anything from my mother. Well, I must've learned some, but mostly from observing her and what she did, not because she actually took the time to teach me anything about art and collecting. Everything I know I mostly self-taught, with my father interjecting here and there with his own opinions.

He collects, but she's the true collector. He pays for it all, but she's the one who chooses almost every single piece they own. They've been a complimentary pair throughout their marriage, though lately things seem a little—off between them whenever I'm around. Like they've lost interest in each other.

And me.

Shaking myself out of my thoughts, I wander through the gallery, stopping in front of each piece and contemplating it with a critical eye. They're all striking. She paints with bold strokes and vivid colors. Bright imagery that leaves nothing to the imagination, the pieces are mostly of people. Women. Men. Pets. One cityscape, though it's already sold, probably because it's the lone painting in that style.

I envy the person who purchased it.

I keep coming back to one painting in particular. The background is a rich, deep green, and there's a woman sitting on the floor, a cat lying just out of reach beside her. The woman's arm is stretched out, abnormally short, and the cat is looking directly at me while the woman stares at the cat.

It's almost unnerving, the image conveyed in the painting, and I walk away from it every time.

Only to find myself standing in front of it once more.

"I think you like this one the best," says a deep, familiar

male voice.

I go completely still, my breath stalling in my lungs as I slowly turn to find...

Crew Lancaster standing next to me, his gaze on the painting in front of us.

Why is he here? How did he know? Where did he come from? I didn't even notice him enter the gallery. I guess I was too wrapped up in looking at each painting.

"What are you doing here?" I ask breathlessly.

"Heard there was an exhibit in Tribeca now until the end of the year. Thought I'd come check it out." He slips his hands into his pockets, glancing over at me. "You're here for the same reason?"

I sort of want to punch him. Or hug him. I feel like I conjured him up in a dream. Is this moment even real? "Yeah. Actually I am."

As if he didn't know.

"Funny coincidence." He returns his attention to the painting, quietly studying it before he takes a step forward to read the information card posted next to it. "Hmm. Interesting. This one's called Two Pussies."

"*No.*" I move toward the painting, shoving past him to read that the name of the painting is...

Two Pussies.

He's chuckling when I turn to face him, my shock obvious, I'm sure. "I can't believe it's called that."

"Oh, I can. Isn't art supposed to be stimulating?"

I stare at him in disbelief. I also still can't believe he's here. Standing in front of me. He looks so good, dressed in jeans and a charcoal gray sweater, with a black jacket over it. Nike Blazers on his feet and a beanie on his head, which he tugs off and shoves in his coat pocket, leaving his hair in complete disarray.

I'm tempted to straighten it for him. Run my fingers through it. See if it's as soft as it looks.

"Why do you think I like this piece?" I ask him.

"Because you keep coming back to it."

"How long have you been here?"

"Long enough to see you return to this particular painting three times already." He takes a step closer, his voice lowering. "Just buy it, Birdy. You know you want it."

His words sizzle through my blood and I turn away so my back is to him, my gaze on the painting once more. "It's the green that I like the most. It's so deep."

"Is green your favorite color?"

I feel him take a step closer, his body heat seeping into me. I keep myself rigid so I don't touch him, even though I want to. "No. I like pink. Or red." I hesitate before I ask, "What's your favorite color?"

"Green." He leans in, his mouth so close to my ear, just like I imagined last night. "Like your eyes."

My legs shake and I lock my knees, tilting my head down as I try to catch my breath. What is he trying to say?

What is he trying to do?

"Are you going to buy it?" He's so close, his breath wafts across my ear. My neck. I lift my head to meet his intense gaze, my mouth going dry the longer we study each other. "You should. Your gut is telling you it's the one."

I press my lips together, afraid I might blurt out something stupid like how my gut is suddenly telling me *he's* the one.

But I keep quiet, swallowing the words that want to burst from my mouth.

"Let's walk around the gallery one more time," I suggest. "I want to really make sure this is the piece that I want."

"Don't you ever do anything impulsive, Birdy?" His tone is soft. Almost suggestive.

"No. Not really."

"You should try it sometime."

"Why?"

"Sometimes, doing something without thinking can be liberating."

I don't know what it's like, to be liberated. To feel free. It's a foreign concept. I'm told what to do, where to do it, and when I should. My entire life, I've been completely controlled.

"Art makes me feel free," I tell him.

He tilts his head. "What do you mean?"

"It's hard to explain." My gaze returns yet again to the painting. "Looking at this makes me feel like I could be a different person. Like maybe I'm the girl lying on the floor, wishing her cat would come closer so she could pet her."

Crew chuckles. "You think that's the message the artist is trying to convey?"

"I don't know what she's trying to say, but that's what I see. Frustration. She just wants to be loved. Isn't that what we all want?" I glance over at him.

He says nothing, but the look on his face speaks volumes.

"We all have different reactions to art," I continue. "That's what makes it so wonderful. It's not just one thing. It's so many things. A million ideas and thoughts and visions."

Crew stares, his gaze appreciative, his voice low and rough when he speaks. "I love how passionate you are about art. And beauty."

I blink at him, surprised by his compliment. "I like pretty things."

"So do I." His gaze sweeps over me, as if he's really taking me in for the first time. "Speaking of pretty things, I like your outfit."

When his eyes linger on my chest, I don't even mind. "Thank you."

"Not what you usually wear."

I lift my chin. "You only ever see me in a uniform."

"True."

"I am trying something different though."

"I like it." His smile is small. "Buy the painting."

I don't even think when I answer him. "Okay."

His smile grows. "And after you buy the painting, we can go to lunch."

"You want to go to lunch with me?" I'm frowning. If we do this, if I go with him, it could change the dynamic between us.

It could change my entire life.

"Yes. Do you want to go to lunch with me?"

My nod is slow, my heart beating heavily. "Yes," I whisper.

"What do you think of the exhibit, Miss Beaumont?"

The spell broken by the gallery assistant, both Crew and I turn to find Kirstin standing in front of us with a smile on her face.

"It's wonderful," I tell her. "I'm having a hard time deciding which piece I want."

"Oh, so you'll definitely be making a purchase? I'm excited to see which one you choose."

"She's thinking about this one," Crew says, indicating the painting we're standing in front of.

Kirstin laughs. "It's very striking, from her use of color to the name. I think the artist wanted to shock a little bit with this exhibit."

"It's the color," I say, glancing over at the painting yet again. Realizing that Crew is watching me very carefully. It's almost unnerving, how he's staring at me. "I love the green."

"It's beautiful," Kirstin says wistfully, her gaze now on the painting as well. I can see it in her eyes. She wishes she could own it. Own all of them. It's why she's working here. She's most likely an art history major, a woman who wants to surround herself with art that speaks to her soul. Pretty things that make her feel like she's going to burst.

I know the feeling.

"I'll take it," I say, and I can see the approval on Crew's face with my choice.

"Wonderful. I'll go write up the bill of sale," Kirstin says before she turns away and heads for the front of the building.

"Great choice," Crew says after she's gone.

"Thank you. I do love it." I stare at the painting—*my* painting— my chest growing tighter the longer I look at it. "I don't know where I'm going to hang it though."

"At your house?"

"I suppose. I just don't want it in my parents' collection. This one is mine." My gaze finds Crew's once more. "All mine."

# CHAPTER SIXTEEN

## WREN

After I've made my purchase and we're about to leave, Kirstin brings me my coat. Crew takes it from her and helps me slip it on, his hands going to my hair, fingers brushing against my nape when he pulls it out from beneath my collar. His fingers continue slipping through the strands, stroking through my hair, and I glance up at him, unable to look away from his heavy gaze.

"Didn't want it to get caught," he murmurs, and I nod in agreement, unable to find any words.

So I remain quiet. Lost in thought. At the realization that this isn't some fantasy that I conjured up in my brain like I did last night. He's actually here, standing in front of me, watching me carefully. As carefully as I watch him.

Can he feel it? The attraction between us? The chemistry? Or is it all one-sided? Am I just a silly little girl with a crush on a guy who has zero interest in me? Is he only humoring me? Toying with me?

Crew came here, to this exhibit, to seek me out. There's no other reason for his appearance than his wanting to see me.

Me.

He escorts me out of the gallery, his hand at the small of my back, guiding me to the curb. He looks both ways before he takes my hand and leads me across the street, heading toward a black Mercedes sedan that sits idling at the curb. A man in a black suit climbs out of the driver's side, a pleasant smile on his face.

"You found a guest, Mr. Lancaster."

"I did," Crew answers. "Wren, this is Peter."

"Nice to meet you," I say to Peter. He's an older gentleman with salt and pepper hair and warm brown eyes.

"Miss." Peter tips his head toward me before he reaches for the handle and opens the back door for us. I slip inside first, Crew following after me and the door shuts, enclosing us in complete silence. The only sound I can hear is the soft purr of the idling engine and my rapidly beating heart.

"Where do you want to go to lunch?" Crew asks, his voice quiet. Making me shiver.

"I don't know." I shrug one shoulder, my stomach suddenly protesting.

I can't remember the last time I ate anything.

"Are you hungry?"

It's the way he stares at my lips that makes me say, "Absolutely starving."

"Me too." His smile is slow.

So is mine.

After we do a little research on our phones, we settle on a restaurant not too far from the gallery that serves breakfast and lunch. The front of Two Hands Restaurant is painted a bright, cheerful blue and when we walk inside, I'm captivated by the light, airy design. It's all white or pale wood, the brick walls white-washed, the giant light fixtures hanging from the ceiling constructed of metal wire.

The hostess leads us to the only open spot in the restaurant—a cramped table for two in front of the windows, overlooking the street. When we settle in our seats, Crew's knees bump against mine, making me flush all over.

"How tall are you?" I ask once the hostess leaves us with menus.

He frowns. "Why do you ask?"

"Oh. You just, uh, bumped into me."

"Sorry."

"I didn't mind," I admit, my cheeks catching on fire, which is so stupid. "You have long legs."

"I'm six-two."

I knew he was tall. I'm only five-five.

"All the Lancasters are tall," he continues. "Mostly blond. Blue eyes. We all look pretty much the same."

If all the Lancaster men are as handsome as Crew, then they must be devastating.

Our server appears, overly cheerful as she asks us for our drink order. Her hair is dyed a vivid pink, cut into a severe bob, and she's wearing pink glasses that match. She's adorable.

"Just water," I tell her with a faint smile.

"Same," Crew adds.

"Great. I'll be back in a minute to take your order." She takes off and I watch her go, noting how confident she seems. You'd have to be to have hair that color.

"Do you like girls with pink hair?" I ask Crew.

He levels that icy blue gaze on me. "I prefer brunettes."

"Really."

Crew nods. "With green eyes and an appreciation for art."

"You're just saying that." I grab my menu and hold it up in front of me, trying to concentrate on what I'm reading, but the words just go blurry. I can feel him watching me, not saying a word, and it completely unnerves me. Finally, I drop my menu. "What?"

"Do you really think 'I'm just saying that' when I followed you to the gallery? You think that was actually a coincidence?"

I blink at him, captivated by his intensity. "No." He goes quiet until I can't take it anymore. "Why are you here anyway?"

"Why do you think?"

"You're stalking me?"

He laughs, the sound rough, and with little humor. It ends as quickly as it started. "No."

Feels like it, though I don't say so. "You said you were going to keep tabs on me after what I—saw."

"That was just an excuse."

"Then why? I don't get it. I'm nothing special." When I spot the incredulous look on his face, I keep talking. "No, really I'm not. I'm naïve and sheltered, and ridiculed at school for my beliefs. People don't like you when you make them uncomfortable."

"You think you make people uncomfortable?"

I nod. "I know I do. They don't like the ring and what it stands for." I hold up my hand for him to see it. This stupid ring that's starting to feel more and more like a burden, especially after what I did last night.

Shame washes over me at the memories.

"I think you're brave."

"Or stupid."

"Not stupid, Birdy. Never stupid."

"Do you ever feel trapped? Like there's all this expectation on you to do all of these—things, sometimes things you don't even want to do. People want you to act a certain way too. They never let you handle things on your own. As if they don't think you're capable of anything." I press my lips together, suddenly wondering if I said too much.

"All the time," he drawls. "As the baby of the family, my father wants to keep me on a short leash."

"As the only child, my father does the same."

"Yet he barely acknowledges me. Half the time, I think he forgets I even exist," he continues.

"I wish my father forgot I existed sometimes." A sigh leaves me. "I don't know what it's like, to be my own person."

"I think you're trying to be exactly that right now," he says.

His words give me hope. "You really think so?"

"Definitely. You're stronger than you think. You just need to stretch your wings, and eventually fly." He settles his hand over mine, rubbing his thumb across my knuckles, electricity sparking where we touch. "When do you turn eighteen?"

"Christmas Day," I admit.

"Coming up then." He doesn't remove his hand from mine, and I like that. His possessive touch, the way he's studying me. "Are you doing anything special?"

"I was going to have a party the day after," I admit.

"Where?"

"At my parents' apartment. But I don't know." I shrug. "I don't have any friends."

"Yeah, you do."

"None of them are real."

He's quiet for a moment, and I take his silence as agreement. Until he says, "I'm your friend."

Until this very moment, I would've never described Crew Lancaster as my *friend*.

"Are you really?" I whisper.

"I'm whatever you want me to be." He curls his fingers around mine and lifts our linked hands, bringing them to his mouth, where he brushes the softest kiss against my knuckles.

I feel that touch all the way to my soul, settling deep in my bones. I lean toward him, my lips parting, my mouth dry, wishing I could find the words to explain how he makes me feel.

Like anything is possible.

"You should have the party," he says.

Pulling my hand from his grip, I settle back in my seat. "I don't think so. I'm going to cancel it."

"Maybe you should let me take you out for your birthday." He settles his hand over mine once more, as if he can't stop touching me.

Why is he being so nice? Why does he suddenly care? It's like he knew what I was doing last night. Touching myself while thinking of him, and now he's here, and I don't understand his mood change.

I wonder if he has ulterior motives...

"You want to take me out for my birthday? Why?" My voice squeaks, and I press my lips together.

The server appears, interrupting us, and Crew lets go of my hand. I sink it into my lap, clutching my hands together, nerves eating at me as the server mentions a few specials while I frantically scan the menu items.

"What would you like?" she chirps at me.

Slightly panicked, I order a salad, earning an incredulous look from Crew before he orders a cheeseburger and fries.

My stomach cramps at the thought of eating a burger, and I immediately regret my choice. But I'm not changing it.

No way can I eat a burger and fries in front of him.

When the server leaves, the conversation turns lighter. We talk about school. Art. The places we've been, the things we've seen. He discusses his brothers. His sister. I tell him about my parents, but I don't go into too much depth. I don't want him to know how lately, our relationship feels fractured. I don't like how it makes me feel.

By the time our meals arrive, I'm starving, and I stare at my salad in dismay, the scent of Crew's lunch wafting toward me, making my stomach growl. I watch as he brings the burger to his mouth and takes a big bite, my gaze lingering on his lips. How he chews. Swallows. Grabs a couple of fries and dips them in ketchup before he drops them into his mouth.

I stab my fork in the bowl of salad like I'm trying to murder lettuce and kale, shoveling it in, frustration rippling through me as I eat, wishing there were at least pieces of chicken in it. It's good, but I bet I'll end up hungry again within the hour.

"You're watching me eat as if you want to steal the burger out of my hands," Crew says at one point, amusement in his voice.

"It looks delicious," I admit.

"Why didn't you order one?" He takes another bite.

"I don't eat a lot of red meat," I admit, which is true.

"Why not?" His gaze narrows. "You don't think you're fat, do you?"

I shake my head. Shrug. "Maybe? I don't know. I need to watch my weight."

"You've got big tits, Bird. That's it. And a nice ass." He drops the crude compliments so easily, making me blush.

"They're too big," I whisper, briefly glancing down at my chest.

"No, they're definitely not." He's staring at them, then blinks, as if shaking himself out of a trance. He holds the burger toward me. "Want a bite?"

I'm dying for a bite. I nod, and he feeds it to me, placing the burger in front of my mouth as I sink my teeth into it. The moment the flavors burst on my tongue, I'm moaning, savoring it as I chew slowly and eventually swallow.

Crew is staring at me, his lips parted. The half-eaten burger still clutched in his hand. "You're sexy when you eat."

My blush deepens. "I'm sure I look like a pig."

"You definitely don't." He drops the burger on his plate and pushes it toward me. "Have some fries."

We share his plate, clearing everything in minutes, the salad long forgotten. When the server stops by, Crew orders more fries and lets me eat most of them, watching me with an amused look on his face the entire time.

Like I entertain him, which is both thrilling and scary. I don't know what we're doing, but I've decided to stop wondering about his motives and just go with it.

"You never did answer my question," I say to him as I'm still devouring fries.

He frowns. "What question?"

"Why you want to take me out for my birthday." I sip from my water glass. "You barely know me."

"I'm getting to know you."

"And sometimes you still act as if you don't like me."

"Right back at you." He smiles.

Ugh, he's too pretty when he does that.

"I just don't go out for my birthday with some random boy," I say, my voice small.

"I'm not just some *random boy*, as you call me. We've known each other for a while," he says, as if that makes all the sense in the world for him wanting to take me out.

"And you've treated me terribly since day one," I remind him.

"Yet here you are, sitting in a restaurant having lunch with me." The smile is still there, and I'm tempted to slap it off his face.

Or kiss it off.

Okay fine, more like kiss it off.

Clearing my throat, I decide to be brave for once in my life.

"Do you like me now, Crew? Or is this some sort of secret trick you're going to pull on me? Is Ezra lurking around the corner, filming us together? Or maybe it's Malcolm. He seems to dislike me more."

Anger flushes his face and his eyes burn as he glares at me. "No one is secretly filming us. Don't put me on the same level as Larsen."

"I'm not, it's just..." My voice drifts and I stare out the window for a moment. "I don't know if I should trust your motives."

That's as real and as raw as I can get. Being with Crew is exciting, but it's also...

Scary.

For all sorts of reasons. Good and bad.

When I return my attention to him, I find he's watching me, his expression serious. He's quiet for so long, I start to wiggle in my seat.

"You should trust me," he finally says. "I like you, Birdy. And I don't go chasing after random girls in art galleries on a Saturday morning. That's not my style."

I dip my head, unable to stop the smile from spreading across my face. A thousand butterflies just hatched in my stomach, their fluttering wings making me giddy.

"I have a question for you," he says, right when I shove the last fry in my mouth.

I pause in my chewing, swallowing before I say, "Whenever you start a sentence like that, it always ends up being an uncomfortable subject for me."

"We're getting to know each other, remember? I'm curious about you."

"Okay." I drag the word out.

"About the ring. How that came about." His gaze drops to my hand. "The purity ball or whatever it's called. Why did you go?"

"It's a long story."

"I've got all afternoon to listen." He leans back in his chair, making himself comfortable.

God, he's so annoying sometimes. Always asking me about stuff I don't want to talk about.

Yet here I am, ready to tell him all about it.

"It started before the ring. I did something that—scared my parents when I was twelve," I admit.

His gaze flickers with interest. "What happened?"

"I got my first phone and I immediately joined a bunch of forums that focused on stuff I was interested in. Mostly boy bands."

"One Direction?"

I nod. "It's a rite of passage for preteen girls around my age."

"I was always partial to Harry," he teases. At my surprised look, he continues, "I have a sister, I know about One Direction."

"Everyone loves Harry. I liked Niall. But anyway." I wave a hand. "I spent a lot of time on these forums and I met a boy on there. He was fifteen."

"That should've been your first clue something was up. What fifteen-year-old dude goes on those forums to talk about One Direction?" Crew rolls his eyes.

"I was only twelve. I didn't know." I shrug, feeling defensive.

"Anyway, we started talking. A lot. He asked me for a photo and I sent him one. He shared his photo with me. Lots of photos. He was really cute. Sweet. He seemed to understand me, when no one else really ever has."

I go quiet, the memories painful. I was gullible. Completely innocent. I believed in him so strongly, I thought we could be together. He would be my boyfriend.

"What happened?" Crew asks quietly.

"He wanted to meet me. In Central Park on a beautiful spring day, so I agreed." I press my lips together, my gaze growing distant. "I took my friends though. They wouldn't let me go alone."

"You have good friends."

"Had. We all went our separate ways when I got into Lancaster." A sigh leaves me. "He never showed, and I was just…devastated. We waited at the park for hours, until it started getting dark. My friends comforted me, but I cried standing in the middle of Central Park, believing I'd been dumped. The moment I got home and finally checked the forum, I had a bunch of direct messages from him, yelling at me in all caps that he actually went to the park. He even saw me, but he was angry because I brought my friends. He just wanted me there alone, he said."

"If he was fifteen, he wouldn't have cared," Crew observes.

"Exactly. And he wasn't fifteen. He was thirty-nine. Married with a couple of kids. The photos he shared with me were of his oldest son." My appetite leaves me and I shove the plate away. "I was so humiliated."

"How did you find out he was a perverted dad looking to get with a little girl?" Crew's expression is thunderous.

"After the missed meeting, I couldn't stop crying, and I was so depressed. I stopped talking to him as much, and he kept trying to get me to meet up with him, but I refused. I thought he would just trick me again and not show up. I'm so glad I didn't go." A shuddery breath leaves me. "My parents were aware that I was upset, but I wouldn't tell them anything. My father eventually did a search of my phone and found out about the relationship I had with the boy. He's the one who discovered who he really was by hiring a private investigator. It was so embarrassing."

"What happened after that?"

"Turns out the guy talked to other girls my age and even met with a few of them—and raped them."

"Holy shit." Crew actually appears surprised.

I nod. "I know. I was lucky. Once that all went down, my parents—my father—went into total protection mode. He wouldn't let me go anywhere alone. I had to report where I was at all times. They put a tracker on my phone. They wouldn't let me spend the night at my friends' houses. I was on complete lockdown," I explain.

"Sounds awful."

"It was, and I was so scared all the time. I didn't trust myself, or my judgment. I was tricked by that guy, and it hurt. My parents made me apply to Lancaster, even though I didn't want to go there. I wanted to stay with my friends and go to the same high school as they did, but my parents wanted me safe. My father didn't trust me."

"Do you feel safe at Lancaster?"

"Lately, no. I was oblivious to what was really going on the last three years, so I guess I did feel safe. Ignorance is bliss, I guess? Right before I turned fifteen, my father came to me, explaining the purity ball and how it works. What it stood for. He wanted me to make a promise to myself, and swear that I wouldn't get involved sexually with any boy until I got married. I think he was worried I'd make bad decisions I'd end up regretting. Like— before."

"That's…kind of heavy," Crew says. "And you shouldn't have to pay for that one mistake you made for the rest of your life."

He's right. I know he is. "At the time, it was exactly what I needed. What I firmly believed in. I thought I still did, but now…I don't know."

Crew frowns. "What do you mean?"

"I'm almost eighteen. And as you already know, I've never been kissed. I can't go through life completely sheltered, can I? I need to experiment. Meet guys. Go on dates. Kiss them. Let them touch me. Right?"

# CHAPTER SEVENTEEN

## CREW

This entire day has been a complete revelation. Discovering Wren's many secrets as she reveals them to me, layer by layer, bit by bit. Until she's laid herself completely bare, and she's asking me if she should go on dates and let guys touch and kiss her.

Just using the word *guys* as in plural, sets my blood boiling. I don't want to see anyone touch her.

Only me.

"That's up to you," I finally say, resting my folded arms on the edge of the table. "Do you want to go out with other guys? Kiss them? Let them touch you?"

"I can't be a virgin forever," she whispers.

"Not like you need to go out and fuck some random guy on your first go," I snap, sounding like a jealous asshole.

"I don't want to do that," she immediately says. "I just—I've had some thoughts lately. Done some things."

She's got me curious as fuck with that statement. "Like what?"

Wren rapidly shakes her head, glancing down at the table. "I can't say."

"Why not?"

"It's too embarrassing." She sounds miserable.

"Come on, Birdy. It's just me. We're in a public spot.

Surrounded by people. How bad can it be?"

"Promise you won't make fun of me?" she whispers to the table.

"Look at me." She glances up, and I keep my expression as neutral as possible. "I won't make fun of you."

I would never make fun of her. Not anymore. Not after she's shared so much with me. She's been so open. So vulnerable.

"Okay." A shaky breath leaves her as she glances up at me. She tilts her head left, then right, as if she's cracking her neck and readying to jump into the ring, primed to fight. "I was alone last night and I—oh God, I can't say it out loud."

Her face is crimson. Whatever she did, she's embarrassed about it. I can only assume a handful of things she could possibly do while alone last night, so I decide to say it for her.

"Did you...touch yourself?"

Her green eyes are wide and fathomless. "Yes."

My dick twitches. "Did you finger yourself?"

She nods.

"Make yourself come?"

More nodding. "A couple of times."

Jesus. My dick is hard.

"I watched a porn too. For the first time. All the way through. I mean, I've seen stuff. Images. Clips. You know how it is on the internet. You can't escape the sex stuff. It's everywhere. But I sat there and watched a twenty-minute video between a man and a woman and it was—it was so hot." She sounds flustered. As if she's still aroused just thinking about it.

I shift in my seat. "What did you like best?"

She frowns. "What do you mean?"

I guess I'm into torture. That's the only logical reason for me asking her these kinds of questions.

"What part of the video did you like the best? What turned you on the most out of what you saw? What they did?"

"Oh." More blushing. She glances around the room, as if

checking to see if anyone's paying attention to us, but they're not. The place is bustling, with the low rumble of multiple conversations lingering in the air. I'm on fucking edge, waiting to hear her answer. "This is so embarrassing. I'm getting hot just thinking about it."

Hot and wet is what I want to say, but I remain quiet.

She actually fans her face with her fingers, and it's the fucking cutest thing.

"Come on, Birdy." My voice drops. "Tell me."

"When he went down on her." The sentence comes out in a rush, the words strung together so they sound like one.

*Whenhewentdownonher.*

If her cheeks get any redder, I swear they'll catch on fire.

"Did she come when he did that?"

"Sort of. I don't know. It looked kind of fake. Really intense." She shakes her head. "When I came, it wasn't like that."

Well damn. Now all I can think about is finding out what Wren's O-face looks like. "Want me to be real with you right now?"

"Yes," she whispers.

"I'm surprised you're admitting all of this to me."

"I am too." She covers her face with her hands for a moment, shaking her head once. "I don't know what's wrong with me."

"I like it." She separates her fingers, so I can see her eyes peeking at me. "Keep talking."

She laughs, dropping her hands into her lap. "I bet you like it."

"Don't worry. Your secret is safe with me."

Her laughter dies. "I hope so. I-I'm probably stupid for admitting this, but I trust you, Crew. And I trust that you won't tell anyone what I just shared with you."

This is my little birdy's problem—she trusts too easily. I show her a little bit of attention, and she's confessing all of her dirty secrets. Why this girl decided to tell me she masturbated and got herself off last night, I don't know.

But I'm thankful as fuck because now I know. I'm not about to let Larsen the asshole slip in and be the one who helps her explore her sexuality. Knowing how easy it was for me to gain her trust, I'm worried Larsen could have an even easier time of it. He's known her longer. She seemed comfortable with him when I saw them talk at school.

I can't let it happen. I need to distract her. Keep her from going to that dinner tonight.

The server shows up with the bill and I hand her my credit card. She takes care of it with her handheld machine, making idle conversation with me, but I'm too distracted. By the sight of Wren smiling at me shyly from across the table, mouthing the words *thank you* to me for paying for her lunch.

I'd buy her more than just a meal, though that had been exquisite torture. Watching her eat. Feeding her. The sounds she'd make, the low moans and murmured words full of appreciation.

It felt like fucking foreplay.

"Let's get out of here," I say once the server hands me my credit card and my receipt. I'm already rising to my feet, slipping on my coat and my beanie. I'm about to help Wren with hers, but she beats me to it, pulling her sleek coat on and grabbing her bag before she heads for the door.

I follow her outside, my phone in my hand as I tap away at the screen, sending Peter a quick message to come pick us up. He's been with the family for a few years and he's a loyal employee. Quiet.

Discreet.

Exactly what I need right now.

Peter pulls to the curb within minutes and I open the door for Wren, allowing her to crawl into the back seat before I follow her, slamming the door behind us.

"Where to?" Peter's gaze meets mine in the rearview mirror.

"Drive around for an hour, would you?" I shoot Wren a quick look to find her already watching me, her brows lowered in confusion. "I don't want the afternoon to end just yet."

Her smile is slow. Beautiful. "I don't either."

"Will do," Peter says with a nod, shifting the car into drive before he pulls back onto the street.

"Where are you taking me?" Wren asks, her voice soft.

I could come up with a long list of cheesy responses, every single one of them crude and sexual, but I don't say any of that. This girl is sweet and kind and so fucking pure, it's almost painful. I treated her like absolute garbage for so long. Chased after her only a few days ago, making her practically beg me not to do anything to her.

We've come a long way, my little birdy and me. I don't want to spook her by coming on too strong. But fuck, I want every piece of her. Her lips. Her tits. Her pussy. Her ass. I want to own her body and soul, and when we're finished, when I've fucked her over and over and made her come so hard, she nearly blacks out, I want her to look at me as if I'm a god. As if I'm *her* god and she'll promise herself to me, not her father. I want to take that ring her father put on her finger and toss it. Make her forget all of her earlier promises.

More than anything, I want to own her.

"Where do you want to go?" I ask her, my gaze catching on her coat. How thick it is. Looks expensive.

What would she say if I laid it out on the back seat and then proceeded to go down on her? Give her a little bit of what she's wanting from that porn she watched last night?

Peter probably wouldn't look.

Yeah. No. I can't do anything like that. Again, I don't want to scare her. And he doesn't deserve to see her naked. No one should see her like that.

Except for me.

"Wherever you want to go." She rests her cheek against the soft black leather seat, smiling up at me with adoring eyes. All of her trust is shining in the green depths. I can't help but see it and feel pain, because if I fuck this up—and I'm bound to, I'm not good at shit like this—I will hurt her beyond measure.

And that is the last thing I want to do.

# CHAPTER EIGHTEEN

## WREN

I press my cheek against the cool leather seat, blatantly staring at Crew Lancaster, not caring one bit that I might look foolish. He doesn't seem to mind.

Drinking in all the male beauty sitting in front of me is almost overwhelming, he's so attractive. I love how his cheeks turned slightly pink thanks to the cold air, making him look younger. Softer.

Though there's not much about Crew's face that anyone could consider soft. He's all hard angles and sharp lines. High cheekbones, firm jaw and square chin. Dark brows that are currently lowered as he watches me, those cool blue eyes growing warmer the longer he stares, as if he likes what he sees.

I like what I see too.

The only thing I can consider soft on Crew's handsome face is his mouth. His lips are pink, the lower lip much fuller than the top, and they're currently parted, his gaze lingering on my mouth until it lifts to meet mine.

My body grows warm, and not just because of the thick coat I'm wearing. He's thinking about kissing me. I know he is. And it's all I want. I want to know what he tastes like. What kind of kisses will he deliver? Soft and sweet? Fierce and rough?

Maybe a combination of both.

"You keep staring at me like that and..." His voice drifts.

"And what?"

His broad chest rises and falls, as if he just took a deep, maybe even nervous, breath. "I can't be held responsible for what I might do."

"Tell me what you want to do to me." Even though it scares me a little, I want to hear every single dirty word he can come up with.

All of them.

He glances over at the driver. "I don't want to say it out loud. You might get embarrassed, Birdy."

"I won't. I promise." I press my thighs together, trying to ease the sudden throbbing, but it only makes things worse. "Whisper it in my ear."

Crew reaches out, his hand going to the seatbelt buckle and undoing it. I shrug the strap away from my body, letting him take my hand and pull me closer. Until I'm sitting in the center of the back seat, and he's strapping me back in, his hand brushing against my chest as he pulls the belt across me, then pushes the buckle into the slot.

We're sitting so close I can see the stubble lining his cheeks. Feel his body heat seeping into my side, making me even hotter. We stare at each other, the tension growing between us, and I swallow hard, ready to say something, when he leans in, his mouth at my ear, his soft exhale making me shiver.

"I want to kiss you. Taste you. Kiss your neck. Nibble it. Run my hands under your sweater, slip them under your bra, until I'm squeezing your tits. Pinching your nipples."

I avert my gaze, my breaths coming faster.

"I'd take off your sweater. Your skirt. Kiss you all over your body. Tell you how fucking beautiful you are, because you are so damn beautiful, Wren. The prettiest little birdy I've ever seen."

I close my eyes, savoring his compliment.

"I'd slip my hand beneath your panties and find you soaking wet. All for me. I'd finger you until you're begging me to make you come, and when you eventually explode all over my hand, I'd make you lick my fingers clean."

My eyes fly open to find him watching me, his gaze dark. Intense. I glance down at his lap to see he has an erection.

Oh God. What would he do if I reached over and touched it?

He moves even closer, his mouth brushing against my earlobe and I bite back the moan that wants to escape. "After I fucked you with my fingers, I'd fuck you with my tongue. I'd lick you from front to back, until you're screaming and coming so hard you almost blackout."

My heart races, my chest rising and falling so fast, it almost hurts. He pulls away, his gaze finding mine once more as he says, "That's what I would do to you. For starters."

There's so much promise in his expression. In his words. And I realize I don't want to be promised to my father anymore.

I want this boy. I don't care if it doesn't last. Maybe I don't want it to.

I just want to know what it feels like to have a man make me come. To feel his soft hair brush against my thighs as he lavishes my most private spot with his tongue. His fingers. I want to touch him. Everywhere. I want to feel his mouth on mine, his tongue thrusting.

Without thought, I lunge forward, reaching for the beanie still on his head, tearing it off, exposing his rumpled hair. I thrust my hands into the silky softness, straightening it as best I can, not saying a word. He lets me, remaining quiet as well, his eyelids falling shut briefly when I continue stroking his hair, as if it feels good.

I hope it does. That's all I want too. To make him feel good, in the hopes he'll do the same for me.

"I'm not doing anything beyond kissing," I warn him, not wanting him to think I'll let this go any farther than that.

"I only want to kiss you," he reassures, his lips quirked up in a barely-there smile.

The smile throws me off. Do I amuse him? I don't know how to feel about any of this. Excited. Nervous. Scared. Ready.

All of the above.

"Okay…good. Because I'm not about to let you do whatever you want to me, just so you know."

"Don't worry, Wren. Your virginity is safe." He pauses. "For now."

I go completely still, staring at him.

If what we're doing progresses further, then yes…

He's right.

When I circle my shaking hands around his nape, he bends down, his mouth hovering just above mine.

"You know this isn't going to end well," he murmurs as he traces my jaw with his fingertips.

I stare at him, hating what he said.

Hating more that I agree with him.

"You sure you want me to be your first?" He drifts his fingers across my cheek, sliding them into my hair, holding the side of my head, forcing me to meet his gaze. "Because after I take one, I'm going to want them all."

I nod slowly, unable to look away from him. He's got me in a trance, and I don't ever want to come out of it.

"I'm going to make you feel so good, Birdy." He returns his mouth to my ear, his voice a guttural whisper as he murmurs, "You promise to do the same for me?"

"Yes," I whisper, a whimper leaving me when he pulls away slightly.

"Then I'm yours." His lips brush mine. "All yours."

The moment our mouths connect, I'm lost. He kisses me once. Twice. He hums low in his throat, and my body responds to the sound with a slow, steady pulse between my legs. I part my lips with every brush of his mouth, my breath catching when his tongue teases mine, then retreats.

Oh God. I want him to do that again.

His hand falls to my cheek, angling my head just so as we continue to kiss, his tongue teasing mine. Every gentle flick or slow circle of his tongue to mine makes me aware of my body. How it's coming to life. Tingles sweeping over my skin. A surge of moisture between my thighs. His hand falls to my neck, his skimming fingers making me shiver as he tilts my head back further, deepening the kiss.

My body catches fire and I grip the back of his head, holding him to me. His other hand is at my waist and he tries to pull me closer, but our coats are blocking us. A frustrated whimper rings in the air and I realize...

It came from me.

He whispers my name against my lips, and I sigh, the sound full of so much longing, I'm almost embarrassed. But it doesn't deter him. He slips his fingers just under the hem of my sweater, his hand on my bare skin making me flush hot everywhere. I drop my hands to his broad shoulders, testing his strength, and he groans. The sound gives me the courage to keep touching him and I run my hand down the front of his chest. Rest it right where his heart thunders beneath my palm, and I have a realization.

I affect him just as much as he affects me.

The car picks up speed, racing down the city streets, and I wonder briefly where we're at. Where Peter is taking us.

I break away from Crew's still-seeking lips, trying to catch my breath, and he kisses my neck, his mouth hot and damp against my sensitive skin. I think of my dad. The car he hired to drive me to the gallery this morning. How I never called that driver to pick me up and take me home. I'm sure he reported back to my father.

They're probably worried about me.

"What time is it?" I ask, panting softly between each word.

Crew lifts away from my neck, studying me. His face is

flushed, his mouth damp and swollen, and I lean in, pressing my mouth to his once. Twice. "Check your phone," I whisper.

He reaches into his coat pocket and pulls his phone out, glancing at the screen before he returns his attention to me. "Almost three."

A wave of panic washes over me, making all of those delicious, needy feelings disappear, just like that.

"Oh no." I glance around the car, stopping to stare out the window, but I don't recognize where we're at. "I should get home."

"Birdy, wait—"

"I need to go," I interrupt. "My dad will be there soon. Or he might already be home. I don't know. Peter?"

"Yes?" the driver asks, his gaze finding mine in the rearview mirror.

I can't even be embarrassed that he witnessed us kissing in the back seat. I'm sure I look a mess. I feel like one. All rumpled and hot and flustered. "Can you take me directly to my apartment?"

"Of course. What's the address?"

I rattle it off to him before I turn my attention to Crew, who looks more than a bit agitated.

And even a little angry.

"I'm sorry," I whisper, a sharp pain stabbing me in the chest. "I hate to rush, but I have to get home. I'm sure my parents are worried."

Are they though? Maybe not, but my father fully expects me to be home, waiting upon his arrival. I've never defied them in my life, and I feel like I'm already in trouble.

Even though I haven't really done anything wrong.

Crew's expression softens, and he touches my hair. Cups the side of my head. "I don't want them to worry about you. Send them a text."

I shake my head. That'll just open me up to a litany of questions I don't want to answer. Not right now, while Crew can bear witness to the interrogation going down. "How far are we from my place, Peter?"

"Twenty minutes if traffic is light," the driver answers.

"Thank you." I settle back against the seat, staring out the window, my mind awhirl with all of the terrible possibilities. I can feel Crew watching me and I hate that I'm in the midst of a panic attack in front of him.

He takes my hand, linking our fingers together. "Don't stress, Birdy."

"I'm not stressed," I automatically say, keeping my gaze on the window.

I'm afraid if I look at him, I might burst into tears.

He shifts closer, his mouth once again at my ear. "Liar. I know you better than you think."

I swallow hard, not saying anything in response.

That's what I'm afraid of.

# CHAPTER NINETEEN

## WREN

As quietly as I can, I creep into the house, slowly closing the door behind me so I don't slam it. The apartment is silent, like no one is here, and I breathe a sigh of relief.

"Where the hell have you been all day?"

Yelping, I turn to find my father standing at the mouth of the hallway, right next to their prized possession—the giant Andy Warhol painting hanging on the wall.

I try to smile at him. "What do you mean? I went to the art gallery."

"That was hours ago." He squints at me, as if he's trying to see inside my head. "You were at the gallery all this time?"

I slowly shake my head, but don't say anything.

"Come with me." He turns and heads down the hall. I have no choice to follow him, entering the sitting room where my mother waits, dressed impeccably in a sleek black dress, clutching a wineglass in her hand. Her smile is brittle when her gaze meets mine, remaining quiet.

She has never been my ally. I don't know why I always think she might be. It's a lost cause.

"How did you get home, young lady?" This is from my father, who has turned to face me, a glower on his face. He's a handsome man. Slightly balding, gray at the temples. Hazel eyes that are always filled with concern when they land on me. I wonder if he worries about me constantly. Sometimes it feels like that's all he ever does.

I think about lying, but in the end, he would most likely get it out of me anyway. Is omitting a few facts also a lie? Maybe not. "I rode home in the car."

He lifts his brows. "Whose car? Because it wasn't mine. The driver called me in a panic a couple of hours ago, Wren. Saying you never contacted him for pickup. When he went to the gallery, he realized you were already gone."

"He went into the gallery?" Guilt swamps me. I'm sure it's written all over my face.

"He drove all over Tribeca, trying to find you, and just happened to see you exit a restaurant with someone."

I'm light-headed at his words, and I fall onto the couch behind me. "Who?"

Daddy steps toward me, thrusting his phone out so it's in my face. On the screen is a photo of me and Crew leaving Two Hands together. I'm smiling.

I don't think I've ever seen myself look so happy before.

"Who is that?" Daddy demands.

"Crew Lancaster." My voice is surprisingly calm.

He frowns, shoving his phone back into his pants pocket. "Wait—Reggie's son?"

"Yes," Mother pipes up, "the youngest one."

"I go to school with him," I add. "He's in my class."

"Hmm." He glances over at Mother. "Might be a better prospect for her than the boy tonight."

She nods in agreement.

My mouth drops open.

What are they talking about? Is there something behind tonight's dinner with the Von Wellers beyond my father wanting to talk to them about business?

"What are you talking about?" I ask when they don't say anything further. "Crew and I are just—friends."

"Why was he at the gallery?" Daddy asks.

"I..."

His phone rings, and he immediately pulls it out of his pocket, glancing at the screen before he says, "I need to take this."

And leaves the room.

The moment he's gone, Mother takes a fortifying drink from her glass. "Next time, you should text your father. He was worried sick."

"I'm sorry," I whisper, hating that I automatically apologize for everything. I never try to explain myself. Or stand up for myself.

"You know how he gets."

"I do." I nod, gathering up my courage to ask the question burning in my mind. "Why did Daddy say that to you?"

"Say what?" She's purposely playing dumb. I can tell.

"About Crew being a better—prospect."

She lifts her chin. "We're exploring all avenues for your future."

I'm frowning so hard it hurts my head. "What are you talking about? Like—marrying me off to Larsen? Is that why we're having dinner at their house tonight? Is that one of the avenues we're seriously exploring?"

Why am I bothering to use the word "we"? Seems to me they were exploring my options, without involving me whatsoever.

"It's not such a terrible prospect to consider. He comes from a good family. They're very wealthy," Mother points out.

"And ours isn't wealthy? Why do I need to worry about money? I don't want to get married straight out of high school. I'll only be eighteen." Just saying the words out loud sounds ridiculous.

"Calm down. You wouldn't get married after high school, darling. That's far too soon. But we want to pair you with someone to ensure your future." She takes another sip of wine, effortlessly cool, as if nothing ever bothers her.

While I feel like my life is imploding right in front of my eyes.

"What if I want to go to college?"

The skeptical look that crosses her face is obvious. "Do you really want to do that, Wren? Such a waste of time."

I flinch at her words. Is she implying she thinks I'm dumb?

"I don't know." I shrug, feeling defensive. I applied to a few colleges, listing art history as my major. "I might want to take a gap year first. I could travel around Europe and explore all of the galleries."

"You won't be able to buy anything though."

I frown. "Why not? I just bought a painting today."

"It's hard to explain." She drops her gaze, fiddling with the giant diamond on her finger. It's not her wedding ring. I don't know where that one came from, but it's so large it almost looks fake. "You wouldn't understand."

My heart drops. She's not behaving normally. "Tell me."

A sigh leaves her and she lifts her head, her misty-eyed gaze meeting mine. "We're having to put a halt on big purchase spending for the moment. Large art pieces are costly. You know this."

"But why? I don't understand. Is business not going well for Daddy?"

A watery laugh escapes her. "Your father's company is fine. Business is booming. The real estate market is doing better than it ever has."

"Then what is it?"

"Your father wanted us to tell you this together, but he's abandoned us as usual." She sits up straighter, her chin tilting up. "We're separated."

I gape at her, the shock of her statement leaving me chilled to the bone. "What? I was just here last week for Thanksgiving and you two acted completely normal. You still live together."

"We didn't want to tell you yet, but he no longer lives here. He moved out a few weeks ago."

"A few weeks ago?" I repeat, my voice weak.

"He wanted to wait until the beginning of the year, to get you through Christmas and your birthday first, but…there's no point in keeping it from you any longer, darling. You deserve to know the truth. We're getting a divorce. We've already hired attorneys and we're currently in discussion about all of the assets we've acquired during our marriage, including the art."

Mother waves her hand at a sculpture standing nearby, one that she loves.

"Divide it up?"

"He refuses to keep any of the pieces or split them up between us. Says if I want all of it, I have to buy him out." A bitter laugh escapes her. "I'm not going to give up millions of dollars of *my* money to pay for art I already own. That's ridiculous."

I'm at a complete loss for words. I almost don't believe her. Why would they get a divorce now? Won't it be too complicated and costly? They've been together for such a long time. Almost twenty-five years.

"For the settlement, we'll end up dividing all of the art work and selling it. Every bit of it. I won't be able to keep any of my pieces," she continues, her eyes welling up with tears.

"Oh, Mama." I haven't called her that in years. Seeing her like this is breaking my heart. "I know how much all of it means to you."

"Yes, yes, that's true, but I'll be fine. It's all right. There will be an auction." She sniffs, her fingers dashing away the tears on her face. "Every piece in the house will go. You probably shouldn't have your new piece delivered here if you want to keep it."

"Wait, what about the Colen piece in my bedroom?"

"It's too valuable, Wren. Anything in the house will be included in the total collection that we acquired during our marriage," Mother explains.

I blink away the tears forming. "But Daddy gave that to me for my birthday!"

"I'm so sorry, darling. There's nothing I can do." She takes another sip of her wine, as if that's the end of the conversation.

Frustrated, I leave the sitting room and go to my bedroom, slamming the door behind me, not caring who hears it or if it makes someone angry. We're not a house where yelling and big fights and slamming doors happens. Everything is discussed civilly. Quietly. With dignity.

Sometimes all that quiet dignity is annoying. Like my mother and how calm she was, announcing their impending divorce.

As I change out of my outfit into leggings and an oversized sweater, I can't stop thinking about what my mother said.

How did I not see it? I know they don't always get along. Daddy is always working. Traveling a lot. Out until late. I didn't see him much at all when I was very young. He tried to be there for me as I got older, especially when the whole phone/forum mess happened. He worked less during that time, and he made sure to be there for our nightly family dinners. Sometimes he even helped me with my homework, though that wasn't often and usually consisted of the two of us sitting in his home office while he worked on his computer. Mother always told him I needed a more solid relationship with him. A positive male role model so I wouldn't grow up and have Daddy issues.

But then they sent me to Lancaster and I don't see much of either of them. I'm not home for the day-to-day interactions. During the summer, they always plan lots of family trips. Though last summer we didn't travel as much. Daddy was working.

Maybe it was fractured even then.

There's a knock on my door and before I can say come in, it's swinging open, Daddy standing there with an annoyed look on his face.

"Can I speak with you for a moment?"

I plop down on my bed, folding my legs close to my body and curling my arms around them. "Yes."

He closes the door behind him and leans against it, watching me. "Your mother said she told you."

I nod, not sure what to say.

"I wanted to tell you. The two of us together, as a united front," he starts, but I talk over him.

"You're really not united anymore though."

A rough exhale leaves him and he scrubs the side of his face. "This isn't how I wanted things to go."

"Why are you forcing her to sell all of the art?" I ask, my voice small. My gaze goes to the piece hanging on the wall. My gift that wasn't a gift at all. "She told me I can't keep that."

He studies it before returning his gaze to mine. "It's a valuable piece. One that could fetch a lot of money."

"Is that what this is all about? Money? Is that why you're selling everything? I'm sure you'll make a ton off of Mom's curated collection she's worked so hard at over the years." Oh, I'm mad. Mad he would betray her like this. Angry he would so callously force her to give up everything she's collected over the past twenty years.

"I invested in those pieces. It was my money she used to purchase them. That collection is every bit mine as it is hers," Daddy says, pushing away from the door. "Don't fall for her sob story. She's just angry things aren't working out in her favor."

"I don't blame her. None of it is fair."

"Life isn't fair, Pumpkin. That's a good lesson to learn now, when you're still young. Bad things will happen to you, and some of the time, it's completely out of your control. It all comes down to the choices you make." He paces my room, pausing to stare at the art piece that no longer belongs to me. "I've made some bad choices in my life, but the very best choice was marrying your mother and having you. I hope you believe me when I say that."

"Then why won't you stay married to her? If she was the best choice you ever made?" I don't realize I'm crying until I feel the tears drip off my face.

"People change. They want different things." His expression softens. "I don't want to hurt you. Neither does your mother."

"Too late," I whisper, my chest aching from holding back the tears.

# *Chapter Twenty*

## CREW

I spent the rest of the weekend in quiet agony, thinking of Wren with Larsen, the fuckhead, at dinner Saturday night, joking and laughing and forgetting all about me.

Because that's exactly what it seems like. She never reached out once. Not after we dropped her off at her house and she ran inside without a backward glance. Not Sunday when I tried to call her.

And I only called her once. A Lancaster doesn't chase. We don't beg and we don't ask what's wrong.

She can come to me.

Monday morning and I'm in my usual spot, leaning against the wall at the front entrance of the school, Ezra and Malcolm flanking either side of me. Natalie is with us, flirting with Ezra all while occasionally eyeing me, but I ignore her. Malcolm is complaining about his parents. While I wait for my little bird to show up.

In other words, nothing has changed.

I feel like I've changed, though no one can see it. Kissing Wren in the back of the car...the sounds she made. How responsive she was. The taste of her mouth. The tentative tease of her tongue. I can't stop thinking about it.

I can't stop thinking about her.

"Christ, you're in a foul mood this morning," Malcolm suddenly says, his words aimed right at me.

"Agreed," Ezra adds.

"I haven't even said much," I mutter, propping my foot against the wall, always on the alert for a certain someone to make her appearance.

"You don't have to. Your negativity is a literal dark cloud, swarming all around you," Malcolm says.

"Oooh, so descriptive," Natalie coos, her gaze appreciative as she sizes up Malcolm. "Why haven't we ever gone out before?"

"You're too busy trying to get up on him." Malcolm waves a hand at me.

"Hey." Ezra snags Natalie's hand, pulling her into his arms. "What about me?"

He's too damn needy. That's why she's not interested in Ezra. He could learn a thing or two from me. The more I ignore Nat, the more she seems to want me.

Not that I want her back.

"Oh, I haven't forgotten you." Natalie giggles, the sound grating on my nerves. "Want to ditch first period? Go back to my dorm room?"

"Hell yeah," Ezra says, way too enthusiastically. "Let's wait a few minutes first."

"Why?" Natalie pouts. "I want to leave now."

Ez can't admit he wants to show off to everyone that Natalie is hanging all over him. He just smiles and kisses her, which turns my stomach.

"Where's your little bird?" Malcolm asks me, chuckling. "That already a done deal?"

"It never started in the first place," I lie.

"I thought you were going to keep watch over our sacrificial lamb and ensure she doesn't tell on us." Malcolm raises his brows. "Should we be worried?"

"I've got it handled," I bite out, hating that he doubts me.

"You better," Malcolm mutters. "I can't afford to get kicked out now. That'll fuck everything up."

I ignore him, my gaze snagging on the pretty face that suddenly appears.

It's Wren, moving down the walkway toward the entrance to school, walking by herself. Not surrounded by her usual posse of freshman girls who consider her their idol. It takes everything in me not to push off the wall and go to her, but I remain in place, letting her approach me.

Her steps are slow, her expression unsure. She doesn't make eye contact with me for the longest time and I can't look away from her. I keep my gaze on her face, drinking in her beauty. The pretty green eyes and the pouty lips. Her hair is pulled up into a high ponytail, a snow-white ribbon wrapped in a bow around the base of it, and she has the same thick coat on she wore Saturday.

I wait for her to walk by me, to ignore me as she usually does, which would be fucking infuriating, but she surprises me by coming to stop directly in front of us, ignoring the mocking looks Ez, Malcolm and Natalie are all sending her.

"Can I talk to you for a moment?" she asks, her sweet voice washing over me. She briefly glances in the direction of my friends, who appear ready to burst at her appearance, the idiots. "Privately?"

"Sure." I push away from the wall and follow her as we enter the building, the cackling of my friends following after us.

Fuckers.

She finds a darkened classroom with an unlocked door and slips inside, and I walk in after her, closing the door behind me. It's a room that wasn't used this semester and there's only a couple of desks inside, along with a podium sitting directly in front of the whiteboards. It's quiet. Private.

No one should bother us in here.

Wren doesn't stop walking until she's in the farthest corner away from the door and only then does she turn around and face me.

"I'm sorry—"

I cut her off with my mouth, kissing her hard. Punishing her for not talking to me for the rest of the weekend. Ignoring me like I didn't exist. Who the fuck does this girl think she is?

A whimper leaves her and she tries to shove at my chest, but I soften my attack, not just for her, but also for myself.

Because damn, she tastes good. And when I feel her slowly melt against me, her hands tugging on the lapels of my jacket as if she wants to get me closer, I know she feels the same. I press her against the wall as I continue drinking from her lips, sliding my tongue against hers, again and again, hoping I can wipe away any evidence of the evening she just spent with fucking Larsen for good.

I end the kiss first, pressing my forehead to hers. "I'm mad at you."

"It was a rough weekend."

A snort actually leaves me. "I'm sure Larsen occupied all of your time."

"I barely talked to him."

"So you did go to dinner at his parents' house." The confirmation is painful.

"Of course, I did. I went with my parents. They expected me there." She makes a choked sound and leans heavily against me. "They're getting a divorce."

"Who? Larsen's parents?" Who gives a shit?

Wren ducks her head, tucking herself against my chest, her hands resting there, right against my heart. "No. Mine. They told me this weekend. It's a mess. My life is a mess."

Ah, fuck.

I wrap my arms around her and hold her close, running a hand up and down her back as she softly cries against my shirt.

"Birdy, I'm so sorry."

"It's okay. It's—it was such a shock. My mother told me first, and she was so calm. It was weird." She sniffs and pulls away so she can look up at me. Her eyes are bloodshot and watery, tears tracking down her cheeks. Going on instinct, I slowly wipe them away with my thumb and she closes her eyes, her lips curving into the smallest smile. "I didn't think they would ever split, but here they are, destroying a twenty-five-year marriage. And there's so much involved. Money and assets. Too many assets. All that art."

"Are they splitting it up between them?"

"They're having an auction, according to my mother. They can't come to a decision over the collection and she refuses to pay for art she already owns, or at least that's what she explained to me." Wren shakes her head. "It's going to be messy. I don't know what to do, or how to feel."

I pull her into me. "You should've called me."

"I didn't know what to say to you," she admits. "After—everything that happened Saturday. I didn't know where we stood."

Slipping my fingers beneath her chin, I tilt her face so she has to look up at me. "I told you I was your friend."

"I need a friend right now, Crew," she whispers. "Badly."

"Tell me what you need."

"I—I don't know yet. Your support? Someone to sit with at lunch?" Her laugh is sad, and it hurts my fucking steel-constructed heart to hear it. "Someone who'll actually be nice to me?"

"Fuck, Wren." I kiss her again because she's so damn sad, but she ends it first, stepping away from me completely. "What's wrong?"

"We should go to class." As if on cue, the bell rings with the five-minute warning. "We can't be late to Fig's."

Fucking Fig. I hate that guy.

"Crew..." She takes a step toward me, her expression pleading. "Can we keep what happened between us a—secret?"

"What?" I shake my head. "What exactly are you talking about?"

"I don't want anyone to think we're in a...romantic relationship. We can be friendly. People will think it's a normal progression from working on the project together, right? I'm just not ready to let people know we made out in the back of a car."

I automatically want to belittle what happened in the back of that car Saturday afternoon. What's a little make-out session? We're in high school. Shit like that happens all the time. All sorts of people who go here hooked up over the weekend and are now pretending nothing ever happened. Hell, I've done that more than a few times myself.

But there's something about Wren telling me she doesn't want people knowing we kissed that bugs me. Like she wants to keep me her dirty little secret.

That's fucked up. A blow to my massive ego, if I'm being real with myself.

Then again, I can't imagine what it's like, to be Little Miss Perfect Wren, the sweet and proud virgin on campus preaching abstinence. Being seen with me puts her reputation at risk, and that's something she values.

Maybe a little too much.

"Whatever you want," I tell her with an easy smile. "We're just friends, right, Wren?"

"Right." She nods. "Just friends," she adds weakly.

"You leave first, okay? I'll wait a minute so people don't see us together," I instruct her.

"Okay." She smiles. "Thank you for understanding."

And then she's gone.

I lean against the wall, steaming as I hit the back of my head on the wall once. Twice. A couple of more times until a growl leaves me.

Why should I care if she wants to keep us a secret? That's how I usually operate, so I should be all for it. Not like I was going to run out and tell everyone what happened. I didn't even mention it to my friends. Hell, I lied to Malcolm earlier.

But Birdy's calling the shots. I don't like it. Not one bit.

As promised, I leave the room a minute later, rushing to class, pushing past the students milling about. Some of them say my name, but I ignore them. A plan clicks into place as I make my way to Honors English, and when I enter the classroom, I'm relieved to see I can go through with it.

Wren is already there, sitting in her usual spot. Front and center. Her cheeks are blotchy from her earlier crying, but otherwise, she looks okay. Barely holding it together, but okay. I make my way over to the desk directly behind hers and settle in, dropping my bag on the floor next to my feet.

Figueroa notices, of course. He observes me from where he sits at his desk, surrounded by his usual harem of girls, including Maggie, who's glaring at the rest of them as if she wants to slit their throats.

Someone's feeling territorial.

I just smile, tempted to wave at him. He doesn't want to see me sniffing around Wren. He's trying to get in on that action himself.

Over my dead body.

The final bell rings and the girls settle into their seats, one of them glaring at me since I guess I took her usual spot.

"That's my seat," she says snottily.

"Sorry, babe. Trying to score points with the teach," I tell her.

She rolls her eyes and finds another desk.

Mr. Figueroa launches into a lecture about *The Great Gatsby*, which I haven't even started reading yet. I figure I'll watch the movie for real this time if I need to. Or someone will share their notes or whatever with me and help me out. I'm a fucking Lancaster. They all do my bidding.

I tune out his droning voice, staring at the back of Wren's head. Her dark hair swept up in that high ponytail, the curling ends brushing against the back of her navy jacket. Giving in, I reach out, curling a tendril around my finger, tugging on it lightly.

She doesn't react. Doesn't even move, and I wonder if she even felt it.

Glancing around, I make sure no one else is paying attention to me. I shouldn't play with her hair in front of everyone. They might get the wrong idea.

*Though, what would be so bad about that? Thinking we've got a thing for each other? So what if we do?*

Jesus, I sound like an idiot, even in my own head. I can't fall for this girl. She's not for me. She's too good, too sweet, too innocent and trusting. And a bit of a mess, thanks to her parents just splitting up.

I should leave her alone. Be her friend and push all hope of getting her naked firmly out of my thoughts.

"Mr. Lancaster. Are you paying attention?"

Figueroa's smug voice startles me and I glare at him, ignoring the soft laughter that fills the class. "Yeah."

"Tell us then, one of the themes from the book." Figueroa crosses his arms, waiting for me to fuck up.

I tried to watch the movie when I was like ten, I think? I can't remember—as in, I also don't remember hardly anything about it. I left the room within five minutes of my arrival, already bored out of my mind. But I do know about a few of the themes it covers. "Greed? Excess?"

Surprise crosses my teacher's face. "That's correct. What else? Anyone?"

Someone else raises their hand and he calls on them, walking over to the other side of the class. Wren turns halfway in her seat, sending me an unreadable look. "Why are you sitting by me? You usually sit in the back."

"Thought I'd sit by my friend." I reach out and tug on the end of her ponytail again, and this time, she notices. "I like your hair like this."

Her cheeks go pink. "Thank you." She turns her back to me once again, and I smile to myself.

She really thinks she'll be able to keep this purely friendly between us?

I'll show her friendly.

# CHAPTER TWENTY-ONE

## WREN

"Wren." Fig stops directly beside my desk, and I glance up at him. "A word?"

Not waiting for my response, he heads to his desk and I follow after him, not daring to look back at Crew. I'm sure I know what I'd see on his face.

Anger. Frustration. Annoyance.

It's the Wednesday after my life changed in a variety of ways and I'm just trying to cope, day by day. My father has called me every evening, his tone soothing as he asks endless questions about my day. I give him minimal responses, not sure how to talk to him, or what to say.

He's worried about me after the divorce news. I suppose I should find that sweet, but there's something about it that makes me feel like he's only trying to cover his butt. Mother sent me a text Monday checking up on me, but otherwise, I haven't heard from her.

Typical.

And then there's Crew.

I can't stop thinking about him, even though I tell myself it'll lead nowhere. I relive the way he kissed me in the back seat of the car every night before I go to bed. Can't help but wonder where things could go between us if I kept seeing him. He was so sweet at the gallery, and when we went to lunch. It felt like a date with a boy who might actually like me.

My parents ruined everything. The divorce announcement kind of soured me on the idea of a possible relationship with Crew—with anyone. The dinner that night at the Von Weller's was a complete bust. Larsen kept trying to talk to me, flirt with me, and I was so cold, I froze him out. Which is not my usual style. I kept thinking about Crew and his warning about Larsen. And how my parents are trying to set me up with him for my future.

Unbelievable.

After Crew kissed me so passionately in that empty classroom Monday, he hasn't tried anything inappropriate since, and I can't help but feel...

Disappointed.

I know I'm the one who said I wanted to keep it as friends-only between us, and I still feel that way because the last thing I need is a potential relationship messing with my head. I don't think I have the emotional capacity to handle something so overwhelming right now.

And the way Crew Lancaster makes me feel is very, very overwhelming.

I still wish he'd kiss me though. Or hold my hand. Hug me. It's comforting, being in his arms. He's warm and solid, and he smells like heaven.

"Wren?" Fig is already sitting at his desk while I'm stalled out in front of the classroom, looking like an idiot, I'm sure.

I scurry over to his desk, clamping my lips together to ensure I don't apologize.

I over-apologize for unnecessary things. Why would I have to say sorry right now? Because I always do? That's not a good enough reason anymore.

I really need to start standing up for myself.

"Is everything okay?" I ask Fig, once I'm standing beside his desk.

"I was just going to ask you the same question." He rests his clutched hands on top of his desk, lowering his voice. "I can tell something is bothering you."

He is far too perceptive. It's dangerous. Like he can hone in on girls when they're feeling extra vulnerable and takes advantage of them. "I'm all right. Really."

"Is someone bothering you?" His gaze shifts over to where Crew sits. His new spot, directly behind me. I quickly glance over my shoulder to see Crew glowering at the two of us, never looking away. Like he doesn't care that he got caught staring. "I can talk to him if you want me to."

I shake my head. "Crew isn't bothering me." I'm not hiding that I know who he's talking about.

"Are you sure about that? I know he can be intimidating. He has a reputation around campus for bullying girls, on occasion."

I'm not surprised. Crew tried to intimidate me many times over the years, though I mostly ignored him, which probably frustrated him even more. "He doesn't bully me. Crew is my friend."

Figueroa's eyebrows shoot up. "Your friend? Oh, Wren. Please tell me you don't actually believe that."

"What do you mean?" I'm hurt by his remark. As if I'm a little girl who's too naïve to know better.

Been there, done that. Still struggling with the aftermath.

"If Crew claims to be your friend, it's merely code for something more."

"Code for what?" I decide to play stupid. Of course I know what he's referring to, but everyone thinks I'm an innocent virgin, so why not play the part.

"He'll—take advantage of you. That's how boys like him operate."

I stare at Fig, hating the way his words make me feel. Hating more that he's just like the very boy he's describing. He takes advantage of his female students, preying on the weakest ones.

Is that how he saw me only a few weeks ago? Weak and unassuming? Too trusting and easy to manipulate?

*Well, too late, sir. I'm on to your games.*

"I know exactly how boys like him operate." It's my turn to lower my voice. "Maybe that's exactly what I want him to do, hmm? Did you ever think of that?"

He struggles to keep his expression neutral, though I can tell I shocked him. "Very well. I just—wanted to warn you."

"Thanks, Fig. Appreciate it." Oh, where did that come from? I sound like I've got attitude.

I kind of like it.

I turn away from Fig's desk so fast, my skirt flares out, flashing a bit of leg. I catch Crew's gaze dropping to my thighs, and my skin warms as I walk back to my desk.

Why am I keeping him at arm's length again?

I fall into my seat, glancing over at Crew to see he's already watching me.

"What the hell did he want?" His simmering gaze shifts to Figueroa.

"He asked if I was okay." I shrug, trying to play it off, but Crew won't let me.

"Trying to make a move on you?"

"Never."

He clenches his jaw. "I'll kick his ass if he says something inappropriate to you, Wren. I mean it."

My entire body erupts in goosebumps at the ferocity in his voice. How protective he is, how he said my actual name. "I blew him off."

"He can pick up on girls who are going through shit," Crew continues.

"I know. I figured that out."

Crew's gaze finds mine, the anger slowly dissipating. "You've got this handled, don't you?"

I nod. "I do. I'm going to be okay. But thank you for watching out for me."

"Anytime," he murmurs, just as Figueroa starts lecturing again.

I turn and face the front of the classroom, thrilled that Crew actually trusts that I can take care of myself.

Something no one ever gives me credit for.

The rest of the day passes just as the last two did, though I decide to switch it up at lunch. I go in search of Maggie, who I find sitting with Lara and Brooke. They all stare up at me as I stop at their table, murmuring uninterested greetings before they return their attention to their phones.

"Can I sit here?" I ask no one in particular, pulling out a chair and settling in right next to Maggie. "How are you?"

She shrugs, staring down at her uneaten sandwich. "Okay."

"Hey." I reach out and settle my hand on top of hers, which startles her. She turns her head, frowning at me. "I wanted to apologize to you."

"For what?"

"Judging you. Lecturing you. Whatever other dumb—crap I've done to you over the last three years or so," I admit. "I don't have any right to look down upon you like I have. I just—I got a little too high and mighty with my morals, and I shouldn't have. I hope you can forgive me."

Maggie stares, no doubt shocked by my apology. While I think I say sorry for way too many things, this one is warranted. I need to apologize to a few more people, even Lara and Brooke, but I'm taking this one step at a time.

"I accept your apology," she finally says, her voice soft.

"Can we still be friends?" I ask hopefully.

She nods, and I pull her in for a hug, squeezing her tight. "If you need someone to talk to, I'm here. I'll listen to you. And I won't pass judgment either. I promise."

Maggie clings to me, her cheek pressed to mine. "Thank you, Wren."

"What's up with the hugfest?" Brooke asks, interrupting us. "You hoping some of her purity rubs off on you, Mags?"

I glare at Brooke, hating how easily she tossed that insult at her supposed friend. "As if you have any room to talk," I say.

"Oh, my bad. Sorry, didn't mean to insult Miss Perfect."

"Shut up, Brooke," Maggie says wearily. "You're so exhausting sometimes."

Lara giggles. Brooke glares, just before she pushes away from the table and takes off. Lara soon follows, running after her.

"Why do I hang out with those two again?" Maggie asks me, just before she starts to laugh.

"I don't know. I hang around them too sometimes, but they're sort of awful."

"They're actually terrible." Maggie shakes her head and sighs, pushing her tray away from her. "I can't eat."

"Why not?"

"So much going on." Her smile is rueful. "I'd tell you all about it, but we'd need at least five hours."

"I've got nothing but time," I tell her, reaching out to pat her hand. "Are you and Franklin still broken up?"

"Yeah. He found out about Fig." And with that one sentence she confirms my suspicions. "He wasn't too happy about it. He even wanted to tell Headmaster Matthews about it."

Oh wow. "Did he?"

Maggie shakes her head. "I convinced him not to, at least for now. I don't know how much longer I can put him off."

"Why don't you let him tell? Then at least you have nothing to do with it."

"Because I'm in love with him, Wren," she admits.

"Franklin?"

"No. With Fig." She sighs. "And there's more."

God, what more could there be?

"You'll freak out though," Maggie continues.

"Just tell me," I say, needing to know.

Her gaze meets mine, and I can see a myriad of emotions swirling in her eyes. Fear and worry and just the tiniest bit of happiness too. "I'm pregnant," she whispers.

My mouth falls open as I struggle to respond.

"With Fig's baby."

# CHAPTER TWENTY-TWO

## WREN

By the time I'm walking into psychology class, I'm an emotional wreck. Crew must sense it from the look on his face as he watches me head for the desk next to his. I don't even bother sitting in the front anymore. What's the point?

"You okay?" he asks when I sit down.

Nodding, I offer him a faint smile. "Fine."

I can't tell him about Maggie and Fig. That would be betraying my friend's trust, and I can't do that. Not after Maggie told me something so incredibly distressing and private. I had to drag her out of the dining hall after she told me, because she started to tear up. We hid away in a bathroom, and I comforted her, holding her close while she cried into my shoulder and told me everything.

How she doesn't want to abort the baby, though that's what Fig wants. She truly believes she can leave school, give birth, and once she's eighteen, they can move in together and live as a happy little family.

That sounds farfetched, even to me.

"You sure?" Crew is perceptive, just like Fig.

No, wait. I shouldn't put them in the same category. That's not fair to Crew. He's not preying upon me and trying to seduce me.

Or is he?

"I'm just tired," I admit, which isn't a lie. I toss and turn in bed every night, and when I do sleep, I have fitful dreams. About my parents. Or Crew. The ones with Crew always end up sexual and I startle awake every time, my body damp with sweat. My hand between my legs.

"Not sleeping well?"

I nod.

"Me either."

"Why aren't you sleeping?"

He shrugs. "Got a lot on my mind."

That's all he says.

And I don't bother asking any more questions, because I might not want to know the answers.

Skov enters the classroom right before the bell rings, just like normal. Once she runs through attendance, she claps her hands together, getting our attention.

"Before you start working on your projects, I have a few things I wanted to go over with you."

I sit up straighter, paying attention, though I can feel Crew's gaze on me. I sort of hate it when he stares at me.

And I sort of like it too.

"Presentations are happening next week, and you're giving them together, in front of the class. No exceptions. You can use any form of visuals you'd like, though don't make it too complicated. I'd like an outline of your project turned in Friday." The entire class erupts in groans and Skov rests her hands on her hips, waiting for the chorus to settle down. "Okay, calm down. You knew this was going to happen. I'm giving you two days. You can handle it."

No, I really don't feel like I can. I don't think Crew and I even have a handle on this entire project. What are we supposed to talk about exactly? And what sort of visuals are we supposed to use? I knew we'd have to present in front of the class, and usually that sort of thing doesn't bother me, but right now, I'm frazzled. Just thinking about getting up in front of the class with Crew by my side makes me nervous.

"You look scared," Crew observes once Skov finishes.

"We have to write an outline in two days," I stress.

"I'm not worried." His tone is so dismissive, it's annoying. "Why? Are you?"

"Do you think we have enough information for our presentation? I don't even know exactly what we're doing."

"I've learned a lot about you over the last ten days, Wren."

I really love it when he says my name, and I really need to stop focusing on that. "I haven't learned much about you, Crew, so consider yourself lucky."

"You actually believe that?"

"You say a lot without revealing much."

His smile is small. "There's something you learned."

I roll my eyes and open my notebook to a fresh piece of paper. "What sort of outline should we sketch out?"

Crew leans back in his chair, stretching his legs out so his knee nudges against mine. My body reacts as usual. I'm always ultra aware of his presence, especially when we're sitting so close. "I was thinking we should do a compare and contrast."

"Of what?"

"Of each other. Remember how Skov mentioned we're similar? I know you do. You brought it up once."

I see it, and then again, I don't. Maybe it's more I don't want to be like him. "That could work."

"We could break it down like this." He leans over my desk and pulls my notebook closer to him, then starts to write with pen. "You'll introduce yourself, and then I'll do the same. You'll talk about our similarities. I'll talk about our differences. Conclude that people who seem like polar opposites on the surface might share some commonalities after all. The end."

He taps his pen on top of my hand. "What do you think?"

"It's a good idea," I admit, reluctantly. "What should we use as visuals?"

"We'll come up with that later. Let's focus on the information first. Then we can come up with the visuals."

I grudgingly agree, not sure why I have such a bad attitude. Crew is actually pretty smart. I guess I never gave him enough credit before, though he's been in my honors classes all four years.

Sometimes I see only what I want to see, not what's actually happening.

I've walked through life with tunnel vision, especially at Lancaster Prep. I had all of these ideas of how I should act, and who I should be. And for most of my high school life, I've been perfectly content with the person I am here.

Until now. Until I started working on this project with Crew and his observations about me. They've been a complete eye-opener.

And of course, then there's Crew. My feelings for him. He makes me curious. He makes me want things I shouldn't.

I'm starting not to care so much about the repercussions anymore either.

"You want to take the similarities or the differences list?" Crew asks me.

"The similarities," I answer.

"Really? I'm thinking that might be the harder one."

"I can handle it."

"I didn't say you couldn't, I just know you've been going through—a lot lately," he says, his gaze dropping to my lips.

My skin grows warm the longer he stares at me, as if he's thinking about kissing me. Which now I'm thinking about too.

"I'm all right," I admit. "This will be a good distraction."

He glances around the room, making sure no one is paying attention to us before he asks, "Still upset about your parents?"

"Yeah. I can't help but think I was blind to what was going on. How did I not see that they weren't happy with each other anymore?"

"You've been here for the last three, going on four years,"
Crew points out. "There's probably been a lot going on with your
parents that you have no clue about."

"Did I mention they were going to hide it from me until the
end of the year? They didn't want to ruin Christmas and my
birthday for me," I admit.

"No, you didn't." He tilts his head. "You reconsidering having
that party?"

I slowly shake my head. "No. That doesn't sound like much
fun. I'll just celebrate my birthday quietly."

My father texted me a list that his assistant put together of
a variety of places I could go for my birthday winter getaway,
but I haven't really looked at any of them. I'm not going to go.
Maggie's world has been completely upended, thanks to her
unexpected pregnancy, and there's no way she's going to want
to go on vacation with me, though she'd probably benefit from
a few days away from her problems.

"You're turning eighteen. That's a big deal," Crew murmurs.

I lift my gaze to his. "Are you eighteen yet?"

He nods.

"And what did you do to celebrate?"

"You really want to know?" He grins, the sight of his smile
making my heart pound.

"Maybe I don't," I say warily.

Crew chuckles. "It wasn't that bad. Spent it at our family
house in the Hamptons with friends. Got really fucking high
and wasted."

I don't even flinch over his use of the f word. I've sort of
become used to it. "You like using substances?"

"I smoked a little weed and drank some booze. I don't mind
using the occasional substance. It's all about moderation. If
you're drunk or high all the time, that's when you're fucked."
He studies me carefully. "Have you ever got drunk, Birdy?"

I slowly shake my head. "Never."

"Not even a sip of champagne during New Year's? Sneaking the occasional gulp from Mommy's wine glass when she's not around?"

How does he even know my mother constantly has a glass of wine in her hand?

"No. I don't like feeling out of control," I admit.

"I won't even bother asking if you've ever smoked weed."

I wrinkle my nose. "That's so gross. I'm not interested in smoking anything."

"There are other ways to do it. Edibles, for one. They make some good ones that you'd probably like."

"No, thank you," I say primly, feeling like the innocent girl that I am.

"You need to learn how to let loose a little," he says. "It's not a bad thing to have fun sometimes."

Normally, when he says that sort of thing, I end up getting offended. But I can tell by his tone that he's not being mean about it. I think he actually believes I do need to learn how to let go, which he's probably right, but I don't want to do it via drugs or alcohol.

"Is that how you let loose?" I ask him.

"Sometimes. Weed mellows me out." He sends me a look. "You could stand to try some. Gets you out of your head. Expands your mind and lets you think about other things. More pleasant things."

I roll my eyes. "That sounds like something a pot smoker would say."

He chuckles. "I guess I'm a pot smoker then. You sound like my mom."

That's probably not a compliment. "Maybe we should talk about our project? The outline?"

"Aren't we doing exactly that? I've got something to add to my differences lists." He grabs my notebook again and starts to write. "Wren doesn't drink or smoke weed. Crew does."

"Shouldn't you be using your own paper to make your notes?" I ask.

"Oh yeah." He lifts his head, his amused gaze meeting mine. "I guess I should."

He's teasing me. Trying to distract me. On purpose?

Well, it's working. This feels like just the distraction I need.

I tear the piece of paper out of my notebook and hand it to him. He takes it from me, his fingers brushing mine, electricity sparking between our fingertips. "You should keep this."

"I've already got it up here." He taps his pen against his temple.

"Really?"

"I remember everything about you, Wren." His gaze turns serious. "Every single little thing."

My mouth goes dry as I think of that moment in the back seat of the car. Or the classroom. My gaze drops to his mouth, and I'm filled with the urge to kiss him again. Right here, in the middle of class.

But of course, I don't. I would never do that. I don't want people talking. I definitely don't want anyone knowing about our earlier interactions.

"Want to work on this after school?" he asks, his deep voice breaking through my thoughts.

"Where?" I ask breathlessly.

"The library."

I should say no. There's no reason we need to work together on this. I can go back to my room and work on my list for the rest of the afternoon, though it probably wouldn't even take me that long. I can complete my parts of the outline, so we can put them together tomorrow in class.

Sitting up straighter, I part my lips, ready to turn him down.

"Okay," is what I say instead.

# CHAPTER TWENTY-THREE

## CREW

She walks by my side as we head to the library, our pace fast since it just started to snow. More like a freezing rain, which means it's still cold as fuck, and stings too. At least snow is soft, most of the time.

"Come on," I tell her, putting my hand at the center of her back and pushing her to pick up the pace. We run the rest of the way, both of us stopping once we're standing under the overhang in front of the library, Wren brushing the top of her head with her hand, water droplets flying.

"It's freezing," she says through chattering teeth, and I don't even hesitate.

Taking her hand, I pull her into the library, the warmth from inside instantly thawing me out.

"Better?" I ask her.

"Yes." She drops her hand and glances around the room. It's one of the original buildings on campus, and it has that musty smell of old books lingering in the air. The ceiling soars high, the shelves tall and filled with so many books it would take someone years to read them all.

There's hardly anyone in here, and I'm thinking the weather is a deterrent. I never come to the library. I can probably count on one hand the times I've been here since I started at Lancaster Prep. Well, maybe two.

"Let's go to the back," I suggest.

She frowns. "Why?"

"So we can have privacy."

"Why do we need privacy?"

"We're talking about some personal stuff, Birdy. You want everyone to find out about your deepest, darkest secrets?"

Her expression turns stricken. "No. But that means I don't want them blabbed during our presentation either."

"We'll keep it surface-level. Don't worry. Come on." I flick my head in the direction I want to go and start walking. She falls into step beside me. "You come here a lot?"

"Not really. I used to more when I was younger. I'd hang out in here with my friends and Miss Taylor would get mad at us," she says, referring to the librarian. "She'd always shush us."

"She's older than dirt. I think she's been here for two hundred years."

"Maybe she's a zombie," Wren suggests.

"More like a vampire," I joke. "Living her best eternal life."

Wren smiles, and I wish I could see her do that more often. She's been so somber, so sad the last few days. Ever since her parents unloaded on her that they're getting a divorce.

I think of my own parents and the fucked-up relationship they're in. Dad's a dick who flaunts his affairs and I'm pretty sure Mom does too. This is why I never want to be in a relationship. They're messy. Unnecessary. Eventually, I'll probably have to get married and carry on the family lineage or what the fuck ever, but maybe I won't have to. Maybe my brothers will take care of that for me.

My oldest brother Grant is involved with someone, and it seems pretty serious, pretty fast. Finn is a total player, so he's not settling down anytime soon. Charlotte just got married to someone she barely knows, but that dude is cool.

I'm barely eighteen. Definitely not interested in anything like that.

But I am interested in getting Wren alone again. Wouldn't mind trying to kiss her again too, though I'm not sure if she'd be down. She's wound so tight lately. I want her to act like she did last Saturday, when she was open and smiling, full of joy as she shared her love of art with me. Our conversation flowed, to the point of her admitting some major stuff I still can't believe she shared with me. Fingering herself in her bedroom all night and watching porn—not very Wren-like behavior at all.

Just remembering her softly-spoken confessions makes my dick twitch.

We eventually find an empty round table in the very back of the library and I go to it, settling into a chair and pulling out the one next to me for Wren. She sits down, setting her backpack on the table, her movements slow. Measured.

"Did you really bring me back here to work on the project?" She shrugs out of her coat, settling it over the back of her chair. Watching me with those big green eyes, her lips slightly pursed in a sexy pout.

Wait a minute.

"Yeah," I tell her, taking my coat off, leaving it slumped behind me. "You told me you just wanted to keep it friends-only between us."

"Right." She tears her gaze away from mine, staring at the shelf closest to us, a sigh leaving her. "I'm so tired of feeling sad."

"You need to take your mind off of it." When she turns to look at me, I continue, "Your parents. Your family. You need a distraction. You said that yourself earlier, in class."

"I'm not going to smoke a joint with you or eat an edible," she says, her tone snotty.

Fuck, that snotty tone of hers is kind of hot.

"I wasn't going to suggest it. Besides, I don't have anything on me. That's against school rules, remember?" I raise my brows, recalling how she caught us passing that blunt during lunch. Something we do occasionally and always on the sly.

I told Ez and Malcolm we need to stop smoking on campus out in the open and they agreed. None of us want to get kicked out, not this late in our high school lives.

"Right. Don't want to break the rules," she murmurs.

"You never do," I point out, and she doesn't answer. Guess there's no need for it, since we know it's true. "Want to break some right now?"

"What are you talking about?" she asks warily.

"Come with me." I stand, holding my hand out to her.

She studies it for a moment before lifting her gaze to mine. "What are you up to, Crew?"

"Come with me, Wren, and I'll show you."

"What about our stuff?"

"We can leave it. No one's going to come back here and mess with it."

She hesitates for a moment before she settles her hand in mine and I curl my fingers around it, pulling her out of the chair. There's no one around and the only person I'd worry about catching us is old Miss Taylor, but she's overseeing everyone at her desk at the library entrance, so she won't notice.

My steps hurried, I lead Wren deeper into the stacks, until we're surrounded by nothing but row after row of books, the aisle becoming narrower. The stacks becoming taller, the lights dimmer. Until we're standing in front of a nondescript wooden door, a shiny new digital lock sitting above the handle. I let go of her hand and enter the code, the green light flashing, and I turn the handle, opening the door with ease.

I glance back at her to see her mouth drop open in surprise. "Where does that lead?"

"Come with me and you'll find out."

"I don't know." She glances over her shoulder, as if fully expecting the dragon lady Miss Taylor herself to be standing there, breathing fire. "What if someone catches us?"

"No one is going to catch us," I say with confidence.

She faces me once more, her gaze going to the open doorway. There's nothing but darkness. "It's not dangerous in there, is it?"

The only thing that might be dangerous to her is me, but I don't say that. "Not at all."

Wren walks through the doorway first and I follow behind her, pulling the door shut, all the light from the library disappearing completely, shrouding us in darkness. She gasps and I come up behind her, settling my hands on her slender shoulders.

"It's okay."

"I can't see."

"I'll guide you." I take her hand and pull her along, my vision clearing the longer we're in the dark. I lead her toward the spot I want to show her, the room growing even lighter until we're standing in front of a wall of windows that overlooks the entire garden that's behind the library. "What do you think?"

She approaches the old windows slowly, tilting her head back, her gaze lifting to the ceiling. "They're so tall."

"A long time ago, this used to be a classroom. They closed it down in the eighties. Then it eventually became a hookup spot. They finally had to put a lock on it a few years ago to keep the students out. Too many people were sneaking in here," I explain.

Wren does a slow circle, glancing about the mostly empty room, her nose wrinkling. "Where would they hook up?"

"Wherever. If you're desperate enough to sneak off with someone, you can get pretty creative." Shit, I'm suddenly feeling desperate to hook up with my so-called friend.

Such a bunch of shit. I don't know why we're dancing around this. Pretty sure she wants me.

And I definitely want her.

"I've never really noticed these windows before," she says as she approaches them. I follow after her, stopping a few feet away from where she stands when she presses her fingers against the glass and stares out at the grounds of the school spread out before us.

"You have." When she glances back at me, I continue, "It's the big wall of windows you can see from the gardens. Ivy covers most of the building itself, so no one ever realizes it's part of the library."

"Oh yeah." She returns her attention to the gardens, the gentle snowflakes falling onto the ground, slowly dusting everything in white. "I don't come out to the gardens much. The statues creep me out."

"Really?"

She keeps her gaze straight ahead, not even noticing that I'm getting closer. "Feels like they're always watching me. It's creepy."

"I figured you'd like them. They're art. From hundreds of years ago." I stop directly behind her, inhaling her scent. Tempted to reach out and grab her hair. Curl it around my fist and pull her in for a drugging kiss.

"You're right. They are art, but they're also sad. Those statues all look like they want to fling themselves over a cliff and die a horrible death."

A chuckle leaves me, yet she still doesn't move. She has to know I'm right behind her. "That's the Lancaster family for you. We're all this close to flinging ourselves off of a building, eager to plunge to a blissful death."

"You Lancasters are moody." Wren rests her hand on the glass, a hiss leaving her when she touches it. "It's so cold."

"It's even colder outside."

"I'm not dressed right to go back out into that."

"Me either." I take another step forward, so close my front presses gently against her back. "The view's pretty, don't you think?"

I'm not talking about the gardens, though they're exactly that, especially with the snow falling. A perfect early winter scene.

No, I'm talking about Wren. She's so fucking beautiful. Sweet.

Interesting. It sort of blows my mind, how much I enjoy talking to her. Spending time with her.

"It is," she admits, her voice soft. She bends her head forward, her hair falling across her face, and I reach out, brushing it aside to expose her neck. "What are you doing?"

"Distracting you," I whisper, bending down to press my mouth on the back of her neck. "I know you appreciate pretty things. I wanted to show you a view you've never seen before."

She's quiet, though I can feel her body trembling. And I don't think it's from the cold windows either.

I kiss her in the same spot again, my fingers tangling in her hair. She lifts her other hand, both of them now braced on the glass, and I subtly nudge her body with mine, until she's fully pressed against it.

And me.

She inhales sharply.

"Too cold?" I ask her, the words murmured on her skin.

"Yes," she whispers. "But you're warm."

Resting one hand on her waist, I touch her cheek with the other, angling her head so she has no choice but to look up at me. "Don't push me away, Birdy."

I see the moment she gives in, how it flickers in her gaze, and she removes her hands from the window, turning so she's fully facing me. "Crew..."

I kiss her before she can protest, or tell me to stop. And she doesn't say anything after that. She gives in completely, her hands coming up to wind around my neck, her entire body leaning into me. Those plump tits press into my chest, and I race my hand up her side, my thumb drifting across her breast. She parts her lips to gasp, allowing my tongue entry, and a low groan leaves me as I deepen the kiss.

"What if someone sees us?" she whispers against my mouth.

I nip at her lower lip, making her whimper. "No one can see us. I promise."

Opening my eyes, I stare out the windows, but there's no one there. The snow is starting to come down harder, the light dimming in the cavernous room, thanks to the darkening sky, and I cup her cheek, tilting her head back, so I can devour her.

Our kisses soon turn into tongues and teeth and nibbling lips and panting breaths. Her hands slip beneath my uniform jacket, sliding down my back, and I press my hips against hers, letting her feel what she's doing to me.

Wren breaks the kiss first, and I open my eyes to find her staring at me, her chest rising and falling against mine, her breaths quick. "We probably shouldn't do this."

"Why not?" I kiss her neck, licking a path to her ear with my tongue. She tilts her head, her eyes falling shut, her expression tortured. "I know you like it, Birdy."

"Kissing leads to...other things. Things I'm not ready for."

"You so sure about that?"

She swallows hard when I nibble her jaw. "I don't know."

"Tell me when to stop then." Ah, I make it sound so easy, but I want this girl to forget herself and get carried away.

With me.

Because she needs it. Because she wants it.

Just like I want her.

# CHAPTER TWENTY-FOUR

## WREN

'm plastered against the cold glass, a warm Crew pressing against me, his hard—yes, he's actually hard—body so close to mine, I don't think you could slip a piece of paper between us. His words are on repeat in my brain.

*Tell me when to stop then.*

He makes it sound so simple, when it's not. I'm finally starting to understand why girls give in so easily to this— to sex. It feels so good, his mouth. His hungry kisses. His tongue. How it tangles with mine. His hands on my body. His rapidly beating heart and accelerated breathing, and those low humming noises he makes when he kisses me. As if I'm the most delicious thing he's ever tasted.

It's heady stuff. I can feel that newly familiar pulsing between my thighs. The wetness growing there. The dull ache forming, and every bit of it, he's responsible for.

I think he's the only one who can ease the ache.

He kisses me until I can't think. Tugs my white shirt out of my skirt, his fingers slipping beneath the crisp, wrinkled cotton to rest against my bare waist before they streak across my stomach.

I can't breathe. Can only clutch his shoulders helplessly, my tongue dancing against his while he slowly but surely undoes me with his fingers. They slide up, skimming the bottom of my bra, and I wish with everything I had that I owned something frilly and pretty. Something that would make his eyes bug out of his head when he first saw it.

But I don't. The nude-colored bra I'm wearing is plain and simple. No ribbon.

No lace.

"You want me to stop, Birdy?" He pants the words into my skin, my neck. His lips are hot, and so is his tongue, and when he licks me at the spot where my pulse throbs, I shake my head.

No. I don't want him to stop. Not ever.

His hands land on my waist and he flips me around so my front is pressed into the window. His erection nudges against my butt, and I stare out at the falling snow, my lips parted, my mind racing with thoughts of seeing him naked. He feels huge.

I don't know what I would do with it if I ever saw it for real.

He slides those expert hands down, until they're playing with the hem of my skirt. And then they're beneath it, his fingers on my backside, tracing the edge of my underwear. One, then the other. Back and forth, his fingers featherlight.

A gush of wetness floods my panties and I close my eyes, pressing my cheek to the glass, needing the cold to ease the heat consuming me. "Crew..."

"I should stop?" He removes his hands from my panties, and I whimper. "Your skin is so soft, little bird. It's hard for me to quit touching you."

I'm conflicted. I know I should say no. This has already gone way too far. He's got an erection. He's touched my bra. His hands were literally just under my skirt. This is everything I promised my father I wouldn't do until I was with the man I plan on marrying.

But then those hands slip back under my skirt, a single finger sliding beneath my panties, and a moan leaves me, muffled by the window.

"Fuck, you're so wet." He dives deeper, his finger sliding into my folds and I arch my hips backward, wanting more. Fighting past the shame that wants to wash over me, my need too great. "Jesus, Wren."

He teases my entrance, barely pushing forward, and shudders wrack my body. I can't even imagine what I must look like, my upper body smashed against the window, my butt thrust out, Crew's finger slowly pushing inside me...

"Oh God," I choke out.

Crew pauses in his search. "You want me to stop?"

"No!" I might die if he stops now.

He slips his finger farther inside me, and I clench up tight. A ragged groan leaves him. "Relax."

I try to, but I'm nervous and scared and excited. I've never let a boy do this to me before and it feels foreign. Odd. Wonderful. Delicious.

Every single one of those things, all at once.

"Am I hurting you?" he asks.

I shake my head, bracing my hands on the glass once again, and I open my eyes to watch the snow fall as Crew fingers me. He slides his finger in, all the way to the hilt, before dragging it back out, and oh God, the friction. I need more.

A shuddery breath leaves me when he pushes back inside, and I can feel him use his other hand to flip my skirt up, exposing my backside to him.

"You're fucking killing me, Birdy. So hot," he murmurs, and I can feel his gaze burning a hole into my skin from the intensity of his stare.

I remain quiet, not sure how to respond. My body starts to move with his finger, my hips rocking, and when he removes his hand from me completely, I want to burst into tears from the loss.

"Turn around," he says roughly, his hands spinning my hips, so I have no choice but to face him. His mouth is on mine, his kiss so hungry, so intense, all I can do is hang onto him and let him consume me.

His hand slips beneath my skirt. Brushes the front of my panties. I cry out against his lips when he presses his fingers against me, rubbing slowly.

"You want me to stop now?" he asks, and I can hear the triumph in his voice.

He knows he's got me.

"N-n-no," I stutter, throwing my head back when he slips his fingers beneath the front of my panties, cupping me fully.

"You like this?"

I nod, unable to speak when he presses his thumb roughly against my clit.

A ringing starts, startling us both, and I crack my eyes open to find Crew already studying me, his brows lowered in displeasure. His fingers are still in my panties, the only sound beyond the ringing phone, our panting breaths mingling.

"That's not mine," he tells me, and I realize he's right.

It's my phone ringing.

"Ignore it," he says, leaning in for another kiss, but I press my hand against his chest, stopping him.

"I should see who it is," I say softly. The ringing stops, and I breathe a sigh of relief. "Or maybe not just yet."

Crew's smile is wicked as he leans in for another kiss, his tongue sliding into my mouth at the same time the ringing starts all over again.

He pulls away from me, his hand still remaining in my panties. "Where is it?"

"In my jacket pocket." I drop my hand into my pocket and pull the phone out to see the word Daddy flash across the screen. I sink my teeth into my lower lip, the guilt coming at me tenfold. "It's my father."

"Jesus." He removes his hand from my panties and steps away from me. "Answer it."

I feel empty without his hands on me and a soft exhale leaves me as I glance down at the screen, imagining how I'll sound to my father if I do answer his call. Breathless. On edge. My mouth still tingles from Crew's kisses and my clit throbs from his fingers. "I can't."

The ringing stops and I shove the phone back into my pocket. Crew reaches for me, but I dart away from him, suddenly unsure.

About everything.

All of it.

He's frowning, watching me carefully. "Are you okay?"

"I should go." I glance back the way we came, hating how dark it looks. Like a scary, fathomless cave to nowhere.

"Birdy, come on…" he starts, but I shake my head and he goes quiet.

"I can't—I can't do this." I'm too conflicted. Having Daddy call right in the middle of the most passionate encounter I've ever had totally ruined the mood. Made me doubt myself—and Crew. "I'm not ready."

"Wren." He runs a hand through his hair, scrubbing the back of his neck. "Don't leave. Not yet."

"I have to. I just—maybe this was a bad idea. I'm not the girl you think I am, Crew. I'm too nervous, too scared. I've never done this type of thing."

"I promised I'd take it as slow as you want me to."

"And you've been perfect." I offer him a tremulous smile, but I feel like I could burst into tears at any moment, so I look away from him, unable to stand looking at his handsome face any longer. "I need to go."

I flee the room, my shoes slapping hard against the cement floor as I run into the darkness. I spot the door and I open it, relief flooding me as I find myself in the main library once again. I make my way through the stacks until our table comes into view, and I hurriedly slip on my coat. Grab my backpack.

And hightail it out of the library, the door slamming behind me so loudly I swear I heard Miss Taylor make a shushing noise.

Only when I'm back in my dorm building, do I send my father a quick text.

**Me:** *Sorry was in the library studying for a project. Will call you after I take a shower? It's snowing here and I got wet on the walk back to my dorm.*

**Daddy:** *Not a problem, Pumpkin. Call me when you can. Just checking on you.*

Seeing his sweet words, the nickname that he's called me since I can remember, I promptly burst into tears.

• • •

"I have news," Daddy announces after we've talked for a few minutes, going over the usual *how are yous* and the *how's school* questions. I'm sitting on my bed after having taken a shower and changing into warm clothes, just like I told him I would.

"What is it?" I ask warily, bracing myself.

"Your mother and I...we're going to try and work on our marriage."

I go quiet, absorbing his words for a moment. "Are you serious?"

"We're starting couples therapy this week. We want this to work. For you. For each other," he says. "We can't just give up now, not after twenty-five years."

"Don't do this for me," I tell him, meaning every word I say. "This isn't about me. This is about you and Mother."

"I know, but you're a part of this family too. Even though you're getting older and about to go out on your own," he says.

Why does that part sound like a lie? Oh, I know why.

"A few days ago, you were trying to pair me up with Larsen Van Weller," I remind him. "In the hopes he'd eventually be my future husband."

It still sounds so completely ridiculous. Even if Crew hadn't warned me about Larsen and said all of those horrible things about him, I still would've been put off. Resistant. The moment I arrived at the Von Weller house and barely talked to Larsen, he knew his chances were shot. He pretty much left me alone.

Thank goodness.

"I cannot make that choice for you. Your mother and I discussed it. We were panicking at the thought of you being on your own, and what might happen to you."

Anger slowly spreads through my veins at his words, and the meaning behind them. He still doesn't trust I know how to take care of myself, believing I'll do nothing but make the wrong choices, over and over again.

Though he might be right to worry. Look at how easily I gave in to Crew earlier at the library. God, he actually had his fingers inside me, and I let him do it. I enjoyed it.

Shame washes over my body like a hot flood of lava, setting me on fire, and not in a good way.

"I'll be okay," I reassure him, dragging in a shaky breath. "I'm almost eighteen. And I want to go to college."

I'm not one hundred percent sold on that plan yet, but it sounds good, and that's all that matters.

"I think you would thrive in college," he says, his voice overly enthusiastic. "You can live in the dorms, and make new friends."

He wants me safely tucked away in a dorm, just like I am here at Lancaster. Then he won't have to worry about me, and he can go about his business, safe in the knowledge that I'm away at college.

"That's my plan," I chirp, my voice reminding me of how I spoke to Fig earlier. All false charm with a hint of sarcasm. Funny how both men don't even notice. "I should go, Daddy. I need to work on my project."

"For what class?"

"Psychology. My partner is Crew Lancaster." I close my eyes at my mistake. Why did I mention him again? For the thrill of saying his name? Knowing what we shared earlier? Despite my shame over what he did to me, I can't stop thinking about him. He's forefront in my mind—what we did together is too. And while I know I shouldn't allow myself to be found alone with him again, I know deep in my heart, I will most likely let it happen.

Maybe I can't be trusted. Maybe I'm too gullible, too easily swayed to be left to my own devices.

"Why does his name keep coming up lately?"

"I don't know, maybe because he's my friend?"

Daddy is quiet for a moment, and I'm about to say something when he beats me to it.

"I very much doubt Crew Lancaster is your *friend*, Pumpkin. He's a hot-blooded boy just like the rest of them, chasing after a sweet, innocent girl."

I remember the sensation of Crew's hot mouth on my neck, the way he licked my ear, and for the first time in a while, I have to agree with my father. "It's just a project, Daddy."

"I know, Pumpkin. Just remember, you're too young to get serious about boys right now. You've got your whole life ahead of you."

"I know." I have heard those same words repeated back to me so many times over the years, I can say them right along with him.

"They only have one thing on their mind anyway," he continues.

Hmm. Maybe I do too.

"I don't like the Lancaster family. You can't trust them." His tone turns bitter.

"What have they ever done to you?" I'm genuinely curious, though knowing him, he won't really tell me.

"We're in the same business. His older brothers have a real estate firm and they're shady." He clears his throat. "None of that should concern you. Just—stay away from Crew Lancaster."

"I have to work on my project with him," I start, but he cuts me off.

"You know what I mean." Daddy sighs, sounding exhausted. "I've got to go. Have a good night. Sweet dreams. I love you."

"Love you too." I end the call before he does, tossing my phone aside before I flop backward on my bed, staring up at the ceiling. Frustration ripples through me, reminding me that I'm not making the best choices, but are they really *that* bad?

So what if I snuck into a room with Crew and kissed him. Let him touch me. Let him slip his hand inside my panties...

God, how am I going to face him tomorrow in class? After what we've done? It's going to be weird, looking into his eyes and knowing what he did to me. How much I enjoyed it.

Did he think I looked dumb, clinging to the window and practically begging him to keep touching me? Does he think I'm a pathetic little creature who's suddenly addicted to his touch, his mouth?

Because that's how I feel. Addicted. Overwhelmed. Needy.

I close my eyes and take a deep breath, reminding myself that I've got this. I can face him tomorrow and act like nothing ever happened between us.

I can.

# CHAPTER TWENTY-FIVE

## CREW

I'm waiting out in front of Wren's dorm building, wrapped up in my thickest coat, a beanie, gloves and a scarf, and I'm still cold as fuck. The sun shines brightly overhead, doing little to warm my bones. The entire campus is covered in a thick layer of snow and thank Christ someone got up at the crack of dawn to shovel the walkways.

She still hasn't come out yet, and I'm getting worried. The bell is going to ring soon. She's usually heading for the school entrance by now, and my friends won't stop texting me, asking me where I'm at.

I ignore them. All I can think about is Wren. How she ran out on me yesterday afternoon. How traumatized she looked when her dad called, interrupting us. I'm sure that fucked with her head, made her feel like a sinner or whatever, though her purity promise has nothing to do with religion, from what I can tell.

It's merely a promise she made to her father, and herself, not to stray with the first guy she's hot for.

If her promise did have religious meaning, then I guess I'm the devil who's leading her straight into temptation.

I can't stop thinking about her. How incredibly responsive she is. The eager way she kisses me. How fucking wet her pussy was—she was turned on yesterday, that was obvious. And that virgin pussy was so tight, so fucking soft and hot...

I'm surprised I didn't explode in my trousers.

Of course, when the word *Daddy* flashed across the screen right in the middle of me getting her off, that was a surefire way to kill a boner.

My phone buzzes, and irritably, I check it. Another text.

**Malcolm:** *Where the fuck are you? Class is going to start soon.*

**Me:** *I slept in late. I'll be there. Don't worry about me.*

**Malcolm:** *Someone has to.*

Not bothering to respond, I pocket my phone, my gaze on the double doors of the dorm building. At this point, I'm practically willing Wren to appear, and when the right door swings open and she appears, I nearly sag with relief. She's as bundled up as I am, with snow boots on her feet instead of her usual Mary Jane's and thick wool tights on her legs, a giant puffer coat wrapped all around her. She has one of those hats on that the girls love to wear with a giant fur puff ball on top of her head and matching gloves and scarf. I can barely see her pretty face.

She doesn't even notice me, too intent on making her way over to the campus buildings.

"Wren!"

Her eyes widen when she spots me waiting for her, and I head in her direction, my steps careful so I don't slip and break a bone from the ice.

"What are you doing here?" she asks, sounding nervous.

"I wanted to talk to you." I stop directly in front of her, tempted to pull her into my arms and hold her close. She actually looks terrified. "Make sure you're okay after yesterday."

"Oh. I'm fine."

"Your dad okay?"

"My dad? Oh yes, he's fine. He was just checking on me. He's been calling daily since the divorce announcement." She mashes her lips together, as if she doesn't want to say anything else about her parents or their divorce.

"Yeah, he kind of—interrupted us." I say it on purpose, wanting to circle back to that moment in the library yesterday. Did it affect her as much as it did me? Is she as rattled by the intensity of that encounter? It didn't even last that long, but I know if it had gone on any longer, I would've made her come.

If she'd have let me, I would've fucked her against that window. And she would've enjoyed every second of it too.

Well, maybe not. She *is* a virgin.

I definitely wanted to fuck her against that window though, that's for damn sure.

"I know." Her voice is quiet and she dips her head, her hair falling forward, the fur ball on top of her head bobbing. "Sorry about that."

I take a step closer, slipping my fingers beneath her chin and tilting her face up so she has no choice but to look at me. "Don't apologize. You do that a lot."

"I know." She visibly swallows. "It's a habit I'm trying to break."

"Are you really okay, Birdy? You look..."

Scared.

Vulnerable.

Fucking beautiful.

"I'm okay. I just—we probably shouldn't have done that." Her voice is so quiet, I can barely hear her.

"Do you regret it? What happened?"

She's shaking her head. "I probably did it all wrong."

"You were perfect." She really was. And I'm repeating the very same words she said to me yesterday.

"I was?"

I hate how this girl doubts herself. Someone did a number on her to make her so self-conscious.

"Yeah." I tug her scarf down, exposing her cheek so I can

touch it. "You were."

The bell rings in the distance since we're a ways away from the main building, where most of our classes are, and the look of panic that crosses Wren's face is almost comical.

"We need to go!" She darts forward, her feet slipping on the ice, and I grab hold of her arm to keep her from falling.

"Slow down. You're going to break something." I loop my arm through hers and we both start walking. "It's okay. We can be late."

"Fig won't like it," she says, her feet seeming to move twice as fast to keep up with my steady pace. I can feel her start to slip again, and I steady her once again.

"Fig can suck my dick," I mutter.

"Oh, that's kind of gross," she chastises, but when I glance at her, I can see nothing but her eyes thanks to her scarf.

And they're twinkling.

"I think you're getting used to my crude ways," I tease her, steering her down the walkway that leads to the back of the main building. I can see the students rushing down the halls through the windows of the double doors and I know we're going to end up being a few minutes late.

We can blame it on the weather, though I'm sure Fig won't buy it. He's not one to care about lateness, but I'm thinking when it comes to me, he's going to give me shit.

He hates me.

Feeling's mutual, so I'm cool with it.

"I actually think I am too," she says sincerely, and I can't help but chuckle.

"I'll have you dropping fucks here and there eventually, Birdy."

"Oh, I doubt that. I can't imagine saying that word."

I can. When she's naked and panting and dying for me to make her come. I'll make her beg. I'll force her to say, *fuck me, Crew* and when I finally slide inside her, she'll come all over my cock.

Yeah, these are the thoughts I've been dealing with since yesterday afternoon. Every single one starring Wren in my dirtiest fantasies.

The final bell rings and now it's Wren who's running ahead, her arm still through mine, so she's almost dragging me along with her. We slam our way through the double doors, turning right to head to our English class. The door is closed, which is unusual, and Wren lets go of my arm to reach for the door handle, me right on her tail.

We race to our seats in the middle of Figueroa taking attendance, and I watch in mute fascination as Wren shrugs out of her coat and leaves it hanging over her chair, the scarf dangling there as well. She pulls the hat off, shaking her head so all of that silky brown hair spills past her shoulders.

I immediately want to touch it. Feel the soft strands curl around my fingers.

Instead, I take off my coat, my gaze finding Fig's, who's glaring at me like he wants to rip my head off.

*Come at me, bro.*

"We're going to work on our essays for *The Great Gatsby* today," he announces as he starts pacing in front of the classroom. "By now, all of you should be wrapping up the book, or already finished. There will be a test next week for finals."

There's some grumbling, but Fig ignores it.

"And the paper will be due the day we get back from winter break."

The complaining is in earnest now. Very rarely do our teachers assign us projects over breaks. They know we actually need the break, and they don't really want to grade assignments when they come back either.

Guess Fig is the exception, the asshole.

"So let's use this week's class time to catch up on our reading, going over what the themes are in the book, and starting to work on the paper. If you've already finished the book and understand the many themes within the story, congratulations. Consider yourself ahead of the game, and you'll most likely have the essay wrapped up by next week before winter break starts." He smiles, ignoring the fact that most of us are disgruntled.

Wren raises her hand, and he smiles at her, his gaze soft. "Yes, Wren?"

I clinch my hands into fists, wishing I could beat his rotten face in.

"What exactly should the essay be about?" she asks in her sweet voice.

"Great question." He turns to the whiteboard, grabbing a blue marker and writing furiously across it before he steps away from the board, tapping the end of the marker against it. "How does Gatsby represent the American dream? That's the theme."

I lean back against my seat, already bored. I can handle that topic in my sleep. I still haven't read the book, and I should probably study for the upcoming final, but I'm thinking I'll be fine. There's enough information on the internet that I can find.

There are a few more questions, but I tune them out, concentrating on Wren sitting in front of me, her head bent, exposing her nape. I remember kissing her there yesterday, making her tremble.

"Mr. Lancaster? A word?"

I glance up to find Figueroa watching me, his hands in his pockets, his posture deceptively casual. I can tell he's tense by the rigid line of his shoulders.

"Sure." Shrugging, I rise to my feet and follow him out of the classroom, Wren's eyes on me the entire time. I send her a quick look, noting the worry in her eyes, and I flash her a quick smile to reassure her.

Her smile is weak. Barely there.

Girl worries too much.

Once we're out in the hall, Figueroa turns on me, his expression grim. "Why were you late?"

This from the teacher who normally doesn't give a shit. Who told us at the beginning of the school year that attendance was a chore he hated but was forced to do. "The weather. Weren't you outside?"

"The sidewalks were all cleared earlier this morning. If you left in enough time, you would've made it." He crosses his arms in front of his chest, on the defensive.

"The sidewalks were icy as fuck."

"Watch your mouth." His eyelids flicker, as if he's got a twitch. "Why did you come in late with Wren?"

That's what this is all about. Good ol' Figueroa is curious.

"That's none of your damn business," I drawl, leaning against the wall. "And what, we were like two minutes late?"

"Late is late."

"From the teacher who doesn't have a tardy policy."

"I still have to follow school rules." His gaze is steely. "As do you and Wren."

"You're just mad," I murmur, so low I almost think he didn't hear me.

But he did. I witness the anger crossing his face that very moment. "Explain to me what you think I'm mad about?"

"The fact that Wren isn't interested in you—that she's interested in me. We've already had this conversation, Fig. And I told you what was going to happen. You don't have a chance in hell getting in her panties." I smile, enjoying the anger I see flashing in his eyes.

"How would Miss Beaumont feel, knowing you talk about her in such a manner?"

Doesn't he sound like a stuffy old teacher who respects his female students? What a crock of shit.

"First, you'll never say anything to her, because you know she'd be more offended by the fact that you brought up her panties to her in the first place. And second, I've been in those panties, so she couldn't deny it even if you mention it to her." Oh,

I'm feeling really smug now, mentioning the 'in her panties' bit, and I fucking love it.

"I don't believe you," Figueroa says through clenched teeth.

"Go ahead. Ask her." I flick my head toward the closed classroom door. "Call her out here."

"I am not about to get involved in my students'—sexual activities," he says.

I laugh. "That's rich, coming from you. Are we done with this conversation?"

"Watch your tone. And don't be late. I'll write you up next time. Wren too." His words are clipped.

Oh, she won't like that. A write-up might send her spiraling.

Standing up straighter, I salute him like the asshole I am. "Yes, sir."

He sneers at me but otherwise doesn't say a word, both of us walking into class at the same time, Wren's curious gaze on me the entire time. She even turns in her desk, lowering her voice to whisper, "What was that about?"

"I'll tell you later." I glance up to find Fig's gaze on us, and I smirk at him as I reach out and tuck a stray tendril behind her ear. "Don't worry about it."

# CHAPTER TWENTY-SIX

## WREN

I can't concentrate with Crew sitting so close to me in psychology. We're supposed to be working on our outline, and I've pretty much put together my part, though he isn't quite finished. I'm trying to help him by pointing out our many differences, but we end up arguing over them.

Then I get distracted by his stupidly handsome face and the delicious way he smells. How rumpled his hair is thanks to that beanie he's been wearing off and on all day. He's currently chewing gum, snapping it and blowing bubbles, and I send him an irritated look.

"Do you have to keep doing that?"

He blows another bubble and pops it with his lips. "That bug you?"

I nod, glaring, though I don't really mean it. More like I'm enjoying giving him a hard time.

"Want a piece?"

"No, thank you." I reach for my backpack, unzipping the front pocket and pulling a fresh Blow Pop from within. My candy of choice. "I'll have one of these."

His gaze narrows. "You're playing with fire by sucking on one of those in front of me, Birdy."

"Really?" I tear the wrapper off and stash it in my backpack before I set the candy in my mouth, my lips wrapping around it.

His gaze settles on my mouth, watching me suck the Blow Pop. The longer he stares, the warmer I get, and I suddenly have a realization.

This probably looks really...dirty to him.

I'm such an idiot.

I pull the sucker out of my mouth. "Maybe I should eat this later."

"No, by all means, don't stop on my account." He props his elbow on the edge of the desk, resting his chin on his curled fist as he continues watching me. "Go ahead. Enjoy it. I know I am."

I hold the sucker to my lips, pausing. "This looks dirty, huh?"

"Fucking filthy, Bird. I can only imagine what you would do with me if given the chance."

My body catches fire at his words, the promise behind them. I'd probably do it all wrong—what he's suggesting. I don't even know if I'd want him in my mouth like that.

Or would I?

That familiar dull ache starts low in my belly and I pull the sucker deeper into my mouth, my gaze never leaving his. I hollow my cheeks, sucking hard on the candy before I let go of the stick.

"Is this all practice?" he asks.

"For what?"

"You know what."

I stare at him, pulling the sucker out of my mouth so I can say, "I never thought of it that way before. I've just always liked lollipops."

His smile is slow and...sexy. "I do too. Especially when you're sucking them."

At least he's not snapping and popping his gum anymore.

I decide to change the subject.

"Are you ready for the test and paper in English?"

"Sure." He shrugs. "I figure I'll watch the movie again and

see if that sparks any ideas."

"Have you read the book?" I finished it a few nights ago.

Crew shakes his head. "Don't plan on it either."

"Crew."

He smiles. "Wren."

"You should read it."

He shrugs. "Bores me. The movie is way better."

"It might not focus on the points Fig wants us to write about."

He makes a face at my mentioning Fig. "Have you seen the movie?"

I shake my head. "No."

"Seriously? You should watch it. I think you'd like it. It's very...pretty."

I laugh. "What do you mean?" I pop the sucker back into my mouth, savoring the sweet cherry flavor, and the way Crew watches me while I suck on it.

"Visually, it's stunning. And Spider-Man is in it." When I frown, he continues, "Tobey Maguire."

"Tom Holland is a better Spider-Man," I automatically say around the lollipop still in my mouth, because I believe it.

Crew scowls. "Hell no. Tobey is the Spider-Man of my childhood. He's forever Spidey."

"How are things coming along?"

We both startle, glancing up to find Skov standing in front of our desks, watching us with an amused expression on her face.

I pull the sucker from my mouth. "Good."

Her gaze goes from Crew's to mine. "You two seem to be getting along."

"She's all right," Crew drawls, making me glare at him.

"Uh huh. Watch it, you two. I didn't plan on starting a romance with this pairing." She takes off before we can say anything else.

We share a quick glance before we look away from each other, and my cheeks feel as if they're on fire.

Are we that obvious? Do we look like a potential romance?

I don't think so. Most of the time, he drives me bonkers with the things he says and the way he acts. I can't deny that I'm attracted to him, and I did let him touch me in a very intimate manner yesterday, but I never thought we were obvious.

"Wren." I glance over at Crew when he says my name. "I have an idea."

"What?" I ask.

"Come to my room tonight. We can watch *The Great Gatsby* together."

I should definitely say no.

"We'll be breaking the rules," I tell him, sounding like the good girl that I actually am. "I can't just hang out in your room. There's no supervision."

"Wren. It's just a movie." He blows a bubble with his gum and I can't resist. I pop it with my index finger, the gum getting all over his handsome face. He peels it off easily and grabs my notebook, tearing out a blank piece of paper and tossing the gum into the center of it before he crumples the paper up around it, forming a ball. "Come on. Say yes."

I suck on my lollipop, mulling over his offer. I should definitely say no. I mean, I guess there are no rules for Crew, considering he's a Lancaster. But what if I get caught in his room? Will I get in trouble? Would they call my parents? God, I'd be mortified. My father would probably ground me for life. Demand I come home and keep me locked up in my room, forcing me to complete my classes online until senior year is over.

No way would I ever want that to happen.

"I don't know…"

Crew grabs the lollipop stick and pulls it out of my mouth. "Hey!" I protest.

"Say yes, and I'll give it back." He holds the candy just out of my reach.

"I don't want to get in trouble," I admit, turning serious.

His expression becomes serious too. "I won't let anything

happen to you, Birdy. We can start the movie early. You can get back to your room before curfew."

"You promise?"

"Yes." He shoves the Blow Pop into his mouth.

"Ew, we can't share that," I protest.

"Why not?" He pulls it out, handing it to me.

I shake my head. "You just had it in your mouth."

"I had my mouth on yours yesterday," he reminds me, his voice lowering, his gaze going hot. "Remember?"

How could I forget?

This movie watching idea is a bad one. I might end up doing something I'll regret.

"Come over at seven," he tells me as he draws the sucker out of his mouth and licks it with his tongue. My breathing starts to accelerate. "You can get back to your dorm by ten."

"How long is the movie?"

"I don't know. Couple of hours? I'll have it set up and ready to stream by seven." He hands the sucker to me. "Sure you don't want it back?"

"Keep it," I murmur. "I shouldn't come over."

"You probably shouldn't," he agrees. "But you will."

. . .

I'm about to enter my dorm building when I spot Maggie walking toward me. I stop and wait for her, glad to see a smile on her face, which I haven't seen in a while.

"How are you?" I ask as we both enter the building. It's so warm inside, I'm immediately unwinding the scarf from around my neck, taking my hat off, and shoving it into my coat pocket.

"I'm good!" Her eyes are sparkling and she grabs my arm, squeezing tight. Her voice lowers. "I talked to Fig."

"Oh yeah?"

She nods. "Want to come to my room so I can tell you about it?"

"Sure."

We both live on the floor where the single suites are, meaning we don't have to share with a roommate. My first three years at Lancaster, I had a roommate each time, and I remember thinking I couldn't wait to get to this point, where I wouldn't have to share.

Now I sort of miss it. A roommate is a built-in friend. Maggie was my roommate sophomore year, and we've been fairly close ever since.

We have our ups and downs, but I'm trying to do right by her and not judge. And I think she's doing the same.

Once we're safely tucked away in her room, without any prying eyes or listening ears, Maggie can speak freely.

"I finally got him alone in his classroom and basically forced him to talk to me," she says as she moves about her room, seemingly restless.

I sit at her desk chair, watching her. "You had to force him to talk to you?"

A sigh leaves her and she goes to the window, staring outside. "I know it sounds bad. It even does to me. But he's been avoiding me the last week or so. The pregnancy thing freaked him out, and I can't blame him."

"So you're really pregnant?"

She turns to face me. "Yes. I'm already two months along. Closer to ten weeks. He tried to convince me to get an abortion at first, but I told him no way. I want to keep his baby."

"But he doesn't want you to keep it?"

"That's what he said at first, but he changed his mind. He wants me to have the baby." She breaks out into the biggest smile, and I wish I could feel her same joy. "He wants to do right by me, and support my decisions."

What does that even mean?

"Are you coming back for the spring semester?" I'll miss her if she's gone. But how can she show back up here and go through the rest of the school year pregnant? With everyone knowing it's Fig's baby, even if she never says so? And how is her ex-boyfriend supposed to react to this? "And when do you turn eighteen?"

"Not until March." She shakes her head. "That's kind of an issue."

Kind of? It's a total issue. He had sex with a minor.

The disappointment that fills me about this is almost overwhelming. I thought he was a good teacher. Kind and looking out for us. Now I feel like he's just on the hunt for a new girlfriend every semester and this one happened to screw up in a major way by getting pregnant.

Did he really think he could've taken advantage of me like that?

"It's a major issue," I murmur, and I spot the irritation flickering in her gaze.

"Look, when you fall in love, age doesn't matter. Not that you would understand," she bites out.

Ouch. "I'm trying to understand. I know you're in love with him. I can see it in your eyes."

Her expression softens. She's just on the defensive, which I can't blame her for. "I am. I'm pretty sure he loves me too, but he's been so weird lately. Until I talked to him today." She's beaming and I swear she seems downright radiant. "We're meeting tonight, and we're going to talk."

"Where are you meeting him?"

"I'm leaving with him later. He's still working, but I'm sneaking off with him in his car back to his house." Her expression turns solemn. "Don't tell anyone, okay? If we get caught…"

She doesn't even need to finish the sentence. They will both be in so much trouble. Especially Fig.

"I won't tell," I promise. "Just—be careful, okay, Maggie? Are you sure he's okay with you being pregnant? If anyone finds out about this, his career is over."

"It's all going to work out, I just know it. He loves me. He promised he would take care of me." She grimaces, running her hand over the front of her stomach.

I'm immediately concerned. "Are you okay?"

"Sometimes I get a weird cramp. I'm fine." Her smile is faint as if she's having to force it. "How are you? What's up with you and Crew?"

I frown. "What do you mean? Nothing's going on with me and Crew."

"Please." She rolls her eyes. "He sits behind you now in English. And he's always watching you. As if he's imagining you naked."

My cheeks go hot. "I don't know about that."

"Oh, I do. I know that look. I think he likes you."

"We've been getting along, for the sake of our project."

I'm such a liar. It's more than that, I just can't admit it. Even after Maggie shared her deepest secret, I don't know if I can trust her.

Or myself.

"Keep telling yourself that." Maggie's smile is knowing. "Want to know my prediction?"

"No."

She ignores my answer. "I have a feeling you're going to have a boyfriend by the beginning of the new year. And his name is Crew Lancaster."

# Chapter Twenty-Seven

## WREN

*Don't go.*

Those two words whisper in my mind when I go to the dining hall early to eat dinner. I sit with Lara and Brooke, not really listening as they gossip about everyone in our class.

Once I'm done with dinner, I head back to my room, those same two words pounding a rhythm in my brain as I walk, the sidewalk slushy and wet from the melting snow. The sky is already dark, and soon, it'll freeze over.

Hopefully I won't break my neck when I head over to Crew's. *No. Don't go.*

I take a shower and wash my hair. Shave my legs and every other area I can think of. Slather my favorite body lotion all over my skin. Blow dry my hair, curling the ends with my rounded brush. Put a thin layer of mascara on my lashes and rub my favorite lip balm across my lips. The one that makes them pinker.

I put on the prettiest underwear I own—a pair of pink cotton panties with a lacy waistband and a bralette I somehow convinced my mother to let me purchase a few years ago when we went shopping together. It's white and lacy and I've never worn it.

Until now.

My intent is clear. I'm going to Crew's and I'm wearing the

sexiest underwear I own, which isn't that sexy, but whatever.

I'm trying.

Once I slip on a black hoodie and my favorite pair of black leggings, I pull on an old pair of black UGG boots, I don't mind getting wet in the snow, and then throw on my puffer coat, going to the mirror so I can check out my outfit.

Boring. Normal. I don't look any different. I definitely don't look like a girl who's hoping a boy will slip his hand in her panties again.

An aggravated noise leaves me and I grab my phone and my dorm building pass, locking my door before I leave.

No one notices me walk out. Not even the RA who sits at the front desk. She's too busy fielding questions from a group of girls surrounding her desk, and I didn't care enough to stand around and listen to what they were complaining about.

It's cold and dark, and I walk carefully along the sidewalk, noting how slippery it is. No one else is out, and there's mist in the air, making me grateful I wore my hat. I pull up the hood on my sweatshirt, giving my freshly dried hair double protection.

Crew's room is in one of the old buildings that used to house staff who lived on campus. Now there are a few suites for Lancaster family members, but it's mostly used for storage. I've never been out here.

Not once.

I tug on the cold metal door handle, opening the door, the creaking sound loud in the otherwise quiet. The moment I'm inside, there's a hushed quality to the lobby, reminding me that it's just me and Crew out here. No one else.

A trickle of fear runs through me, but I push it aside. He's proven that he knows how to be nice to me, though I've witnessed his anger and meanness too.

Maybe that's half the appeal. I never know what I'm going to get when I'm with him.

I walk down the hall, spotting an open door up ahead, the light from within the room shining onto the floor. Suddenly he appears, standing there in the beam of light, looking way too handsome in a navy hoodie that looks just like mine and a pair of gray sweats with the Property of Lancaster Prep logo on his right hip.

"You made it." He smiles faintly as I draw closer. "Didn't think you'd show."

"I didn't think I would either," I answer truthfully. I stop directly in front of him. "Should I leave?"

"You want to?" Before I answer, he adds, "Don't think too hard about it. Just say yes or no."

"No." I straighten my spine. "I don't want to leave."

He holds his hand out toward his room. "Then come in."

I enter the suite, glancing around, trying to take it all in. The room is huge. There's a massive bed in the center of it, at least a king-size, with nightstands flanking either side of it, both lamps lit. There's a desk to the left with an expensive chair, and a dresser to the right. An open doorway to the right of the bed leads to a bathroom.

"Your room is nice," I say, feeling nervous.

"Thanks." He comes toward me. "Want to take off your coat?"

"Oh. Yes." Crew helps me out of it and I smile up at him. "Thank you."

"Don't look so scared, Birdy. It's just a movie." He takes my coat and hangs it on the rack by his door, which he shuts.

And locks.

I notice the laptop sitting in the middle of his bed. "Where are we watching the movie?"

"Thought we could kick it on my bed," he suggests, his tone casual.

"Your bed?" I squeak out, trying to swallow down my nervousness.

"I won't try anything you don't want me to," he says.

See, that's the problem. I might want him to try all sorts of things...

"No, that's fine." I play it off because I can. I'm not scared of him. Or of this—connection that's growing between us. It's overwhelming, and okay, it's a little frightening too, but I'm so tired of being scared of boys and kissing and naked bodies and sex.

It's natural. I'm almost an adult. Less than a month until my 18th birthday. Shouldn't I have kissed a couple of boys by now? Fallen in love, only for the boy to break my heart into a million pieces?

Not that I want my heart broken, but I should be further along than this.

"You want any snacks?" He heads over to a shelf I didn't notice when I first came inside, and I realize there's a mini fridge in his suite. He grabs a bag of popcorn off the shelf, along with a box of Milk Duds, handing them over to me. "I've got more."

I take the bag of popcorn from him. "We can share."

"Want anything to drink?" He bends down and opens the mini fridge, and I see a few bottles of water and cans of Coke. A couple of bottles of beer.

"Just water, please."

When he stands and hands me the water bottle, I take it from him with a murmured thank you, our gazes locking. He seems nervous. To have me in his room?

This is very un-Crew-like of him.

I watch him settle in on the bed first. He's got a pile of pillows and he leans against one stack, then pats the empty spot beside him. "Sit down."

I set my bottle of water on the nightstand before I join him, tossing the bag of popcorn in his direction. He catches it, settling it next to him before he leans over and grabs his laptop.

Leonardo DiCaprio's face is huge across the screen, elegant in a tuxedo, his golden hair swept to the side.

"Ready to play, just like I promised," Crew says, and when he glances over at me, I smile.

"Push play then. I have to be back in my dorm by—" I check the time on his laptop. "A little over three hours."

"You showed up early."

"I was worried it would take me a while to walk over here. The sidewalks are getting slick."

"It's cold out there."

"Nice and warm in here though."

He says nothing. Just hits the space bar on his laptop and the movie starts playing. He holds it in his lap, angling it toward me and I give in to comfort, leaning my head against the pillows behind me, rolling on my side as I reach for the bag of popcorn. I tear it open, grabbing a handful before I hand it over to him, and we share it, occasionally dipping our hands inside at the same time, our fingers colliding. Tangling.

I'm achingly aware of his presence, and I can't even concentrate on the movie, though Crew was right. It's visually stunning, and I want to pay attention, but he's a complete distraction.

He's so close, I could reach out and touch him easily. I study his face, the way his hair falls over his forehead, and he keeps shoving it back. He smells fresh and clean, as if he took a shower before I arrived, and I'm half-tempted to bury my face in his neck, so I can inhale his scent.

Crew changes position, mimicking mine, resting his head on a stack of pillows and lying on his side. He sets the laptop in between us before he glances over at me to find I'm already watching him.

And I don't look away. It's like I can't.

His gaze drops to my mouth, lingering there before he finally looks me in the eyes. "You shouldn't look at me like that."

"Like what?" I whisper, my skin prickling with awareness when he reaches over and pushes my hair away from my face, his touch so gentle, I briefly close my eyes, savoring his closeness. The fact that I'm here with Crew. Just the two of us. Lying on his bed.

It goes against everything I've ever said. Every girl I've looked down upon for succumbing to a boy. How weak I thought they were.

Now I'm just as weak as them, and I understand.

I get it.

"Like you want me to kiss you," he murmurs as he traces my jaw with his fingertips. "Open your eyes, Birdy."

I do as he says, sucking in a breath when I see how close his face is to mine.

"You're so pretty," he murmurs, drifting his thumb across my bottom lip. "I thought you hated me."

"I did," I say with hesitation.

He smiles, the sight of it warming my insides. "I hated you too."

"Why?" I'm genuinely curious. "I never did anything to you."

"You came onto campus a complete stranger. No one knew who the hell you were, yet they all wanted to know you. Wanted to get closer to you, copy you, be your friend. It annoyed me." A flash of irritation appears in his eyes, there and gone in an instant.

His words make me feel bad. Does he still feel that way about me? I didn't like him because he would always glare at me. He scared me.

"I thought you were full of shit. No one could be that sweet, that nice, that beautiful. I figured you were hiding a dark, ugly secret." He curls his fingers around my chin, tipping my head up. "But you're not. You really are that sweet."

I frown. "I'm not always sweet."

"I know." He leans in, his mouth barely touching mine. "Sometimes you're dirty, aren't you? You liked it when I had my fingers inside you."

A shuddery breath leaves me and he kisses me again, his mouth lingering, his tongue sliding out for a teasing lick before he pulls away. "You were so wet."

My cheeks go hot. It's embarrassing, how he's bringing up every mortifying detail of that afternoon.

"Wet for me," he whispers into my mouth before he kisses me deep, his tongue thrusting, stroking against mine. He scoots closer, his foot kicking the laptop shut, cutting off the movie, so there's nothing but silence in the room. The only sound is of our lips connecting. The rustle of clothing as he pulls me into him, a sigh falling from my lips when he kisses my throat.

"You drove me crazy in class today," he admits against my neck.

I wrap my arms around him, daring to slip my hand beneath his sweatshirt, so I can touch his hot, bare skin. "How?"

"With that damn lollipop. The way you kept licking it. You don't even want to know what I imagined you really doing." He lifts his head so his gaze meets mine.

"Tell me what you wanted me to—" He silences me with his lips, stealing another deep, tongue-thrusting kiss before he breaks away, his breath hot in my ear.

"I imagined you doing the same thing to my cock." He nips my earlobe, making me whimper. Or maybe that's just his words making me feel that way. Needy and restless and wanting more than just his kisses. "You'd be on your knees in front of me, sucking me off. Licking me like that lollipop."

I never thought I wanted to do anything like that but the visual he's putting in my head is making me throb between my thighs. "You think I'd be any good at it?"

"I know you would." He rolls me over, so he's lying half on top of me, his mouth on mine, kissing me as if he can't get enough. I kiss him back with matched enthusiasm, running my hand up and down his lower back, marveling at how smooth he is. How warm.

I want to get closer.

The heater is going full force in the room and I start to get hot. Hotter. Maybe it has something to do with the fact that Crew is lying on top of me and he's as hot as a furnace, I don't know. I wish I could take off my hoodie. But I didn't wear a T-shirt underneath and it's not like I can wear my bralette and my leggings while we're kissing.

Or maybe I could...

"Fuck this, I'm burning up." Crew leaps off the bed and goes to turn down the heat before he rips off his hoodie, revealing he doesn't have a shirt on underneath his either. I sit up, blatantly staring at him, my gaze darting everywhere, not sure where to land first.

All the air seems to back up in my throat, leaving me unable to speak. His body is beautiful. There's no other way to describe it. Broad shoulders. Wide, firm chest. Sculpted pecs and the lightest bit of chest hair in the center. Not a lot. Just enough to make me curious.

Make me want to touch it.

His stomach is washboard flat, and ripples with muscle when he moves. There's a thin path of dark hair just below his navel, trailing into the waistband of his sweats, and I'm suddenly filled with the urge to follow that path with my fingers. Slip my hand beneath the front of his sweats. Touch his thick, hot—

"You're staring, Birdy." His deep voice settles between my legs, pulsating. Reminding me of what he did to me with his fingers the last time we were together.

A shiver moves through me at the memory.

"You're shirtless, Crew."

He glances down at himself, rubbing his hand across his rib cage before he returns his gaze to mine. "Does it bother you?"

I shake my head. "No. I'm just—"

"Shocked?"

"I didn't expect it." I squeeze my thighs together, feeling...

Achy.

Needy.

"I don't want to watch this movie anymore." He leans over and grabs his laptop, setting it on top of his desk. He doesn't rejoin me on the bed.

"Me either," I admit softly.

We stare at each other for a moment and I let my gaze drop to his chest again, fascinated. My fingers literally itch to touch him and I sink my teeth into my lower lip, trying to fight the feelings coursing through me.

The pretense of hanging out with Crew to watch a movie for class is long over. The make-out session proves that. I know why he invited me over. And I know why I showed up.

"Come here," he demands, and I don't protest.

Why would I?

I climb off the bed and walk toward him, letting him take my hand. He pulls me in close. I reach out, resting my hand on his side, his hot flesh burning my palm, and I lift my head to find him already watching me, his lips curled into a mischievous smile.

"I got you a treat."

"What is it?"

He reaches into his pocket and pulls out a Blow Pop. Cherry flavored.

My favorite.

I lift my gaze to his. "Why did you get me a lollipop?"

I know why he did. I just want to hear him say it.

Crew leans in close, his mouth right at my ear, making me shiver. "I want to watch you suck it."

My entire body flushes hot. "Why?"

"I wasn't lying when I said I couldn't stop thinking about you in class, sucking on that Blow Pop. How fucking sexy you looked. How red your lips and tongue got from licking the candy." He nuzzles my face with his. "I want to kiss those pretty red lips," he whispers in my ear. "Taste you."

I'm breathless when he pulls away, a smirk on his face as he pulls the wrapper off the sucker and tosses it over his shoulder.

"Crew—" I'm about to give him a lecture about littering, but he cuts me off.

"Suck." He rubs the lollipop across my lips. Back and forth. Tracing their shape. I part them and he slides the candy just inside. "Do it, Birdy."

I wrap my lips around the Blow Pop, sucking on it. His eyes are fixed on my mouth, and they flare with interest.

"Show me your tongue. Lick it." He pulls the candy from my mouth but leaves it resting there.

As usual, Crew is taking something that started out as innocent—and something I do often—and turned it into something dirty.

For some reason, I don't mind. I want to do this.

I want to show him what I can do with a lollipop.

Pushing past the embarrassment, I slowly circle the top of the candy with my tongue, our gazes locking, my heart racing. I close my eyes and lap at the candy, enveloping it with my lips before I let it pop out again.

"Jesus," he mutters, sounding pained. I open my eyes to find his tortured expression, and a heady rush flows through me, along with a realization.

There's power in sex. In me and my sexuality. I was always so scared of it. Afraid I'd give myself to the wrong person. That I'd be humiliated and ashamed of sharing my body with someone who didn't deserve it.

And maybe Crew Lancaster doesn't deserve it, doesn't deserve *me*, but I'm giving myself to him anyway. I've given him a part of myself already, and by participating in this now, tonight, I'm about to give him another piece.

I can see it in his eyes that he wants me, and that's heady stuff. That he feels as strongly as I do.

Because I want him too.

Crew removes the sucker from my mouth and kisses me, his tongue thrusting in between my lips, a groan sounding low in his throat. That same hungry sound he always makes when he kisses me, as if I he can't get enough. I open to him, letting him devour me, my tongue sliding against his. He sucks on it, and I run my hands up his chest, marveling at the strength I feel shifting beneath my hands. Smooth warm skin and hard, unyielding muscle. That tease of soft hair between his pecs.

He breaks the kiss first, breathing hard as he stares at me. "You taste like cherries."

I nod, my mind empty, my entire body tingling. I stare at his mouth, rising up so I can press my lips to his once again, and he cups the back of my head, letting me take control. I test the varying ways I can kiss a boy. Soft. Hard. I bite his lower lip, and he growls.

The sound only encourages me to bite harder.

I suck his upper lip between mine. Trace the shape with the tip of my tongue. Thrust my tongue between his lips, sliding it against his. Grip his head with my hands, running my fingers through his silky hair.

His hands come to my hips, guiding me toward his bed and I let him, not thinking. Not caring.

Once I lie back down on that bed with him, anything could happen.

Anything.

I end up sitting on the edge of the mattress, Crew standing in front of me, his erection stretching the front of his sweatpants, practically in my face. I stare at it. He's so big. Thick.

I wonder what he wants me to do with it.

"Don't look so scared." His voice is low and growly and so incredibly sexy. "Tonight is all about you."

I watch as he grabs the bag of popcorn and drops it on the floor, the bag tipping over, spilling popcorn everywhere. He doesn't seem to care.

His focus is one hundred percent on me.

Before I can think too hard, he's practically on top of me, my back against the mattress, Crew rising above me, darkly handsome, and all mine.

At least for tonight.

From out of nowhere, the lollipop returns, and he drags it across my lips. I dart my tongue out, licking it with enthusiasm and I swear I can feel his erection thickening against my leg.

"You're talented with that tongue," he rasps.

I laugh, heady power coursing through my veins. Then I give the sucker another good lick.

"I have an idea," he says, reaching for the hem of my hoodie. "Let's take this off."

Panic slices through me, and I rest my hand on top of his, stopping him. "Wait."

He takes off my hoodie and things will shift even more between us. Though they've already changed after what happened before. When he slipped his fingers inside my panties and stroked me until I was moaning, straining toward him like the weak girl I apparently am.

He goes still, his gaze finding mine. "I won't push you. You know that."

Fear trickles down my spine. I want to trust him. I did in that secret room in the library, when he had his fingers between my thighs.

"What do you want to do?" I ask.

"Take your shirt off. Your bra." His gaze darkens the longer he stares at me.

I melt at his words, how simple yet effective they are. What he said shouldn't sound so good, but it does.

Removing my hand from his, I nod, giving him permission.

He takes the sweatshirt off, pulling it over my head and tossing it aside. I'm lying there in just my delicate lacy bralette, my nipples straining against the thin fabric, my entire body growing hot when he stares at my chest.

Without warning, he bends down, dragging his mouth across one breast, his tongue darting out to lick the stiffened nipple over the lace. He reaches for the front of my bralette, undoing the clasp, and the cups spring free, exposing me completely.

He lifts away, staring down at my bared chest, his hands moving to shove the straps from my shoulders. I squirm out of it, pushing the bralette out of my way, breathing a sigh of relief when he returns his attention to my chest, his mouth everywhere, trailing fire wherever it touches, making me whimper when he pulls one nipple into his mouth and sucks it deep.

I'm lost to the sensation of his lips. Pulling and tugging. His hot tongue licking. Circling. He lifts his head from my breasts, the lollipop somehow still in his hand and he holds it toward my mouth.

"Suck it."

I do as he says, giving it a good lick before he pulls it away, bringing it to my breasts, dragging the shiny damp candy across my nipple. Circling it over and over.

Then he drops his head and sucks my nipple back into his mouth.

Groaning, I shove my hands into his hair, holding him close.

He keeps up his torture as if he enjoys driving me out of my mind with lust. Toying with my flesh with the candy. Rubbing it against my nipples. Sucking and nibbling and driving me crazy. He pays so much attention to my breasts, I soon become restless, my legs working. Scissoring, trying to stave off the painful throbbing between my legs. I'm wet. Drenched from his attention, and when he finally reaches for the waistband of my leggings, I practically sob with relief.

Finally, I think.

"I'm going to do something," he says like a warning, and I go completely still. "Don't freak out, okay?"

When someone tells you not to freak out, you want to do exactly that. "O-okay."

He lifts his head, his gaze meeting mine. "I mean it. It's going to feel good. Trust me."

I nod, closing my eyes when he yanks my leggings down my

legs, his hands caressing my exposed flesh. They fall onto the floor with a soft plop and then he's kissing his way up my body. The inside of my knees. The tops of my thighs. When his mouth lands on the front of my panties, I throw my arm across my eyes, the slightest bit ashamed.

But I'm also aroused. A flood of moisture escapes me, and I know I'm embarrassingly wet. I don't even care, though.

I can't.

The sucker is back in play. He rubs it against the front of my panties, pressing hard. "I'm going to take these off." His fingers slip beneath the waistband. "Unless you don't want me to."

I don't protest. I want him to take them off. I want to see what he might do next. I have no clue. This is all so new to me, and I have no experience. I'm surprised he hasn't told me to stop because, surely, I've done something stupid by now.

He tugs the panties from my waist. I keep my arm over my eyes as he pulls them off, until I'm completely naked in front of him.

"So beautiful, Birdy," he whispers reverently, his hands curving around my hips. My waist. Goosebumps rise on my skin, from the combination of his touch and the chill in the air since he turned off the heat. "Do you even know how gorgeous you are?"

I say nothing. Can only revel in his compliments. The sweetness in his voice when he talks about me. As if he cares.

As if I matter to him.

He takes the sucker and pops it into his mouth. I can hear him sucking on it before he pulls it free.

"Need to get it nice and wet first," he whispers, his words sounding extra filthy.

Just before he brushes it against my most private spot.

I cry out, shock and pleasure racing over my skin.

"Spread your legs," he commands, and I automatically do it, putting myself on complete display. "Look at me."

I remove my arm from my eyes and slowly open them to find

him kneeling between my spread legs, his eyes locked with mine as he holds the sucker up. He licks it, his tongue lapping at it in an overexaggerated way before he pulls the Blow Pop from his mouth and returns it to the spot between my thighs.

A shuddery moan leaves me. I've never made a sound like that before, but Oh. My. God. It feels so wrong, so *good*—what he's doing to my body with the lollipop.

I'll never look at a Blow Pop the same way again.

He traces me everywhere with the candy. Through my folds. Across my clit. Up and down, around and around until he pauses at my entrance before slowly inserting the sucker just inside my body.

"Does that hurt?" he asks.

"N-no." I shake my head.

He pushes it in farther. A whimper leaves me, and I close my eyes, letting the sensation wash over me as he pulls the sucker almost all the way out before sliding it back in.

In and out.

In and out.

Crew removes the candy and I open my eyes in time to watch him slip the lollipop back into his mouth, tasting me. My lips part. I can't believe he just did that.

I want him to keep doing it.

He does, thank God. He teases my clit with the sucker, rubbing it in tight circles, ratcheting up my pleasure. My entire body is liquid, loose and languid and completely out of my control. I'm melting into the mattress, completely undone, and when he thrusts the sucker back inside my body, I lift my hips, wanting it to go deeper, though I know it won't.

It's too small.

"Jesus, do you know how fucking sexy you are, letting me fuck you with this Blow Pop?" He does exactly that with the candy, and just when I begin to move with him, he pulls it out, holding the lollipop out toward me. "Want a taste?"

Do I? I'm about to ask if I do, but when I part my lips, he slips the candy between them.

Tentatively, I suck on it, tasting the cherry and myself mixed together. A hint of salt and sour with the sweet.

"Fucking hot," he murmurs, his gaze on me as I continue to suck on the lollipop. When he removes it from my mouth, his lips come crashing down on mine. He kisses me with a ferocity I don't expect and I drown in his taste, in his fierceness. His need.

He's on top of me, slowly thrusting against me in time with his searching tongue, his erection pressed directly against my center. I spread my legs wider, accommodating him. I'm naked and wet and aching, and it's as if he's the only one who can take care of me.

He's the only one who can fulfill my needs.

"Wren," he whispers once he breaks the kiss, sliding his mouth down my neck. "I want to make you come."

"I'm so close," I admit, tingling when he lifts his head so he can stare into my eyes. "I am."

"You didn't come last time."

I press my lips together, remembering how I ran away from him. "I got scared."

The feeling was so overwhelming, I didn't know how to deal with it.

He kisses me, his lips gentle. "I'm going to make you feel good."

A steely determined glint fills his eyes and then he's sliding down my body, his mouth and hands everywhere. The sucker leaves a sticky trail across my skin, but I don't mind. I raise my arms above my head, gripping the pillow resting there, lifting my hips. My body knows what it wants without having any experience, and when Crew pauses, his gaze lifts to mine, dark and full of promise.

"Did it look like this?"

I frown, confused. "What do you mean?"

"That porn you watched. When he went down on her." His gaze becomes hotter the longer he watches me.

"This is better," I admit, and he smiles.

Just before he settles his mouth on me.

A ragged sigh leaves me and I thrust my hands in his hair, holding him to me as he devours my flesh. His tongue licks and teases. He thrusts it inside me, pulling out. Pushing in.

It feels so good, but it doesn't seem like enough.

He slips the sucker between my thighs, thrusting it inside me before he pulls it out, rubbing it along my folds. I'm whimpering, my eyes falling closed, the sensations overwhelming me again, just like last night.

But I push through, straining toward release, my mouth falling open on a silent scream as he increases his pace, his face smashed against me, his mouth working me into a frenzy. He replaces the sucker with a finger, pushing inside, and I cry out. When he adds another finger, I practically scream.

It's too much. It's not enough. My muscles are taut, my skin coated in sweat, and when he wraps his lips around my clit and sucks, that's all it takes.

I'm coming. My body shudders uncontrollably as I chant his name, smashing my lower body against his face. I'm helpless, completely out of control, and he grips my hips, holding me to him as he continues his delicious assault.

It's as if I'm in complete freefall. I have no sense of control over my body. I'm trembling, drawing air in big gulps, my heart beating so hard it feels like it could fly out of my chest.

I try to push him away, my skin so sensitive his attention almost hurts, and he does what I silently request, pulling away from me. I peek down to witness Crew rubbing his hand against the side of his face, and when he drops it, I see that his skin and mouth shine.

From me.

He catches me watching, his eyes narrowing as he studies

me. I'm still shivering, my breathing erratic, my heart racing. I wish he'd say something.

Anything.

He moves, so he's lying beside me, his hand on my hip, pulling me toward him. I go easily, still boneless as he tucks me into his body. His mouth is at my forehead, his fingers in my hair when he murmurs, "You okay?"

I nod, curling into him, pressing my cheek to his chest. I need him to hold me. To say the right things. To reassure me that I'm going to be all right.

I don't feel all right. I feel like I'm coming out of my skin. As if the world had shut its doors to me all this time, and I finally caught a glimpse inside.

To find it's all I could ever want.

# CHAPTER TWENTY-EIGHT

## CREW

I turn away so I'm facing my dresser, my reflection staring back at me in the mirror that hangs just above it. I'm supposed to be giving Wren privacy, so she can pull her clothes back on, but I can't help watching her get dressed. All that creamy smooth skin on display, those perfect tits with the pink nipples that are probably still sticky from me rubbing the Blow Pop on them.

Can't believe I did that. Or that I fucked her with a lollipop. She liked it though.

She liked it a lot.

I gave her what she wanted by going down on her, just like she mentioned to me about the porn she watched and how it was her favorite part.

Glancing down at myself, I realize my hard-on is still throbbing, and I readjust myself. Try to think of other things. The frigid temperature outside. How pissed off I got at Fig earlier.

Some of the tension eases and I take a deep breath, reaching for my hoodie and pulling it back over my head.

"I should probably go."

I face Wren, noting how unsure she looks, her gaze cast downward, that flush from her orgasm still coating her skin.

"We didn't finish the movie," she continues, talking to the floor.

"Maybe you should come over tomorrow and we can finish it then," I suggest, not talking about the movie at all.

Her lips curl into a small smile and she sends me a quick glance, clutching her hands in front of her. "Maybe."

I'm surprised she agreed. "You definitely should."

"What time is it?" she asks, before moving to the nightstand and grabbing her phone from where she left it. "It's already nine-forty-five."

"Better walk you back then."

Her eyes go wide as she shoves her phone into her hoodie pocket. "I can walk back myself."

I slowly shake my head, approaching her. "No way am I letting you walk back to the dorm building this time of night by yourself."

"No one will be out there."

"You don't know that."

"I'll be fine." She pauses. "What if someone sees us together?"

Annoyances flares through me, making my erection deflate for good. It bothers me, how she doesn't want anyone to know what we're doing. Though what exactly are we doing? I'm not sure yet. "I won't walk you all the way to the door."

"I don't know…"

"I'm walking you to your building. Stop arguing." I go to my closet and grab my boots, falling onto my desk chair, so I can pull them on, despite the fact that I'm not wearing socks.

Wren watches me, her expression sad. "I made you mad."

"I'm just trying to make sure you're okay. I don't know why you have to argue with me about it."

"Everyone always takes care of me. Teachers. My parents. Especially my dad. He's the worst." She lifts her chin. "I'm trying to learn how to take care of myself."

I lean back in the chair, immediately feeling like a jackass, but I push past it. "What if something happened to you on the walk back? I'd never forgive myself."

She studies me, shoving her hands into her hoodie pocket. "You've changed a lot over the last few weeks."

"What do you mean?" I frown.

"You're a lot nicer."

I rise up and go to her, pulling her into my arms. "And you're a lot meaner."

Before she can complain, I'm kissing her, murmuring my approval when she opens to me without hesitation. Damn this girl is so fucking sexy. We are making all the right steps, and it's all leading to exactly what I want. I predict I'll take her virginity before winter break starts.

At the rate we're going, it'll be easy to get her to have sex with me.

And then what? What happens next? I forget all about her, like the other girls before her?

I don't know if I can do that with Wren. She sticks with me. Within me.

All the time.

I can't stop thinking about her. And after what happened between us just now? Forget it. She'll consume me. I know she will.

She already does.

When she breaks away from me, her lips are swollen, her breath hitching in her throat. "We need to go."

"Yeah." I kiss her one last time, then let her go, grabbing my coat while she slips on that black puffy jacket she wore over. She puts on a pair of beat-up UGGs and then we're headed out the door, out the building, and into the bitterly cold night.

I haul her close to me, draping my arm around her shoulders as we walk along the iced-over sidewalks, our steps careful, so we don't slip. We don't say much, our breaths forming little clouds when we exhale, and she's shivering next to me, despite me holding her close.

When her dorm building comes into view, I have to restrain her so she doesn't break free of me.

"I need to get inside," she says to me when I grab hold of her hood and don't let go. "It's almost ten. I don't want to get in trouble."

The pleading look she sends my direction has me letting go of her hood, but she doesn't run away.

Instead, she throws herself at me, her arms sneaking in beneath my coat to give me a hug, the fur ball on her hat smacking me in the mouth. "I had fun," she murmurs.

Fun. That's one way to describe what we did tonight.

She tilts her head back, her gaze meeting mine. "Please don't make it weird between us tomorrow."

"I should be the one telling you that." I kiss her fast, then gently push her out of my arms. "Go. Before you're late."

A smile crosses her lips, her eyes sparkling as she takes a step backward. Then another. Her footing slips, her expression turning downright comical, and I'm about to go catch her, but in the end, she remains upright.

"Be careful," I hiss at her, and she just laughs.

Such a pretty sound.

She turns and runs—carefully—to her building, disappearing through the double doors. I start to make my way back to my room, slowing my steps when I spot a flash of car lights pulling into the parking lot.

Odd. It's late. No one is allowed off campus during the weeknights, unless they have special permission.

Forgetting about going back to my building, ignoring the cold, I creep closer to the parking lot, until the car comes fully into view. A late-model Nissan sedan sits there idling, two people sitting inside. I can make out their heads, how they're bent close together, but not their features, though I recognize the vehicle.

It's fucking Figueroa's car.

I duck behind a bush, slowly tilting my head around it to see who might pop out of the passenger side door. Figures the pervert would take a girl off campus on a weeknight. Can't even control himself and wait until the weekend, when the rules are lax. It's probably Maggie. Rumor around campus is that they've been hooking up all semester, and I heard her boyfriend recently broke up with her because of it.

Messy.

The door finally swings open, and I wait to see Maggie's familiar dark blonde head.

But it's not Maggie who's climbing out of Fig's car.

It's Natalie.

I hide behind the bush, confused. Since when has she been hanging around Fig? She's never been in his English classes—he tends to go for the smart ones. The vulnerable girls who are quietly desperate for attention. Yeah, Natalie's always looking for attention, but I wouldn't call her quiet or desperate.

Wouldn't necessarily consider her vulnerable either. Girl goes after what she wants, when she wants it.

Maybe that's what she did with Fig.

And how the hell does this asshole get so much pussy anyway? He must have a way with words to convince all of these girls to spread their legs for him so easily throughout the years.

He's such an asshole. If I could, I'd beat the shit out of him for all the girls he must've destroyed over the years.

Piece of shit.

Natalie is headed in my direction—her dorm is in the same hall as Wren's—and she's about to go marching past the bush I'm hiding behind when I step out, revealing myself.

She comes to a complete halt, her eyes wide. "Crew. What are you doing out here this time of night?"

"I should be asking you the same question, Nat." I glance toward the now empty parking lot, Figueroa's car long gone. He didn't even wait to see if she got inside safely. "Who'd you sneak off with?"

She turns on the sass, despite the freezing cold and how bundled up she is. "Wouldn't you like to know?" Her tone is flirtatious.

"I think I already know." She smirks, as if she's daring me to figure it out. "Dark gray Nissan? An Altima, I believe? Pretty sure there's only one teacher who drives a car like that. Figueroa?"

Her smirk fades, her gaze turning pleading. "You can't say anything to anyone."

"Are you seriously hooking up with that piece of shit?"

She glances back at her dorm building, completely freaked out when she faces me once more. "Keep your voice down."

"No one can hear us. I can't believe you. You know he's been with Maggie all semester," I tell her.

Natalie flinches. "He swore they broke up."

"You really believe him? And what about Ezra? I thought you liked him."

"That's all just for fun. He likes to flirt." She shrugs.

I shake my head. "You're fucking with him. I thought you were nicer than that."

"Come on, Crew. You know better. I'm not nice." She turns away from me, heading for the dorm building.

Like a complete idiot, I follow after her. Yeah, we hooked up in the past, and yeah, I also find her annoying most of the time, but she needs to watch out. Figueroa is a piece of shit. Only out for himself. "You need to watch out for him, Nat."

"Oh, watch out for him?" She whirls on me, her expression fierce. "We need to watch out for all of you. That's all guys want, am I right? A quick piece of ass, then you dump us. At least Fig is a man. He knows how to treat a girl. Make her feel good. He's not some insensitive asshole like the rest of you."

"Oh, come on. You really believe he's something special because he's an adult? He's a middle-aged predator who fucks around with underage girls. He finds new ones every single year, and I don't know how the piece of shit doesn't get caught."

Her eyes are wide and she's panting, she's so upset. "It's not that deep, Lancaster."

"Right. That's why you look ready to tear my eyes out for insulting your pedophile hookup. Do you really care about this dickbag, Natalie? You need to wake the hell up."

She comes for me, her fists swinging, screeching at the top of her lungs. I duck, avoiding her fists, grabbing her with both arms and holding her against me as she struggles and fights. She's calling me all kinds of names, and I swear to God she's sobbing.

Pretty sure I've never seen Natalie cry.

"You're such an asshole, Lancaster!" she screams, and I'm about to cover her mouth with my hand to keep her quiet when a bright white light flares on. A cluster of people exit the dorm building, flashlights illuminating us.

"Natalie? Is that you?" one of the women call.

All the fight leaves her as she sags in my arms. "Oh shit," she whispers.

# CHAPTER TWENTY-NINE

## WREN

I'm still in bed, half asleep, when there's rapid-fire knocking on my door.

Cracking one eye open, I grab my phone and check the time.

It's not even seven o'clock. School doesn't start for another hour.

The knocking starts all over again, then stops.

"Wren. Open your door."

It's Maggie.

Climbing out of bed, I put on my slippers and cross the room, unlocking and opening the door to find Maggie standing on my doorstep, dressed in her uniform and ready for the day, though her face is streaked with tears. "What's wrong?"

She rushes inside, shutting the door behind her and leaning against it. "Fig never came to meet me last night."

I'm almost relieved he didn't, though I can't tell her that.

"What happened? Did he give you a reason?"

Maggie shakes her head. "He said something came up, and he couldn't talk about it. I kept trying to text him, but he ignored me for the rest of the night." She hesitates, her eyes full of fear. "Do you think he found someone else?"

"No," I say automatically, because I can't imagine him moving that fast. "He's been too busy with you to find someone else."

Well, he was hoping to recruit me, but I think I shot him down. Maybe he did actually seek someone else out?

"Yeah, that's what I keep telling myself, but maybe I'm wrong. Maybe he's not happy with me wanting to keep the baby. Maybe I shouldn't." She drops her head, but I still see the tears dripping down her cheeks.

"Oh, Maggie." I go to her and wrap her up in a big hug, letting her cry on my shoulder. I'm so glad whatever is happening between Crew and me isn't as complicated as what Maggie's going through. He still confuses me and I'm not sure if we're trying to be in an actual relationship or if he only wants to hook up with me, but at least I'm not crying over him.

"It's okay," she finally says when she pulls away from me, hurriedly wiping the tears from her cheeks. "It's why I got ready early. I'm going to go talk to him."

"You think that's a good idea?"

"Not talking to him about it is worse," she practically wails. "I need to know what he's thinking. What he was doing last night. The not knowing is the worst."

I go to my dresser and grab the tissue box sitting there, then hand it to her. "I'd hate that."

"It's awful." Maggie takes a tissue and wipes her face, then blows her nose. "I could barely sleep last night, I was so upset. Oh my God!"

"What?"

"Something else happened last night. Since I'm on the ground floor, I heard everything. A bunch of girls came out and watched it go down."

I'm frowning. "Watched what go down?"

"Natalie was caught in front of the dorm in a big argument with Crew. Can you believe it? I thought you two had something going on, but maybe they've been hooking up the entire time?"

I fall heavily onto the bed, her words on repeat in my brain.

With Crew.

Natalie was outside with Crew.

Maybe she was trying to sneak in and he saw her since he walked me over? That has to be it.

"What exactly happened?" I ask. "Do you know?"

"I guess they were fighting? I heard Natalie scream. We all did. She was yelling at the top of her lungs, like she didn't even care, though it was past curfew so she had to know she would get in trouble. Not sure why Crew was out in front of the building. For Natalie, maybe?"

No, for me, I want to tell her. We watched a movie and forgot all about it. He kissed me until I was breathless, and I could feel his erection against my thigh. We did inappropriate things with a Blow Pop and he made me come with his mouth and the candy. It was the hottest experience of my life.

Ruined by him ending up getting caught with…Natalie?

I can't even begin to understand what happened after I left him outside last night.

"I'm glad I wasn't the one caught sneaking back into the dorm," Maggie says, oblivious to my shock. "I would've been if I'd gone and met with Fig like I was supposed to."

"Yeah," I say numbly. "You're lucky."

"I know." She grabs another tissue and mops up her face, then goes to the full-length mirror on my wall, checking herself out. "I look like I've been crying."

"You don't look that bad," I reassure her, wishing she could reassure me too.

But that would mean I'd have to tell her everything that happened between Crew and me last night, and that's the last thing I want to do. Especially with everything else that happened on top of it.

"I could look better." She keeps her gaze on her reflection, sighing. "I guess this will have to do. I'm going to go talk to him."

"You think he's already here?"

"He always gets here early. If he's not in his classroom yet, I'll go grab a coffee in the dining hall first," she says as she starts for the door.

I don't bother telling her to stay or try to convince her she shouldn't talk to him. Make him come to her. She wouldn't listen to me anyway. She's going to do what she wants.

"Okay. Good luck." My voice is weak, my thoughts turbulent, but she doesn't even notice.

"Bye, Wren. See ya in class. Wish me luck!" She shuts the door before I can say anything else.

I flop backward on the bed, overwhelmed. I don't even know what to think. Will Natalie and Crew get in trouble? Suspended? Oh God...expelled?

They wouldn't expel a Lancaster, would they? I know he's claimed they have zero tolerance with drugs, and even he could get kicked out, but what about a situation like this?

What if he's gone already and I never get a chance to talk to him again? What then? I don't even have his phone number, which is so stupid. I suppose I could contact him via social media but...

Okay, I'm getting way ahead of myself here. I need to get ready for school and leave a little early to see if he's waiting out front for me like he usually does. If he's not there...

I don't know what I'll do.

I get ready in a hurry, pulling on a thick pair of white wool tights and the bralette I wore last night, then I don my uniform. I slip a navy sweater over my white shirt, forgetting the jacket, then my skirt, rolling it up a little to show off more leg.

Tight-covered leg but who cares? I'm trying to catch someone's attention.

Hopefully he'll be there. Waiting for me by the entrance like he normally does. Before, when he used to level that cold stare on me, I'd run by him, just to get away.

Now I walk slowly, savoring that one-sided smile that appears on his face when he first spots me. He makes me feel beautiful.

What in the world was he doing with Natalie last night?

Once I'm finally out of the dorm hall, I make my way toward the main building, my steps careful thanks to the slushy mess the sidewalks are. The sun is out again, a little warmer this morning, and even though it's still cold, it's causing the snow to melt.

There are people all around me, most of them with their heads bent as they walk, whispering to each other. I hear Natalie's name mentioned time and again, along with Crew's.

It's all anyone can talk about. The gossip is going to be rampant.

If they all think Crew and Natalie are together, I'm going to feel like a fool. Even if it's not true.

Holding my head high, I pick up my pace, marching toward the building when I spot Ezra and Malcolm standing in Crew's usual spot, frowns on their faces as they watch everyone walk by them.

There's no Crew in sight, and I can't fight the disappointment sinking in my stomach like a stone.

"Wren."

Malcolm calls my name in that crisp British accent of his and I go to him, nerves making my entire body shake.

"Yes?" I ask, shoving my gloved hands into my coat pockets.

"You heard what happened to our boy?"

I like how he calls Crew our boy. He must be aware of what's going on between us, and any other time, that would be embarrassing. Not right now, though.

Now, all I want is information about Crew. Where he is. If he's all right. What in the world he was doing with Natalie.

"I know he was caught with Natalie last night," I admit, taking a step closer, so I can speak to him more privately. "Where is he?"

"He's got a meeting with Matthews," Malcolm answers, referring to the headmaster of the school. "Right at eight o'clock. He wanted me to tell you."

"Oh." Hope rises within me, but I tamp it down. I can't read into this too much. "Thank you for letting me know."

Malcolm sends a quick look in Ezra's direction before he returns his attention to me. He holds out a folded yellow Post-It Note between his fingers. "This is his phone number. Don't know what the two of you are doing if you're not texting or Snapchatting with each other on the phone like normal fucking teenagers, but he wanted you to have it."

"Thank you." I clutch the piece of paper in my hand, the edges biting into my palm. "Is he going to be all right?"

"Don't know," Ezra says, earning a dirty look from Malcolm for his oh-so-reassuring contribution. "Might get suspended. Fucker deserves it."

"He's a Lancaster," Malcolm adds, ignoring Ezra. "He'll be fine."

I see the hostility filling Ezra's gaze and I remember how he was always flirting with Natalie. The almost desperate edge to it, and how she ignored him.

How she was always staring at Crew instead.

"Thank you again," I tell Malcolm because I'm polite to the point of being annoying and I can't help myself. He nods. Ezra sneers.

I leave them where they stand, entering the building and immediately leaning against the wall, opening the Post-It Note to study Crew's phone number.

He also wrote something else.

*Text me when you can, Birdy. I need to talk to you.*

My heart flutters in my chest and I grab my phone, punching in the number, and immediately send him a text.

**Me:** *It's Wren. Text me back when you can talk.*

I wait for a few minutes, leaning against the wall, watching everyone walk past me, headed to class. They're all talking among themselves, whispering and gossiping. Laughing and reveling in the downfall of Natalie and Crew.

It makes me sad. Worse, it makes me angry, because they don't know what actually happened. They're all assuming Crew and Natalie were together last night, and I know that's not the case.

He wouldn't just drop me off and pick up Natalie, would he? No. No way.

Not after everything we just shared.

I walk into English class in a daze, my head bent, not paying attention to what's happening. I fall into my desk chair, hating that the desk behind me is empty, that Crew is nowhere to be found. I glance around the room, my gaze snagging on Figueroa's. He's already watching me, and I realize as I look around the classroom, once again, that Maggie isn't here.

Without thought, I rise to my feet and approach his desk, noting the pleasant smile on his face, the way his eyes flicker with interest when they land on me.

I wish I had the courage to slap his face and call him out for his bad behavior. He's getting careless.

"Wren. How can I help you this morning?" His tone is light, as if he doesn't have a care in the world.

I was with Maggie not even an hour ago. Upset, pregnant-with-his-baby Maggie, who left my room to come talk to him, and here he sits, not traumatized in the least, while she's not even here.

What happened with their conversation? Did he blow her off?

"Where's Maggie?" I ask him, my tone flat. Unfriendly.

Totally unlike me.

He frowns, sensing my hostility. "I don't know. She hasn't shown up to class yet. The bell hasn't rung—"

It does exactly that, silencing our conversation.

"She has three more minutes," he says once the bell shuts off. "She should be here any second."

"But I know she came straight here from the dorm to speak with you," I say, wanting him to understand that I know everything.

Something flickers in his expression but he smooths it out. Like a blank canvas. "No, she didn't."

"She told me she was going to."

"We have nothing to talk about."

"She was upset because you didn't meet with her last night."

The irritation is full-blown blazing in his dark eyes now. "You don't know what you're talking about."

"Oh, but I do. You were supposed to meet with her last evening, and you cancelled. She wanted to talk to you about the ba—"

"Stop. Shut up." His voice is fierce, his eyes almost black. "Stay out of it, Wren."

I stare at him, startled he would speak so harshly to me. "Where is she?"

"I don't know."

He's lying.

"Did she leave? Should I go find her? Make sure she's okay?"

"She'll be fine," he snaps. "Go sit down."

It's like I don't even care anymore. I've tossed all niceties aside, just as he has. I need him to know that I know...everything.

"You're going to pay for what you've done to her," I tell him, my voice even. My emotions completely under control. "You need to do what's right and take care of her."

He doesn't say a word, but he curls his right hand into a fist, pounding it lightly on top of his desk.

"She's only seventeen and hopelessly in love with you," I continue, quickly glancing over my shoulder to see if anyone's watching us. No one really is. They're all used to girls talking to Fig during class. "I don't know why, considering you have a reputation. You do this every year."

"Like you were even aware of what was going on until that asshole boyfriend of yours told you," Fig snarls, basically admitting what I just accused him of. All pretense of the friendly, cool English teacher is gone. Now he's just a pitiful, angry man.

He lowers his voice, though I'm not sure anymore if he cares if someone hears him. "Where is Crew anyway? Oh, that's right, he got caught sneaking around with Natalie Hartford last night. Both of them will most likely get suspended."

His words are like a stab to the heart. He said it just to upset me and it worked.

Turning away from him, I go back to my desk, settling in my seat, staring at the door, willing Maggie to appear.

Willing Crew to appear too.

But neither of them ever do.

# CHAPTER THIRTY

## CREW

I'm sitting in Headmaster Matthews' office, slouching in the chair that sits in front of his desk, watching as he speaks on the phone with my father. He's got it on speaker, I can hear every shitty word Reginald Lancaster has to say about me, but I don't care.

I just want out of here. I need to talk to Wren. Clear the air with her and make sure she understands what actually happened last night.

"Normally we would suspend students caught out on campus after curfew," Matthews says after my dad wraps up his three-minute tirade on my lack of focus and how I don't give a damn about school or other people. "But we're so close to finals week and winter break. I'm thinking the time off will be a good time for both your son and Miss Hartford to think about what they've done and come to terms with their mistakes."

My father makes a harumphing noise. "You're too soft on 'em, Matthews."

Matthews can't win. He suspends me, and my father will be pissed. He lets me go and my father's pissed.

"I'll put them in detention then," Matthews suggests, his gaze meeting mine. If I could, I'd give him the finger, but I restrain myself. "For the rest of the week."

That's a whoppin' two days. Big deal.

"Whatever you think is best." I can tell my father is done with this conversation. "Crew!"

"Yes, Sir?" God, I hate him.

"Quit fucking around and get your head on straight for once in your goddamn life. Do you understand me?"

Matthews flinches at the choice words my father uses. Such a cool, calm dude when he wants to be.

Not.

"Will do," I tell him.

Dad ends the call, and with a sigh, Matthews punches a button, shutting off the phone. He rests his elbows on top of his messy desk, pressing his hands together. "You know I'm taking a chance with this."

I lean forward in my chair, taking my opportunity. "And you know I'm telling you the truth. Natalie was sneaking back onto campus after meeting with Mr. Figueroa. I saw his car. I saw him inside the car. Pretty sure I saw him kiss her too."

Matthews winces. "You sure about that?"

"Not one hundred percent."

"You don't think he was helping her with a paper?"

Oh sweet, idiotic Headmaster Matthews. Why is everyone in denial when it comes to Figueroa?

"It was ten o'clock at night. I don't think he was helping her with a paper," I tell him, my voice dry. "I don't even think she's in one of his English classes."

Matthews sighs. "She's not. I've already checked."

"Told you."

"This is a serious allegation, Crew. You could put a man's entire career at stake if this comes out."

"It'll come out, because now that I've told you, by law, you have to report it to the authorities." I'm feeling pretty damn good for ratting Fig out. I don't even care if it fucks with his career. That's exactly what it should do. "He has no business teaching here. These rumors have been going on for years. Haven't you ever heard about them?"

Matthews sighs. "There have been rumors swirling around him for years. A friendly English teacher, who actually cares, garners a lot of attention, some of it negative. The man is an institution at this school. He's been here longer than I have."

"And that means it's okay that he's preying on underage teenage girls." I nod. "Gotcha."

"I want you to know no one has ever come to me about Figueroa—ever. I've heard rumors, but I've never seen actual proof."

"Well, now you've got to make your report, and you've got your proof. Me. I saw them." I rise to my feet. "Can I go to class now?"

"What's your first period?"

"Honors English." I grin, not giving a shit that I'll see Figueroa. Might be fun, knowing that I'm destroying him, yet he has no clue.

Plus, I need to talk to Wren. Make sure she's okay. All the rumors must be flying around campus, and I'm sure they're all talking about me and Natalie.

Malcolm already warned me Ezra is mad, thinking I'm trying to steal his girl by meeting up with her last night.

The dumbass has no clue what's really going on. He needs to blame that asshole Fig for stealing Natalie from him.

I leave Matthews' office a few minutes later, spotting Natalie sitting in the admin office, I assume waiting to speak to him next. The moment her gaze meets mine, she stands, rushing toward me.

"What did you tell him?" she asks, her voice hushed as she glances over at Matthews' secretary, Vivian, who's watching us with obvious interest.

"Everything."

Natalie's eyes widen. "What exactly are you referring to?"

"Had to rat out your lover, Nat. Sorry, but I'm tired of

watching this guy destroy girls' lives every semester. He deserves to go down." I start to walk away, but Natalie grabs my sleeve, her grip surprisingly strong. I look back at her, shaking her hand off. "What's wrong with you?"

Her expression is panicked. "You can't do that. You just—you can't."

"Too late."

She's shaking her head. "When my parents find out what happened, they're going to kill me. It's like you didn't even think about what you're doing. You don't care about anyone else. Just yourself."

"Come on, I was telling the truth," I remind her. I had to come clean with Matthews over what I saw. "I'm not about to take the fall for him."

We're basically in a stare off, and I can tell she wants to smack me. Slap my face. Stomp on my foot. Something. She's so pissed off at me right now, but I don't even care. I had to do the right thing.

Natalie's entire demeanor transforms. Suddenly she's standing a little straighter. Her expression clears. Her voice is calm. "You're lying." She says this loud enough for Vivian to hear her.

I frown. "What do you mean?"

"We met up last night. We hooked up. And we got caught. You just don't want to admit it. Don't want your precious little virgin to find out you've been fucking me on the side," Natalie says, her tone as sweet as her smile.

"Miss Hartford, please watch your mouth," Vivian reprimands.

Matthews comes out of his office, halting when he spots me and Natalie talking. "Come in, Miss Hartford. We have much to discuss."

"Yes, we most certainly do." The smile Natalie flashes me is smug before she turns and enters Matthews' office, shutting the door behind her.

I storm out of the admin office, snatching the pass from Vivian before I leave, and head for Figueroa's class.

Fucking Natalie. She's going to tell Matthews a completely different story and make me look like a lying asshole, all to protect her precious Fig. Confirming all the rumors swirling around campus this morning.

That I was hooking up with her, not Wren.

I wonder if Wren would vouch for me. Of course, this would mean she'd have to come clean about her sneaking into my room last night, and I'm sure she wouldn't want to do that, even though she's a reliable witness. Matthews would believe her over all of us.

But my little birdy doesn't get in trouble.

Ever.

I'm a bad influence. I should probably leave her alone, let her be. But fuck.

I've had a taste. I want more.

Within seconds I'm entering the classroom, marching up to Figueroa's desk and tossing the pass at him.

"You're late yet again," he says, a faint smile curling his lips.

"No thanks to you," I bite out, wanting him to know I saw him with Natalie last night.

He's not even paying attention to what I'm saying. "Go sit down and work on your essay. Or read. Whatever it is you need to do. And don't talk to anyone. Understand me?"

"You're not my boss," I retort, annoyed. Hating how he's making me feel like a little kid, when I know I could take this asshole.

If I ever get a chance, I'm going to kick the shit out of him. He would deserve it.

"I am your teacher, and you'll listen to what I have to say. I've had enough of your backtalk these last few weeks. Sit down." His gaze never strays from mine. "Now."

I can feel Wren's gaze on me and I glance in her direction, noting the pleading expression on her face. She looks sad. Of course she does. Shit's gone sideways in a matter of hours.

I go sit down behind her, leaning over my desk, getting as close to her as I can. "I need to talk to you."

She turns her head to the side and I stare at her profile, wishing I could kiss her. She nods but doesn't say a word.

Fuck. This is a mess.

A complete mess.

# CHAPTER THIRTY-ONE

## WREN

It's agony, having Crew so close, yet I'm unable to talk to him. I have so many questions to ask, every one of them having to do with last night and what happened between him and Natalie.

I want to believe it was just a coincidence, that they somehow ran into each other, but the doubt creeps in, as it usually does. Only a few weeks ago, he hated me. Antagonized me every chance he got. Who's to say it isn't some sort of trick on Crew's part? A way for him to get close to me, only to make me the laughingstock of the entire school?

My stomach roils at that thought. God, I think I'm going to be sick.

He taps me on the shoulder and I turn, my gaze meeting his, and he must see the worry on my face, though he chooses to ignore it. His expression is deadly serious. "Can I borrow a piece of paper?"

Frowning, I say, "Sure?"

"I forgot my bag in my room," he explains. "I don't even have my book."

"Do you want to borrow my copy?" I offer, wishing I could smack myself.

I need to stop being so nice to him. He might not deserve it.

"Yeah. Please."

"Wren. Crew." Figueroa's expression is stern. He's being extra strict this morning, though I'm sure a lot of that has to do with me and how I just confronted him. I sent a quick text to Maggie earlier asking where she was, and she still hasn't answered me.

I'm worried.

"I forgot my stuff. She's helping me out," Crew says to Fig.

I hand Crew a few sheets of paper, a pencil and my copy of *The Great Gatsby*, his fingers brushing mine during the exchange, making me shiver. "Thank you," he murmurs.

"You're welcome." I turn around, taking a deep breath, feeling stupid. I remember everything that happened between us last night. Every single thing, and I don't want to regret it.

But something is telling me I could. Maybe things aren't what they seem between us. What if he's been using me the entire time? If Crew didn't mean any of things he said or did these last couple of weeks…

I'm going to die of humiliation. I will never want to face him again.

He's quiet for the rest of class, which is only around fifteen minutes since he arrived so late. By the time the bell rings, he's bolting out of his seat, dropping the book on top of my desk, a folded piece of paper in it, the edges just showing. I glance up at him in question.

"Meet me at lunch, out back where you caught me and the guys. You know the spot?" He lifts his brows.

I nod slowly. "Okay."

He taps the book with the pencil I gave him. "Read what's in there."

I nod again. I assume he's referring to the note.

His gaze locked on my mouth, he murmurs, "Bye, Birdy."

He's gone in a flash and I gather up my things, shoving everything in my backpack and am about to leave the classroom when Fig speaks up.

"You know you should avoid him. He's only going to break your heart."

I send him a look. "Is that a warning?"

"Just want you to be safe, Wren. And that boy is definitely not safe. He's already toying with your heart *and* Natalie's."

I hate that he brought her up. He's believing the rumors just like everyone else.

"Is that what you want?" he asks when I still haven't said anything. "To share him with someone else?"

His words, his assumption that I want his opinion about my personal life, is infuriating. The man crosses boundaries all the time, as if he has the right.

"You know what you should do?" I stand, slinging my backpack over my shoulder.

Fig frowns. "What?"

"Mind your own damn business."

I flounce out of there before he can say anything else, shock coursing through me at the way I just told off a teacher. How I actually cursed at him. I never do that.

I *never* say bad words. It's like I spend a little time with Crew and I'm changing. Becoming stronger. Finding my voice.

I think I like it.

I race to my second period class, falling into my chair in record time, my hands shaking as I pull the paperback out of my backpack and crack it open to find the folded note inside. With trembling fingers, I open it, my gaze trying to decipher his bold, messy writing.

*Don't let anyone read this. Last night after you went inside, I saw Figueroa drop off Natalie in the parking lot. I confronted her about it and she got mad. Tried to attack me. That's what happened when we were caught. I wasn't hooking up with her. She's hooking up with Fig. Don't believe the rumors. I'll tell you more at lunch. Please believe me.*

*PS – I can't stop thinking about you and that Blow Pop.*

A tiny smile curls my lips and I shove the note back between the pages of *The Great Gatsby*, then put the book away in my backpack.

I believe him. I have to. There's no way he could do everything that he did with me, and then get with Natalie immediately afterward. I just—I can't even wrap my head around it.

It's like my brain won't let me.

I pass through the rest of the morning in a haze. Always searching for Maggie—she still hasn't texted me back—or trying to tune out the rumors about Crew and Natalie. They're rampant.

It's all anyone can talk about.

By the time lunch rolls around, I'm an internal mess, trying to keep it together. Still no Maggie to be found. I'm supposed to meet Crew and I'm scared to hear what he has to say, but there's no way I'm not meeting with him.

I have to see him. I need reassurance.

As I'm leaving my fifth period class, I spot Natalie in the hall, our gazes locking for the briefest moment, hers knowing. That devilish smile on her face, as if she's aware she's messed up my world and there's no coming back from it.

And she really doesn't care.

I look away from her first, hating that I gave in, but I don't want to have a confrontation in the hall with her that everyone would witness. That'll make everything even worse.

Gosh, I really, *really* don't like her.

Heading outside, I tuck my coat around me, glancing over my shoulder to make sure no one's paying attention to where I'm going. But it's so cold, everyone is pretty much in the dining hall, where I wish I was too.

Or maybe not.

Honestly, I wish I could run away from this place and never

look back. Preferably with Crew by my side.

I walk behind the building where I found Crew and his friends doing drugs, and that moment seems like such a long time ago. So much has happened in such a short amount of time, it's overwhelming.

I come to a stop when I see Crew standing there, his back to me, his face tilted toward the sky. He turns, as if he can sense I'm behind him, and then as if I have no control, I'm running toward him, his arms going wide as I practically throw myself at him. He holds me close, his mouth at my forehead, his hard, hot body warming the chill I haven't been able to shake since I woke up this morning to Maggie knocking on my door.

"Birdy, you're shaking," he murmurs against my temple, just before he kisses it.

I melt against him, closing my eyes, savoring how tight he's holding me. "Everything is a mess."

"I know. But we have options." He slips his fingers beneath my chin, lifting my face up. "We either ignore it and wait for another scandal to replace this one or…"

I frown, hating that option. "Or what?"

A sigh leaves him. "Or I expose Figueroa publicly and tell everyone he was with Natalie last night."

Oh, that's right. We haven't even discussed that yet.

"You really saw him with Natalie last night?"

"After you went inside, I saw a car pull into the parking lot. I ducked behind a bush when I realized it was Figueroa's and waited to see who would get out of his car. I thought it would be Maggie."

"He was supposed to meet her last night," I whisper. "He texted her, said something else came up. She told me this morning."

"Yeah, because he was with Natalie." Crew's expression is thunderous. "I told Matthews what I saw. He'll have to report it to the authorities. She's a minor."

"This will devastate Maggie. She's in love with him." I don't tell him about her being pregnant.

"In the end, she'll know it was the right thing to do. He's a creep. He's playing two girls this semester, and he's been doing it for years." He scowls. "He was going to try and get with you next. I know he was."

A shiver moves through me at the thought. Would I have fallen for it? Before Crew came along and disrupted my world, I might've. I don't know. We'll never know. "He probably hates me now. I told him to stay out of my business at the end of class, after you left."

Crew's brows shoot up. "You did?"

I nod, feeling bad over what I said to him, even though he deserved it. I don't mention he was warning me off Crew. "And I never talk back to a teacher."

He smiles. "My little birdy is getting her wings."

"Stop." I roll my eyes.

"It's true." He slowly runs his fingers through my hair. "I hate the rumors that are out there right now. Natalie's not stopping them. She told Matthews we were meeting up last night before we got caught."

My stomach cramps. "Seriously?"

He nods. "She doesn't want Figueroa to get caught. I know it. Why the hell do they all protect him so much? He doesn't deserve it."

I grab hold of the front of his coat, clutching the heavy wool. "Be real with me right now, Crew."

His expression turns somber. "About what? I've told you the truth."

"So you really didn't—hook up with Natalie last night?" My voice is a whisper, barely heard. Carried away on the wind.

"No," he says vehemently. "I was with you. All I could think about was you. And how good you tasted."

My cheeks go hot, despite the cold air. "Crew."

"I'm serious." He ducks his head, nuzzling my face with his, his breath hot against my ear. "I can't stop thinking about you."

"I can't stop thinking about you either," I whisper.

"Natalie is fucking everything up. I should've minded my own business and kept walking when I saw the car lights pull in, but I had to know." He presses his mouth to my cheek, seeming to breathe me in.

I close my eyes, pressing my forehead to his chest. "I don't like her. But you're doing the right thing, Crew."

"You really think so?"

I nod, then look up at him. "Yes."

He kisses me, so gently I almost want to cry. Who knew this boy could be so sweet?

"You coming over tonight to finish watching the movie?"

I'm sure that's code for messing around.

"I shouldn't," I answer. "Everyone's probably watching you."

I can sense the disappointment radiating off of him, but we can't risk it—and he knows it. "Maybe tomorrow? It's a Friday. Curfew isn't as strict. Or are you going home?"

"I'm not going home until winter break."

He stiffens, squeezing me closer to him. "Where are you going for break?"

"Nowhere. We're spending it at home." I hesitate, wondering if I should ask. Then I do. "Are you going home?"

He nods. "I'll be at my parents' apartment on the Upper East Side."

"Oh." Our parents are practically neighbors. "Maybe we could see each other."

A slow smile spreads across his handsome face. "You want to, Birdy?"

He sounds surprised.

"I don't know." I shrug one shoulder, and he clutches my waist beneath my coat, trying to tickle me. "Stop! That tickles!"

"Stop trying to act like you don't care, when I know you do."

He pulls me in so close I'm completely pressed against him, our lower bodies stuck together like glue. "It's okay to admit that you like me."

"I shouldn't," I tell him truthfully. "After everything you've put me through lately. For the last three years, actually."

His expression turns somber. "I'm an asshole."

"Yes, you are," I agree.

"Birdy." He sounds shocked.

"I didn't say it. I just agreed with it." I smile.

So does he.

"Everything's going to be all right," he tells me, his mouth hovering above mine. "I promise."

He kisses me.

And I can't help it.

I believe him.

# CHAPTER THIRTY-TWO

## WREN

I haven't been this grateful for a Friday in years.

Sometimes Fridays make me sad. They would make me miss my family when I was stuck at school. It was hard at first, adjusting to going to boarding school. Having to share a room with a virtual stranger, never feeling like I got time by myself. I did my best though, and eventually got used to it.

But Fridays were hard. Sometimes they still are, especially lately, as my friends grow more and more distant. I was so excited to have my own room, until I started missing having a roommate. Someone to talk to, even if it's forced.

That's how pitiful I was feeling only a month ago, if that.

At least we'll have a shorter schedule next week so that's something to look forward to, with winter break starting the week after that.

Will Crew and I actually see each other over the break?

I hope so.

I go to the dining hall early to pick up a muffin and coffee, stopping short when I see Maggie already there, standing in line. I immediately go to her, and when our gazes connect, she walks straight out of the line and wraps me up in a tight hug.

"I'm sorry I didn't text you. Yesterday was—rough."

I slowly pull away from her, glancing around the room, noting the curious gazes as people blatantly watch us. "Want to talk somewhere private?"

She shakes her head. "I'd rather pretend none of it is happening."

I want to argue with her, tell her that's probably not the healthiest way to handle this situation, but I don't know what it's like, what she's going through. She has to be overwhelmed.

And I don't think she knows about the Natalie part of her and Fig's equation.

"I'm going home this weekend," she tells me as we make our way to the back of the line. "I need to talk to my mom."

"Are you going to tell her?"

"Not everything," she whispers. "Just this part."

She waves a hand in the general vicinity of her stomach.

I can't imagine telling my mother I was pregnant while still in high school. She'd freak out—in the most elegant way, of course. "Won't she be curious about who..."

"I'm going to tell her it's Franklin."

Wait a second—now she's going to lie? I'm sure she can see the shock on my face.

"I don't know what else to do. I don't want to get Fig in trouble," Maggie stresses. "We'll figure it out. Eventually."

I don't tell her about Natalie being with Fig. That would devastate her, and I don't know how to break it to her. What if she doesn't believe me?

I've gone through high school blissfully unaware of all the drama. Ignorant to the problems people are facing daily. Now I'm neck deep, and it's...

A lot to take in.

"Are you upset with Crew?" She makes a sympathetic face and I realize she's referring to the Crew and Natalie situation.

The gossip has settled down from twenty-four hours ago, but there are still whispers in the halls and giggles in the classroom.

Psychology was torture yesterday, with Natalie in there with us. She spent all of her time glaring at the two of us from across the room, completely ignoring poor Sam, who was trying to engage her in conversation. Ezra kept dropping insults here and there, all of them aimed at Crew.

It was a nightmare.

One I'm going to have to face again, but at least I always have Crew by my side, glowering at all of them. He's so intimidating when he's angry.

It's kind of hot.

I shouldn't find something like that attractive, but I do.

"It's not true," I tell Maggie, hating how she frowns. "He wasn't with Natalie that night. They ran into each other."

"Oh, Wren. Is that what he told you?"

She feels sorry for me, I can tell. Which is kind of hilarious, considering she's pregnant with our English teacher's baby.

"I have my reasons for believing him," I say, my tone a little snotty. I feel defensive, and I don't like that. "Just like you have yours for your situation."

That renders her silent for the rest of the time we wait in line. Once I order my coffee and muffin, I go stand beside her as we wait for our names to be called.

"You think I'm dumb, don't you?" Maggie says, looking anywhere but at me.

"What do you mean?"

She turns toward me. "What you said, how I have my reasons for believing him. My situation is different from yours, Wren. I'm in love with him. Things are serious. Our whole lives are changing, while you've got the meanest boy in class chasing after you like he's trying to corrupt you," she explains, her nose wrinkling.

I'm offended. The last thing I want to do is fight with her, but I can't believe she said that.

"I know that you're going through a lot, but that doesn't mean you can belittle my problems," I say.

"Mine feel a little bigger than yours," she retorts.

"And what, is it a competition? There is so much going on that you don't even know," I tell Maggie. "I can't explain it all now, but later I will."

"Whatever." The barista calls her name and she marches over to the counter, grabbing her coffee. Decaf, I might add. She turns to look at me, a pitying expression on her face. "Hope you have fun getting your heart destroyed."

I almost say, *right back at you*.

But I keep my mouth shut.

Crew didn't show up to English, and when I tried texting him, he didn't answer, which hurt.

Made me angry too.

I'm probably being too sensitive, but I'm worried. Scared. Where is he? What's going on? Has anything changed?

I just hope he's all right. It's so foreign to me, caring about Crew. Of course I've worried about friends and family, but never someone I've become romantically involved with. It's a different kind of feeling. All-consuming.

A little heartbreaking.

I go through the motions the rest of the day, hiding away in the library during lunch, finishing up my paper for English. Crew and I worked on our project presentation in psychology yesterday and I feel pretty good about it. We turned in our outline to Skov, and she's returning them today with tips and suggestions. I'm so grouchy though. I can't stop thinking about Crew and where he could be. Why didn't he text me? How busy is he, that he can't even manage to send me a quick response?

This is probably why I should avoid boys. They cause us nothing but trouble.

When I'm walking into my last class, I'm apprehensive, knowing I'll have to deal with Natalie most likely alone, since Crew has been MIA all day.

But to my surprise, Crew is sitting at his desk, laughing with Malcolm and even Ezra, who was furious with him only yesterday.

Natalie isn't there at all.

The moment Crew sees me, his eyes light up. I make my way to the back of the classroom, trying to keep my composure so I don't throw myself at him and hug him tight. I've been worried about him all day, yet here he sits, smiling and joking.

"Birdy," he greets me as I fall into my chair.

I stare at him, but don't say anything in greeting.

Malcolm chortles. Ezra makes a low *ooooooh* sound.

Crew frowns. "You okay?"

"I really don't want to talk about this in front of them." I send a look in Ezra and Malcolm's direction.

"Ah, come on, Wren. We're his best mates. If you can't talk about it in front of us, who can you talk about it with?" Malcolm lifts his brows.

"Shut up," Crew snaps at him. "Leave her alone."

Malcolm holds his hands up in front of him. "Sorry. Just trying to keep the mood light. Didn't know there was already trouble between you two."

"I didn't either." Crew's gaze settles on mine.

I look away, vaguely annoyed with all three of them.

I don't know how to act around him, and I'm uncomfortable talking about any of this in front of his friends. I wish we were alone, so he could hold me and tell me everything was going to be okay.

Skov enters the room seconds later, far ahead of the final bell for once. She appears flustered, settling her stack of binders and books on top of her desk before she comes to stand in front of the class, her hands on her hips as she studies all of us.

"I can't believe I'm saying this," she says, loud enough to get all of our attention. "But I read over all the outlines last night and...you're all on the right track. I don't really have any major suggestions for any of you."

We all start cheering. There's clapping and yelling, and I can't help but smile, relief flooding me.

"Okay, okay. Settle down. I'm going to pass back your outlines now, and there are a few suggestions on them, so please read and take what I said into consideration. My biggest concern is time. You've all seemed to learn so much about each other, I'm worried we won't be able to get to all of the presentations next week during your scheduled exam time," Skov explains.

She goes to her desk and grabs a stack of papers, then starts passing them out. "I was hoping a few of you might feel confident enough to give your presentation today, though I totally understand if you don't feel up to it. I am springing it on you unannounced."

Just thinking about making the presentation right now makes my legs go weak. I need to gear up for something like this, presenting in front of the class, especially since I'm doing it with Crew.

I'm still irritated with him for never texting me.

Skov stops by my desk, dropping the outline on top of it. "Excellent work, you two. I can't wait to see this presentation."

She walks away and I pick the paper up, looking at her suggestions. She really didn't make any. Just lots of glowing comments and a few red exclamation points by specific parts on the paper.

"I think she liked it," Crew murmurs, leaning over to scan the paper.

I turn toward him, not realizing he's so close. "I'm mad at you."

"I know." He drifts his fingers across the top of my hand. I snatch it away from his reach. "I'll explain everything later. I got called in. I was interviewed all morning."

I'm frowning. "Interviewed? By who?"

"I'll tell you later. Hey." I blink at him. "You want to give this presentation now?"

"What? No way." I shake my head.

"Come on, we can get it out of the way. Looking at her lack of constructive comments, I'm thinking we've got this thing on lock. We could give it in a couple of minutes, tops."

"I don't like speaking in public," I admit.

"Are you serious? You're always talking to people."

"Not in front of a full class of students. Talking about myself and comparing and contrasting between the two of us. That's just—intimidating."

"Look, we're going to be fine. Just follow the outline. Follow me. I won't lead you astray." He smiles, and I think with that smile alone Crew could lead me astray forever and ever.

"I don't know..."

"We're doing it." He shoots his hand up despite my cry of protest. The moment Skov spots him, she nods in his direction.

"Please tell me you two are volunteering."

He sets his hand on his desk. "We are."

"All right. I'll give you a few minutes to prepare. Let me know when you're ready." Skov makes her way to her desk, the rest of the classroom talking among themselves.

I glare at Crew, anxiety over this sudden presentation leaving me cold. A little shaky. "I am so not ready for this."

"Wren." He grabs hold of both of my hands and gives them a shake, his gaze boring into mine. "You've got this. It won't be that hard. We'll talk for three minutes tops, and we'll be sharing that time. Ninety seconds. That's it. I know you can do it."

The way he's looking at me, as if I can conquer the world, fills me with the tiniest flicker of courage.

"I don't know..."

He squeezes my hands again. "Let's go over the outline."

So we do, me reading my parts to myself while he gives me pointers. I've seen Crew talk in front of a class before and it never seems to bother him. He has this effortless way about himself, a confidence I only wish I had.

"You've got this. Come on." He rises to his feet and I follow on shaky legs, walking behind him to the front of the classroom. Skov watches us, a faint smile on her face.

"Are you ready?"

Crew nods. "Yep."

Her gaze falls on me. "How about you, Wren?"

I nod. "Yes," I lie.

No matter how much I prepare, I won't be ready. I guess Crew is right.

We should just get this over with.

Crew starts talking and I follow his lead, interjecting with my observations. He explains our differences, while I offer our similarities, and after a while, we've established a rhythm, bouncing back and forth between each other. I'm feeling more confident. Standing taller, speaking louder. There are a few bored faces in the crowd, but for the most part, they seem interested and I have a realization near the end.

At least we're doing this without Natalie here.

We're just about to wrap it up when Crew mentions one last observation.

"I know I've talked mostly about our differences while Wren spoke of our similarities. I do have to mention that before I got to know Wren, I wasn't a big fan of lollipops." His gaze meets mine, a smirk on his face, and I suddenly want to die. "But she's convinced me that they're delicious, especially when she shares them."

He pulls a couple of Blow Pops out of his pocket and starts tossing them, one directly at Ezra, who catches it with one hand.

Okay. He's trying to make me die of embarrassment. Clearly.

"And that's it," I say, my voice weak.

Skov starts clapping and so does the rest of the class. "Interesting last point, Crew. Not sure why you felt the need to make it, but I'm glad you two could find some commonalities after all. I knew you would."

"Thanks, Ms. Skov," he drawls.

"Not the best usage of visuals, but I did spring this on you so I won't mark you down for it," Skov continues.

Smiling briefly over at Skov, I rush back to my seat, Crew following after me. I'm mortified he mentioned the lollipop thing, but no one else knows what it means.

Just us.

And if I'm being honest with myself...

I like that we have a secret, only the two of us can share.

"We still getting together tonight?" he asks once we're both seated and Skov is trying to con more people into giving their presentation early. "We have a lot to catch up on."

"You're right. Like where you were earlier today." I let my emotions shine through, my irritation obvious.

It doesn't even faze him.

"I can't talk about that now. Maybe later? Like tonight?"

This is a moment of truth. Agreeing to see him later means our "relationship" is most likely going to progress.

Sexually.

Am I ready for it? Is this what I really want?

"I've missed you," he adds when I still haven't said anything.

I lean in closer to him, not wanting other people to hear me. "I can't believe you brought up the lollipops."

"Blow Pops are now officially my favorite candy." He's smiling. Actually, it's more like he's—

Grinning.

"It was embarrassing," I whisper.

"No one caught on, Birdy. Don't worry about it." He slouches in his seat, something he does often, and I hate to admit it but, he does it really well. Why do I find his sprawling so attractive? "You're cute when you blush."

"You used to hate me. Is that why you still torture me?"

"I don't hate you anymore," he murmurs, his gaze warm. "I actually kind of like you."

I arch a brow. "Only kind of?"

"Do you still hate me?" he asks, avoiding my question.

"When you do stuff like drag me up in front of the classroom and mention one of my most embarrassing moments, yes." I sniff.

"Most embarrassing? Really? I thought it was hot."

I'm growing hotter just thinking about it.

"Been thinking a lot about a repeat performance," he continues. "Though we don't have to involve candy this time."

I glance down at my desk, letting my hair fall forward. I've been thinking about doing it again too. I've been curious about his body. As in, I want to see it.

All of it.

"Don't get shy on me now," he teases.

Turning toward him, I brush my hair away from my face. "You know I'm shy."

"Shy and sexy. A good girl with a secret bad side. I like that about you, Birdy."

"Really?"

He nods. Changes the subject. "I wish we could get out of here for the weekend."

I frown. "What do you mean?"

"I'm sick of this place." His voice drips with disgust. "It's been a rough week. Today was brutal."

I wish I knew what happened, but I'm sure he'll eventually tell me.

"This week has been…a lot," I agree.

His hot gaze lingers on me. "Would you run away with me for the weekend?"

I laugh at his joke, but he doesn't laugh with me. His expression remains deadly serious.

Wait a minute.

"You actually want to run away?"

"We could leave tonight. Come back Sunday."

"What would I tell my parents?"

"Nothing. You wouldn't tell them at all."

I glance around the room, watching as Skov goes over an outline with someone. She's not paying attention to us. No one is.

"Finals are next week," I remind him. "We can't just leave. We need to study."

"Really, Wren? You're going to turn me down to *study*?" He arches a brow.

"I've never just—ran away before, Crew. My parents know where I am, at all times."

"Tell them you're going out of town with a friend, because that's what we are, right? Friends?" His sly smile reminds me we are anything but friends.

"I'm not an impulsive person," I say primly.

"Sometimes we need to change it up. Come on. I'll make a couple of calls. Find us a hotel somewhere."

"In the mountains?" The words slip from my mouth as if I have no control.

"You want to go to the mountains?"

I nod. "That's what I originally wanted to do for my birthday. Go on a little trip with my friends."

"Let's do it then. We can leave tonight. We can use the plane if we have to. Hopefully it's available."

My family is wealthy. We have money. But we don't have a plane.

The Lancaster wealth is unfathomable.

"I don't know…" My voice drifts and a soft gasp leaves me when Crew settles his hand over mine.

"Come on. Just say yes."

I stare at him, conflicted. If Daddy found out I went away on a weekend trip with a boy, he'd be devastated. Especially if that boy was someone like Crew.

Angry.

Disappointed.

And I never want to disappoint him. Especially after the

promise I've made.

But that promise is starting to feel more unimportant, the longer I spend time with Crew.

He interlocks his fingers with mine, basically holding my hand in front of everyone in class, his middle finger brushing over the diamond ring my father gave me, and I give my answer before I can overthink it.

"Yes."

# CHAPTER THIRTY-THREE

## CREW

Normally, I don't do this sort of thing.

Like plan a weekend getaway with a girl I'm hot for.

When I usually spend time with a girl, it's at a party, or some sort of social gathering. Always in a big group. Never one on one—until I sneak her into an empty bedroom or whatever and we hook up. I've had plenty of moments like that in my life, and they leave me mostly satisfied. I lost my virginity at fifteen, at the end of freshman year, and I've been fucking on the semi-regular ever since.

My brothers taught me that it's easy to get pussy, with our family name alone, and I realized quickly they were right. Once they hear you're a Lancaster, the girls will come flocking without hesitation. With that kind of pull, there was never any reason to get tied down by just one person, not when there were so many options out there.

But then there's Wren.

I hated her—and maybe I felt that way because deep down I knew I was attracted to her and there was nothing I could do about it. I do not fit the mold of a possible boyfriend when it comes to Wren Beaumont. I'm the one her precious daddy warned her about, and with reason. She avoided me as much as possible.

Until she didn't.

And somehow, we're helplessly caught up in each other.

She's in my thoughts. She haunts my dreams. With her sweet smiles and softly spoken words. The way she watches me with those luminous green eyes. That sexy body hidden under the uniform. Her ripe lips wrapped around a Blow Pop, right before I fuck her with it. The way she looks when she comes.

The fact that I'm the only one who's ever made her come fills me with this unfamiliar, downright possessive feeling. She was untouched.

Until me.

I don't want another guy looking at her, let alone talking to her. Even when Malcolm mouthed off to her earlier, I wanted to bash his face in.

And he's one of my best friends. What he said was essentially harmless.

I'm not used to feeling like this. Hung up on one girl. Thinking about her constantly. Wondering what she's doing, where she's at, how she's feeling.

It fucking killed me, having those rumors go around campus that I was hooking up with Natalie. I know they hurt Wren, but I couldn't come out and say I was meeting with her instead. She's a good girl who never gets in trouble.

I refuse to be her downfall.

Thank God all the shit that's happened the last couple of days is about to be put to bed for good. I missed class most of the day, stuck in the admin office, either being interviewed by police detectives or waiting around for them to talk to me. They interviewed Natalie first, and she wouldn't break, no matter how much they badgered her.

How do I know this? Shit, I was sitting right outside the room, and I could hear them coming down on her hard. No matter what they said or what tactics they used, the girl would not give.

They tried to do the same to me, making me out to be the

liar, but I never gave either. Natalie finally confessed all when her mother showed up.

Then they called Maggie in. And that's when the shit really hit the fan.

Pretty sure they're going to arrest Figueroa this weekend. The dude is in huge trouble. I wonder if he even knows what's about to go down.

That's half the reason I want to leave. I'm tired of it. Sick of the drama that I was unwittingly drawn into. If I had my choice, I'd never see Figueroa again. Or Natalie.

Pushing all thoughts of the twisted love triangle out of my mind, I grab my phone and make a call to my oldest brother, Grant.

"What do you want?" is how he greets me.

"Great to hear from you too. So glad you keep in touch." The sarcasm is heavy. This is how my brothers and I operate. We act like we can't stand each other, but I know they'd be there for me no matter what.

"Do you need something, Crew? Or are you calling just to piss me off?"

I get right to the point. "Is the plane available this weekend?"

"You want to use it?"

"Yeah. Just tonight and then we're coming home Sunday afternoon."

"Ask Dad." He sounds amused.

"Hell no." His answer is always no when I ask him for almost anything. "That's why I'm calling you."

"What exactly are you doing this weekend? And where are you going?"

"Just a quick trip with a friend. We're going to Vermont."

I found a town that has snow, an overabundance of Christmas spirit and a luxury hotel with room service. The only rooms they had left all had single king beds. Hopefully Wren doesn't mind.

I know I don't.

"With a woman?"

One thing about Grant is that he treats me like I'm an actual adult, which I like. "Yes."

"I'm warning you. Don't do it, little brother. You'll dazzle her with your wealth and then you'll never be able to shake her. You're too young to tie yourself down."

With Wren, it doesn't feel like I'm tying myself down. I like spending time with her. When I'm not with her, I'm thinking about the next time we're together. Shit happens and I want to tell her about it.

I've never felt this way before. My parents' relationship is more like a business deal. She tolerates him, he barely tolerates her, they don't really talk, they cheat on each other...

I could go on and on.

My father is a controlling fucking monster. He tells people what to do and they do it. Grant got older and basically told our dad to fuck off—which he respected. Finn did much the same. Charlotte was just bartered off to the highest bidder.

And then there's me. The baby of the family. Dear old dad has zero expectations for me. Most of the time, he forgets I exist, which is fine.

I'd rather avoid him every chance I can.

"Her parents are wealthy. She's used to it."

"There is nothing like our family, and you know it."

He's right, but fuck it.

"Is the plane available or not?"

"It's available. I can have it headed your way in thirty minutes. The pilot is on call," Grant says.

"I need it at the airport by around five. I want to leave by five-thirty," I tell him.

"I'll let them know."

I can tell he's about to end the call, but I stop him. "Hey, Grant."

"Yes?"

"Thank you."

"Consider it your Christmas present."

There's a clicking sound and then he's gone.

I call Wren next.

"I have a surprise for you," is what I say when she answers.

"Are you actually planning a trip, Crew?"

"That's what I told you, right?" Does she doubt me? I need to make sure she never does again.

"Yes, but I don't know. This is all so last minute." The worry in her voice is obvious. "And I don't know how to tell my parents."

"Like I mentioned earlier, tell your parents you're going on a trip with a friend. Just for a few days."

"With what friend?"

"I don't know—Maggie?"

A sigh leaves her. "I guess I could. Where are you taking me?"

"I want it to be a surprise."

"That's sweet and all, but when I call Daddy and tell him I'm leaving for the weekend, he's going to ask where I'm going. And I can't say it's a surprise, because that's just weird."

This girl is so damn aggravating sometimes. She worries too much about what other people think of her—especially her precious daddy.

"We're going to Vermont," I tell her.

"Oh really? I've never been! I've heard it's so pretty. The mountains and the snow. Some of the towns really get into Christmas too."

"Does that mean you're definitely coming with me?"

"I want to." She hesitates. "Let me call my father first and tell him. I'll see what he says. He has to sign me out anyway so…"

That's true. I'm eighteen and can sign myself out. Well, that and I'm a Lancaster.

When your name is on the school, they let you get away with a lot of stuff with no arguments.

"Call or text me when you've got an answer, okay? And hurry.

I already ordered the plane," I say.

She's quiet for a moment. "We're actually going to fly there?"

"I didn't want to drive."

"Oh my God, Crew."

"Have you never flown private before?"

"No, never."

"You're in for the ride of your life then."

In more ways than one, if I have anything to say about it.

# CHAPTER THIRTY-FOUR

## WREN

I have never lied to my parents before, until I met Crew. Now I'm sneaking around and hiding what I'm doing from my mom and dad, specifically my father, because I know he would be incredibly disappointed in me.

Worse, he'd flat out tell me no about this trip. Going away for the weekend with a boy, all alone?

Daddy would never let that happen.

Bringing up his contact info, I hit call and wait, holding the phone to my ear as I go to my closet and pull down the bag I use when I travel.

"Pumpkin, how are you?" His voice is warm and edged with faint concern, which makes me feel guilty.

"Hi, Daddy."

"How was your day? How's school going? Glad the semester is almost over?"

"Definitely." I need to get this over with. "Um, I wanted to ask you a question."

"What is it? Is everything okay?"

"Everything is great," I reassure him. He's been worried about me ever since the divorce announcement—and retraction. "A friend of mine invited me to go on a trip this weekend."

"A trip? The weekend before finals? Are you sure that's a smart idea?"

No, it's a terrible idea. And a wonderful one too.

"I'm ready for finals. I already completed one today," I tell him. "I have an A in psychology."

"Of course you do." He says it as if he never had any doubt about my abilities. "Where are you going? Somewhere close?"

"Vermont."

"Are you driving? Another storm is coming in, you know. It'll be dangerous on the roads. And who are you going with?"

"Maggie." I close my eyes, praying he believes me. "And we're flying. Her family—has a plane."

I have no idea if that's actually true. Maggie's family comes from money, but it might not be we-have-a-private-plane-type money.

"Oh. Well that should be safer if you're flying out tonight. The storm is coming in tomorrow."

"We'll be careful, Daddy. We just want to get away for a bit. Relax before our intense finals week."

"Are you ready? Do you need to study?"

"I'll be okay," I reassure him. "Really. Can I go?"

He's quiet for a moment, which makes me nervous. I start pacing around my room, afraid of his answer.

"I normally would never allow something like this," he starts, getting my hopes up. "But you're almost eighteen. Almost done with high school. You deserve to have a little break. Especially since Veronica wasn't able to find proper accommodations for your birthday trip."

Oh. Veronica. His assistant. The trip she was supposed to be planning for me, even though I wanted to do it. "What do you mean, she wasn't able to find proper accommodations?"

"Everything I wanted for you was sold out or too expensive."

Since when does expense matter to my father? I know I sound like a spoiled brat, but he's usually able to get me whatever I want, no matter the cost—save for that art piece I wanted so badly last year.

"It's okay. This trip will be for my birthday," I tell him.

"Then enjoy it, Pumpkin. We can't wait to see you next weekend. Your mother has held off decorating the house. She wants to wait until you're home."

I frown. That doesn't sound normal either. Mother usually starts decorating right after Thanksgiving. She'll hire out a professional to come into the house and decorate with a theme in mind. It looks like something straight out of a magazine layout. Almost too beautiful to touch.

I've always sort of hated it.

"I'd love to help her," I say, meaning every word. I can't remember the last time we decorated for Christmas on our own. Do we actually even own any Christmas decorations anymore? Normally Mother pays for the decorating service, has the house featured in some sort of online publication for publicity, and then gives the decorations back when the holidays are over.

"Good. I'll let her know. I'll tell her about your trip too," he says. "Have fun, Pumpkin. Be safe."

The guilt is real. "I will. Thank you."

"Love you."

"Love you too."

He ends the call, and I immediately text Crew.

**Me:** *I can go.*

My phone starts ringing and I answer quickly.

"Pack your bags fast, Birdy. We need to be at the airport by five-fifteen," Crew explains.

Panic floods my veins. That means I don't have a lot of time. "I can be ready by then, but I need to go so I can pack."

"I'll pick you up at your building in a half hour, okay?"

"Okay. Sounds good."

• • •

We arrive at the airport, with the plane scheduled to take off by five-forty-five. The flight to Vermont is only about thirty minutes. From there, we have a twenty-five-minute drive to our hotel, which fills me with both excitement and dread.

Will we have separate beds? Knowing Crew, I think that's doubtful.

Pretty sure I'm in over my head.

I enter the Gulfstream jet first, Crew right behind me, and we're greeted by a male flight attendant who's dressed in a black suit.

"Mr. Lancaster, good evening. Welcome. My name is Thomas and I'll be serving you and your guest during your flight." Thomas glances over at me, his gaze friendly. "Would you care for anything to drink?"

"I'd like a glass of champagne," Crew answers Thomas.

"And you, Miss?" Thomas's gaze meets mine.

"She'll have the same," Crew answers for me.

"Will do." Thomas offers a little bow and leaves to go fix our drinks.

I turn to Crew. "Champagne?"

"Let's celebrate."

"We're underage."

"They're not going to check our IDs. My family owns the plane. We can do whatever we want," Crew says before he starts checking out the plane. "This is nice. I haven't been on this one."

"Do you fly private often?" He's right. This plane is very nice. The leather seats are a rich cream, clustered in pairs facing each other with a small table in between them. The windows are oval shaped and large, and there's a cabinet with a TV.

"Most of the time," Crew answers, and I marvel at the casualness of his answer. What it must be like, to come from such wealth. My family has plenty of money, but nothing like this.

I think of what my father said on the phone earlier and I'm

starting to think we don't have as much money as I originally thought.

Thomas brings us our drinks and I take mine with a murmured thank you, settling into the seat closest to the window.

"We'll be taking off shortly," Thomas announces.

"Thank you, Thomas," Crew tells him, settling into the seat beside me and taking a sip from his glass.

I follow his lead, taking a tinier sip, the bubbles tickling my throat. My nose. It tastes almost bitter, but at least it goes down relatively smooth.

"Ever drank champagne before?" Crew asks me.

I slowly shake my head. "I don't drink alcohol."

"I am thoroughly corrupting you." He clinks his glass to mine. "What do you think?"

"It's okay." I take another sip because he's watching me, and I make a face. "It tickles."

"It's the bubbles."

I study the glass, the tiny bubbles in the golden liquid. "I don't know if I like it."

"I bet you'd prefer something sweet. A tropical drink."

"I drank lots of virgin pina coladas when we went on a Caribbean cruise a couple of years ago," I tell him, immediately feeling dumb for admitting that.

He sets his glass on the table in front of us and then takes mine from my hand, setting it on the table next to his. "You're nervous."

This isn't asked as a question. He can sense it. I don't bother denying it either.

"I am," I admit. "I feel bad, lying to my father. Going away with you for the weekend. This is a huge step for me, Crew. I don't do things like this."

"I won't push you for anything you don't want to do," he says, and I know he means it, but he also knows how easy it is for me to get carried away when I'm with him.

I know it too. Maybe I feel guilty because I want to do this. I want to run away with him for a couple of days and forget the rest of the world. Spend my time with Crew and no one else. I think of the day he showed up at the art gallery, and how much fun we had. Just the two of us.

I also think of the night in his room, when we kissed in his bed and he went down on me. That was fun too. A different kind of fun, something I want to explore more, if I'm being honest with myself.

I didn't know it could be like this. That he could feel like a friend and a—lover, both at once. How much I'd want to spend time with him. How lonely I feel when he's not around. How happy I am when I first spot him, when he shines that smile on me, looks at me with those all-knowing blue eyes. Filled with a combination of affection and lust. Sometimes amusement. Sometimes irritation.

All I ever wanted was for someone to see me for who I really am. Everyone has their own expectations and eventually I fell into those roles, giving them what they needed from me. No one makes me feel like I'm just being myself when I'm with them.

Except for Crew.

"Wren." His deep voice pulls me from my thoughts and I glance up to find Crew watching me, his gaze steady, his expression serious. He touches my hair. Tucks a strand behind my ear, his fingers lingering. "I'm glad you're coming with me. You need to get away from reality for a little while."

"So do you," I say, then I frown. "Wait. I'm still supposed to be mad at you."

A sigh leaves him. "What did I do now?"

"You never responded to my text this morning. I was worried about you. I didn't know where you were." That's another thing I'm not used to.

Caring about someone—a boy—and wondering where he is when he doesn't reach out. I was truly worried. Even a little panicked. What if something happened to him? Something awful? The relief I felt upon first seeing him blotted out all of my anger and frustration.

But that's all coming back to me now.

"I was in the admin office all morning. I didn't get out of there until after lunch," he admits, reaching for his champagne glass and draining it, as if he needs the liquor coursing through him to even talk about it.

"Why were you in the office?" I almost don't want to know.

"I was being questioned by police detectives. About Figueroa."

"Oh." That sounds ominous. "Are they going to arrest him?"

"Probably. That's half the reason I wanted to get away from here. I'm sick of dealing with that shit. Natalie and her lies. Figueroa and his sleazy ways." His upper lip curls with disgust. "I can't stand him."

"Forget about him." I pluck the empty glass from his fingers and return it to the table before I turn my full attention on him. "Let's focus on the weekend. I don't even know where you're taking me exactly."

"Manchester, Vermont. I hear they go all out for the holidays."

"Really?" Excitement bubbles up inside me, much like the bubbles in my champagne glass. "And there's snow? Mountains? Pine trees?"

He nods. "I've never seen someone so enthusiastic for the mountains."

"I'm a city girl. My family never goes to the mountains."

"Not even to Vail?"

"You sound like such a snob right now," I say with a soft laugh. "And no, we don't go to Vail."

"You're missing out then." He doesn't even seem offended by me calling him a snob. Not like I really meant it.

"Can I ask you a question?"

Crew nods, turning in his seat so he's facing me more fully.

"Did you do this for me? This trip to Vermont? Or for yourself?"

He reaches for me, his hand landing on my cheek, his fingers stroking my skin, leaving me breathless. "I did it for you."

I blink at him, my eyes wanting to fill with tears, though I don't know why.

"I did it for us," he admits.

Just before he kisses me.

# CHAPTER THIRTY-FIVE

## WREN

The hotel is more like a resort, and when we enter the lobby, I glance up at the giant wrought-iron chandelier hanging overhead, the heat from the nearby massive stone fireplace immediately warming me up. Outside the snow has already started, the flakes small but abundant, and I wonder what we'll wake up to tomorrow.

I still can't believe we're here. Together.

Alone.

Crew arranged for an SUV to be waiting for us when we arrived at the small airport and I couldn't stop staring at him as he drove the snowy roads with calm expertise.

Who knew I would find a man driving so sexy? The word sexy wasn't even part of my vocabulary until a few weeks ago.

But everything he does is undeniably sexy. From the way he takes command of every situation to the smooth sound of his voice as he talks to the hotel employee, who is currently helping him. She's an older woman with a sharp Vermont accent who seems quite taken with him.

I can't blame her.

I go and wait by the fireplace while Crew finishes up with the front desk clerk, our bags near my feet. He makes his way toward me, two key cards clutched in his fingers, a faint smile on his face. When he gets closer, he hands one of the keys over to me.

"I upgraded us to the cabin suite," he says.

"A cabin?" If it's a log cabin, I will absolutely die of bliss.

"Yeah, it has a living room. A fireplace. Only one bed, though it's a king."

Nerves make my stomach flip but I push past the feeling. "That sounds nice."

"I hope so. Ready to go?"

When I nod, he takes our bags and we go back to the SUV, hopping inside. He drives around the resort, and we end up near the back, close to what I assume is a lake, considering the snow-covered dock I see in the near distance. Once we're parked and he's shut off the engine, Crew turns to me.

"Let me go open the door, turn on all the lights, and bring in our bags. Then I'll come out and get you," he says.

"Okay." I watch him climb out of the car, and open the back door. I can hear the sound of the snow pelting his jacket as he pulls our bags out and then he slams the door. He jogs toward the building directly in front of us and unlocks the door, slipping inside.

Lights come on from within, and in minutes, he's back outside, heading toward the car, opening the passenger side door for me. "Ready?" he asks.

I nod and he takes my hand, shutting the door for me and leading me inside our cabin for the weekend. I like how attentive he is. It's actually very...

Sweet.

The moment I'm inside, I spin in a slow circle, taking it all in. There's a gas fireplace that Crew must've turned on when he first came in here, giving the space a warm, cozy glow. A stairway leads to what looks like a loft and I glance over at Crew to see him unzipping his duffel and pulling out a couple of liquor bottles he must've taken from the plane. "Where's the bedroom?" I ask him.

"Up there." He clutches what looks like a bottle of vodka and a bottle of tequila in each hand, nodding toward the stairs. "And there's a bathroom up there too. Plus, there's a small bathroom down here. And a kitchenette, though I doubt we'll be doing much cooking."

"I don't even know how," I admit.

"Me either. We could use some glasses though." He lifts the bottles in his hands and heads for what I assume is the kitchenette.

"Looking to party?" I call after him.

"Whatever you're up for, Birdy. I'm game," he yells back.

I head up the stairs, a little squeak of happiness leaving me when I see the massive bed that takes up most of the space. There's a giant faux fur blanket draped across the bed and I run my hand over it, marveling at the softness. "It's so cute up here," I tell him.

"You want that bed?"

I go to the railing, so I can frown down at Crew. "What are you talking about?"

"The couch folds out into a bed, if you'd rather I take that so you can sleep alone," he suggests.

"Oh." Our gazes collide and we stare at each other in silence until I say, "The bed up here is really big."

"Yeah?" He shoves his hands into his jeans pockets. He already got rid of his jacket and beanie, while I'm still in my coat, and he looks so handsome in the black and gray flannel shirt. I'm so used to him always being in his uniform, it's still a bit of a shock seeing him in regular clothes.

I nod. "Come up here and check it out."

He does as I ask, his heavy-booted footsteps loud on the stairs as he heads up here. He comes to stand next to me, and I suddenly feel awkward. A little uncomfortable. Not because of him.

Because of my own insecurities and nerves over the sleeping situation.

"You're right. It's nice up here." Crew goes to check out the bathroom. "I think this place was recently remodeled. Everything looks new."

I follow him to the bathroom, silently agreeing with him. The marble countertops, the massive glass-encased shower and giant white tub, all of it looks modern and sparkly brand-new.

My imagination kicks into gear and I immediately envision the two of us sitting in the tub, Crew behind me, his arms wrapped around my middle, our naked, wet bodies covered in soapy bubbles.

I feel very grown up right now.

"I don't want you sleeping on the pull-out sofa," I announce.

His smile is slow. "Oh yeah?"

I slowly shake my head. "We can share the bed." I exit the bathroom, and he follows after me. "Look how big it is. We have plenty of room."

"Yeah, we do." His tone is suggestive and my entire body flushes hot. I can't even look at him right now.

I'm afraid if I do, he might tackle me onto the bed and show me everything he wants to do to me.

And I won't protest. Not one bit.

He settles on the end of the bed, his legs spreading wide. "Come here."

I let him snag my hand and pull me in close, letting go of his hand, so I can settle mine on his shoulders.

"You look nervous," he says.

My smile is tremulous. "Are you surprised?"

Crew slowly shakes his head, his hands settling on my hips. "You need to relax. Want to order room service?"

I nod. "I'm hungry."

"Me too." He grabs hold of me, making me squeal as he basically tosses me on the bed. I land with my back on the mattress, breathless when he hovers above me, his face in mine, his gaze locking on my lips.

"Is this your idea of room service?"

He laughs. "Did you just make a dirty joke?"

That wasn't my intention but...

"I guess so."

Dipping his head, he delivers a drugging kiss upon my lips. One full of plenty of heat and tongue, accompanied by those low murmuring sounds he makes, as if he can't get enough.

Can't get enough of me.

His hand slips beneath my sweater and I don't push him away. I lean into his touch, wishing he'd take it further.

I want to feel his hands all over me.

We kiss for I don't know how long, until my mouth starts to ache and my chest feels tight. I can feel him as he slowly grinds his hips against mine and my body responds, that slow, throbbing ache between my legs making me restless.

He grabs hold of my hands, interlocking our fingers before he holds them above my head. When he breaks away from my still seeking lips, I lie there trying to catch my breath as he studies my face, his eyes dark.

"If I had my way, we'd never leave this cabin for the entire weekend," he murmurs.

"We'd eventually have to eat," I remind him.

"There's room service."

"I thought I was your room service." I smile.

So does he.

"I want to see the Christmas stuff," I admit. "You said the town was cute."

"From what I could tell, it's straight out of a Hallmark movie," he says.

I frown. "What do you know about Hallmark movies?"

"I have a mother. And a sister. I've seen a few in my lifetime," Crew admits, somewhat grudgingly.

I suddenly have a great idea. "We should watch some this weekend," I suggest.

"The only thing I want to watch is you." He nuzzles my neck, his breath hot on my skin. "We should take a bath. That tub will fit the both of us."

My earlier fantasy flares to life, but is quickly doused by a serious case of nerves. "I don't know about that."

He lifts away from my neck, so he can look at me. "What if I feed you first."

I'm tempted.

"Then give you an orgasm or two." He grins.

I blush. "Crew…"

"I should've brought Blow Pops." He thrusts against me again, nice and slow, and I close my eyes, breathing deep when I feel his fingers tighten around my wrists. As if he wants to keep me captive.

"Surely you're more creative than that," I tease.

He pauses for so long that I open my eyes, worried I said the wrong thing.

"You want me to be more creative?" His brows shoot up. The devilish expression on his face is almost scary.

Almost.

But not quite.

"I don't want to scare you, Birdy," he continues. "But if I had my way, I'd strip you naked. Then I'd take one of those ribbons you're always wearing in your hair and tie your wrists together."

He squeezes them for emphasis.

My entire body flushes at the image he's putting in my head. I love it when he tells me what he wants to do to me. "Then what?"

And I think he knows it too.

"I'd kiss you everywhere. Make you come with my fingers. Then my mouth." He kisses me, his tongue searching. "What do you want to do to me?"

I don't know if I can say the words out loud.

"I can tell you what I want."

"Tell me," I murmur.

"I want you to make me come with your fingers. Then your mouth." He basically repeats what he just told me, and my panties flood with moisture at the thought. But...

"I don't know what to do. I've never done anything before," I admit, hating how closely he's watching me. If I had my choice, I'd run and hide after such a confession.

"I can show you."

"You want to show me?" My voice comes out squeaky, and I close my eyes.

The humiliation is almost too much to bear.

"I will show you whatever you want," he says, his voice rich with promise.

"Will you get undressed for me?" The words are out before I can stop them.

His smile is faint. "Is that what you want?"

I nod. I'm in this far, and once I see him naked...

There is no going back.

# CHAPTER THIRTY-SIX

## CREW

My sweet little innocent Birdy is adorable.

Adorably sexy.

Completely teachable.

Utterly fuckable.

I can mold her into everything I could ever want, and it's tempting, so fucking tempting, to completely corrupt her and take her virginity tonight. It wouldn't take much. She's so damn responsive, I know I could do it.

But I want to take this slow. I want to make it good for her. And while I've done nothing but that the last couple of moments we've shared, my sexual frustration is through the roof. I've never had such a raging case of blue balls in my life.

I need relief.

I can't be too demanding though. She'll cut and run, and I can't have that. I need her to want me, to want to do this with me. Despite my stance on relationships and never committing myself to just one girl, I'm starting to care about her.

And I want Wren to care about me too.

From the glow I see currently in her gaze, she's hot and bothered. Needy. She likes how I'm holding her captive, my fingers circling her wrists. Her arms above her head make her thrust her chest out and I'm dying to see those tits again. They're perfect.

Everything about her is perfect.

I remember what my brother said. How I shouldn't let myself get tied down by a girl. It's not the first time he's said something like that, and most likely won't be the last either. I know he's right. I'm only eighteen.

But this girl...

I'm addicted.

I can't get enough.

I release my hold on her and roll off the bed, standing next to it. She scrambles into position, sitting up and leaning against the headboard, her gaze never leaving mine.

"You want me to strip?" I sound amused because hell, I am amused. Everything Wren does tends to surprise me.

And I like it.

She nods. "Yeah. I do."

I reach for the front of my shirt and start unbuttoning it, undoing each one slowly, revealing the white T-shirt I've got on underneath. She watches me with her hungry gaze, focused on my chest, and when I shrug out of the shirt, letting it fall to the floor, she releases a soft sigh.

A chuckle leaves me. "I haven't even shown any skin yet."

"Your arms." She waves a hand at me. "I really like them."

"You just say whatever's on your mind, don't you?"

"Only with you," she admits, her cheeks turning pink.

"I like it, Birdy." I grab the neck of my T-shirt from behind and yank it off in one smooth move. "You should join me."

"Join you how?"

"You strip too."

"Oh." She glances down at herself. "I don't know. I'm self-conscious."

"And you don't think I am?" Well, I'm really not. The appreciation I see in Wren's eyes is a total ego boost for one.

Everyone needs a girl like Wren staring at you as if she thinks you're a god.

"No, I don't. Look at you." Her gaze slides over my pecs, down to my stomach.

My cock twitches almost painfully against the front of my jeans.

"Look at you," I return, my voice low. "You're sexy as fuck with your innocent words and fuck-me eyes."

She blinks. "What do you mean?"

"You stare at me like you want to fuck me." I reach for the front of my jeans, undoing one button. Then the next. And the next one after that, relieving the pressure off my dick.

Her gaze tracks my every movement. "I don't mean to look like that."

"It's okay to admit you want to fuck me, Wren." I undo the last button, letting my fly hang open, revealing the top of my black boxer briefs. "I want to fuck you."

"You do?" She sounds surprised.

Laughter bursts out of me. "Of course, I do."

Her smile is small. "You want me to strip with you?"

"If you want." I keep my tone casual, so I don't seem too anxious.

She sits up straighter, shedding her sweater and letting it fall to the floor. She's wearing the bra she had on a couple of nights ago. The one that barely restrains her perfect tits that I can't help but stare at.

"This isn't so bad," she admits, sinking her teeth in her lower lip. "I like the way you're looking at me."

"And I like the way you're looking at me." I keep my distance, trying to pace this right, when all I really want to do is jump her.

Nervous laughter leaves her. "We're being a little ridiculous."

"Just having fun." I shrug.

"Is that what sex is to you? Fun?"

I can't describe any of my previous sexual experiences as fun.

I was always just looking to get off, and to make sure she got off too. No savoring or lingering necessary.

"Not really."

"Oh." She rubs her fingers in between the valley of her breasts, seemingly lost in thought. "I've always taken it so seriously. Sex."

"I know. You've got a ring on your finger to prove that." I nod toward her left hand.

Wren glances down at the diamond ring her father gave her, twisting it around and around her finger before she slowly starts to pull it off. "This has felt like a burden lately. A reminder of what I shouldn't do."

"If you don't want to—" I start, but she shakes her head, cutting me off.

"No. I want to. I do." She climbs off the bed, dropping the ring onto the nightstand before she slowly approaches me.

Toeing off my boots, I wait for her, my breath stuck in my throat, my gaze pinging everywhere, too many pretty places to look at once. Her smooth, creamy skin. Her tits straining against the lace. The dip of her waist, the flare of her hips in those jeans. She kicked off her boots when we first entered the cabin and she seems shorter than usual. Smaller.

The need to protect her is fierce. Piercing my steely heart and filling me with all sorts of unfamiliar urges. I want to haul her into my arms and never let her go. Protect her from every other asshole out there who wants to steal her from me. Because if they knew, if they knew just how sweet she is, how sexy, they'd all want her.

She reaches out, settling her hands on my rib cage, her fingers spanning wide, as if she wants to touch as much of my skin at once as possible. It's like she's counting my ribs, memorizing the pattern of my skin, her touch featherlight. Goosebumps rise, a shiver stealing over me, and my heart thuds harder. Faster.

Her hands slide down, fingers curling around the waistband of my jeans, her knuckles brushing my skin. I swallow the groan in my throat, holding my breath as she spreads the front of my jeans open wider. As wide as the denim will go.

Wren lifts her gaze to mine, holding steady as she slides her hand inside the front of my jeans, her fingers curling around my cock, lightly holding me. Her breaths are coming rapidly, I can tell by the quickening rise and fall of her chest, and this time around, I let the groan escape when she gives me a squeeze.

"You're big."

What every guy wants to hear.

Her brows lower in concern. "Will it fit?"

"It'll fit," I rasp. "As long as you're wet and relaxed."

Her tongue sneaks out, licking the corner of her lips. "I'm wet right now."

Jesus Christ, this girl. She is unbelievable.

"So are you," she continues. "The front of your boxers is damp."

I close my eyes. She keeps talking like this and I'll come where I stand.

"You touch me like that and that's what happens," I tell her through gritted teeth.

"Hmmm." She continues her exploration, her other hand tugging down my jeans. I help her out, pushing them down past my hips, until they're crumpled around my ankles and I'm kicking them off. "Oh wow."

Her gaze is glued to the front of my boxer briefs, my cock straining, dying to be freed.

"You can touch it," I encourage her.

"This is...you're impressive." She lifts her gaze to mine. "I didn't expect you to be so big. I think you're bigger than that guy I watched in the porn."

I want to laugh. I want to groan in absolute agony. The innocent things she says. The simple yet highly effective way she touches me. The lust in her gaze.

She's driving me out of my mind.

Giving in, I cup the side of her face, tilting her head back so I can kiss her hungrily. She responds immediately, her lips parting, her tongue swirling around mine. I groan, taking a step closer, my hand falling to her chest, fingers curving around one luscious tit, brushing my thumb across her nipple. It's already hard, and I circle it again and again, making her whimper. Her fingers tighten around my dick, and she gives it a tentative stroke.

My balls clench tighter, as if I could blow at any second.

With my other hand, I reach for the front of her jeans, undoing the snap with fumbling fingers, lowering the zipper. I dive my hand into her open jeans, my fingers encountering silky material, and I press my fingers against her pussy, the material already wet.

Just as she said it would be.

"Oh my God," she whispers when I cup her fully, my fingers pressing hard. "That shouldn't feel so good."

"You like that, Birdy?" I stroke her up and down, using the friction of her panties to help get her off.

She nods, a helpless whimper leaving her, and I can't stand it any longer.

Removing my hand from her panties, I crowd her, pushing her with my body to the bed, so her ass falls heavily onto the edge. She glances up at me, her eyes wide and unblinking as she reaches for me, sliding her hand up and down the front of my boxer briefs. I thrust my hips, pressing my cock into her palm, so she knows I like that.

"Tell me what to do next," she whispers.

"Pull me out," I demand and her eyes flare with heat.

Wren removes her hand from the front of my boxers, so she can pull them down, slowly but surely. Until my cock springs free, bobbing directly in front of her face.

Her mouth.

She lifts her gaze to mine, once again, before she returns her attention to my eager dick. She wraps her fingers around the base, her touch gentle, her gaze curious as she studies me. Her brows lower in concentration when she squeezes me tight, and I hiss in a breath, my stomach muscles contracting.

"You like that?"

"Tighter," I grit out, and she holds me tighter, her thumb running along the distended vein, exploring. Like my cock is a fucking science experiment.

"Doesn't that hurt?"

I shake my head. "Feels good."

She squeezes me from root to tip, a clear drop of pre-cum forming, and she stares at it in fascination. Then she does the craziest fucking thing.

Brushing her hair back, she leans in and drops a kiss on the very tip of my dick.

"Fuck," I groan, wishing I could grab hold of her hair with both of my hands and force her to suck my cock. But that would most likely scare the crap out of her and I can't do that.

"Tell me what to do next," she encourages, her fingers slowly sliding up and down my cock. "I could give you a—hand job."

I could tell it took a lot for her to say that, my sweet, innocent Wren. She's not used to asking for what she wants, and my goal is to make sure she feels comfortable with me. That I won't judge her.

I'll give her whatever she wants.

Taking a deep breath, I tell her, "I'd rather have a blow job."

That mouth of hers would look so damn good wrapped around my dick.

"I'll mess it up."

"You could never." I close my eyes and tilt my head back, wanting to laugh at myself for standing in the middle of the room without a stitch of clothing on, save my socks. My girl sitting on the bed, arguing about giving me a blow job while she jacks my cock as if she owns it.

What the hell is happening to me right now, thinking of her as my girl. And why am I enjoying it so much?

"Oh, I could," she says, sounding amused. "I didn't expect it to be so veiny."

"Wren." Her name comes out of me as a groan, and when I glance down, I see she's watching me, her fingers still around the base of my cock. "Whatever you want to do, just do it."

"You want me to stroke you faster?" She does exactly that, her fingers sliding up and down, keeping a steady pace. Like I have no control of my body, my hips start to move with her and I'm basically fucking her hand.

I can't speak. It's been weeks of buildup. Years, really. Of wanting Wren like this. Dying for her to touch me. And now that she is, I can barely stand it. This girl is about to make me lose all control, something a Lancaster never does.

My father beat that into my head from a young age. So did my brothers. We have the upper hand. Always. Never let anyone get by you.

This girl? The sweet, beautiful girl with the mouth made for sin has totally slipped by my defenses, and I let her. Hell, I practically begged her to do it.

And I don't care.

I'd do it all over again—for her.

She leans forward, her mouth on the tip of my cock again, and slowly, she envelops it with her lips, pulling it just inside her mouth.

Holy fuck.

She trains those big eyes on me and I grab hold of my cock, her fingers falling away, her mouth staying on me. I stroke myself into a frenzy, my body coated in sweat, my chest aching from how hard I'm breathing. I can't look away from her, and when she pulls slightly away, her tongue coming out for an exaggerated lick, I feel the need to warn her.

"I'm going to come."

The warning goes right over her head as she continues to lick the flared head of my cock, her tongue tracing every curve.

That familiar feeling starts at the base of my spine, spreading everywhere, my skin electrified, and I know without a doubt I'm going to come.

All over her pretty face if she doesn't watch it.

"Wren," I bite out.

She doesn't move.

I warned her twice.

"Fuck," I groan as my orgasm barrels down. All the air leaves my lungs and I choke out a strangled sound, that first spurt of cum hitting her on the cheek.

She jerks away from my cock, her eyes full of surprise as I keep coming, my body shuddering, completely overcome. I squeeze my shaft, just beneath the head, and one last drop falls before I'm spent.

The room is silent, only the sound of our heavy breaths in the air. I lost complete control, something I never do with a girl. I made a fucking mess. Of myself and Wren and the bed.

She touches her cheek, her fingers coming away cum-covered, and I nearly lose it when she brings them to her mouth and gives them a lick.

I don't know if I'll survive the weekend, let alone the night if she keeps this up.

# CHAPTER THIRTY-SEVEN

## WREN

We clean ourselves up and put our clothes back on before we order room service. The moment we shared still hangs heavily in my mind, though we haven't really talked about it. And I have no idea how to approach the conversation so...

I don't bring it up.

Can't stop thinking about it, though. He seemed to lose all control earlier. He actually came on my face, which I think is an actual thing, from what I remember seeing on that one porn site the night I explored its category menu.

I didn't mind, though it was shocking when it happened. I'm so curious about everything. All of it. It's interesting, how internalized a woman's orgasm is for the most part, while a man's is incredibly obvious. To the point of exploding everywhere.

Literally.

Crew is so incredibly patient with me, and while my body is still aching for something only he can fulfill, I'm okay with waiting. I know more will happen between us. Tonight. Tomorrow.

Besides, I'm hungry.

Our food arrives relatively fast and we eat it in the living room, both of us sitting on the floor in front of the coffee table, our backs leaning against the couch as we stuff our faces. We both got cheeseburgers, fries and Cokes, and I could tell Crew was pleased I didn't order a salad.

Probably only because he wouldn't have to share his meal with me again, like last time.

The fries are delicious and I keep dragging them in the puddle of ketchup on my plate, a little moan leaving me with every bite. Eventually I realize Crew has stopped eating and is watching me, his eyes slightly glazed over, his lips parted.

"What's wrong?" I ask, my mouth kind of full, which is totally rude. I swallow it down, then wipe my mouth with a napkin.

"You're so fucking sexy when you eat, Birdy. I can't take it." He leans in and grips the back of my head, pulling me in for a quick kiss. "I feel like everything you do is sexy as fuck."

"I am not a sexy person," I say primly, thinking of what we did not even forty-five minutes ago. Which was absolutely, one hundred percent sexy.

I still can't believe I did it, but I couldn't resist. Seeing him like that…he was just so *big*. I wanted to know what he tasted like. And while I didn't give him a full-blown blow job, he seemed rather pleased with what I did do.

And I like that, pleasing him. Making him feel good, even though it's scary and I worry I'll make a mistake, I'm realizing that he seems to enjoy everything I do. I liked seeing the blissed-out expression on his face, and how he lost control. The sounds he made and the commanding way he took over. It was hot.

Sexy, like he says.

"Wren." His voice is flat, and I glance over at him once again, frowning. "Please. You're the sexiest woman I know."

I sit up straighter, thrilled by his praise. At the way he called me a woman. I'm close enough to eighteen that I guess I should get used to that, though in some ways I still feel like a kid.

Not tonight though. Not even close.

"Thank you," I murmur.

He pulls me in for another soft kiss, our meals soon forgotten as we lose ourselves in each other. Is this what the entire weekend is going to be like? We can't do this so freely at school and maybe he feels all pent-up. As if his want for me is now spilling all over. On campus, I don't want people to see us and I'm sure he doesn't either.

Or maybe he doesn't care who sees us. Maybe I shouldn't care either.

It's wild, to think how much we've changed. With each other, and how we feel.

When he ends the kiss, I blurt out the first thing that comes to mind.

"A few weeks ago, you hated me."

He frowns. "I told you before I never hated you. Not really. You just—frustrated me. All the time."

It still bothers me that I would affect him so terribly while I was completely oblivious—only at first. After a few short weeks, I knew Crew Lancaster didn't like me. I just never understood it.

"Why? I never even talked to you. And once I realized you had it out for me, I avoided you as much as possible."

"Because I wanted you, though I was in complete denial." His smile is slow. A little arrogant. "And look. Now I've got you."

Is that the only reason though? He supposedly hated me? It's odd. Was he so disgusted with his supposed attraction for me that he masked it by acting like a complete jerk and treating me terribly? Glaring at me if I even dared to look at him? If that's the case...

That's kind of messed up.

"You think you've got me?" I raise my brows.

"I convinced the last virgin in our senior class to come away with me for the weekend." The heat in his gaze tells me he's thinking of all the things we've done together so far that takes me closer to losing my virginity, once and for all. "Pretty sure

I've got you."

"You're very cocky, Crew Lancaster." I kiss his cheek, darting away from him when he tries to recapture my lips with his own.

"Did you just say the word cock, Birdy?"

I'm immediately horrified he would even suggest such a thing. "Absolutely not. I said cocky."

"Nope. I heard it. I heard cock." He's grinning. "Go on. Say it. You know you want to."

I'm shaking my head. "No way. I don't say words like that."

"That's too bad," he murmurs, his gaze focused solely on my mouth. "I would love to hear you say a string of dirty words in that sweet voice of yours."

"You think my voice is sweet?"

He nods. "Maybe you could whisper them in my ear."

I slowly shake my head. "I couldn't."

Crew ignores my protests. "You know what I'm really looking forward to?"

"What?"

"Watching those lips wrap around my cock again." His gaze lifts to mine. "Hopefully you'll suck me deep next time."

My cheeks feel like they're on fire, thanks to what he said. "You're embarrassing me."

"Don't ever be embarrassed." He pulls me in close, until I'm practically in his lap. "Get used to it, Birdy. This is all we're going to do for the entire weekend."

I form my lips into an exaggerated pout. "You promised to show me the Christmas lights."

"And I will." He kisses the tip of my nose. "For like an hour. Tops."

"Crew." I shove at his chest, but he doesn't budge.

"Wren." His tone is teasing, his eyes sparkling as he studies me.

I've never seen him look so handsome.

Handsome enough to make my heart hurt.

God, what are we doing? He said it so himself, that Saturday afternoon in the back of the car before he kissed me for the very first time.

*This probably isn't going to end well.*

I'm scared he's right.

# CHAPTER THIRTY-EIGHT

## WREN

It's late afternoon and we're checking out the shops downtown, strolling by the gorgeously decorated window displays hand in hand. Crew humors me every time I stop to marvel at the pretty Christmas decorations, or when I have to look inside the store, though I never buy anything.

There's really no one I want to buy Christmas gifts for. My grandparents on both sides are gone. I don't have siblings. I'm not that close to any of my aunts and uncles. There are only my parents, and what do you buy the people who own everything they could ever want?

It was so much easier when I was younger and I could make them gifts in class. The pressure was off. Now I'm on the hunt for something special and unique, and I'm coming up empty.

The air is crisp and bitingly cold, the sky heavy with clouds. Snow lines the sidewalks, and the spindly trees are strung with twinkling white lights. Christmas decorations are everywhere. Large pine wreaths trimmed with simple red ribbons. Beautifully decorated Christmas trees stand tall in store windows. When the door opens of almost any shop, the sound of Christmas music wafts in the air, filling me with excitement.

I've never had a boyfriend during the holiday season—and my

birthday—before. Well, I've never had a boyfriend, period. And while I'm not sure if I can consider Crew Lancaster my actual boyfriend, it feels like he could be.

And that feels more magical than the holiday season.

I think of last night and what we shared. How we ate dinner and kissed for a little while. Tried to watch a movie but we both could barely keep our eyes open. We ended up going to bed and never really did anything. Woke up and got ready for the day like it was perfectly normal for us to have slept together.

It was kind of nice, sleeping with Crew. Studying his face before he woke up. How sweet he looked, like the little boy he used to be. I woke him up by touching his cheek, and when he first cracked his eyes open, he looked at me as if I were the most wondrous thing he's ever seen. It made my heart expand, filling me with far too much hope, which I needed after the doubt I struggled with last night.

He's been patient with me all day, indulging my every whim. We ate breakfast at the hotel restaurant. Went driving around looking at all the stately houses in the area, all of them decorated for the holidays. We finally ended up here in the downtown area, which is bustling with people out shopping for gifts. It all feels so natural, spending time with Crew like this. Having him smile at me, wanting to touch me. I could get used to this.

And that's terrifying.

I'm wandering around a shop full of useless but beautiful knickknacks, Crew patient by my side, when I come to a stop, exhaling loudly. "I don't know what to get my mother for Christmas."

"Is that what you've been looking for? Gifts for your mom?"

"And my dad." I pick up a rustic bird carved out of wood, turning it this way and that, appreciating the technique. "They're impossible to buy for."

"So are mine."

"What are you getting them?" I glance over at him expectantly.

"Nothing." He shrugs.

I frown. "You aren't buying them anything?"

"There's no point. They don't expect any of us to. Especially me."

"Why especially you?" I set the bird down on the shelf, only for Crew to immediately pick it up.

"I'm the baby of the family. They don't expect me to do much of anything," he admits, weighing the carved bird in his hand. "I think I want this."

"It is beautiful," I agree. "And I'm pretty sure everything in this store is handmade by local artists."

"It reminds me of you." He holds his hand out, the bird sitting on his wide palm. "My little birdy."

My heart swells and I do my best to mentally tell it to calm down. "That's so sweet," I murmur.

"I'm getting it. You should get one too. Give it to your parents. Tell them it represents you." He nods toward the other birds sitting on the shelf.

"That's a good idea." I look over the remaining birds, choosing my favorite one before I follow after Crew. A question suddenly pops into my mind and I hesitate before blurting, "Do you want anything for Christmas?"

He turns to face me. "From you?"

"Well, yeah." I roll my eyes. Like this is no big thing.

But it feels like a very big thing. A scary thing.

"If you want." He starts heading for the short line to get rung up and I fall into step behind him.

"Are you getting me something for Christmas?" Oh, I sound pathetic. Silly. Maybe even a little desperate.

The smile he sends in my direction makes me catch my breath. "I've considered it. Even came up with a few options."

My curiosity is piqued now. "Like what?"

"I can't tell you. It should be a surprise."

I'm scowling. I can feel it. "I hate surprises."

He just laughs, stopping at the back of the line to purchase the bird. I'm standing next to him, thinking of all the things he could possibly get me for Christmas/my birthday. I wish I could spend it with him. I'll be expected to spend the day with my parents and any other year, I would have no problem with that. I didn't need guests on my special day. We always planned a small party afterward with my friends, and this year, for my eighteenth, I planned on having a big bash.

All of those plans went away. Evaporated, just like most of my friendships did. Now the only person I want to spend my birthday with is Crew.

Would he want to join us? Would my father even allow it? Even if Daddy approved, it would be a big deal, having Crew come meet my parents. I don't know if he would even want to. That makes our relationship seem so serious.

I don't think we're to that point yet.

"What are you doing for the holidays?" I ask, my tone casual. As if I'm just making light conversation.

Really, I'm digging.

"I'll be at my parents' house, like I told you. I think we're all getting together on Christmas Eve this year, since Charlotte has plans on Christmas Day," Crew says. "She'll be with her new in-laws."

I remember seeing the photos from her wedding a few months ago. It was beautiful. Her dress, stunning.

"When I was younger, we'd all get together at my uncle's house in Long Island. We'd stay there for days and it was fun. But as we got older, we didn't do it as much. Especially after my aunt and uncle divorced. Then things really fell apart," he explains.

I think of my parents and their divorce announcement—and Daddy telling me they're going to try and repair their marriage. I don't even know what to believe anymore. Will this make the holidays weird and uncomfortable? I hope not.

Once we leave the store, we find a bakery that also serves

coffee, so we get in line, ordering frosted sugar cookies and lattes before we're back outside, leaning against the brick building and enjoying our treats.

"It's so cold out here." I set the bag holding our cookies on the window ledge and wrap my hands around my to-go coffee cup. "Too bad there were no tables available inside."

Crew pulls his cookie out of the bag. It's a giant pale blue star. He holds it out to me and I bite off one of the points, chewing. It's an explosion of sweet sugar and crisp cookie, and I can't help the moan that escapes me.

"This is so good," I murmur after I swallow.

He's watching me with hooded eyes as he bites off another star point, and I realize this was his plan all along. He likes to watch me eat.

"It is good," he agrees, dropping his cookie back into the bag before he grabs his coffee and takes a swig. "You want to go to dinner tonight?"

"Maybe." I prefer to stay in, like he suggested. This is our last night. And we haven't done anything since last night before dinner.

I sort of want to do more. Take it further. I feel so comfortable with him, and everything between us feels so right. He seems to care about me, and I definitely don't think he's using me.

I think of my father and his reaction. If he knew we were together this weekend, just the two of us, he would be furious. I'd probably be banned from ever seeing Crew again. And the thought of that, of never seeing him...

Fills me with panic.

"Maybe? Are you turning down a chance to go out for a meal?" I think he knows how much I like going out to eat.

"I think I'd rather stay in for the night."

He raises a brow while I take a sip of coffee. "You don't want to look at Christmas lights?"

I shake my head. "Not really."

"I thought that was on your agenda."

"Agendas can change."

His smile is slow. Almost wolfish. I can imagine him taking a bite out of me, and enjoying every minute of it. "I don't mind staying in with you."

"Maybe we could pick up a pizza," I suggest, peeking inside the white bag and contemplating if I want to eat my ornament-shaped cookie or not. I think I'll save it for later.

"Or we could order room service," he says.

"Whatever works." I glance across the street, noticing the lingerie shop. The beautiful displays in the windows of scantily clad mannequins. Inspiration strikes and I send him a look. "There's a store I want to check out real fast. Mind if I go?"

"Sure." He glances in the direction I was just studying, a gleam forming in his eyes.

Leaving my coffee behind, I'm about to cross the street when he calls out to me.

"Find something sexy, okay?"

Oh my God.

He's got me all figured out. Though I was also terribly obvious about it.

The moment I enter the store, I'm overwhelmed with all the many color options. Red and black lace. White and pink. Lots of green too, for the holidays, even a few plaid options. I don't know where to look first and I wander around aimlessly, picking up a hanger here and there, shocked to find a pair of panties split right down the crotch.

Guess those offer easy access.

"Can I help you find anything?"

Startled, I immediately put the hanger back on the rack and turn to find a seemingly elegant woman dressed all in black smiling at me politely. "Oh I was just—looking."

"Have something in particular in mind?" The woman's brows rise.

Old Wren would've told her no and run out of the store. But I really want to find something to wear for Crew. Tonight.

"I'm looking for something…sweet," I say. "And sexy."

Her smile is faint. "What color?"

"Red. Or pink." My favorites.

She shows me a few options, never passing judgment that I'm an almost eighteen-year- old girl shopping for something to wear for her first time having sex, which is a little…

Awkward.

"We have lots of pretty panty sets right now in the colors you like," she says as she shows the rack to me.

I thumb through them, pausing on one set in particular. It's constructed of sheer pink fabric trimmed with red lace, and it hides nothing. Which is sort of my intent.

I don't want to hide with Crew. Not anymore.

Setting the hanger back, I continue browsing, but nothing else appeals. I grab the pink and red set, pleased to see my size is available and I pluck the hanger from the rack, showing the saleswoman.

"I think I'll take this."

She looks pleased. "A perfect choice."

I follow her to pay for my items, glancing out the window to see Crew waiting for me where I left him across the street, scrolling on his phone. The wind ruffles his hair and he brushes it out of his eyes and I can't help it.

My heart swells with emotion.

I like this boy.

So much. And maybe we're moving too fast, but I don't care.

When something feels right, you shouldn't deny yourself. And I refuse to deny myself of spending time with Crew.

• • •

By the time we're back at the resort, it's dark outside, and I'm carrying in the bags filled with my purchases while Crew brings in a pizza we picked up on the way. The smell of it has me ravenous and I drop my bags by the door, reaching for the box before Crew can set it down.

"I'm starving," I tell him as I lift the lid, grabbing a piece and taking a bite of it.

Oh man, it's delicious.

Crew watches me with an amused expression on his face. "You're always hungry."

"I know." I set the half-eaten piece back in the box, disappointment filling me. "My mother says I eat too much."

"Don't listen to her," he says, his voice ferocious. "Swear to fucking God, our parents are always trying to fuck us up."

I frown, reaching for my pizza slice once again. "You think they do it on purpose?"

"Sometimes it feels like it, especially with my parents. My dad." He shakes his head, and I mentally will him to keep talking. To reveal more. "Like I mentioned, they have zero expectations when it comes to me, but I can't fuck up. Ever."

"I think my parents want to marry me off to a rich man so they won't have to worry about me anymore," I admit.

Maybe I shouldn't have said that, considering how rich his family is, but I want to be honest with him.

"Don't they have a lot of money already?"

"The whole divorce thing." My appetite leaves me just thinking about it. "Daddy claims they're trying to work on their marriage, but I don't really believe them. I think…"

I clamp my lips shut, not wanting to say the words out loud. It's okay to think them, but putting them out there, letting them hang in the air and enter the universe, makes it feel like it could actually happen.

"You think what?" Crew asks when I still haven't spoken.

"That it's actually going to happen. They're just trying to

protect my feelings or whatever. Get through Christmas, through my birthday and then at the beginning of the new year, they'll spring it on me," I explain. "They're definitely getting a divorce. I can just feel it."

"Sounds like a shitty way to spend the holidays, pretending everything's okay when it's not," Crew says.

I like how he always keeps it real with me. Not trying to protect my feelings all the time, which is how my father always treats me. Like I'm a delicate little flower who can't handle bad things.

Maybe I was that sort of person not so long ago, but I feel like I've changed. Since school started, and especially lately. Spending time with Crew, learning what's really going on around me, has opened my eyes.

To some things I don't want to see.

And others that I'm so glad I know now.

Like the taste of his lips. The way his hands feel when they're on my body. Inside me.

I want to know all of that again. And more.

"It does sound pretty shitty, huh?" I say in agreement.

Crew's eyes are so wide they nearly bug out of his head. "You just said shitty."

I shrug. Grab my pizza slice and shove it into my mouth, chewing and then swallowing it down. "I can't lie. It's going to be an awful Christmas. And birthday. Not what I expected at all."

"What did you expect?"

"I wanted everything to be perfect," I say with a sigh, envisioning it. "I even made a Pinterest board for my eighteenth birthday celebration. Pink and gold and white. Everything sparkly and beautiful. A gorgeous cake covered in flowers made of frosting. Glitter everywhere. A dazzling dress and matching shoes that would make me feel so grown up. Like I'm an actual adult. My hair would be perfect and we'd drink champagne to celebrate. It would be cold and snowing outside but inside, it would be warm and inviting, and I would be surrounded by my favorite people."

"Sounds nice," he says.

"Sounds like a fantasy. Like a birthday and New Year's celebration combined, which is what I've always dreamed of doing, but it's silly, right? I don't even like New Year's Eve, but if I had a birthday party on the same night, maybe it would make me like it more. I don't know. I never approached my parents with the idea because I knew they'd turn me down."

"Why would they turn you down?" Crew asks, finally reaching for a slice of pizza. At least I'm not the only one eating.

"Because they always have plans, and they never include me. I used to think a New Year's Eve party was so glamorous, especially the parties my parents would attend. But now I realize there is something rather ominous about New Year's Eve. Don't you think?"

He doesn't say anything. Just watches me with that cool, steady gaze of his as he keeps eating.

"It's almost the end of a year. Sometimes even an era. My birthday has come and gone, not that anyone cares about it. All of us are too busy making plans for the future. Bogus promises to ourselves we'll never fulfill. Then there's the countdown at the end of the night, and the frantic search to find someone to kiss at midnight. How we promise to be good and stick to our resolutions, even though we know deep down we won't keep them." I stop talking, realizing I sound pessimistic, which isn't my normal style.

"You've thought about this a lot," he murmurs.

I shrug one shoulder, suddenly uncomfortable. "I sound like a selfish brat."

"You sound like someone who really doesn't like this time of year," he corrects.

God, he's so right. I actually hate this time of year.

"I make all of these promises to myself, and now I'm

breaking them," I admit. "Maybe I'll become nothing but a disappointment."

"You're not a disappointment."

"To you." I don't bother mentioning my parents.

 Specifically, my father.

"Come here." Crew holds his hand out and I take it, letting him pull me to him, a gasp leaving me when I'm fully pressed against him. He sneaks his arm around my waist, his hand resting on my backside and I stare up at him, at a complete loss of words from the intensity in his gaze. "I don't like seeing you look so sad."

"I'm not sad," I admit, and I mean it. "I just—"

"Want to forget everything else? Everybody else?"

I nod, resting a hand against his chest, my palm directly over his thundering heart. "Maybe I am a little sad."

He dips down, his mouth at my ear. "What would make you feel better?"

I turn toward his mouth, my lips brushing his when I whisper, "You."

# CHAPTER THIRTY-NINE

## CREW

I hold her close and let Wren control the kiss at first, sensing that she needs it. That semblance of control, of being in charge of her life, which I don't think she experiences much. Her sadness is obvious, palpable. About to steal all of the oxygen out of the damn room until I distracted her.

She needed that. Needs this. Me. My hand slides up and down the perfect curve that is her ass, her tongue darting out to lick at mine. I hum my approval when she sucks on my tongue, and then I can't hold back any longer.

I take over, my hand going to the side of her face, angling it for a deeper kiss. Our tongues dance, our breathing quickens, and she slides her hands up my chest, curving them around my shoulders, so she can cling to me.

This entire day has been foreplay, Wren-style. Shopping, eating. Lots of eating, which drives me out of my damn mind. Watching her face light up when she *oohed* and *aahed* over the Christmas decorations everywhere. The determined look that took over her face when she spotted that small lingerie store and came out of it not even fifteen minutes later, clutching a tiny red bag in her hand.

I can't wait to see what she got there.

There is so much more to this girl than meets the eye, and I like that she's comfortable enough to reveal those things to me. I'm trying to be more open with her too, and I wonder if she realizes that.

If she knows how much she affects me.

Wren is unlike any girl I've ever known, and I want to know more. I feel as if I've barely scratched the surface, and tonight's mini-rant was telling.

Though I shouldn't call it a rant. She was being real and raw and vulnerable. Something she's done with me often, which I like.

Damn it, I like everything about this girl, and that's scary as fuck.

I don't let people into my life, especially a girl. I have friends, but I keep most of them at surface level, worried to let them get close. I don't trust people, even guys who are almost as rich as I am.

But no one I know is as wealthy as my family, and it's hard to let them into my inner circle. Every girl who's ever shown interest in me I always figured was after my money.

Shitty but true.

Not Wren though. She wanted nothing to do with me at first, but I guess I wore her down. It's as if we can't help ourselves when we're around each other.

And now that we've gone this far, I'm not about to let her go without a fight.

She breaks the kiss first, her chest brushing against mine with her every breath. "I have a surprise for you."

I raise my brows. "Does it have anything to do with that bag over there?" I incline my head toward the cluster of bags she left on the coffee table.

She nods, biting her lower lip. "I hope you don't think it's stupid."

"Anything involving you and whatever you found at that store, I know it won't be stupid."

Her smile is small, her gaze locking on mine. "I've had so much fun with you today."

I don't think anyone's ever called spending time with me fun before.

"And I'm so glad you convinced me to come with you, even though I was scared." Her hands tighten on my shoulders. "I like how you push me."

I run a hand through her hair, cupping the side of her head. "I don't think you know what you're capable of."

"I'm starting to realize, thanks to you." Her smile grows and then she's ducking out of my hold and practically running over to the bags, plucking up the one from the lingerie store before she heads for the stairs. "I'm going to take a quick shower. Meet me up there in thirty?"

"Sure," I tell her, smiling at her before she zooms up the stairs.

I settle onto the couch with another slice of pizza, checking my phone while I wait. I have text messages I've been avoiding. Ones from Malcolm and Ezra, both of them asking where I'm at. One from my sister, asking if I'll be at the house for Christmas Eve.

I shoot her a quick text, because I never ignore Charlotte. She's my closest sibling and I've been worried about her ever since she married that Perry dude.

There's an ominous message from my father, one that fills me with dread.

*We need to talk. Call me when you get a chance.*

I consider ignoring it, but realize quickly that avoiding my problems is not the answer.

I bring up his number and call him, hoping he won't answer.

Just my luck, he picks up on the second ring.

"Why didn't you tell me detectives interviewed you yesterday?" he barks at me.

Damn it, I'm probably going to need alcohol after this conversation.

"You already knew about the situation, so I didn't think I needed to call you. Plus, I'm eighteen. An adult," I remind him.

"I deserved a call. That way I'm not caught unaware when some asshole reporter reaches out, looking for a reaction from me."

Shit. I didn't expect that.

"Why would anyone care? This doesn't really involve us."

"Because we're Lancasters, son. And what we do, people pay attention to, even when we're only involved on the sidelines," Dad explains, his tone rough. I can tell he's losing patience with me.

"Well, it was nothing. I was interviewed, I told my side of the story and what I saw, and that's the end of it." I glance upwards at the loft, hearing the telltale sign of the shower running, and I imagine Wren standing under the hot spray of water, her slick, naked body shrouded by steam.

Reaching between my legs, I readjust myself.

"The reporter was kind enough to tell me the story is hitting the papers Monday morning. You will be named as a witness. You will most likely have to testify in court when it goes to trial. I hope you're prepared to make an appearance," Dad says.

"I look forward to it. Anything to put that slimeball away for good." I relish the thought of Figueroa behind bars. It's what the asshole deserves.

"Where are you anyway? I saw that you used the jet."

Damn. Busted.

"Vermont."

"With who?"

"A friend."

"Don't you have finals next week?"

"Yeah, so?" I sound like a fucking little kid, but this is what happens when my dad does this sort of shit to me.

I revert.

"So I don't think it's wise that you're out partying the weekend before finals," he says, anger lacing his tone. "You can't be a fuck-up during the important moments in your life, Crew. You have to straighten out sometime."

I press my lips together to keep from saying something I'll regret.

"You should go back to campus," he continues. "Study for your finals and make sure your grades are in good shape. You've applied to colleges and I'm sure they're watching you."

I doubt that. Every single one of them will let me in if my family donates a building in our name or whatever the fuck.

"Right," I tell him, just to get him off my back. "Okay."

"Go home," he asserts. "Tomorrow."

"Will do." That was always the plan.

"And keep out of trouble."

"Always."

He goes silent for a moment. I'm sure I've made him angry. "Are you being flippant with me? You should know better, son. I don't like it when you give me attitude."

"I'm agreeing with you. That's all," I say, my voice hollow.

Kind of like my heart.

"As long as you understand then. Good night."

"Night," I say to nothing.

He already ended the call.

Pocketing my phone, I go to the kitchenette and pull out the bottle of vodka from the fridge, then grab a glass from the cabinet. I pour a healthy amount into it and take a deep swig, swallowing hard before I wipe the back of my hand across my mouth.

Fuck, I need another.

Talking to my father always leaves me full of doubt, and I hate it. He goes from completely ignoring me to questioning every move I make, and I end up feeling like a complete fuck up.

I'm not. I've got my head on straight, and for the first time in my life, I know what I want.

Wren.

I'm falling for her. I'd do anything for her. Does she know

that? Does she realize how important she is to me? I should tell her.

I should. Tonight.

I've had a couple of glasses by the time I hear Wren's sweet voice calling from the loft.

"Crew? Where are you?"

Taking one last swallow directly from the bottle, I leave it on the counter and head up the stairs, pushing my father from my mind. My family. All of it.

I want to concentrate on Wren. No one else but her matters.

When I get to the top of the stairs, I come to a stop, watching Wren as she stands by the foot of the bed, wrapped in one of the hotel robes. Her hair is down, falling far past her shoulders, and her face is scrubbed clean save for a shiny red lip-gloss that's been applied to her lips.

My dick stands at attention.

"Is that what you got at the store?" I tease her.

She glances down at herself, her mouth curved in a smile. "Not quite."

"Show me what you got then."

Wren returns her gaze to mine. "You really want to see?"

I nod.

She reaches for the front of her robe, toying with the cloth belt. "It might surprise you."

"I love a good surprise."

Her laughter is soft. Sexy as fuck. "I hope you like it."

"Drop the robe and let me see, Birdy."

With shaky fingers, she undoes the belt, the white terrycloth parting slightly, giving me a view of sexy legs, a flat stomach and plumped-up tits. She shrugs out of the robe completely, so it falls in a puddle around her feet, and I stare at her, all the air from my lungs sticking in my throat.

The bra she's wearing is made of the palest, sheerest pink trimmed with red lace. I can see her nipples. The panties match, and I can see her pubic hair too. She may as well be naked, but fuck, she's not.

She's the hottest thing I've ever seen.

"You like it?" Wren asks shyly.

Nodding, I start to approach, pausing when there's still a few feet between us. It's now or never. I want to pounce, and I assume she wants me to, considering what she's wearing, but fuck.

I need to make sure.

"I love it." The gentle curve of her stomach, that small indentation of her belly button...I want to stroke her there. With my tongue. "I'm afraid once I get my hands on you, I won't be able to control myself."

Something unfamiliar shimmers in her gaze, and she licks her lips. "That was the reaction I was hoping for."

Her permission given, I go to her, settling my hands on her hips, toying with the thin lacy waistband of her panties. "You make me feel out of my fucking mind, Birdy."

She tilts her head back, smiling up at me, though her eyes are wide. I see fear in them, and I want to banish that. Banish everything that scares her so she feels safe with me. "I like that you make me feel confident."

I pull her into me, her body colliding with mine. "You are the sexiest woman I've ever seen."

Her eyes flare with heat.

"I can see you." I cup her left tit, gently squeezing, making her eyelids waver. "Your nipples." I place my hand over her pussy, the heat from her body radiating, coating my palm. "Your pussy. You wanted me to see you."

She nods, her lips parted.

"And your mouth." I touch the corner of her lips, pulling away to find faint red gloss coating my fingertips. "You remembered what I said."

"I want to do something," she whispers. "Will you let me?"

"Yes." I don't even hesitate.

Whatever she wants, I'll give her.

Wren shifts away from me to go grab her phone off the nightstand, her ass cheeks jiggling as she walks. My dick surges against my jeans, and I reach between my legs, cupping myself. Trying to get comfortable.

"I want to take a photo," she starts, and I lift my brows.

"You fucking serious?"

She seems mildly aggravated. "Let me finish. I want to take a photo of you. And then me. Us. Together."

"That's called photographic evidence, baby."

Her smile is sassy as she approaches me. "I'm not scared. Okay, take off your sweater."

I do as she says, whipping it off over my head and letting it drop. Her appreciative gaze skims over my shoulders. My pecs. Dips down to my stomach. All that wide-eyed wonder as she takes me in makes me want to rip off my jeans and show her what she really wants to see.

"Okay, hold still." She takes a few steps toward me, her mouth close to my left pec. Pursing her lips, she leans in and presses a long, sticky kiss to my skin before pulling away.

Then she snaps a photo of the mark she left.

"Trying to brand me?"

"Making a memory with you." She kisses me again, in a different spot, yet close enough to the first one. She takes a photo of that as well, then checks it out, her brows furrowed in concentration as she studies the image.

"How did it turn out?"

"I need darker lipstick, I think." She holds the phone out to me.

I check out the photo. "You do. I can see it, but not very well."

"I'll wear a darker one next time," she murmurs, her voice loaded with promise.

"You want to do this again?"

"There are lots of things I want to do with you." I see the

emotion shining in her eyes, and I realize this is my moment. I need to be open with this girl, and tell her how I feel.

"I want to do a lot of things with you too." I pull her into my arms, just holding her. "You know I care about you, right?"

She blinks up at me. "You do?"

"Well, yeah. I—don't do relationships. Not normally. My parents..." My voice drifts and she waits patiently for me to continue. "They aren't the best example. There wasn't a lot of love in my house growing up. Just money."

Always money.

"We're not our parents," she murmurs, and I wonder if she's thinking of her own.

"Yeah, but they influence us, and how we act. My dad was—is—such a controlling prick. He's not a nice person." That's putting it mildly.

"You are though." When I start to argue she shakes her head, and I go quiet. "You are. You're sweet and kind. With me."

"That's because I like you." Those words don't seem big enough for how I really feel about Wren. It's more than like. Or care. It's...

I don't want to put a label on it. Not yet.

"Then I guess I should feel honored." She laughs, the sound soft.

Sexy.

I don't answer her. Instead, I kiss her until she's out of breath, my tongue doing a thorough search of her delectable mouth. Fuck, I can't get enough of her. This feeling is so overwhelming, it almost fucking hurts.

Even worse? The thought of losing her. That's downright unbearable to even imagine.

When she pulls away, she smiles, thrusting her phone in between us and taking a photo of me.

"What the fuck, Birdy?"

She's already opening up the photo, smiling. "Your lips are

covered in gloss."

When she shows me the photo on her phone, all I see is a lust-filled idiot who's left in a daze by the girl who just kissed him. "I look stupid."

"More like stupid hot." She tosses the phone on the bed, smiling up at me. "Thank you for indulging me and my little project."

"Are you done?"

"I think so," she says shyly.

"Good." I lean in closer, stealing a kiss. Then another. "Because now it's my turn."

# CHAPTER FORTY

## WREN

shiver when he grabs hold of my butt and hauls me up, then tosses me onto the bed as if I weigh nothing. I land with a bounce on the mattress, bracing my hands on it, so I won't tip over, my knees bent. He stands at the foot of the bed, his gaze only for me, and I position myself in a more provocative pose, clamping my knees together before I slowly part them.

His gaze grows hot as he stares at the spot between my legs, and I can feel my panties grow damper and damper the longer he looks.

"You are a bad girl," he murmurs. "I knew I could bring it out in you."

I spread my legs as far as they can go, my feet planted firmly on the bed. "You like it?"

"I fucking love it." His gaze turns molten. "Slip your hand in your panties."

Shock courses through me. "Really?" I squeak.

He nods. "Show me what you like."

"But...you won't be able to see where I'm touching myself." I can't even believe I said that. Or that I'm contemplating actually doing it.

"I like the idea of watching you touch yourself, your hand

busy beneath the panties. And I can see. The fabric is sheer."

Oh. That's right.

Taking a deep breath, I rest my hand against my stomach, right above the top of my panties. I trace the thin band with my index finger, sliding it back and forth. The way he watches me, the way I'm teasing myself, already has my breathing coming faster. My heart pumping harder.

"Do it, Wren," he demands, and my fingers slip beneath the thin fabric, sliding through my pubic hair. Going deeper, until I brush my clit.

I hiss in a breath, closing my eyes.

"Look at me," he says, and I flash my eyes open once more, held captive by him. "Start stroking."

I do as he says, sliding my fingers up and down, nice and slow, gathering up all the wetness. A whimper leaves me when I flick my clit, and then I'm sliding back down, teasing my entrance, my middle finger pushing inside, just barely.

"Are you fucking yourself with your fingers?" he asks, his voice rough.

"Not really."

"Do you want to?"

"I'd rather it was your fingers," I admit, the need to be truthful overwhelming any bit of embarrassment I might feel at making the confession.

My touch feels good, especially with the way he's watching me.

But it would feel even better if it was his hand between my legs. His fingers stroking me.

"Fuck, you're hot." He shakes his head, like he can't believe it. "I need you to beg."

I frown. "Beg?"

He nods. "Beg for my fingers, Birdy. Tell me how much you want me."

"I want you so bad," I whimper, all the shame I've ever

experienced when it comes to this boy leaving me so rapidly, I feel weak. "Please, Crew. Touch me."

He's on the bed in an instant, his jeans half undone, revealing his navel and that intriguing dark path of hair that disappears into his blue boxer briefs. His erection strains against the cotton as if it's trying to break free, and unable to help myself, I lean forward and reach out, trailing my fingers down the front of him.

Crew bites back a groan, thrusting his face in mine before he kisses me as if he's a starving man, and I'm the only one who can ever satisfy him. His tongue thrusts rhythmically against mine, his fingers circling around my wrist and yanking my hand out from under my panties, replacing it with his own.

His touch is rough, making me cry out, but I don't mind. He searches and thrusts, his thumb pressing against my clit at the same time he slips a finger inside my body. His finger matches the rhythm of his tongue, in and out at a rapid pace, and I cry out against his lips, the orgasm already drawing closer.

"You like that?" he whispers against my lips, and I nod, frantic. "Fuck my hand, Wren. Do it."

I move my hips, awkward with my movements but eventually getting it. I push forward at the same time he does, wincing at first, until it starts to feel better.

So much better.

"Oh God," I murmur, my eyes tightly closed as I do exactly as he says. Moving with his hand helplessly. Desperate to get off.

He increases his speed, shoving two fingers inside me, stretching me wider. It hurts, only because it's so tight, and I pause in my movements, trying to calm my breathing. My racing heart.

"Birdy." He kisses me, softer this time, his touch turning softer too. He rubs gently against my clit, sliding his fingers back and forth, coating them with my wetness before he pulls his hand out, his fingers suddenly at my mouth. "Taste."

I part my lips and his fingers are inside my mouth. I lick them, tasting myself, a moan leaving me. I'm throbbing between my legs, so hard it hurts, and he knows it.

I'm sure he does.

"You'd do anything for me, wouldn't you?"

I nod, not even caring anymore. I just want him. "Yes."

"I'd do anything for you too," he continues, his fingers drifting across my belly, making goosebumps rise. "Will you give me this?"

He cups me between my thighs, holding me tight, and I open my eyes, staring up at him, breathless at the darkness I see in his gaze. "Yes."

"I want to fuck you."

I nod. "I know."

"Do you want me to fuck you?"

Another nod. "Yes." I close my eyes, faintly embarrassed. Even after everything we've shared.

"Open your eyes." I do so, and he continues, "Tell me, Wren. Say you want me to fuck you."

Pressing my lips together, I swallow hard before I whisper shakily, "I want you to fuck me, Crew."

He's pleased by me saying such a thing. It's written all over his face. In his smile. "I don't want to hurt you."

I know he won't.

"I'm going to make you come." He kisses me. "Once. Twice. You need to relax."

His mouth wandering all over my body does wonders for my nerves. The tension racing through me. He kisses me everywhere, removing my bra. Sliding my panties off, careful not to rip them. I melt into the mattress, at the touch of his mouth on my inner thigh. My hip. My belly button.

"You smell so fucking good," he murmurs against my skin, just before he slides in between my legs and opens his mouth, his breath tickling my most sensitive spot when he asks, "Do you want to come?"

"Y-yes." I slip my hands into his hair, holding him to me. Like I never want him to leave.

He laps at my clit. Gentle, soft strokes that have me moaning. He pauses, and I want to die. I never want him to stop. "Like this?"

"Harder," I encourage, and he presses his tongue flat against me, licking and then sucking. "Oh yes. Like that."

I'm shameless, rubbing myself against his face, his low groans only encouraging me. It feels so good, what he's doing. *He* feels so good. It doesn't take much until I'm coming, my body wracked with shivers, his name falling from my lips as I thrust my hips up, trying to get closer to his magical mouth.

He holds me to him, his mouth never wavering, his tongue lashing at my clit as I ride out my orgasm against his face. He slips a finger inside me and I arch up, closing my eyes.

"I don't think I can take it," I protest.

But he doesn't let me go. A second finger joins the first and he pushes them deep inside me, pulling out before sliding back in. His tongue is everywhere, licking my still throbbing clit. Searching every part of me slowly.

Another orgasm builds, this one slower. More gradual. I keep my fingers in his hair, twisting the strands tightly, moving with him as he drives me out of my mind with his tongue and fingers. Until I'm a gasping, crying mess, coming again, so quickly after the first one.

He kisses the inside of my thigh, wiping his face against my skin before he rises up and kisses my mouth. My response is enthusiastic. I can't get enough of him, and the heavy weight of his erection against my stomach tells me he's ready.

He's probably been ready since this all started.

"You taste good," he murmurs against my mouth, making me smile. "I can't get enough of you."

"I want you," I whisper, not holding back.

"I'll be right back." He drops a kiss on my forehead before

he climbs off the bed.

I rise up on my elbows, watching as he strips off his jeans and socks before going to his bag and pulling out a box of condoms. Shock courses through me and he must see it on my face as he tears the box open.

"I was hopeful."

The smile that curls my lips is one of pure satisfaction. I love that he was hopeful.

He plucks a condom out of the box and tosses it on the bed before he drops the box back into his duffel. He makes quick work of his boxer briefs and I watch, gnawing on my lower lip as he tears into the condom wrapper and slips the ring of rubber over his thick length.

I swallow hard, fighting the fresh nerves fluttering low in my belly. This has been fun and all, but knowing he's about to enter me for the first time is making me apprehensive. I think of all those promises I made long ago. How I swore this would never happen.

But I'm almost eighteen, and I know what I want. And what I want is...

Crew.

He glances up, catching my gaze, and he must see the fear written all over my face. Without hesitation, he comes to me, wrapping me up in his arms, our damp with sweat skin sticking to each other as he cradles me close. His hand is on my stomach, and his mouth is at my forehead. I close my eyes, savoring the closeness, not able to ignore his erection nudging against my thigh.

"Don't worry." He kisses my temple. "I'll be careful."

"Crew..." My voice fades, and I squeeze my eyes shut tightly, trying to tamp down the panic that threatens. "This is a big deal to me."

He says nothing. Just squeezes me closer.

"I've never done this before, and while I definitely want to, I can't help but feel...scared."

Crew strokes my hair, his fingers tangling in the wild strands. "I know."

"Please don't ignore me when we get back to school." I blurt out my biggest fear, and it hurts, how scary that was. My chest is so tight, it feels like it could burst. "I think I might die if you pretend I didn't exist."

His body stills, and he reaches beneath my chin, tilting my face up so I have no choice but to meet his gaze. "I won't. I promise."

There are no more words after that. Nothing decipherable, that is. Plenty of murmured sounds and soft moans as he kisses me until I can't think. He runs his mouth all over me. Down my neck. Across my collarbone and chest. He licks and sucks my nipples, giving them so much attention, I start to become restless. My legs tangle with his, the throbbing between mine unbearable.

I want him. I want to feel connected to him.

He rises up, his fingers curled around his shaft as he drags his erection through my folds. I moan, my hips lifting, seeking more while he teases me. His brows are lowered in concentration, and when the head is nudging at my entrance, I automatically tense up.

His mouth is on mine once more, his tongue thrusting before he pulls away. "Relax," he murmurs.

I do my best, relaxing my shoulders, imagining the rest of my muscles slowly easing. I spread my thighs wider as he fits himself more firmly between my legs, and then he's nudging again, the head just inside, filling me. Stretching me wide. I close my eyes, wondering if this is what it feels like to be split in two.

Wrong mental path to take, I know.

He works his way in, one excruciating inch at a time, and I'm breathing deep, long exhales leaving me until he's fully inside me.

I crack my eyes open to find Crew watching me carefully, his entire body shaking, his cock throbbing. Hot and thick and unmoving. The undeniable reminder that he's completely claimed me.

I feel incredibly full. Like I can't even move—and neither can he. I'm scared it'll hurt, and maybe he won't care. Maybe he'll become too wrapped up in his own pleasure that he won't pay attention to me.

"You're so tight." He curls his arm around the top of my head, his fingers playing softly with my hair. His gaze is tender as he studies me, but I see the strain bracketing his mouth. He's holding himself back. For me. "I'm afraid if I move too fast, I'll come."

"Be careful with me," I whisper, because that's what I need. If he was to ram himself deep, I might cry.

He does as I ask, pulling out before he pushes back inside. I try to move with him, awkward as can be, becoming frustrated though I know it all takes time to learn. He's patient with me, his hand falling to my hip, guiding me, and after a few minutes of false starts and stuttering stops, we're moving together.

Slowly.

Smoothly.

I'm still not fully comfortable. He still feels thick inside me, but the more he moves, the easier it gets. The looser I become. The bed springs creak rhythmically with our movement, the squeaky sound filling the room and making me smile.

"Why are you smiling?" He pauses, dipping his head to kiss me.

"I don't know." I loop my arms around his neck. "I'm happy."

I am. I'm so happy with Crew. Knowing he's my first. I never thought this would happen. Not this fast. Not like this. Certainly not with him.

His smile is sweet, unlike any smile he's ever given me before. And then he buries his face in my neck, his breath hot against my skin as he picks up the pace. Pumping himself inside my body, the slow drag of his erection in and out starting a fresh wave of tingles washing over me.

I clutch him closer, his heart racing against mine, our mouths finding each other, tongues thrusting. The kiss is filthy. Sloppy. He's lost all control and I'm encouraging it. Encouraging him.

"Oh fuck," he whispers against my throat, bucking against me, his cock buried deep. His body goes tense, a choked groan falling from his lips just before the shivers take over.

He's coming. And all I can do is hold on to him, witnessing this miracle. It's mesmerizing to watch him, knowing that not many have seen him look like this. I squeeze my inner walls around him, causing a strangled sound to leave him, and he collapses on top of me, his weight heavy and hot. His skin sweaty and sticking to mine.

"Jesus. I'm sorry. That happened way too fast." He's breathing hard, his heart racing, I can feel it.

"Don't apologize." I drift my fingers up and down his wide back, tracing his shoulder blades. "It felt good."

"Did you come? You didn't." His voice is flat, his disappointment palpable.

"I came twice already," I remind him, kissing his forehead. I can't stop touching him. I love having him lie on me like this, as if he owns me. It all feels so perfect.

He feels like mine.

Crew is about to pull out of my body, but I hold him to me, keeping him in place with my hand on his butt. Good lord, his muscles are hard.

"Can we do it again?" I ask hopefully.

He smiles, his mouth finding mine as he murmurs, "Hell yeah."

# CHAPTER FORTY-ONE

## WREN

I think I have a problem.

Pretty sure I'm falling in love with Crew Lancaster.

Maybe it isn't love. Maybe it's just a serious case of infatuation that's perfectly natural, considering he's the one who took my virginity. He's very important to me. The one boy I can never, ever forget. The one who I will remember until I'm an old lady on my death bed, my memories running through my mind, filtered, altered. Broken.

Except for that one boy. The one who I had sex with for the first time.

The rest of Saturday night is a haze. After round two, where we both made sure we came, he cuddled me close as we dozed off. We slept in each other's arms, and when I woke up Sunday morning, he was tucked up behind me, hard and poking me in the butt, his fingers between my legs, touching my sore, sensitive skin.

He still made me come, and I returned the favor before we took showers and got ready to leave. We had breakfast and couldn't linger for long. The plane was ready to take us back to Lancaster Prep.

Back to reality.

...

Once we returned to campus, I went to my room, collapsing into bed and sleeping the afternoon away. I only woke up to my phone buzzing, the room already dark since it was after five.

It was my father, checking in on me and asking about my trip. I lied about the fine details and got him off the phone quickly, grabbing the cookie out of my duffel bag that I got at the bakery yesterday afternoon and devouring it before I fell back into bed.

Now it's Monday morning and another school day is about to start. At least it's a shortened day—all week we get out at twelve-thirty because of the finals' schedule. Today is first and sixth period, so we get to kick it off with Figueroa.

God, I don't want to face him, knowing what he's done. Will he even be there, or did they already arrest him?

I take a shower and blow dry my hair. Get dressed in my uniform. Tie my hair back with the ribbon, remembering what Crew said. How he wants to tie my wrists together with it one day.

My skin goes hot at the possibility.

I slip on my boots and am about to put on my jewelry when I realize something.

Where is my ring?

I unpacked at one point last night and don't remember pulling it out of my bag. I go to the bathroom and dig in my toiletries bag, but it's not in there. I check my purse to see if I dropped it in a small pocket inside, but no.

It's not there either.

I remember taking it off. Leaving it on the nightstand at the hotel.

I don't remember picking it up before we left.

Panic fills me, making it hard to breathe. My father is going to kill me. That ring is a family heirloom. It was his mother's original engagement ring, and it has so much sentimental value attached to it. If I lost it...

I throw on my uniform jacket and my thick winter coat. Wind the scarf around my neck and don a hat before I'm leaving my dorm room and eventually exiting the building, a little earlier than usual.

I need to talk to Crew. Ask him if he remembers grabbing the ring for me. Anything is possible, right?

If he didn't, I can call the hotel and ask if someone turned in a ring. There are still good people in this world who would turn in a lost item. I'm sure of it.

My steps are hurried as I run across the slick sidewalk. It rained for the better part of the weekend and some of the snow still remains, though now it's slushy and dark with debris and dirt. Not fluffy and white like it is when it first falls. When it feels magical and wondrous.

No, now it's just ugly. The air is cold and damp, the sky a dark, steely gray. There aren't many people out this early, so it's easy for me to make my way to the main building. When I see the entrance, no one is lingering in front of it, not even Crew's friends. I trudge my way up the steps, going just inside and waiting by the door, so I can see his approach.

We texted briefly last night, but I could tell he was tired. I was too. Plus, I don't want to come across as too clingy.

Oh my God, I sound like every other girl I know who's had sex and then wants to play it cool. Like it's no big deal. And the sex thing isn't what's bothering me today. No, it's the fact that I lost my ring and I'm scared of my father's reaction.

He's going to be mad. I just know it.

Five minutes pass and there's still no sign of Crew. I send him a text, asking where he's at, but he doesn't respond.

He's driving me out of my mind with worry.

Finally, I spot him, walking with his friends toward the building, Crew standing in the middle. I walk outside, barely able to repress the smile that wants to appear when I note the way his gaze lights up when he first sees me.

How he tamps it down so his friends won't notice.

Well. That's disappointing. Though it's originally what I wanted, so I can't complain.

Chewing on my lower lip, I wait until he's closer to say something.

"Hi, Crew." I glance over at his friends. "Ezra. Malcolm."

They both nod and murmur their greetings, Crew watching me with the slightest frown.

"Can I talk to you?" I ask him.

"Sure."

"Privately?" I send a pointed look in Ezra and Malcolm's direction.

"Yeah, definitely."

Crew lets me take his arm and we walk down the hall, hiding away in the abandoned classroom he dragged me into that one time, when he kissed me so ferociously. Like a jealous lover.

Once the door is shut, Crew is on me, his hands cradling my cheeks, his mouth landing on mine. He devours me like a starving man, consuming me completely.

I eventually push him away, needing a clear head, hating how he frowns, worry crossing his face.

"What's wrong?" he asks.

I stand up straighter, my tone somber. "I lost something this weekend."

His smirk surprises me. "You sure did."

My cheeks burn. "Stop."

"What did you lose?"

"My ring. The one my father gave me. He's going to be so mad if it's gone. It belonged to my grandmother. It was her engagement ring, and it's really special to him. That's why he gave it to me," I explain, my head starting to hurt.

I will never forgive myself if I lost it for good.

"I know where it is," Crew says, calm as ever.

Relief floods me, though not enough to ease the fresh headache. "Oh my God, really? Where is it? Can you give it to me?"

He slowly shakes his head. "I can't."

I blink at him. "Why not?"

"Because." He unzips his jacket and reaches for the knotted tie at his neck, loosening it so he can then unbutton his shirt.

I'm so confused. "What are you do—"

The rest of the word sticks in my throat when he pulls out a chain that's hanging around his neck, my ring dangling from it.

My gaze meets his, surprise coursing through me. "Why are you wearing it?"

"It belongs to me now." His expression is grim.

"What?" Okay, he's really making no sense. "It's mine, Crew. It belongs to my family. My father gave me that ring."

"And I'm taking it. Because I took you." He glances down, sliding his finger through the ring, though it barely fits. "This is mine, just like you are."

I blink at him, startled by his declaration. The tiniest bit thrilled by it too. "Crew..."

"Don't argue with me, Birdy. You're mine." He kisses me fiercely. "You don't belong to him anymore."

The him he's referring to is my father.

Crew slips his fingers beneath my chin, his thumb rubbing. "You belong to me," he whispers.

• • •

After we kiss for far too long in the darkened classroom, we slip back into the hall, me leaving the room first and Crew waiting a few minutes before he followed after me. I'm already in English by the time he appears, his smile smug as he struts in and slips into the desk directly behind mine.

Fig is nowhere to be found, which is extremely unusual.

Maybe he finally got in trouble and that's why he isn't here.

I turn in my seat to talk to Crew. "Did you turn in your paper by midnight?"

It was due online by the end of the day yesterday.

"Yep." He nods. "I even wrote it last night."

"Crew!" I can't help but chastise him for waiting so long.

He shrugs. "At least it's done."

"Are you ready for the final?" His casual attitude about grades and assignments is mind-blowing to me, especially because of how well he does.

"Do you think we're actually going to have one?" He nods his head toward Fig's empty desk.

"I don't know. Even if he's not here, I'd think they would still give us the final."

"Maybe." He shrugs again, like it's no big deal.

I want to ask him about the possible arrest. What his suspicions might be on where Fig is. But I don't want to say anything he told me in private that someone else might hear, so I keep my mouth shut.

It's easier that way.

Mr. Figueroa finally shows up right as the final bell rings, seemingly frazzled. He drops his book bag on top of his desk, scanning the room, his gaze settling on me for a beat too long.

Then I realize he's actually looking at Crew sitting directly behind me.

Fig clears his throat. "Sorry I'm late. Give me a few and then we'll start the final."

The class erupts in whispered conversation, and I can feel a prickle between my shoulder blades. Crew is watching me.

I slowly turn toward him, once again, the weight of someone else's stare heavy upon me. I barely flicker my gaze in his direction, correct in my assumption.

Fig is watching us, his lip curled into a faint sneer. He glances down at his desk when I catch him, but it's too late. I saw the disgust on his face. He really can't stand the idea of me with Crew.

"He doesn't like seeing me talk to you," I whisper.

"Well, that's too fucking bad." Crew puts a possessive hand on my arm, claiming me in front of Fig.

"Crew..."

"No, don't tell me to stop. And don't make excuses for him either." Crew lowers his voice, his intense gaze meeting mine. "If we're lucky, his ass is about to get arrested. Maybe even today. I thought they were going to do it over the weekend. He needs to know he can't come around you anymore. He even looks in your direction and I don't like it? I'm kicking his ass."

I'm gaping at him, shocked by the words he's saying. "Are you serious?"

"I protect what's mine," he says through gritted teeth, his eyes blazing with anger.

Everything inside me melts at the way he said that. The look on his face, how he's touching me. The fact that he's wearing my ring around his neck. His behavior is so archaic and sexist, yet a part of me loves it.

That he believes I belong to him.

There's a rapid-fire knock on the closed classroom door, and just as Figueroa stands to answer it, Headmaster Matthews strides inside, his gaze frantic when he scans the classroom before he says, "We need you in the office, Mr. Figueroa. Right away."

Fig stands, swallowing visibly. I pull away from Crew's grip, facing the front of the classroom, my gaze going to the empty seat beside me.

Maggie isn't in class. That's probably a good thing.

Two men and a woman suddenly enter the classroom, all of them wearing dark suits. They give off that cop vibe, and when the female pulls out a pair of handcuffs, I realize my instincts are correct.

"David Figueroa, you're under arrest," the woman says as

the two males flank either side of Fig and grab his arms before he can get away.

Not like he was trying. Defeat is written all over him.

"Hands behind your back," she says as the other detectives turn Fig, so his back is to her. The woman lists the charges. Contributing to the sexual delinquency of a minor. Inappropriate sexual behavior with a minor. Sexual misconduct. The list goes on for a while.

Our teacher is in massive trouble. I don't see him ever recovering from this.

And them arresting him in front of us is sending a message to the entire school. He's been caught.

Finally.

They haul him out, Fig's head hanging down the entire time, all of us in the classroom deathly quiet. We're all in shock. I know I am, and I even had a heads-up.

Matthews stops in the open doorway, contemplating all of us. "Don't worry about the final. You all got an A on it," he says.

Right before he turns and leaves.

# CHAPTER FORTY-TWO

## WREN

The rest of the day is uneventful, thank goodness. We have a shorter lunch break because of the shortened schedule, and Crew never leaves my side. He's very possessive, slinging his arm over my shoulders as he sits next to me in the dining hall and talks to his friends. Claiming me in front of everyone at school.

There are stares and whispers and gossiping behind hands, but a lot of it has to do with Fig's arrest and not because of Crew's obvious attention—and affection—towards me. This is a big deal, having a teacher arrested in front of our class, during school hours. Hauled off in handcuffs and paraded around the entire school.

Because that's what those detectives did. They walked Fig down the main hall, hoping to catch the eye of everyone they could. Totally unexpected.

But then again, not surprising.

When the final bell rings, I walk out of my sixth period final to find Crew waiting for me, leaning against a row of shiny blue lockers. He pushes away from them to approach me, and I frown.

"What are you doing here?"

"Walking you to your dorm," he says, taking my hand and falling into step beside me.

I marvel at this new Crew. We have sex and this is what happens? He becomes super possessive and wants to spend all of his free time with me? It's so...weird. And thrilling.

Something to get used to, that's for sure. I'm not used to this sort of attention, and while I like it, there's also a small part of me that wants to run and hide.

People seeing me with Crew will eventually realize that something happened between us. Something sexual. My role model days are over.

I fell, just like the rest of them.

And I sort of don't mind. I get it now. I understand why it happens, and how all other things cease to matter when the boy of your dreams, the boy you're falling for, smiles at you and makes you feel like nothing else matters to him.

Just you.

Once we're outside, I pull my hand from his and slip my gloves on. He tries to grab my hand again, but I won't let him.

"What the hell, Birdy?"

The irritation in his voice is obvious, but I ignore it. "You should put gloves on first."

"Oh." His annoyance clears and he pulls a pair of black gloves from his coat pocket, putting them on and then taking my hand. "Is this your way of taking care of me?"

"I have to try sometime, since all you want to do now is take care of me." I should sound more grateful. He needs to understand this will take some getting used to for me.

He shrugs, seemingly uncomfortable. "I feel protective."

"Why? Because of what happened over the weekend? I can still handle myself, you know," I remind him.

"I never thought you couldn't," he agrees. "But...I can't help the way I feel."

"And how do you feel?"

"Like you're mine and I want everyone to know it," he answers seriously.

I absorb his words. The fierce way he said them. I believe he cares about me. That he feels possessive of me. But we've gone from nothing to everything in a rapid amount of time and I still need to process this.

When we arrive at the dorm hall, I turn to face him, grabbing hold of the front of his jacket and giving him a little shake. "I love how protective you are, but you have to be patient with me."

Crew frowns. "What do you mean?"

"I'm not used to it. A few weeks ago, you were chasing after me. Threatening me and always shooting me dirty looks. You've even admitted you hated me."

His exasperation is evident. "I didn't shoot you dirty looks."

I love that's the point he got stuck on. "You so did. Every morning when you waited for me to show up before school."

"I was trying to get your attention."

"As in, staring at me like you wanted me to die?" I laugh.

He doesn't.

"I guess I approached it—*you*—wrong," he admits.

"You still got me in the end though." My smile is small.

He kisses it away.

"I could come inside and hang out with you in the common room," he suggests, pressing his forehead to mine.

"I would love that, but I have a paper to finish." My history essay is due tomorrow, plus we have an actual final. "Plus, I need to study."

"You do not," he teases, delivering another kiss to my lips.

"I do. The paper is only two-thirds finished and I barely remember what we learned in class this semester," I explain. "I need to read over my notes."

"I have that final tomorrow afternoon," he says. "Maybe I should study with you."

"We won't get any studying done together and you know it." I smile up at him, not wanting to hurt his feelings. "Once I get through tomorrow, the rest of the week is easy."

"And then we'll hang out." He says this firmly, as if I can't argue.

I won't. I want to spend time with him. As much as I can before winter break starts.

"Yes. We'll hang out." He kisses me again before I can say anything else.

"I want to plan something for your birthday. Something special. Just for the two of us," he says.

I don't know how my father will feel about that, but I don't mention that. "Okay."

"Good luck with studying. And your paper." Yet another kiss, this one long and filled with tongue. "Text me later."

"Bye," I whisper.

I watch him walk away before I finally turn and head into my dorm, waving at the RAs sitting behind the desk as I walk past. I'm in my room in minutes, changing out of my uniform and pulling on sweats. I crack open my laptop and settle in, opening the paper I've been working on for history.

This is the absolute last thing I want to do, but I remind myself once tomorrow is over, the rest of the week is fairly simple. I can handle this. A paper. Some studying. A final. Then it's easy-peasy until we're out of school for break.

I can't wait. I want to spend time with Crew before we have to leave. And then I want to spend more time with him when we're both home. Winter break can be so depressing for me sometimes, even though it's my birthday and Christmas and all of those good times, where you're supposed to be making memories and having a great time.

I'm usually just with my parents. We don't have much extended family, and the last few years, Daddy never wanted to go on vacation over the holidays, claiming he had too much work to catch up on.

Now I'm actually excited for break. For all the possibilities that come with it.

Like spending ample time with Crew.

I'm going to have to tell Daddy about him sometime. Mom probably won't care so much, but Daddy will. He has all of these expectations on me that I can no longer meet.

I can't meet them. Not anymore.

Really don't want to anymore either.

I'm staring at my laptop screen, trying to get up the energy to finish writing this history paper when my phone rings.

It's Daddy.

I answer immediately, greeting him with, "Hi. I was just thinking about you."

"Really? Looks like you weren't thinking much about me over the weekend, am I right?" His tone is harsh, full of barely-restrained anger.

I frown, slamming my laptop shut. "What do you mean?"

"You think I don't know?"

My heart lodges in my throat, making it hard for me to breathe. "Don't know what?"

"Who you were with this weekend? What you two were doing? I'm disappointed in you, Wren. You broke your promise."

Oh God. How does he know? How did he find out? Who told him?

"Daddy, wait—"

"I don't want to hear your excuses or your lies. Because that's what you did, Wren. You lied to me. You told me you were going to Vermont with Maggie when you didn't. You went with that insufferable—boy and did inappropriate things. You shared a bed with him. I know you did. I saw the proof."

My brain is scrambling, trying to keep up with what he's saying. "How do you know?"

"I'm glad you're not trying to deny it. You're doing the right thing." He hesitates only for a moment. Long enough for me to realize tears are running down my face. "I have access to your iCloud. I logged in and saw the inappropriate photos."

I briefly close my eyes, my heart sinking fast. I remember the photos I took of Crew that Saturday night. With his shirt off and my lip-gloss imprint on his chest. Much later that night, after we'd had sex twice and we were about to fall asleep, I took one last photo of the two of us lying in bed, my head resting on his naked shoulder, our gazes sleepy, our smiles full of satisfaction as I took a selfie. I wanted to document the moment. The night I gave my virginity to Crew.

And my father saw all of it. Even the photos I took Saturday afternoon of us downtown. The decorations. Crew sitting across from me at lunch.

None of those photos were meant for anyone else's eyes but mine. And Crew's.

"Do you have anything to say for yourself?" Daddy asks when I remain quiet.

"What am I supposed to say? I can't defend myself. You've seen all the evidence." I swallow hard. "I didn't know you had access to my iCloud."

"That's clear," he retorts. "From everything I saw on your most recent camera roll, I almost regret looking."

That's false. I'm sure he doesn't regret it, since he finally caught me in a lie. Like he's been hoping to catch me in one all of these years. Why else would he need access to my iCloud account?

Because he doesn't trust me. He's never fully trusted me after I did something so incredibly stupid when I was twelve.

Well, I'm not twelve anymore. I'd like to think I'm smarter than I was. I'm definitely stronger.

I think.

"You're coming home now," he demands. "Tonight."

"Daddy! I can't. I have finals to complete. I'm writing a paper right now!"

"I'll call the school and you can do everything online. I'll tell them it's a family emergency—which it is," he says. "Don't argue with me, Wren. You're coming home early."

"Daddy, please. Listen to me. I have to finish this paper and study for the final. It's all happening tomorrow. It's my first class since we're on a finals' schedule this week. How about I come home after that? The rest of my classes, I'm pretty much done."

He's quiet for a moment, and I rest my head on my desk, anxiously waiting for his answer. It's not a lie. I do need to complete everything I listed.

But I also need a chance to explain to Crew what's happening. He deserves to know.

To know my father most likely hates him.

"I'll send a car to pick you up at noon. You better be on time with that driver, Wren. I'll make sure he reports to me," my father says, his voice firm.

"I'll pack tonight," I say, my voice shaky, my head aching.

So is my heart.

"And stay away from Lancaster. That boy is trouble. I've done my research. His brothers are always trying to steal my clients. I wouldn't doubt that's why he's getting with you. He's just using you to get closer to me, to help his brothers," Daddy explains.

I lift my head, anger suffusing me, though I keep quiet.

The world doesn't revolve around him. Something he still doesn't quite get. Not everyone gets close to me or my mother in order to get to him. It doesn't work like that. Not always.

"Okay," I mumble, not meaning it.

"We'll discuss this further tomorrow." He blows out a harsh breath. "I'm so disappointed in your choices, Pumpkin. You were on the right path, and you've ruined everything."

"Having sex doesn't ruin your life, Daddy," I bite out, annoyance filling me.

"Don't talk back," he snaps. "Who are you right now?"

Before I can tell him, *I'm your daughter,* he ends the call.

And I burst into tears.

# CHAPTER FORTY-THREE

## CREW

I wait for her outside the front of her dorm, unreasonably keyed-up. Anxious.

Words I don't normally use to describe how I'm feeling.

I tried texting with Wren last night, but she wasn't very responsive. Even distant. She blamed it on the paper she finished and all the studying she was doing for the history final, but I don't know.

It feels like something's wrong. I just can't put my finger on it.

She was a little odd yesterday too, and I'm still not quite sure why. I get that I'm acting different, and I understand why. Spending the entire weekend with her, having sex with her, fuck. I'm obsessed.

I want her again. In any way I can get her. I can't stop thinking about her. Yesterday I couldn't stop touching her. I wanted the whole damn world to know she's mine. She belonged to me.

Wearing that damn purity ring her father gave her on a chain around my neck felt like the right thing to do. Before we left the cabin, I found it on the nightstand and snagged it up, slipping it into my pocket. I forgot to tell her I had it, and when I got into my dorm room that afternoon and shed my clothes to take a shower, the ring fell onto the floor with a soft pinging sound.

I grabbed it, holding it up to the light, the idea forming. What the ring symbolizes, she no longer is.

Because of me.

I deserve to wear that damn ring around my neck. Maybe she doesn't like that I did that, but I don't want to give it back.

If she wants it back though, I'll give it to her. Reluctantly.

The doors swing open and a group of girls come striding out, but they're not Wren. I smile grimly at them as they pass by me, a couple of them saying good morning.

I check my phone for the time, realizing she's running later than usual. Where's my girl at?

That I even think of her as my girl is mind-blowing. We haven't made an official declaration to each other, but it feels serious to me. I care about her. I'm worried about her.

Where is she?

The doors swing open again, and she appears. Wearing the black puffy coat and the Mary Janes on her feet, her legs clad in white wool tights. She spots me almost immediately, her expression unreadable and dread consumes me as she draws closer. She's not smiling. Her eyes are rimmed red.

I go to her, reaching for her, but she dodges away from my hold.

"What's wrong?" I ask her, not bothering with niceties.

She shakes her head, her eyes filling with tears. "I have to go home today."

I frown. "You *have* to?"

"Yes. My father, he's—mad at me." She sniffs, the tears now falling freely.

I take a step closer, wiping them away with my thumb as I rest my other hand on her hip. "Why?"

"He—he knows about us, Crew. And he was so upset. I broke my promise to him and he's angry."

"How does he know?"

"He has access to my iCloud. I didn't know about that. He

saw my camera roll. The photos I took of us over the weekend. Saturday night." She shifts closer to me, pressing her forehead against my shoulder. "I'm so ashamed."

Irritation fills me. Nice word choice. "You're ashamed of us being together? Or that we got caught?"

"Both. More that we got caught." She takes a deep, shuddering breath before she lifts her head, her tortured gaze meeting mine. "I told him I wouldn't do that."

"What, have sex with someone? Where's the shame in it? You're almost eighteen, Wren. Yet you still act like a little girl."

Her mouth sets in a firm line. "That's not fair."

"See? You're still doing it." I grab hold of her shoulders, pulling her into me. She rests her hands on my chest, her touch light. "Life isn't fair, Birdy. You should know this by now. He shouldn't be mad at you for doing something that's natural. You're a good girl. He should be proud of you for holding out for this long."

"It's not about holding out, Crew," she says, her tone bitter. "It's about making the right choices."

What the hell? "Are you calling me the wrong choice then?"

"No. I don't know. I shouldn't have done that..." Her voice drifts, and she averts her head. As if it pains her to look at me.

"You shouldn't have done what? Fucked me?"

Her gaze immediately returns to mine. "You don't have to put it so crudely."

"That's all your father is doing. He's taken all of the human emotions out of it. Like maybe I want to be with you because I care about you. And you care about me," I say. Putting it all on the line. Something I don't normally do.

More like I never do it.

"Do we really though? We barely know each other. It's only been a couple of weeks," she points out.

"When we're lucky enough to find someone that makes our world brighter, shouldn't we grab hold of that person and never let them go?"

She's staring up at me, confusion in her gaze. "What do you mean?"

"I'm talking about you. And me." I kiss her, and naturally she responds. I end the kiss before we get too carried away. "You don't have to listen to every word your father says. His expectations on you are impossible to maintain."

"But he's my father," she whispers. "I love him. Knowing I disappointed him just…it hurts. I don't like it when he's angry with me. He's all I've got."

He's going to make her choose. Him or me. I can sense it.

I can also sense what her answer will be.

Fuck. That hurts.

"Well, what about me?" I ask her.

"And what are you to me? What am I to you?"

I remain quiet, my thoughts a confused jumble in my brain. I've been real with her so far. Admitting things I probably shouldn't have, yet here I am. Opening up the veins and letting myself bleed.

"That's what I thought," she says when I still haven't replied. The disappointment is written all over her face. "Maybe we moved too fast."

"Is that what you really think? Or are you only saying that to make yourself feel better?" Shit, I don't mean it. Yes, we moved fast. Too fast? I don't know about that.

"I don't know what to think!" she wails, more tears raining down. "I have to go. I can't be late for class."

She starts walking, leaving me where I stand. I watch her go, knowing I should chase after her. Yet I stay rooted in place.

Wren keeps going, never looking back, and I fight the anger that simmers just below the surface. How easily she walks away from me, as if I don't matter. All she can think about is her father, and how she can't disappoint him. His standards are impossible for her to meet. He wants her to be his little girl forever.

She's my girl now. He needs to understand that.

So does she.

"Birdy!" The nickname bursts out of me, and she whirls around, her sad eyes meeting mine. "I want to see you when we're in the city."

"I don't know if I can," she says, loud enough for me to hear.

Loud enough to pierce my steel-walled heart.

I'm going to see her. Before her birthday. After. On New Year's Eve. I'm going to make sure these next few weeks are good for her. Prove that I haven't forgotten her like everyone else. When I said I was her friend, I meant it.

When I said I cared about her, I meant that too. No way can I lose her now.

Pulling my phone out of my pocket, I bring up my brother's number and call him.

"What now?" Grant barks.

"I need your help," I tell him, my voice dead serious. "Hopefully you can find it."

"I can find anything you need, little brother," Grant says with that Lancaster confidence we all have. "Tell me what you need."

# CHAPTER FORTY-FOUR

## WREN

I'm a prisoner in my own home. Forgotten. Neglected. Daddy demanded I come home and I did as he asked, leaving Lancaster the moment I finished my history final. The second final scheduled was for psychology, and I already did my presentation with Crew, thank goodness. It was easy for Daddy to call into the administration office and have me excused early.

And now here I am, in the sterile apartment with my sterile parents. It's only been a few days since I came home, and already, I've just become another piece of furniture. Or maybe I'm a painting hanging on the wall.

Pretty to look at. Enough to invest in. Otherwise, it doesn't matter.

It's Saturday, and I'm bored. Restless. I slept a lot the first couple of days. It was either that or cry, especially since my father took my phone away from me the moment I arrived. I can't communicate with anyone.

Crew.

He probably hates me. Thinks I'm a little baby who can't stand up for herself. I pretty much proved that by the dumb things I said to him when we got into that fight. Was it even a fight? I don't know how to describe it. All I know is I'm devastated that it had to end like this. With my father witnessing the photos, seeing me lying there naked with Crew, even though nothing is shown in the photo.

It was so obvious though. The image is imprinted on my brain. I can see the way my head is lying on his bare shoulder, our lazy smiles and half-lidded eyes. My own naked shoulders, making it obvious I have no clothes on. The rumpled sheet beneath us.

I miss him. My heart aches to see him. Talk to him.

Yet, I'm trapped.

Giving up on my pity party for one, I leave my bedroom and wander around the apartment, glaring at every piece of art I pass by. My parents—specifically my mother—care more about the art hanging on their walls than about me. She hasn't come to talk to me once since I've come home. No reassuring words like, "I'll speak to your father," or even a, "You'll be okay," mentioned.

She's letting me suffer on my own.

I approach her sitting room, hearing the voices coming from the open doorway, and I pause, pressing myself against the wall when I realize it's my parents.

And they're talking about me.

"When are you going to give her phone back?" Mom asks.

"If I had my choice, never," Daddy mutters, the disgust clear in his voice.

"She's almost eighteen. Just give it back to her. What's the worst that could happen if she has it?"

"That boy will text her. Call her. He's been doing it nonstop since I took the phone from her."

My heart swells with hope. He hasn't given up on me.

"At least he's persistent."

"That means nothing. She had sex with him, Cecily. Of course he's persistent. He's hoping for more," Daddy explains.

I wince, hating how he thinks Crew only cares about me because we had sex. When it felt like so much more than that...

"Well, she attracted a Lancaster, which I have to admit is a solid choice. At least she picked well," Mom says.

"She should've never done that. She promised herself to me," Daddy says vehemently.

"Your archaic ways can't stick forever and you know it. She's a beautiful girl. Smart. Interesting. It doesn't surprise me at all that Crew wanted to land her in his bed."

I'm shocked by my mother's words. She thinks I'm beautiful? Smart? Interesting? Most of the time she acts as if she can barely stand me.

"Don't say that," Daddy says bitterly. "I can't stand the idea of her being with him."

"Well, it's true! She's almost a woman, Harvey. You're going to have to let her go sometime. You two have a very close relationship, but if you prevent her from seeing this boy, she'll resent you," Mom says. "Give her the phone back. Let her talk to him. We'll see what happens. She's a wise girl. She won't make a stupid decision."

"We don't know that. I've protected her all these years. It terrifies me, thinking of her on her own. Making bad choices, putting herself at risk." He sounds tortured, and I immediately feel bad.

"You've created this by protecting her for far too long. Give her back that phone. Tell her you're sorry for invading her privacy. And let her make her own choices, her own mistakes. If we've done anything right, she'll do well. Like I said, she's a smart girl. She can handle herself, and this boy. And if he breaks her heart, then so be it. That's life. She'll hurt, she'll heal and she'll move on."

Tears prick the corner of my eyes, listening to my mother's support. If I could, I'd run into that room and hug her. Thank her for believing in me when my father still refuses to.

Instead, I return to my room and stare out the window, watching the rain fall. It splatters against the glass with the wind, the clouds a dark threatening gray, and I hold my old teddy bear to my chest as I sit curled up on my bed.

There's a soft knock on my door and then my mother appears, a kind smile on her face. "May I come in?"

I nod, not saying anything.

She glides in, holding something behind her back. "A package came for you."

I frown. "Really?"

"Yes." She holds it out in front of me and I frown at the small white box, wondering who it came from. She waves it at me. "Take it."

I do as she says, opening the box carefully by pulling off the lid.

"It was delivered by courier," Mom says as she watches me. "From someone local, I assume."

I push back the layers of white tissue to reveal a small black box. Picking it up, I read the label.

"It's Chanel," Mom says. "Looks like lipstick."

I immediately know who it's from.

The lipstick is Chanel Rouge Allure Luminous Intense Lip Colour. I open the small box and pull out the tube, taking the cap off and rolling it up to see it's an intense, crimson red.

"Looks like 99 Pirate." I glance up at my mother in confusion. "It's their iconic red. I own it."

I'm not surprised. My mother likes wearing bright red lipstick, and she can do it well.

"Who would send you that?" she asks.

I send her a look but don't speak. And I can tell she knows.

"He has good taste," she says with a faint smile. "He should, considering how much he's worth."

I smile. I can't help it.

"I won't tell your father. It'll be our little secret," she says as she heads for my door. "I've also been trying to convince him to give you your phone back. He can't treat you like a little girl forever."

She's about to exit my bedroom when I call out to her.

"Mom?" She turns to look at me, her delicate brows drawn together. "Thank you."

Her smile is slow. "You're welcome, darling. I think the color could look good on you. Give it a try."

"I will."

Once she closes the door, I cap the lipstick and search the box, finding a small envelope buried at the bottom. I pull the card out with shaking fingers, recognizing the bold handwriting immediately.

*You can kiss me with this color the next time we're together. It'll show up on my skin better.*
*X,*
*Crew*

I close my eyes, my lips curling into a smile. Oh my God. Oh my *God*.

I hop off the bed and go to my bathroom, opening the lipstick once more and applying it to my lips, careful to keep my hand steady. When I'm finished, I take a step back, staring at myself in my gray sweats, my hair in a sloppy bun on top of my head, and my lips painted a bright crimson.

With the right outfit and makeup, I think I'd look pretty.

Like I'm all grown up.

• • •

It's at dinnertime when my father finally hands over my phone, his expression grave as he gives me a lecture about responsibility and doing the right thing.

I just keep my head bowed and nod occasionally, enduring the speech I've heard so many times over the years. My mother interjects every once in a while trying to defend me, as if that's going to get him to stop.

It doesn't, but I appreciate her support.

"Do I still have to stay home?" I ask when he's finished speaking. "Or can I go out?"

"Who do you want to go out with?"

Do I even need to say?

I shrug one shoulder. "Friends."

"Anyone specific?"

"Harvey," Mom snaps. "Leave her alone. Yes, darling, you're allowed to go out. I'm sure you have plenty of friends to see and catch up with."

Daddy sighs heavily. "Fine. You may go out, Pumpkin. Not too late though."

If I could roll my eyes without consequences, I would. But I keep myself under control. "Thank you, Daddy."

"Thank your mother. She's the one who convinced me I need to give you more freedom," Daddy mutters.

I glance up to find her watching me and I mouth a silent thanks. I'm so glad she's an ally. I can't remember the last time she's been on my side.

We eat dinner, my parents talking while I stare at my phone, wondering what mysteries it might contain. Who's texted me? According to my father, I know Crew has. How many times, and what did he say? Does he still want to see me? He must want to, considering what he said in that note.

My lips are still stained with that lipstick. Talk about long lasting. Daddy either didn't notice or didn't want to acknowledge it, and neither did Mom, but I'm sure they can tell I'm wearing lipstick, something I never do.

There are a lot of things I haven't done until lately.

Most of them thanks to Crew.

Once dinner is finished, I escape to my room, wanting to be in there for the first time since I came home. I immediately see a string of texts from Crew, most of them asking how I am. Where I am. Why I won't talk to him. And if I'm ignoring him on purpose or if my dad took my phone away.

I'm sure that text made my father burn with anger.

I also have texts from Maggie and I read them, hating that I missed them.

**Maggie:** *I saw Fig got arrested. I had everything to do with that, and while I regret everything that happened, I don't regret that. I'm sorry if I treated you badly. I was going through a lot and I know I snapped at you that one time when you walked in on us. I was just jealous. Our relationship was so toxic. I'm glad to be away from him. I hope you understand. Maybe we can get together over break?*

She sent another text the next day.

**Maggie:** *Or maybe not. I hope you're not mad at me.*

Before I respond to Crew, I send a text to Maggie, wanting her to know what happened. I explain how my father took my phone away and how scared and worried I've been for her. And that I'm glad she's doing okay. I don't bring up the baby, or the arrest that I witnessed. When she's ready to talk about all of it, I know she'll tell me.

**Me:** *I miss you, Mags. Let's definitely try and get together over break. And I'm sorry I didn't respond sooner. Just know I'm here for you no matter what.*

She responds almost immediately.

**Maggie:** *I can't believe he took away your phone! Then again, I can. Your dad has always been kind of strict. Let's get together in the next few days. I'm already bored and dying to hang out with you.*

**Me:** *Sounds good. We have lots to catch up on.*

I smile, telling myself I really need to make sure and meet up with Maggie in the next couple of days. Sounds like she needs a friend.

I need one too.

I contemplate how I should approach Crew next, but first things first. Going into my phone's settings, I change my password for my iCloud. No way do I want my father spying on me anymore.

It's still hard for me to believe he did that. Such a violation of my privacy. Especially when I had no idea he was doing it. How many times did he check up on me? Scroll through my photos, my texts, my email? Nothing was off-limits to him and it hurts so much, that he would spy on me like that.

Finally, I come up with something to say in my notes and I copy and paste it into the text box and then send it, my heart pounding in my throat the entire time.

**Me:** *I'm sorry I didn't respond to you sooner. The moment I got home my parents took my phone away from me. That's why I haven't texted or called. I hope you understand. I'm sorry about our fight we had before I left. I feel so awful about everything that happened, but the one thing I never feel awful about is you. I don't regret what happened last weekend. I wish we could do it again. I miss you so much. Thank you for the lipstick. I can't wait to wear it for you.*

I'm gnawing on my lip, staring at our text thread when the gray bubble appears, indicating he's responding. My nerves amp up, leaving me feeling sick, and I hope to God I don't throw up the dinner I just ate.

What if he says he's through with me? That he doesn't care anymore? I can't half blame him. I haven't talked to or texted him since Tuesday. But he is the one who also sent me a gift today...

**Crew:** *I want to see you.*

A little sigh leaves me and I can't contain the smile spreading across my face.

**Me:** *I want to see you too.*

**Crew:** *Tomorrow?*

**Me:** *Yes. Tomorrow.*

# CHAPTER FORTY-FIVE

## WREN

I arrive at the Lancaster building just before one, thanking Peter as he holds the door open for me to get out of the car Crew sent. The building is tall, imposing, and I tilt my head back, my heart racing at the knowledge that in a matter of minutes, I'll see Crew.

"Give your name to the man at the front desk and he'll instruct you to the penthouse elevator," Peter advises after he shuts the door, his smile warm when he turns to me.

"Thank you again," I say with a faint smile, pushing past the nerves that are dancing in my stomach.

I walk into the building, the lobby similar to where I live, and when I give my name to the man behind the massive wood and lacquer desk, he nods as if he's been waiting for me, the instructions for the penthouse elevator rattling off his tongue as if he's said it a thousand times before.

Tucking my coat around me, I make my way to the elevator, the doors sliding open immediately after I hit the button. The elevator is incredibly fast, making my knees wobbly when I exit, and I'm about to knock on the black door directly in front of me when it swings open, revealing Crew.

His hot gaze races over me, and now my legs are wobbly for a different reason.

"Birdy. I've missed you." He opens the door wider, allowing me entry, and when I walk in, he immediately shuts it.

And is on me in a flash.

I'm pressed against the wall, his mouth finding mine, his tongue delving inside. I match his excitement, my tongue circling his, a whimper leaving me when he breaks the kiss to run his mouth down the length of my neck. His hands are on my waist, pinning me to the wall, his thumbs stroking my front.

"What the fuck are you wearing?" he asks, his tone full of wonder.

"A dress," I admit shakily as I reach for his face, needing his mouth back on mine. "Do you like it?"

"I don't know yet." He kisses me again, and we stand there in the foyer, devouring each other for I don't know how long until I'm finally pushing him away, desperate to catch my breath. To get my bearings.

One passionate kiss and I'm overwhelmed—in the very best way.

"Is no one home?" I ask as he wipes at the corner of his mouth. I wore the lipstick but chewed half of it off on the drive over, so his lips only have a trace of red on them.

"I told you they were all gone. I'm the only one left at home. My mother is in Mexico for a girls' getaway weekend." He rolls his eyes. "She claims the stress of the holidays sends her over the edge and that's why she needs the trip, but come on. My mother doesn't have to do anything to prep for Christmas. She hires out people to do all that stuff."

"My mother and I decorated the apartment for the first time in years," I say. "She used to always hire someone out to do it."

"Why didn't she do that this year?"

"I don't know." I start to take off my coat and Crew comes behind me, slowly helping me out of it. "But it was kind of fun. We haven't done that since I was a little kid."

"Hmm, that dress." His tone is appreciative, and when I turn to face him, I see the lust in his eyes when they drop to the deep square neckline, the tops of my breasts on blatant display. "Fuck, Birdy, you look good enough to eat."

"Um, thank you?" I laugh. I don't think I've been this happy in a long time.

"It's a compliment." His gaze is still stuck on my chest. "Seeing you in that dress makes me want to fuck your tits."

Shock courses through me at his comment. I don't know how to answer him so I change the subject. "Take me on a tour of your place."

"It's my parents' place, really," he reminds me, his gaze dropping to the lug sole boots on my feet. "You're going to have to take those off. You stain my mother's white rugs, she'll freak."

"I don't want to do that." I start to take them off, placing my hand on the nearby wall, so I can pull one boot off, then the other.

Crew offers me a pair of fuzzy slippers and I step into them. He takes my hand and pulls me along with him, taking me around the massive apartment that puts my parents' place to absolute shame. It's huge and luxurious, with amazing views of Manhattan.

Our art is still better though. I see a few pieces by artists I recognize and they're gorgeous. Extremely valuable.

"I see you eyeing the art." We stop in front of an original Keith Haring, and I'm immediately taken with it. It's not one I recognize, and I consider myself familiar with his art. "It was originally untitled, but it's known as the *Dancing Dogs*."

"I don't think I've seen this one before." I take a step closer, my gaze unable to land on one spot for too long. There are so many things happening all at once. The dancing dogs are the most prominent, but there are men dancing as well. He only used three colors in the entirety of the painting and there's a few radiant babies crawling across the bottom of the canvas. "I love it. My mother has one of his pieces. It was my favorite when I was younger."

"My parents bought this at an auction a few years ago. My

mom has a thing for Keith Haring. She says she loved him when she was a teen," Crew explains.

I glance over at him to find he's already watching me. "I didn't realize your family has so much art."

"Not as much as yours, but they own some pieces." He says it so casually, just like a rich person would. I only recognize the casual tone over something so valuable because my parents do the same thing. "My mother is always looking for an investment."

"She's smart."

"Sometimes. Sometimes not." He grabs my hand once more. "Come on. I'll show you my room."

"You never did mention where your father is," I say as we walk down the corridor, past the wall of windows that overlooks the city.

"He's in town."

I come to a stop, forcing Crew to do the same. "Could he come home at any time?"

"Maybe." Crew shrugs. "He doesn't care if I have a girl over, Wren."

"I might care." Has he had other girls over? I probably shouldn't ask.

It's none of my business.

He turns toward me, his hands on my waist guiding me so I'm against another wall, his hot, hard body pinning me in place. "I've missed you and your fussy ways."

I'm frowning. "I'm not fussy—"

He kisses me, stealing my words. "You're adorable. And fussy. Oh, and by the way...I've never had a girl over here before."

Smiling at his confession, I touch his mouth, my finger sinking between his lips. When he nips my fingertip with his teeth, I yelp, yanking my hand away. "I don't want to make a bad first impression on your father, Crew. Us being here alone might make him question my...morals."

"As long as you don't greet him naked, I think you'll be fine."

I'm sputtering, about to complain further, but I'm silenced again by Crew's mouth. That humming sound he makes when our lips first connect, as if he can never, ever get enough of me. I'm lost to the taste of him. The feel of him. His hands grip my hips, his mouth hungrily moving over mine, and I wind my arms around him, clutching him close.

He slides his hands down, his fingers catching on the fabric of my dress, pulling it up, exposing my thighs. I moan when he slips his knee in between them, lifting up, rubbing it against me. A moan leaves me, and I turn away from his mouth, tilting my head back against the wall as I try to catch my breath.

"You're wet," he observes, his knee nudging the front of my panties.

"I've missed you," I admit as I strain toward him.

His gaze darkens as he stares at me. "I could fuck you right in this hallway."

"In front of the art?" I glance around. "The paintings of your ancestors?"

He looks over his shoulder, scowling at the massive portrait of the man with ice blue eyes that resemble Crew's. "He's the original Augustus Lancaster."

"He looks mean."

"You have to be, to amass a fortune like he did." He dips his head, his mouth brushing mine once. Twice. His tongue sneaking out for a lick. "I don't want to talk about him."

"Take me to your room then so we can do it on a bed," I suggest, my fingers curling into the front of his expensive hoodie.

The smile on his face is wicked. Breathtaking. "Let's go."

I pause, grabbing hold of his sleeve to stop him. "I forgot my lipstick."

"You actually brought it?"

I nod, suddenly shy. "It's in my bag. I left it in the foyer with my boots."

"Let's go get it."

We grab my tiny purse I left on top of my boots and take it back to Crew's room, which is massive. He has an entire wall of windows too, with that same spectacular view of the city. The walls are painted a rich, deep gray and his bed is draped in a pale gray duvet. The furniture is low and sleek, made of dark wood and there's a giant mirror that hangs over the dresser. I can see the entire bed, meaning we could probably...

Watch ourselves, if we wanted to.

Crew walks up behind me, slipping his arms around my waist, his mouth on my neck. I keep my gaze glued to the mirror, watching him as one hand slips up, toying with the ruffled neckline of my dress. "I liked that you dressed up for me."

"I wanted to look pretty," I tell him and my reflection.

He's got both hands on my breasts now, cupping them, drawing his thumbs back and forth across the front of my bodice. "I always think you look pretty."

I tilt my head back until I'm resting it on his shoulder, my gaze still on the mirror as Crew molds my breasts with his hands. My body aches, that delicious throb between my thighs increasing in tempo with every touch. His mouth is on my neck, his teeth and tongue, and I hiss out a breath when he bites my earlobe.

"Are you watching us in the mirror?" he murmurs in my ear.

I nod, not even embarrassed.

"Kinky girl." His voice rings with approval and there's no containing the smile that spreads across my face. "Let's take these off."

He hitches my dress up a little, exposing my white lacy panties and he studies me in the mirror, his gaze zeroed in on my crotch. The way the fabric clings to me because I'm wet.

The dress falls over my panties, hiding them from my gaze when he reaches for the waistband of my underwear. He kneels behind me, easing my panties down, until I'm stepping out of them and he's kissing the back of my knees.

My thighs.

I choke out a gasp when he slides his finger inside me from behind. I clench around him, making him groan.

"Spread your legs," he demands, and I do as I'm told, the skirt of my dress confining me, my thighs only parting a few inches. It doesn't deter him. His hands come up to my hips, gathering up the fabric, so it's out of his way and mine before he starts to lick me from behind.

"Oh God," I moan, my eyelids heavy as his tongue spears inside me. His hands grip me tight enough to bruise, my entire lower half exposed. I can hear him lick and suck, the sound of his tongue slicking through my juices, watching him kneeling behind me in the mirror, feeling him do what he's doing to me sends me closer and closer to the edge.

I lean forward, pressing my butt against his face as he consumes me. Until I'm shuddering, coming with a whimper. A moan. Grateful he has a hold on me or else I would've slipped to the floor. The orgasm left me weak.

He rises up to tower over me, spinning me around so I'm facing him. I stare up at him in a daze, letting him kiss me, his hand slipping between us to stroke me from the front this time. "So easy, making you come."

"It felt so good," I whisper.

"When I fuck you, I want you to watch in the mirror, okay? I know that's what got you off, Birdy." His dark tone tells me he likes that I watched. That I enjoyed it.

"Okay," I agree weakly, not even protesting when he unzips my dress and pushes it off my shoulders, revealing that I'm not wearing a bra.

My nipples are hard and aching. My entire body throbs, demanding his attention. He sheds my dress quickly, until I'm completely naked, and he's got me on the bed sprawled out while he stands beside it and removes his clothes.

"I wanted to take my time with you," he murmurs as he studies me. "Savor you. It's been a week since the last time we were like this."

I nod, shifting my legs, restless. There's a buzz beneath my skin that makes me squirm and it has everything to do with him.

"But you make me too impatient," he continues, his gaze drifting down the length of me. "Touch yourself."

I go completely still, remembering how he asked me to do this last time. "Do you like watching me touch myself?"

"I want to see you rub your clit. Make yourself come again."

I settle my hand in between my legs, suddenly shy. It's the middle of the afternoon. There's so much light spilling into the room, I can hide nothing. I'm on complete and total display.

"Spread your legs wider. I want to see all of you." He settles on the bottom of the mattress, his gaze zeroed in on the spot between my legs.

I push them open wider, my jaw dropping when I watch him wrap his fingers around his shaft and begin stroking. I brush my fingers against my clit, whimpering at how sensitive it is.

"Hurts?" he asks.

I nod. "A little."

"Keep rubbing," he urges, and I do.

We stare at each other as we touch ourselves, and it is the hottest thing I think we've ever done. My fingers are busy while he watches with rapt attention. My complete fascination with the way he strokes himself, his thumb coating the head with leaking pre-cum.

My mouth waters. My body vibrates. I want him inside me. I want to feel him move within me, our bodies connected, our mouths fused. I want to feel him come and I want to come again too.

I want all of it. Now. I feel greedy for it. Greedy for him.

He must feel it too because he suddenly gets up, his cock hard and curving upward as he makes his way over to the nightstand and pulls out a condom. I watch him put it on as I stroke myself, my skin growing hot and itchy.

"Come here," he says as he settles on the edge of the mattress, his feet planted on the floor. "Sit on me."

I do as he asks, scrambling across the bed and adjusting myself, so I'm straddling his lap. His cock nudges against my backside and his face is at breast-level, which is too much of a temptation for him to ignore. He draws my nipple in his mouth and sucks, murmuring around my flesh, "Look in the mirror."

I glance over and see my reflection. The rosy flush to my skin. My hair wild and Crew's head at my chest. His lips tugging on my nipple before he lets it go, his tongue darting out for a long, sensual lick.

"Oh," I choke out, completely overcome. My skin breaks out in goosebumps when he pays attention to the other nipple, his mouth working wonders on my flesh.

"Rise up, baby," he whispers, and it's the way he calls me baby that has me melting. I brace my knees on the edge of the bed and lift up, his cock nudging at my entrance. He reaches around, adjusting himself, and when I slowly lower myself down on his length, we both groan in pleasure.

He's deeper inside me like this, and I pause for a moment, allowing my body to readjust. This is only the third time we've had sex, and I feel as if we're going from zero to sixty with this position, but oh my God, I don't want to stop. I love how deep he is. How close we are.

I glance down at him, swooping in for a kiss, and it turns dirty in seconds. His tongue, his teeth, his lips. He's trying to consume me, and I want to let him.

I want him.

"Rise back up," he urges, and I do so, that slow glide of my body riding his cock nearly making my eyes cross with pleasure. I keep doing it. Up and down. Nice and slow. My gaze going to the mirror, zeroing in on the spot where our bodies are connected.

I can actually see him enter me, and that's all it takes.

I'm coming, clutching him close, my inner walls milking him, wrenching the orgasm right out of him until he's coming too. It's too much. Not enough. I'm shaking so hard I swear to God I'm going to black out, and when it's finally over, when all I can do is slump against him, my heart thundering in my ears, he slides his hands down my butt, touching the spot where his cock is still embedded inside my body. He slides his fingers up, along my crack, teasing that forbidden spot and sending a jolt of electricity racing through me.

"You like that?" he asks, his voice full of smug satisfaction.

"I-I don't know," I answer truthfully. I'm shocked he would touch me there.

He does it again, and I bite back a moan.

Though I have to admit, I liked it.

I liked it a lot.

# CHAPTER FORTY-SIX

## CREW

This girl, goddamn.

She is dirty and agreeable to anything, and so fucking responsive. The sounds she makes, the way she arches against me, as if she can't get enough. When I went down on her from behind, her pussy was soaked, drenching my face as I ate at her flesh.

Fuck, I'd do it again. Right now, if she let me.

I took a risk, touching her asshole like that after she milked the orgasm right out of me. I wanted to test her. See what she was up for. I'm probably moving too fast.

But her pussy clenched up on me when I touched her there. She squirmed and whimpered and practically begged for more when I kept it up.

My little former virgin is up for anything.

How the fuck did I get so lucky?

Once we get cleaned up, we end up lying in my bed, lazing the rest of the afternoon away. She eventually grabs the lipstick and goes to the mirror above my dresser, bending over to watch herself carefully as she applies the deep red shade. Her ass is sticking up in the air and I can see the sweet shadow of her pussy in her pose.

My cock rises to the occasion, eager to get back inside.

She turns to face me, rubbing her ruby red lips together, the lipstick still clutched in her fingers. "What do you think?"

"Hot as fuck," I say, my gaze on her tits.

She knows where I'm staring because she rests her empty hand on her hip, a frustrated noise leaving her. "I'm talking about my mouth."

I level my gaze on her made-for-sin lips, painted a deep, rich red. "Come over here and wrap them around my dick. Then I'll tell you what I think."

Laughing, she caps the lipstick and sets it on the dresser before she saunters over to the bed. When she gets close enough, I grab hold of her, pulling her on top of me. I'm about to kiss those pretty lips, but she dodges away from my mouth.

"I have a plan," she practically purrs.

"What is it?"

"I want to try and do the same thing I did last time." When I frown, she explains, "I want to kiss you. Leave lipstick imprints on your skin. You said this shade would show up better, remember?"

I do remember. Wait until she sees what else I have in store for her.

"Have at it." I open my arms wide and let them fall by my side, as if I'm helpless. She repositions herself, straddling me once again. She touches the ring—her ring—that hangs on my chain, her expression thoughtful.

"Do you want it back?" I ask, knowing what my answer will be if she says yes.

A firm no.

Wren slowly shakes her head. "I don't know what I'm going to say when I'm asked where it is though."

"You lost it?" Which is true.

She lost it—her virginity—to me.

"He'll be mad."

"He'll be mad no matter what you tell him. What would he

do if you told him the truth?" I raise a brow.

"Rip this right off your neck." She traces the gold chain.

"I wouldn't give him the opportunity." My smile is smug. I could take Harvey Beaumont. That man doesn't scare me. I've had to deal with my father and uncles my entire life. Those guys would slay Beaumont dead with just a fucking look.

"Ooh, you're so tough," Wren teases.

"You like it."

"I do," she whispers before she leans in and presses her mouth to my chest once. Twice.

A few more times.

I bend my head down, watching her leave her mark, pleased to see the red lipstick shows up, vivid against my skin. She leans back, studying her work, her lips curled up in a closed-mouth smile.

"I like it."

I lift my gaze to hers. "You're a little weird, Birdy."

"I don't think you mind though," she says, her cheeks turning a faint pink.

"I like anything that makes you happy." I reach for her but she leaps off my lap and grabs her phone. "You sure your dad won't find these photos?"

"I'm positive." She nods. "I changed my password."

"What to?"

"Oh, I'm definitely not going to tell you." She aims her phone at me, taking a few steps closer to focus tightly on where the kiss prints are. "This is going to look good."

"And you said you didn't want to recreate it," I murmur.

She frowns. "Recreate what?"

"Your favorite piece. A million kisses in your lifetime. You're doing that right now. I'm your canvas."

She blinks at me. "I guess you are."

"I don't mind."

"I want to do your back next," she says as she checks out

the photos on her phone. "Oh, this looks amazing. Just how I wanted it to."

"You know what I want to do?"

"What?" she asks, her gaze still on the photos.

"I want to see those bright red lips wrapped tight around my cock."

Her wide-eyed gaze lifts to mine. "No photos, right?"

I would love photos. I would never share them with a soul. Only her.

"If you don't want me to take your picture, then I won't," I say. I'm no Larsen Van Weller, that's for damn sure.

"I don't." She slowly shakes her head, and I realize in this instant, she still doesn't fully trust me.

And I also realize in this instant, just as she dips her head and wraps those red lips tightly around the head of my cock, that I want her trust more than anything else in the world.

How did she get past the iron fortress and worm her way into my heart in such a short period of time? I was the one who refused to believe in relationships and love and all the bullshit that comes with it. When you're in a family like mine, you witness fake love on a constant basis. With the generations before us, marriages were made as business transactions. Powerful families coming together and becoming that much more powerful. Hell, it still happens. Look at my sister, married to a man because of our family name and his.

I don't want a fucking merger. I want someone I can laugh with. Someone who's admittedly a little different and likes to press her lip-sticked mouth to my skin. A sweet, innocent girl who has a dirty mind.

Like Wren.

I push her hair away from her face so I can watch. She has no idea what she's doing, but it doesn't matter. Her enthusiasm more than makes up for any lack of experience.

She grips me tight and licks me like a fucking lollipop. Swirls her tongue around the head before she envelops it completely with her mouth, sucking on it. Making slurping sounds that make me clench up, knowing the end is already coming closer.

Damn this girl. Despite her inexperience, she makes me come faster than anyone else ever has. Is it because I care about her? Is that why?

How do I tell her this? How do I express myself when I grew up in a house where feelings were mocked, especially if you're a guy. We're supposed to be cold and unfeeling.

This girl makes me feel the complete opposite of that.

She draws me deep into her mouth. A little deeper. Until she almost gags and my cock is sliding rapidly out of her mouth.

"Sorry," she murmurs, blinking hard.

I touch her cheek, tilting her face up to look at me. "You don't have to deep throat me, Birdy."

Her cheeks flush pink. "I might've watched more porn last night."

Oh, fuck me. "In private mode, I hope."

She laughs. "Yes, definitely."

"I don't plan on coming in your mouth," I tell her, pushing her hair away once again. "Just—play with it. Until I can't take it anymore and I have to fuck you."

And damn, does she ever play with it. She pushes me to the brink in a short amount of time, until I'm practically tearing her off my dick, positioning her so she's flat on her back and I'm hovering above her. I slide inside her with ease, going completely still when I feel all of that hot, wet heat grip me.

"I didn't put on a condom." I glance down to find her wiggling beneath me, like she's trying to take me deeper.

"I'm on birth control," she admits.

I'm shocked. "Seriously?"

"I had irregular periods when I was younger." She seems embarrassed. "My mom took me to the gynecologist and I've been on the pill ever since."

Goddamn, I love her mom. "I've never had sex without a condom. Ever."

"Me either."

I kiss her smiling mouth. "You're funny, Bird."

"I try," she teases, lifting her hips so I do actually sink deeper inside her body. "Are you telling me the truth?"

"About never having sex without a condom?" When she nods, I say, "Yes."

"Then let's try this. It feels good this way."

Once we do it this way, it'll be hard to go back to condoms. I can feel...everything. No barriers, just flesh on flesh.

And fuck, it feels amazing.

"I love being inside of you," I whisper in her ear, because that's as close as I can get, using that word. And I mean it—I love being inside of her. Fucking her. Kissing her and making her come. Knowing that I'm the only one who makes her feel good.

"I love being with you like this," she answers, her hands roaming up my chest to curl around my shoulders. "No one knows me like you do, Crew."

No one knows me like she does either.

Not a single soul.

I start out gentle at first, not wanting to hurt her. She's still so new at this, and I'm sure she's sore. She's already come twice.

Eventually, I lose control. I fuck her hard. And she doesn't complain, not once. She moans and whispers my name, clutching me close. I disentangle myself from her grip and rise above her, wrapping my hands around her hips as I fuck her senseless. Until she's writhing beneath me, her shaky whimper indicating that she's coming.

I'm coming too. So hard.

Falling for her too.

So damn hard.

# CHAPTER FORTY-SEVEN

## WREN

I wake up first thing Monday morning to my mother knocking on my bedroom door promptly at nine, pushing her way inside with a large, pure white box clutched between her hands.

"Wake up, sleepyhead," she chirps. "You have a delivery."

I push the hair out of my eyes, squinting at her as she sets the box on my desk and goes to my window, pushing open the curtains. It's a gray day outside but still bright enough to make me groan and fall back onto the pile of pillows.

"I'm on break," I tell her. "Let me sleep in."

"I couldn't stand waiting any longer." She goes to my desk, grabs the box and hands it to me. "This came for you about an hour ago."

I sit up, the box in my lap. I know who it's from, but I have no idea what's inside. Anticipation makes me feel downright giddy, and I stare at the lid, wondering what he could've sent me now.

"Oh my God, open it, darling!" Mother practically screeches.

Laughing, hoping it's nothing dirty, I pull the lid off and push away the layers of white tissue paper to reveal a slightly smaller box inside, wrapped in glossy black paper. I pull it out, tearing off the paper like a little kid at Christmas, to see it's a Polaroid Now Instant Camera. A special edition featuring Keith Haring.

"I didn't even know this existed." I examine the box, staring at the photo of the camera. It's a bright, vivid red, with one of Keith's trademark radiant babies on the front. The back of the camera is a black and white composite of his art. It's beautiful.

Meaningful.

My heart literally pangs at the sight of it.

"A camera? Oh, it's Keith Haring." Mother plucks the camera box out of my hands, studying the box as she reads the description. "This is so fun. I assume it's from the Lancaster boy?"

Nodding, I reach inside, pushing past the tissue paper to find another slender black box containing a Chanel lipstick. When I open the box and pull the lid off the tube, I see it's a bright, rich pink.

That'll look good on his skin, I can't help but think.

There's a note, and I hurriedly open it, hoping my mother doesn't notice.

*For our next photo session, I think that pink will look good on your lips.*

*xx,*

*Crew*

If he's trying to make me swoon, he's doing a good job.

"He likes you," Mom says.

I glance up to find her watching me carefully. "I like him too."

"I told your father you could do worse." She sets the camera box beside me on the bed, then settles down on the edge of the mattress. "Is he nice? I ask, because he's a Lancaster. They're notoriously not nice."

"He's nice to me," I admit softly, pulling the camera box back onto my lap. "I just wish Daddy wasn't so upset over this."

When I came home last night after my afternoon with Crew,

my father barely spoke to me. I'm sure he assumed who I was with, and I didn't confirm or deny it. I never told him anything. But he can keep tabs on me still.

He had to know I was with Crew. At his apartment.

"You're his little girl. He doesn't want you to grow up. I keep telling him you have to become your own person sometime," she says.

I decide in that moment to ask her the question that's been on the tip of my tongue since the last gift arrived. "Why are you being so nice to me?"

Her expression turns contrite. "It's tough to hear your daughter call you out for your cruelty."

"I truly believed you didn't like me," I admit, my voice small.

"It had nothing to do with you and everything to do with your father." Her tone is faintly bitter. "He's busy working. Or worrying about you. I didn't see where I fit into the equation, so I lashed out at you whenever I could. And that's awful. I was jealous of your relationship with your father. I felt pushed out of our family of three."

I hate that she felt that way, but I hate worse that she took it out on me when I was just a kid who wanted both of their attention.

She releases a deep, shuddering breath. "I'm sorry, Wren. I hope you can forgive me."

When she grabs hold of my hand, as if that's all she could dare to touch for fear of being rejected, I pull her closer and wrap my arms around her, resting my head on her shoulder. We cling to each other for a long, silent time, and I think she might be crying.

I'm a little misty-eyed too.

Eventually she pulls away first, sliding her fingers under each eye to catch any stray tears, a watery laugh leaving her. My mother has never been an overly emotional person. "Why did he give you a Keith Haring camera? I'm curious."

"I went to his family's apartment yesterday," I admit. "And I was admiring the Keith Haring painting they have."

"Two Dancing Dogs?" she asks.

I nod, not surprised she'd know which one it was. "It's beautiful. I told him I liked it. And he sends me this."

I hold up the camera.

"How sweet." A soft sigh leaves her. "Young love. First love. Enjoy it, darling. There's nothing else like it."

"Oh, I don't think he loves me," I'm quick to say. "It hasn't been very long...whatever this is that we're doing."

"Modern love." Another sigh leaves her and she slowly shakes her head. "This is where I admit I feel old and don't understand the ways of teenagers anymore."

"I don't think we're that different from when you were a teen," I say.

"There are a few differences. Social media, for one." She stands and starts heading for the door. "You can go back to sleep now. I was just curious over what he sent you today."

Mom shuts the door behind her and I flop back onto the bed, reaching for my phone so I can send Crew a text.

**Me:** *Got your gift. I love it. Thank you.*

He responds almost immediately.

**Crew:** *You're welcome. Want to come over for a photo sesh?*

I'm smiling so wide it hurts.

**Me:** *I'm surprised you're awake.*

**Crew:** *My brother called me at seven. Such an asshole.*

**Me:** *What did he want?*

**Crew:** *He's been helping me out with something.*

**Me:** *???*

**Crew:** *Can't explain it over text. I'll tell you later.*

**Crew:** *Did you like the camera?*

**Me:** *I LOVED IT. A Keith Haring camera? So awesome.*

**Crew:** *This way you don't have to risk saving the images on your phone. In case your dad figures out your password.*

**Me:** *No one will figure out my password. Not even you.*

**Crew:** *What about the lipstick?*

I drop my phone and grab the lipstick, slicking it on my lips and using my phone as a mirror. I take a selfie and send it to him.

**Crew:** *Hot.*

**Me:** *Not too pink?*

**Crew:** *On you? It's perfect. Come over.*

**Me:** *Right now?*

**Crew:** *We're both awake. No one is at my house. Get your pretty ass over here.*

I should not find it attractive that he says things like that, yet here I am.

Enjoying it.

**Me:** *I need to get ready first.*

**Crew:** *I'll send a car over.*

**Me:** *Peter?*

**Crew:** *Yeah. He's a good dude. Knows how to keep a secret.*

His words make my stomach sink. Is that all I am to him? A secret?

Does a boy buy you gifts and indulge you in your weird urges to cover his body in lipstick kisses think of you as a secret? I don't know.

I can't worry about it.

**Me:** *I'll text you when I'm ready.*

**Crew:** *I'll keep Peter on standby. Don't forget the camera and the pink lipstick.*

I drop my phone onto my nightstand and crawl out of bed, heading for my walk-in closet. I don't know what to wear today. Definitely not a dress, though that had been fun. And cold.

Especially when I went home last night. I was freezing by the time I walked into our apartment. The look on my father's face was one of utter disappointment as he watched me take off my jacket, revealing my outfit.

I don't know what Mom said to him to keep him quiet, but I'm grateful for it.

I quickly dress in jeans and a sweater, pulling my hair back into a high ponytail. I slip on my lug sole boots and exit my bedroom to find my father standing in the hall. His hands are in his jacket pockets, his gaze on the painting hanging on the wall. He glances over at me, his expression flat.

"I was waiting for you."

There goes Mom keeping him quiet.

I pause near my bedroom doorway, almost afraid to get closer. "What's up?"

Why is he here? It's a Monday. He should be at work.

"What do you want to do for your birthday?" His smile is hopeful, which worries me.

I don't know how he wants to spend it, but I want to be with Crew. Maybe not on my actual birthday, but that's okay. I can spend the next day with him. I want it to just be me and him, doing whatever I want to do.

My entire body flushes hot at the possibilities.

"Oh, I don't know." I shrug, hoping I don't have to come up with an answer at this very moment.

"You said you wanted to go out of town."

"I've changed my mind. I'd rather stay here."

"You want to have the party here, after all? We can get invites out today."

I slowly shake my head. "I don't want to do that either. Not anymore."

"But it's your eighteenth birthday." Daddy frowns. "It's a special day. We should celebrate."

He's pushing me into a corner I won't be able to get back out of. "Don't you have to work?"

That's always his excuse. He's constantly working, and for once, I want him to be too busy to spend time with me.

"I can take some time off. I own the damn company." He chuckles. "I wanted it to be a surprise, but I can't contain it any longer. We're going on a trip."

"Who?"

"Me, you and your mother. For your birthday. To Aruba. We leave Christmas day. Your birthday." He grins, looking pleased with himself.

While my heart falls. "I don't want to go to Aruba."

"It's a beautiful resort, Pumpkin. I got us a family suite with three bedrooms. A private chef. The best they had available, which took some finagling since we planned this so last minute. We'll be there for a week."

A week without Crew. Leaving on my birthday. "Does Mother know about this?"

He shakes his head. "I haven't told her yet. I'm sure she'll be excited."

I don't want to sound ungrateful, but...

"I don't want to go."

He frowns. Takes a couple of steps toward me. "Why not? It'll be fun, Pumpkin. A chance to get away. Get some sun and sit by the ocean. Forget all your troubles and school and snow."

"I'd rather stay home. I don't mind the snow. I can see what few friends I have while I'm here, and that's enough for me."

"I heard about your teacher. Figueroa?"

I go completely still. I'd forgot all about that. Out of sight, out of mind. "Oh."

"You didn't even tell me."

"I sort of forgot, with everything else that happened." I'm implying that he's the reason I forgot, with his demands that I come straight home.

"You used to tell me everything. Now I have to find out from the news that your teacher was arrested for having sex with a minor." He visibly shudders. "Imagine if he tried that with you?"

I don't bother telling him he wanted to. He'd just put me under lock and key if he knew that. "I have to go, Daddy."

"Where are you going? It's so early. I'm surprised you didn't sleep in. I know how much you like to." His smile is gentle, and he's trying. I can tell. But it's almost as if he's trying a little too late.

He spied on me. He's never trusted me. He saw the photos of me and Crew together and that's just so...

Embarrassing.

It's going to take me a while to forgive him for that.

"I'm going to see Crew." I stand up straighter, practically daring him to tell me I can't.

His mouth thins into a firm line and he just stares at me for a moment. As if he can't believe this is what I've turned into.

"We're going on that trip."

"No." I shake my head. "You and Mom can go. I'm not."

"I already paid for your ticket."

"Well, ask for a refund. I don't want to go. You can't make me. I'm going to be eighteen in a few days. An adult." I lift my chin, hoping he doesn't see how this confrontation is making me shake.

He looks furious. I don't do this—defy him. Ever. "You still live under my roof."

"I'll go live with someone else then, until I have to go back to school. I don't really live here anyway." I try to push past him, but he stops me, his fingers circling around my upper arm, keeping me from escaping.

"Who would you go live with, hmm? That supposed boyfriend of yours?"

I try to jerk out of his hold. "He's not my boyfriend."

"You two are just fucking then? Is that what he tells you? He's only using you. And you're letting him."

My father's eyes lock with mine and I physically recoil, desperate to get away from him. Why is he acting like this? Saying such awful things?

"You changed your iCloud password because you've got something to hide," he continues. "I thought I raised you better than this."

"It's not that I have anything to hide, it's that you don't trust me so you think it's okay to invade my privacy! That's not right."

"I am your father. I can do whatever the hell I want. I made you."

I jerk out of his hold, right as my mother appears in the hallway.

"What in the world is going on?" She is so calm. Like ice. Impenetrable.

"I'm leaving."

"Going to the Lancaster residence?" When I nod, she smiles. "Have fun, darling. Don't stay out too late."

Daddy is gaping at her like a dying fish, his mouth opening and closing as if he can't find the right words. "You're just going to let her—leave?"

I march past him, stopping to give Mom a brief hug before I keep walking.

"You need to stop treating her like a little girl, Harvey. I've already told you this. The tighter you hold onto her, the more you'll make her run," I hear her say.

She's so right. He keeps holding me too tight.

And I keep wanting to run away.

# CHAPTER FORTY-EIGHT

## WREN

I ignore my father the best I can for the rest of the week, which is…awful. It's almost Christmas and my birthday, and I should be happy. Eager to spend time with my family and friends—well, Maggie—and creating new memories.

And while I am happy with certain aspects of my life, my relationship with my father is not one of them.

He cancelled the trip to Aruba with Mother's encouragement. Instead of taking the next two weeks off as he originally planned, he's back at the office, which means I don't have to sneak out of the house when I want to leave, which is a relief. And I'm not just seeing Crew either. I also got together with Maggie on Tuesday. We met for lunch and she told me how she ended up having a miscarriage, tears streaking down her face when she told me.

My heart broke for her, but deep down, I wonder if she was relieved. At least she's not forever tied to the man who manipulated and molested her.

If I'm not sleeping, or spending time with Mom or Maggie, I'm with Crew. Which means I'm with him almost every single day, and it's wonderful. Perfect. We already used up all the film that came with my instant camera. I have a ton of photos of Crew with lipstick prints all over his chest and back. I took a couple of selfies with him of me kissing his cheek, my lips vibrant with color. He's sent me a Chanel lipstick every day this week. My mother has enjoyed the gifts too, bringing them to me each time with anticipation dancing in her eyes. Pretty sure she thinks he's worth keeping.

I feel the same way.

I'm with him now, and we're shopping in midtown, strolling past the luxury designer shops, me having to stop and look in every single window, marveling at the gorgeous Christmas displays. Some of the stores are even worthy enough for me to walk into, though I really don't want anything.

"Let's go in here." Crew steers me into the Cartier store. "I need to buy my mother something."

"In Cartier?" I stop in the entryway and tilt my head back, taking in the cream-colored interior. The hushed quality of the room. The giant, sparkling chandeliers hanging from the ceiling.

I've been in high-end shops before. Plenty of times, mostly thanks to my mother. But there are shops that are on a whole other level, and Cartier is one of them.

I feel like I'm in a sacred place. Like church.

"Yeah. This is one of her favorite stores." He's strolling slowly by the glass cases, the glittering jewelry beckoning. A salesperson says hello to him, using his last name and I'm impressed.

He walks into a store on Fifth Avenue and they automatically know who he is. What's that like?

I help him pick out a necklace for her and we wait as they gift wrap it for him, me dawdling over the glass cases full of diamond rings. They glitter and sparkle, mostly simple bands paved in diamonds, though there are some larger rings included in the display.

Crew slides in next to me, his shoulder pressed into mine. "You like?"

"They're beautiful," I admit, wondering if I'm throwing him into a panic. What eighteen- -year-old boy wants the girl he's spending all of his time with looking at diamonds?

"Not as pretty as you." He nudges me. "You haven't seen yourself naked in my bed only wearing lipstick. Now that's beautiful."

My cheeks warm and I duck my head. He took a photo of me the last time we were alone in his room. The sheet draped over my lower half, my hair covering my breasts, the bright pink lipstick coating my lips as I posed for the camera without smiling. Completely natural. He convinced me I was the prettiest he'd ever seen me in that moment, and I believed him, trusting him enough to let him take that photo, nerves jangling deep inside me the entire time.

He studied the photo once it developed, an undecipherable look on his face. When he finally lifted his head, his gaze finding mine, I saw so much emotion in his eyes.

It was almost scary.

Then he attacked me and I sort of forgot all about it.

Until right now.

"Want to go to Chanel?" he asks, once the salesperson hands him his shopping bag.

"Do *you* want to go to Chanel?"

"I want to watch you walk around Chanel if it makes you happy," he says.

"Are you my dream man?" I rest my hand against my chest and bat my eyelashes, making him laugh.

"Fine. I'm partial to their lipsticks. And the girl who wears them." He kisses me and takes my hand, leading me out of Cartier.

We're entering the store minutes later, the imposing security guards standing at the entrance watching us as we walk by them.

"Do you own a Chanel bag?" Crew asks me.

"I have a black wallet on a chain I got for my sixteenth birthday. My mother owns a few and I want them, but she won't give them to me." I laugh. "I don't blame her."

"I'm surprised your father hasn't bought you a bag," he

murmurs as we stop in front of the counter, staring at the various bags on display. "If you could have one, what color would it be?"

"Pink," I say without hesitation. "A mini flap, I think. I don't want it to be too large."

"You've been thinking about this." Crew sounds amused, and I smile at him.

"Every girl at prep school dreams of a Chanel bag at one point or another, don't you think?" I make a face. "I sound like a rich snot."

"You are one," he teases, his expression turning serious when the salesperson approaches us.

"May I help you?" She's a tall, reed thin blonde with deep red lips and a French accent.

"Do you have any pink bags? Specifically, the mini flap?" Crew asks, like he shops for Chanel bags every day.

"Let me check." She turns her back to us as she slides open the compartment that holds an exorbitant amount of Chanel bags.

I wander around the store while Crew waits, stopping at the various displays. The shoes and the jewelry and clothing. It's all so beautiful, like little pieces of art. But if I'm going to invest my money, it's going to be on items that are actual art, not designer clothing or accessories.

I can't lie though. I do love the occasional designer item.

When I come back to stand beside Crew, I see that there are three pink bags sitting in front of him on the counter, the saleswoman hovering nearby.

"Which one do you like best?" he asks me.

The mini flap size is a deeper pink than I would like so that's out. There's a medium Boy bag that's gorgeous, but it's more of a hot pink, and I'm not a fan of the heavy chain strap.

There's a medium flap bag in lambskin with silver hardware that is the most gorgeous pale pink. I pick it up, admiring it before I unlock it and peek inside.

"This is beautiful," I breathe, setting the bag onto the counter.

"It's a gorgeous color," the saleswoman agrees.

"A little big though." I press my lips together, glancing over at Crew.

He's watching me carefully. "You like it?"

"Oh, I do. But it's so expensive. I can't imagine owning something like this. Not yet anyway." I smile at the saleswoman who watches me with faint disdain. She takes the bag and slides it back toward her like I'm going to try and steal it. "Thank you for your help though."

"Of course," the woman says snippily.

"Let's get out of here," Crew mutters, taking my hand. He pulls me out of the store, the two of us laughing once we've escaped, though I can see faint scowl lines at the corners of his eyes.

"That bitch was rude to you."

"It's fine." I wave a hand, dismissing her. "She just thinks we're dumb teenagers wasting her time."

"Maybe I wasn't wasting her time. Did she see what I was carrying?" He holds up the Cartier bag. "I can buy out that entire store."

"Oh stop, Mr. 'I'm a Very Important Man' Lancaster." I push myself into him, sliding my arm around his back. "You sound like such a snob."

"I am a snob." He smiles down at me, some of the tension easing from his features. "I don't like how she treated you."

"It didn't bother me."

"It bothered me." He stops in the middle of the sidewalk, forcing me to do the same, and he cups the side of my face, kissing me gently. "Why are you so damn nice all the time?"

"Why are you so scowly all the time?" I lift up, pressing my mouth to his, and people dodge past us on the sidewalk, most of them grumbling under their breath. "Come on. Let's go get a snack."

"I'd rather snack on you," he murmurs.

I roll my eyes. "We can't go back to your place again."

"Why not? No one is ever there." He grabs my hand and we resume walking. "I can call Peter. He'd be here in ten."

I'm hesitant, not because I don't want to get him alone, but more that I'm worried that's all he wants from me.

Sex.

His actions don't say that, but I also need the words.

Desperately.

Crew lets go of my hand so he can tap away on his phone. Sending a text to Peter, I'm sure. Completely oblivious to the war that's currently raging inside my head.

The doubt pops up every other day or so, when I wonder what exactly Crew is doing with me, and how serious his intentions are. I should be playing the cool girl. The one who doesn't have a care in the world, who knows how to keep it casual and never be too demanding when it comes to a boy.

But I'm not that girl, and Crew knows it.

By the time we're in the back seat of the car and Crew is trying to kiss me, I push him away, earning yet another scowl for my efforts.

"What's wrong?"

I chance a look in Peter's direction before I return my gaze to Crew's. "Is this all we're going to be? Each other's hook-up partner?"

"Is that all you want it to be?" he asks carefully.

I don't want it all put on me. I need input from him. I need to know how he feels about me. I can't make this decision on my own. This is the first time I've ever done anything like this, and I'm completely clueless on how to handle it.

"I—"

He cuts me off. "Because it's not what I want. You really think I want you to be a casual hookup when I'm sending you Chanel lipsticks every day?"

"I don't know how any of this works." I feel helpless. Worse?

I feel dumb.

"I'll tell you how it works. At least with me." He slips his arm around my shoulders, tucking me close to his side, so he can whisper in my ear. "There's this girl, you see. She's sweet. Beautiful. I don't know how she tolerates an ass like me, but she seems to like me all right. And I really, really like her."

Warmth spreads through my veins and my heart swells.

"This is the first time I've ever wanted to spend all of my time with a girl, and it's leaving me feeling...consumed. I can't stop thinking about her. All I want to do is make her smile. Make her laugh. Make her like me," he continues.

I angle my head toward his and whisper, "I do like you."

Crew kisses me, his lips clinging to mine. "I like you too. And I definitely don't want you to be a casual hookup."

Another kiss. This one deeper, with tongue.

"I want you to be mine. And no one else's," he whispers against my lips.

I reach for the neck of his sweater, tugging out the chain with my ring on it. I slip my finger into the ring and gently pull, staring up at him. "No one else has this."

"I know. It means you belong to me. I already told you that."

"I just feel...unsure sometimes," I admit.

He gathers me closer, until I'm practically in his lap. I never did put on my seatbelt. "I never want you to feel unsure again."

"You don't?" I tilt my head back when he presses his mouth to my throat.

"No," he murmurs against my skin. "You belong to me."

He licks the length of my neck, making me shiver.

"And don't ever forget it."

# CHAPTER FORTY-NINE

## WREN

I wake up on Christmas Eve to my mother rushing into my room, her eyes wide, her white silk robe billowing behind her.

"You have a gift," she announces.

Rubbing my eyes, I blink at her, still half asleep. "Where is it?"

"I couldn't carry it into your room. You'll have to come out and see it." She is giddy, practically jumping up and down in one place. And giddy is never a word I use to describe my mother.

I leave the bed and pull on the hoodie that's draped over the back of my desk chair, then slip my feet into the slippers I got for Christmas last year. I follow Mom and she leads me into the foyer where a large brown box is leaning against the wall right by the door.

"Is it one of your paintings?" I ask her.

She shakes her head. "Your name is on it. I had to sign for it."

"Maybe it's the piece I bought from Hannah Walsh." Though I was told it wouldn't be delivered until the beginning of the new year.

Mom goes to the nearby console table and pulls a drawer open, withdrawing a box cutter. "Let's open it."

"Wow. You're prepared," I say with a huff.

"I'm opening boxes like this all the time." She pushes up

the blade and goes to the box, careful as she cuts it open. I watch, anticipation curling through my veins, curiosity leaving me stumped.

I seriously have no idea what's inside this box.

"Do you think it's from Crew?" I ask, not wanting to get my hopes up.

Hasn't he given me enough already?

"It came from a different delivery service, so maybe not," Mom says as she slices the box open with the blade. "Oh, I think it's a painting."

She pulls at the cut cardboard, tossing it aside.

"It's not large enough to be the one I bought," I say, staring at the canvas wrapped in white.

"Tear it off and let's see what it is!" My mother is practically vibrating with excitement. This is the kind of thing she lives for.

My mind is scrambling, but I'm drawing a complete blank. I have no idea what this could be or who it's from.

Crew has sent me plenty, so I doubt it's from him…

"If you don't open it, I'm going to open it for you," she finally says, reaching for the painting.

"Hey, that's mine." I push her out of the way with my hip, making her laugh.

Carefully, I pull the gauzy wrap from the painting, which isn't really a painting at all. My heart's starting to race as it's slowly revealed and my hands begin to shake. I recognize it immediately, of course. The lip prints in multiple colors on white canvas, how they almost cover the entire space. The way all of those lips clustered together seem to undulate.

It's the piece I've wanted for so long.

My heart is beating so fast, it threatens to pop straight out of my chest.

I rest shaking fingers to my lips, tears springing to my eyes the longer I stare at it. Is this moment even real right now? "Oh my *God*."

"*A Million Kisses in Your Lifetime*," Mom whispers, staring at it. "Oh, it's lovely."

"Who sent this? Where did it come from?" I can't tear my eyes off of it. I can't believe it's actually here, sitting in my parents' foyer.

And that it belongs to me.

"I don't know." Mom starts for the discarded box that she left in pieces on the floor. "Let's check the—"

"It was me."

We both turn to find my father standing there, beaming at us.

Mom frowns. "You never told me you were going—"

"Oh Daddy!" I run toward him, wrapping him up in a big hug, crying tears of pure joy against his dark green sweatshirt. I'm guessing he didn't plan on going into work today, and I'm so glad.

I can't believe he did this for me. That he found this piece for me, after all.

"Do you like it?" he asks, squeezing me tight.

"I love it. You know how badly I wanted it." I pull away from him so I can stare at it again, completely enchanted. It's so beautiful. All the various shades of Chanel lipstick. The different shapes of the lip prints. Some of them hard, others soft. All of them on top of each other, layers upon layers of kisses.

And it's all mine.

I could never recreate this, despite what Crew has said. It would never look the same. Would never be as beautiful as this.

"I do, Pumpkin. And now the piece finally belongs to you. Happy early Birthday." Daddy glances over at Mom, who's still frowning. "We should celebrate this moment, don't you think? Let's go out to breakfast."

"I'm not even dressed yet, Harvey." She's watching him carefully, as if she can't...what? Believe he bought it for me? Is she mad that he did? I remember her saying last year when I wanted it so badly that she thought it might be too pricey as a starter piece for me. "And neither is Wren."

"I can get dressed quickly. We'll just go to the diner down the street, right?" It's my absolute favorite, though Mom hates the place. But they have the best French toast, and I'm suddenly hungry.

"Perfect. Whatever you want, since tomorrow is your birthday." He turns to Mom. "Get dressed, Cecily. It's Christmas Eve! We should spend it together as a family."

I stare at the piece once more, unable to look away. I'm as giddy as my mother was only a few minutes before. "Can I take it to my bedroom?"

"Of course, darling," Mom says, her smile brittle. "It's yours now. You can do whatever you want with it."

I carefully grab hold of the piece and slowly walk back to my bedroom, praying I don't trip and put a foot through the canvas.

I would never be able to forgive myself if I did.

Once it's in my room, I prop the canvas against the wall and take a step back, admiring it. It's gorgeous.

Stunning.

All mine.

I clutch my hands in front of myself and start jumping up and down like I'm five, a weird squealing noise leaving me. I can't contain myself, or my excitement. This is like...the best birthday present *ever.*

I should text Crew. Tell him all about it. He'll be so happy for me, though I know he's busy today. He has plans with his family and they were supposed to leave earlier this morning to go to his uncle's house to celebrate Christmas Eve.

Daddy knocks on the door and then barges into my room, a false smile on his face. "Come on, get ready, Pumpkin. We don't have time to waste. I'm starving."

"Hold on." I check my phone to see I already have a text from Crew.

*Hey lazy bird, you up yet?*

I snap a photo of the piece leaning against my wall before I send him a response.

**Me:** *Look what my father got me for my birthday! Can you believe it? I'm in L O V E.*

I then send a string of kissing lip emojis to him.

"Let's go," my father practically demands, and I set my phone down on the nightstand, turning to face him.

"Give me just a minute. Okay?"

"Put on some sweats and let's go. You look fine. I'm going like this." He waves a hand at his sweatshirt and jeans. "And your mother isn't dressing up. It's just the diner."

"I know. Okay, hold on." I find it odd he doesn't leave my room when I change, but I do it in my walk-in closet so I have privacy. I kick off my pajama bottoms, slip on a pair of black sweats, put on my favorite Nikes and I'm out of the closet in less than two minutes. "I'm ready."

He strides toward me, grabbing my arm and steering me out of my room. "Let's go. Like I said, I'm hungry. Can't wait to dig into my favorite chicken fried steak."

We pause in the foyer, waiting for my mother.

"The one dish that Mom says will give you a heart attack?" I'm teasing. Mom used to say that to him all the time when we were on a kick one summer and went there almost every Sunday morning for breakfast. She forced us to break the habit, and I remember thinking she was such a buzzkill.

"That's the one." He smiles and taps his index finger against my nose. "You like your present?"

"I love it so much." I wrap him up in another hug, holding him tight. "I know we haven't really gotten along lately, and I'm sorry. It means so much, that you got me this. It's all I could ever want."

"You're welcome. You know I love you more than anything, right?" He runs his hand over my hair, clutching my head against his chest for a brief moment. The way he does it, just like he used to when I was little and he was my true everything, makes my throat tighten up. And I don't want to cry.

I'm too happy to cry.

"I love you too," I whisper, slowly pulling away so I can smile up at him. When I extract myself from his arms, I turn to find my mother watching us, her gaze flashing with irritation.

What, is she jealous of our relationship again? After we just had that talk? All over a piece she probably didn't want me to have? I don't get it.

I don't think I'll ever understand my mother and her mood swings.

. . .

The French toast is to die for, just as I remember, and the diner is packed with people, every table full and a line of customers waiting to be seated. Christmas music plays over the speakers so loudly, everyone is trying to talk over it, which makes the restaurant beyond noisy, but I am relishing every moment.

Despite my mother's bad mood.

And my father's seemingly cagey nervousness.

I'm too happy to let them bother me for long, still giddy over my early Christmas gift. Or birthday gift. I devour my bacon and French toast, drenching it with maple syrup. Tiny pockets of powdered sugar explode in my mouth with the occasional bite, and I have to hold back the rapturous food moans that want to leave me.

Maybe everything tastes better because I'm so happy. This is like...the best day ever. And it's not even my actual birthday yet.

The only thing missing is Crew. I wish he were here with us to share in this. To celebrate with me. I know he would understand my love for the piece Daddy gave me, and he would be happy for me too. This piece is now mine, forever and always.

It belongs to me.

Like an idiot I forgot to grab my phone when my father

rushed me out of my bedroom, eager to get to the diner, and I left it on my nightstand. He wanted to get here quickly since he figured the restaurant would be packed. Who knew so many people went out to breakfast on Christmas Eve?

"Are you happy, Pumpkin?" Daddy asks at one point, when I'm almost finished eating my breakfast. He's sitting across from me, smiling in that nostalgic way he gets, like he can't believe I'm not his little girl anymore.

"You don't even know how happy I am right now," I tell him with a beaming smile. "I still can't believe you got it for me."

Mom has totally checked out, too busy scrolling on her phone.

Unease slips over me and I can't ignore it, even though I want to. This all feels so familiar, like it used to be between the three of us. What hurts is that I thought we'd fixed this. At least, fixed what was broken between me and Mom. My relationship with my father needed some repair, but I wasn't too worried about it. I knew he'd come around.

Look at him, making me come around first with his present— like a peace offering. He knew I couldn't stay mad at him if he gave me the one piece of art I wanted more than anything else in the world.

I'm still having a hard time believing that it's mine.

My father gets a phone call right when the server drops off our bill at the table and he answers it, rising from the booth seat and covering his phone to whisper to us, "I'll be right back," before he exits the restaurant.

The moment he's gone, I glance over at Mom, who's sitting directly across from me, her concerned gaze meeting mine. "What's wrong? Tell me you're not mad at him for getting that piece for me. I know it must've cost a lot, but I love it so, so much and I swear I'll—"

She interrupts me.

"He didn't get it for you."

I blink at her, silent for a beat. Trying to comprehend what she just said. "What?"

"He's lying to you. I knew it from the start, though I didn't want to believe it."

"I don't understand." I shake my head, baffled.

Mom glances around as if looking for him before she continues, "I know when your father isn't telling the truth. He didn't buy that piece for you. I never thought he did."

"I'm so confused." My chest aches. I feel like I could burst into tears at any moment. If Daddy didn't buy it then...

"It was the Lancaster boy, Wren. It had to have been him."

# CHAPTER FIFTY

## WREN

"No." I slide out of the booth and stand, searching the diner for my father, remembering that he's outside. "No, no, no. He wouldn't lie to me."

"Darling. Sit down." Her voice is firm, her gaze pleading. "We need to talk this through before he comes back."

I plop on the edge of the booth seat, gripping the table in front of me with achingly cold fingers. I'm numb. Humiliated.

Infuriated.

"Your father has been too busy to go in search of it. And he's not going to spend that kind of money on a piece right now, no matter how badly you want it. That piece came from Crew Lancaster. And it makes all the sense in the world, don't you see? He's been sending you Chanel lipsticks for a week. All leading up to the grand finale. *A Million Kisses in Your Lifetime*, indeed. The boy is a genius."

Oh God. She's right. I know she is. Why didn't I see it? Because my father interfered and made his claim so quickly? Did I want to believe he would do that for me so badly that I forgot how it didn't necessarily make sense? Am I that desperate for my father's love and approval?

"I think I'm going to be sick," I croak, swallowing down the nausea that threatens.

She scoots my water glass closer to me and I grab it, gulping down half of it in seconds.

"He knows how upset you are with him, and I've been upset with him too, with his treatment of you. His treatment of me. I ignored it for far too long and allowed him to spy on you and treat you like an incapable child rather than the smart young woman you've become, but no more. You have a good head on your shoulders. Your father doesn't need to constantly monitor what you want to do. You can make your own decisions," Mom says with a finality I've never heard before.

"You really think so?" My voice is small, my emotions chaotic.

She nods, reaching out to rest her hand over mine. "You believe your father can do no wrong, but he has his faults. We all do. He's human, just like the rest of us. I didn't want to cause a scene here, or in front of you, but I couldn't stand it any longer. Allowing him to take credit for a gift he didn't give you is—wrong. I don't understand why he's lying, but he is, Wren. And it's all going to catch up to him."

My chest hurts at his deceit. He had to know he would get caught. "Do you think he took credit for the gift to make me happy? So I wouldn't be mad at him anymore?"

"That's not a good enough reason, but perhaps? He has to know you would find out the truth quickly. Crew will mention it to you—he'll want the credit he deserves. I'm surprised you haven't heard from him yet, asking what you thought of your gift."

I sag against the booth. "I left my phone in my bedroom. Daddy rushed me out of there."

"I'm sure he did," she retorts, shaking her head. "Ah, here he comes now. Pretend you don't know. We can discuss this at home."

I try to keep my expression neutral, but it's hard for me to lie, especially when I'm face to face with the person I'm lying to.

My father slides back into the booth, a smile on his face like he's never done a single wrong thing in his life.

How can he lie to me? I can't take it.

I can't.

"Are you okay, Wren?" he asks, frowning. "You seem upset."

"When did you purchase it?"

"Purchase what?"

Oh, he's playing dumb. He already looks guilty.

"The piece. *A Million Kisses in Your Lifetime.* When did you buy it? How did you find it?" I cross my arms in front of my chest, waiting.

"I bought it...recently."

"From who?"

"The previous owner."

Duh. "And where do they live? How did you find it?"

He chuckles, though he sounds nervous. "Well, we do have connections in the art world, your mother and me."

"I had nothing to do with this," Mom adds, earning a stern look from him.

"Tell me how you found it," I demand.

"Like I said. I have connections. I did a little digging and made a few calls." He's starting to sweat. I see it dotting his hairline.

"Perhaps Veronica assisted you?" Mom asks, her voice dripping with disgust. "I know how helpful she is."

"Leave her out of this," he snaps, his cheeks turning red.

Veronica. The new assistant. Maybe there's more there than I know?

"How much did you pay for it?" I ask him.

"Why are you both ganging up on me? And it's rude to ask how much the piece was, Wren. It was a *gift*," he says, chastising me. He's out of the booth and on his feet in seconds. "Let's go."

"But—"

"We're leaving," he interrupts before he turns and exits the diner.

Mom and I share a look. "It's going to be all right," she tells me. "We can finish this conversation at home."

My stomach sinks. I wish I didn't need to have this conversation at all.

I'm silent the entire walk back to the apartment, as is my father. Even my mother. We're all quiet, the mood somber.

Completely ruined.

How could he lie to me like that? How? I don't understand. I don't know if I ever will. He gets angry at me for my perceived betrayals, and then does the same exact thing and expects us to all accept his lies.

He can't have it both ways.

We're approaching our building when I notice someone standing near the entrance. A very familiar someone, clad in a black coat and jeans, that beanie he always wears covering his hair. He turns to face us and my heart soars.

It's Crew.

Our eyes connect and the thunderous look on his face fills me with worry, though I realize quickly his anger has nothing to do with me.

And everything to do with my father.

"Oh dear," I hear mother say when she spots Crew.

My father, of course, is completely oblivious.

I break away from my parents and run to Crew, a soft cry falling from my lips when he yanks me into his arms and cradles me close. I press my face to his chest, inhaling his familiar, delicious scent, hating what's about to happen, but knowing it has to happen just the same.

"Birdy." He runs his hand over my hair. "We need to talk."

Slowly, I pull away so I can look into his eyes. "I know."

"Crew," my mother calls as they approach. "It's so nice to finally meet you."

I turn, staying in Crew's embrace and my father is watching us, all the color draining from his face when he sees who I'm standing with.

"Nice to meet you too, Mrs. Beaumont." Crew releases his hold on me to go to my mother, shaking her hand.

My father doesn't say a word, but his grim expression is telling. He has to know he's been caught.

"Sir." Crew nods toward him, showing respect, though he probably doesn't deserve it. "I believe there's been a misunderstanding."

Oh, he's being way too polite.

"You didn't buy that piece for me," I throw at my father, unable to contain myself. "I know you didn't."

His expression turns indignant. "Are you calling me a liar?"

I can't believe he's still sticking to his story, especially in front of Crew.

"Harvey, please. Give it up. You've been caught." Her tone is weary. She looks tired, and it makes me realize she's been putting up with him for a long time.

And she might be finally over it.

Crew turns to me, his expression earnest. "I'm the one who bought it for you, Wren. I figured it would all come together, with me sending you the Chanel lipsticks all week? Since that's what the artist used in the piece."

"I should've known." I am in complete disbelief that he did this for me. All for me. Yet it also makes complete sense. The lipsticks. The camera. How he let me kiss him and cover his skin with my lip prints, never complaining. Deep down, I always sensed he liked it.

He would do anything for me.

Everything.

"Who the hell do you think you are, buying *my* daughter such an expensive piece of artwork? She doesn't even know you, and here you come along, always sending her things. Showing off and trying to buy her with extravagant gifts. It's pathetic." My father's face is beet red. I think this is the maddest I've ever seen him.

"*I'm* pathetic? At least I'm not some dried up old man trying to hold onto his daughter by lying to her when controlling her no longer works," Crew retorts.

I touch Crew's arm, hating how cruel he sounded just now, but I guess he's only speaking the truth.

And sometimes, the truth hurts.

"You're really going to fall for this boy, Pumpkin? You know what the Lancasters are like. Heartless. Cruel. He will toss you aside when he grows tired of you, just watch," Daddy says, his gaze pleading. His words are like a punch to the stomach, as if I'm not worthy to keep Crew's attention. That my father thinks so little of me. And Crew. "I only want the best for you, Wren. I'm trying to protect you from him."

My heart sinks, the tears leaking from the corners of my eyes. That he would say such awful things about Crew when he doesn't even know him, just...

Hurts.

"Listen to me, Wren. You are the most important thing in my world. I would never purposely try to upset you. You know this." Daddy takes a step forward, his gaze landing on where Crew's hand rests on my hip when he pulls me into him, his touch possessive. A claiming, like it always is.

It has more meaning now, though. He's sending an unspoken message to my father. I don't belong to him anymore.

"You lied," I tell my father. "You claimed a gift that you never actually gave me. You tried to take credit for something you had nothing to do with."

"I was losing you!" The words explode from my father's lips, shocking me. "You were slipping right out of my fingers and there was nothing I could do about it. I don't want to lose you to—*him*."

"You lied. To. *Me*." I shake my head once when he takes a step toward me and he goes still. If he touches me, I don't know what I might do. Scream? Push him away? Kick him in the shins? "After all this time, you were supposedly worrying about me. Tracking me. Spying on me via my phone. Telling me what I can and cannot do. Claiming you can't trust me over something I did almost six years ago, when all along, I'm the one who shouldn't trust you!"

My breaths are coming fast and I'm dizzy, the anger consuming me so strongly I can barely think straight. I know we're most likely making a scene out in front of our apartment building, but I don't care. The truth needs to be told.

My father needs to know how I really feel.

"You're right."

I gape at him, shocked he would admit his fault so quickly.

"It was wrong, and I'm sorry," he continues, and at least he's owning up to his lie.

But it's a little too late.

I don't have the strength to tell him that though. I'm too overcome with emotion. Crew holds me close, making me feel safe. He doesn't cling too tightly, ever. He gives me the freedom I need, and he respects my decisions. My thoughts. My body. All of me.

Every single bit.

"You're breaking my heart," my father croaks, tears shining in his eyes. Any other day, seeing him like this would destroy me. But not today. "I've always been your hero, Pumpkin. The one you come to when you need help. Don't ever forget that."

"You don't have to be her hero anymore," Crew says, tugging me even closer to him. "That's my job now."

The pain on my father's face is unmistakable. He actually flinches, his gaze narrowing into slits as he studies us.

"You've destroyed my family," he accuses Crew.

"No, Harvey." My mother steps forward, her eyes blazing with anger. "You did that all on your own."

His shoulders sag and he hangs his head.

Just before he turns around and leaves.

• • •

The moment the three of us enter the apartment, Mom marches over to the discarded box where we left it, digging through the mess until she's clutching a tiny white envelope between her fingers, no doubt with a card waiting inside. "For you," she says, bringing it to me.

I take the envelope from her and glance over at Crew, who's watching me carefully.

"Open it," he urges.

With trembling fingers, I tear into the envelope and pull out the card.

*An early birthday present for my Birdy. A million kisses in your lifetime, from me to you.*

*Love,*
*Crew*

I clutch the card to my chest, completely overwhelmed with emotion. The tears flow freely, streaming down my cheeks and I blink hard to clear my blurry vision as I stare at Crew.

"I love it," I whisper. "Thank you."

He touches my cheek, his fingers drifting down to trace along my jaw. "You're welcome."

Emotion swirls between us, seeming to fill the entire room as we continue staring at each other.

My mother clears her throat, drawing our attention. "Wren. Why don't you take Crew to your room and show the piece to him."

I turn to look at her. "That's okay with you?"

Her smile is small. "Of course. I trust you, darling."

I go to her, wrapping my arms around her and squeezing tight. "Thank you. For everything."

"Go," she says, gently pushing me from her arms. "Show him."

She knows how much this means to me. This moment. This piece.

And Crew.

"I love you," I whisper to her before I go to Crew and take his hand, leading him down the hall and to my room. He follows me without a word, but the moment I pull him inside and shut the door, he's on me, pressing my body against the wall, his arms wrapped tight around my waist.

"I'm sorry," he says, raining kisses all over my face. "That I had to show up and confront your father like that, but I couldn't let him take credit for my gift for you."

"It's okay." I revel in the softness of his lips, the sincerity in his voice, and the careful way he's holding me. "I'm glad you came. I'm just sorry I didn't figure it all out sooner. My mom had to tell me."

"Don't apologize. I get it. Really, Birdy. You wanted to believe he would do that for you." He leans back, studying my face. "Are you all right?"

"It hurts, how little respect my father has for me." My throat is raw, my eyes burning.

"I wish I could take away your pain," he says, and I can't help it.

I stare at him in disbelief, wondering where the cruel, brooding Crew went. He's been replaced with this sweet, sexy, thoughtful man who only wants to take care of me, and...

I love it.

I love him.

I do. I'm in love with him.

"I'm just glad you're here." I glance over at the piece leaning against my wall, and he does the same. "I love it so much."

I love *him* so much, but how do I tell him that?

It's scary, how strongly I feel about him. Does he feel the same way about me?

"I knew you would." He kisses my temple and I lean into him.

I should've known Crew gave it to me. All the clues were right there, staring me in the face, and I was so blinded by the idea of my father wanting to earn back my trust and forgiveness, I went along with his lie.

But my eyes are open now. Thanks to my mother. I would've found out eventually, and I still can't believe I didn't see it, but now I know.

Crew was the one who went in search of it and found it, and God knows what he paid for it, but he gave that piece to me because he wanted to see me happy. He said that to me, only yesterday, at the Chanel store.

"Happy Birthday," he whispers, and I return my gaze to him.

"I still can't believe you did this."

He hesitates, frowning. "It's what you wanted, right?"

A sob escapes me and I cover my mouth, nodding as yet more tears spill.

Crew presses my head against his chest, and I can feel the steady beat of his heart. "Aw Birdy, don't cry."

"I'm fine. I'm perfect." And I'm still crying. This day has been so completely overwhelming. Good. Bad.

Wonderful.

"I don't like it when you cry." Crew's voice is strained. "The piece was supposed to make you happy."

"*You* make me happy," I tell him, pulling away slightly so I can stare at his handsome face. "I can't believe you would do this for me."

His voice lowers, his expression gravely serious. "I would do anything for you, Wren. Just to see you smile. Hear you laugh. Remember what I told you?"

I nod, sniffing loudly.

"Instead, you're crying like I killed your cat."

"I don't even have a cat," I mumble, making him smile.

"Soon you'll have two pussies," he says, referring to the painting I bought at the gallery that day, when he followed me. Took me to lunch.

Kissed me in the back seat of his private car.

I laugh. Cough. Sniff. I'm a mess. "You're right. I will."

We're quiet for a moment and I eventually disentangle myself from his arms to grab a tissue, wiping the tears from my face.

"I love the note you wrote me," I say.

God, that note. Who knew Crew Lancaster could be such a romantic? I didn't realize he had it in him.

But that's what he's been doing. Romancing me for the last couple of weeks. Making me feel special. As if he thinks I'm special. That he cares for me. Maybe he even loves me.

I think he does.

I really, really do.

"I've been on the hunt for it since you told me about it," he admits.

I'm gaping at him. "You hated me then."

"I did not," he retorts.

I laugh, all the sadness leaving me at hearing him get all growly and grumpy. "You found it all on your own?"

"Actually, Grant helped me locate the owner." He smiles. Shakes his head. "He's such a dick."

"The previous owner?"

"No, my big brother. He put me through some shit while we were trying to get it. But all I cared about in the end was owning it, and now it's yours."

"It's such an extravagant gift," I murmur, my gaze returning to the piece, drinking in all of those kisses on the canvas.

"You gave me something you can never give anyone else, and I wanted to do the same for you," he admits, his voice low.

Oh God. When he says stuff like that, I don't know what to do, or how to react.

Now I really want to jump him.

"Thank you," I whisper, smiling at him when he enfolds me back into his arms. "I'll cherish it forever."

"Just like I'll cherish you." He doesn't add the word forever, but I think I know what he means.

A realization hits me and I glance up at him. "Weren't you supposed to go to your uncle's house today?"

He shrugs one shoulder. "I came back when I got your text."

"What?"

"When you sent me that text and it said your dad got you that piece, there was no way I could spend Christmas Eve with my family while your dad was lying to your face." His expression is fierce. "I had to tell you the truth. In person."

Rising up, I press my mouth to his, kissing him with everything I've got. His lips part and I tangle my tongue with his, until his hands are roaming and I'm whimpering, shoving him away from me.

"We can't get carried away," I say, breathless.

His grin is devastating. "Always my good girl."

My cheeks go warm. "Stop. We'll take things too far and you know it. I don't want to break my mom's trust."

He runs a hand through his hair, blowing out a harsh breath. "Let's go and hang out with her then."

I frown. "You want to hang out with my mother?"

"Sure. We need to get to know each other. And I get the feeling she approves of me. I mean, look what I got you. Pretty impressive."

Joy flows through my veins and I laugh.

"You don't mind if I hang out with you and your mom, right?" He raises a brow.

"I want you to," I say, smiling.

"Tomorrow afternoon, you want to come over to my place? It'll just be me and my parents and brothers. Charlotte won't be there, which is too bad. I really want you to meet her."

The tears threaten yet again. He wants me to be with his family. And he wants to spend time with my mother. Oh God, this is serious. "I want to meet her too."

Of course, it's serious. He bought a painting that cost him well over five hundred thousand dollars. Maybe even a million.

I know he's a Lancaster and that is probably like, twenty dollars to him, but still.

What he's done for me is just...no one has ever made me feel so special.

So loved.

"Thank you again for my gift," I say again, hating how meaningless my words feel. "I absolutely love it."

"You're welcome." The look on his face is one I've never seen before, and I wish I could take a photo so I'd have it forever. "Happy Birthday, Birdy."

# CHAPTER FIFTY-ONE

## WREN

Christmas morning.

My birthday.

I wake up slowly, not wanting to get out of bed and face the day. Not yet. I roll over and crack my eyes open to find the piece of art staring back at me, and I smile.

*A Million Kisses in Your Lifetime.* That's what I want. I want someone to promise me a million kisses and more. Someone who will cherish me and love me and only want to see me happy.

And I think that someone is Crew.

I sit up in bed, brushing the hair out of my face as I reach for my phone to see I have a text from him.

**Crew:** *Happy Birthday.*

**Crew:** *Merry Christmas.*

**Crew:** *I sent you something.*

I actually gasp out loud. He needs to stop spending money on me.

I also love how he said happy birthday first.

**Me:** *Thank you. Merry Christmas! Stop sending me gifts.*

**Crew:** *Stop telling me what to do.*

So grouchy.

**Crew:** *When are you coming over?*

**Me:** *I need to spend some of the morning with my mom.*

I don't want my mother to be alone on Christmas. How depressing. My dad? I don't really care what he's doing.

Okay fine, I care. I want to be callous and unfeeling, but that's not my style. I'm still hurt by what he did with Crew's gift to me. I think he came home late last night, long after I went to bed, and never actually spent Christmas Eve with us beyond the disastrous breakfast, which I know hurt Mom. She didn't say anything to me about it, and we got dressed up and went out to dinner after Crew left, just the two of us, which was fun, but I know she had her suspicions on where Dad went.

And I think some of them have to do with Veronica, the assistant.

If he's actually cheating on her, after everything they've struggled with lately, I know...

This will be the end of their marriage.

**Crew:** *It's a low-key day for us. There will be food and my asshole brothers. My parents. My dad is an asshole too, but he'll be on his best behavior when he meets you.*

I love how he calls all of the males in his family a-holes. Sometimes, he acts like one too, ha.

**Me:** *I'll text you when I'm ready to leave.*

**Crew:** *Want me to send a car?*

**Me:** *Tell me Peter has Christmas Day off. Please! He deserves it.*

**Crew:** *He does. It'll be someone else driving.*

**Me:** *I can find my own way over there.*

**Crew:** *No. Let me send a car. I want to make sure you get here safely.*

I smile. Why is it when my father does stuff like this, it feels controlling and belittling, yet with Crew, it feels like he's only protecting me?

Maybe because he believes in me. Tells me I can do things no one else can. When he looks at me, I can see the respect in his gaze. The admiration.

I feel the same way about him.

**Me:** *Okay. Send me a car then. I'll text you when I'm ready.*

**Crew:** *Text me after you open your gift.*

**Me:** *I will. Or do you want me to wait? I can bring it over to your house.*

**Crew:** *No fucking way. You open it in front of my brothers? They will give me endless shit.*

Hmmm. I wonder what it could be.

**Crew:** *Go open it, Birdy. And when you can, text me. Or even better, FaceTime me. I want to see your pretty face.*

**Me:** *Okay. I lo—*

I backtrack that last statement, deleting it hurriedly. I was about to tell him I loved him. What in the world?

Wait.

There's no denying that I *do* love him. I'm in love with Crew Lancaster, and I need to tell him how I feel. Does he feel the same way?

I hope so.

**Me:** *Okay. Give me a few.*

I send the text, my heart racing from my realization.

I climb out of bed and put my slippers on before I leave my bedroom. I head for the living room, where I hear Christmas music playing softly. The sound of my mother talking to someone—she must be on the phone. Maybe calling her sister. My aunt lives in Florida and I wish I could see her more, but I'm always away at school when Mom goes to visit her.

Which lately has been often.

When I enter the living room, the Christmas tree is lit with twinkling white lights, an array of presents lying beneath, all wrapped in cream and dark green wrapping paper. There's one gift that stands out though.

The stark white box that is signature Crew.

"Oh, she's awake. I should go. Yes, I'll talk to you later. Merry

Christmas!" Mom ends the calls and smiles at me. "Happy Birthday, darling. Your aunt says Happy Birthday too."

"Thank you. I should call her later." I settle on the floor, staring at the presents.

At one in particular.

"Oh, she'd like that. We can call her back." Mom smiles, reaching out to brush my hair away from my face.

"Where's Daddy?"

Her expression hardens. "He's not here."

My mouth falls open. "Where is he?"

She shrugs. "He never came home."

"Oh, Mama." My heart breaks for her. I rise up and scoot over to her chair on my knees, wrapping her up in a hug. We cling to each other for a moment, and I close my eyes, disappointed in my father. That he would abandon her—us—so completely. On Christmas Day.

On my birthday.

"It's okay, sweetie. It's been bad between us for a while. I was trying to keep it together through the rest of the year like your father asked, but I am definitely filing for divorce in January. I can't pretend any longer." She pulls away slightly so she can look at me. "We haven't been in a good place for at least a year. Maybe longer."

I frown. "He told me you were trying to work it out after all."

Her frown matches my own. "When did he tell you that?"

"After your divorce announcement. He called me and said he had good news. That you two were going to counseling and wanted to make it work," I explain.

A sigh leaves her, and she shakes her head. "We never had that conversation. It was always going to end in divorce. He knew that. He asked if we could be civil to each other for the rest of the year. Specifically, when you were home. I agreed only because he seemed so concerned for your wellbeing."

"More like was saving face in front of me," I mutter.

"Or trying to convince himself that things would eventually be okay. It's hard to face your problems, especially when you're the one creating the majority of them." Her smile is faint, tinged with sadness. "Let's forget about him and focus on your birthday. And Christmas."

I force her to open her present from me first—the little carved wooden bird I found at that store in Vermont.

"Is it a wren?" she asks as she studies it. "It looks like one."

"Maybe? Crew found it. Said it reminded him of me," I admit.

Her expression softens when her gaze meets mine. "I think he really likes you."

Such an understatement.

"I think so too," I admit.

"It's not every day someone buys a very expensive piece of art for someone else, just because they're friends," she continues.

"I know. He said he just wanted to make me happy." I'm feeling misty-eyed just thinking about it.

"Is he kind to you? Honest with you? Does he make you laugh?"

*Yes. Yes. Yes.*

"He is the very last person I ever imagined myself with," I say, blinking back the tears. What is with me and crying the last couple of days? I'm so emotional. "But now I can't imagine my life without him."

"Ah, darling, I'm so happy for you. And I love my gift." She smiles down at the wooden bird. It looks so rustic now that it's in our showcase of an apartment, but hopefully, she really does like it.

"I have more for you." I hand over a small box with a pair of earrings I found here in the city, and she loves those too.

I open the presents from my parents. Some clothes. A Louis Vuitton scarf with lip prints scattered all over it—I sense a theme here. A couple of gift cards to my favorite stores. A necklace I admired a long time ago that I forgot all about it, which makes it extra special since she remembered and bought it for me.

I've unwrapped everything for me except the box from Crew, and I stare at it, letting the anticipation curl through me.

"Aren't you going to open it?" Mom asks.

My heart starts to thump extra hard when she hands it over. "I almost don't want to know."

"Of course you want to know. Don't be silly." She waves a hand at me, clearly impatient. She's enjoyed this week and my gifts almost as much as I have. "Open it."

I pull the lid off to find another black and white box almost the same size, wrapped with the signature white ribbon and camellia flower that indicates it's from Chanel.

Oh God, I think I might know what it is.

I pull the lid off. Push back the tissue paper to see a black protective bag surrounded by boxes of lipstick. I pull out the bag, the lipsticks falling to the bottom of the box, and open the drawstring.

"He got you a bag? Oh, he is so, so clever. I love this boy. I do," Mom says, making me laugh.

I pull the bag out to see it's the pink one I admired in the store only a couple of days ago. And when I undo the clasp and peek inside, there's no paper stuffing filling it.

Just box after box of lipstick.

"Is there a note?" Mom asks.

I find it at the very bottom. A small white envelope, as usual. I open it, his familiar handwriting scrawled across the card.

*Merry Christmas. I bought you every shade of lipstick Chanel carries, so you can create your own million kisses in your lifetime. Hopefully you'll share some of those kisses with me.*

*Love,*
*Crew*

"I'm keeping him," I announce, making my mom laugh.

"You definitely should," she says, her gaze on the pink bag sitting on my lap. "He chooses well."

"I picked out the bag. I told him if I could have any Chanel bag, I wanted it to be pink," I admit.

"You've always loved pink. And the lipsticks. That's very romantic. He understands you, doesn't he?"

"I guess he does." For the first time, I feel understood. Utterly and completely.

"I need to call him."

"Go on, call your boyfriend," Mom urges as I get up, the purse clutched in one hand and my phone in the other. "You're going to see him today, correct?"

I stop and turn to face her, suddenly sad. "I don't want to leave you alone."

"Oh, darling, don't worry about me. I'll be fine. Go be with him. Spend your birthday with him. I know that's what you want. I'm grateful we had last night together. And this morning." Her smile is sad. "I've wasted too much time being upset with you and your father when I should've inserted myself into your life more. I'm sorry about that."

"You don't have to apologize," I tell her. "Not anymore."

She shakes her head. Sits up straighter. "Go call him. I'm sure he's waiting to hear from you."

Smiling at her one last time, I dash off to my bedroom, closing the door for privacy. I FaceTime him and after a couple of rings, he picks up, his handsome face filling my screen. He's a little more disheveled today compared to yesterday. His hair is rumpled and stubble lines his cheeks and jaw.

I hold the pink bag up in front of me, showing him.

"You got it."

"I love it." I drop the bag onto the bed beside me. "And all the lipsticks. You really bought every color Chanel makes?"

"All four hundred of them. Didn't you notice how full of lipstick that box was?"

"There were lipsticks in the bag too."

"That was a special request. They don't normally put anything in the bag when you purchase it. I bought it from another salesperson by the way. A much kinder, older woman who helped me," Crew explains.

"I love it." I pause, the words heavy on my tongue, and he sends me a knowing look.

"Don't say it, Birdy. Not now, when we're FaceTiming each other." His smile is smug. "Save it for when we're actually together."

I burst out laughing. "How did you know?"

"Because I feel the same way."

# CHAPTER FIFTY-TWO

## CREW

"You're pathetic."

This is the first thing Grant says to me when I return to the living room after my quick conversation with Wren.

"Oh, leave him alone." This comes from Grant's girlfriend, Alyssa. She has no fear in telling him what to do, and I think he respects that. Begrudgingly. I know I respect it. No one talks to Grant like she does. "He's in love."

Even a day ago, I might've denied it, but come on.

I am definitely in love with Wren Beaumont.

Purchasing *A Million Kisses in Your Lifetime* for her birthday present more than confirms that. Sending her a Chanel bag and spending a shit ton of money on four hundred lipsticks more than proves it too.

The piece proved tough to find. Tougher still to actually purchase it from the previous owner. That guy did not want to give it up, no matter what we quoted, and he held out for a while. He also made me sweat, and Grant loved every second of it, the dick.

But money talks and Lancasters have plenty of it. I eventually acquired that piece my girl loves so damn much. For a cool 1.2 million dollars.

"If being in love makes me pathetic, then I guess you are too," I tell my brother, sounding like I'm five.

"Stop fighting," Mother says, her tone mild. "When is she coming over, Crew? And will she be here for dinner?"

"She should be here soon. And yes, she'll stay for dinner. It's her birthday."

Mother's eyebrows shoot up. "What? Today?"

I nod.

"We must celebrate then. I'll talk to the chef. We already had something planned, but it needs to be extra special. And we should have a cake! Oh my." She rises to her feet and scurries to the kitchen, calling out to her staff.

"You really spent a million bucks on a painting for her?" This comes from Finn, my second oldest brother. He's kicked back on the couch, clutching a glass of orange juice loaded with vodka.

It's not even noon yet. Guess he needs it to cope with all the family time we've experienced the last couple of days, which he normally tries to avoid.

Not that I can blame him. It's the one good thing about being trapped at Lancaster Prep. I only see my family for major holidays.

"I did," I say with a nod as I make my way over to the windows that face the city, stopping next to the massive pine tree that's strung with white lights. Mother went all out this year. The entire place reeks of pine, which isn't a bad thing. "And it's not a painting."

"What the hell is it then?" Finn asks.

I turn to look at him. "The entire piece was made with lipstick."

Finn frowns. "Come again?"

"Someone kissed the canvas. Over and over and over again in different shades of Chanel lipstick," Alyssa explains, her sheepish gaze meeting mine. "When Grant told me about it, I had to do a little research. I was intrigued."

"It's her favorite piece." I shrug. And all I ever want to do is make that girl happy.

No matter the expense.

No matter what.

"I can see why. It's beautiful," Alyssa agrees, bringing it up on her phone and showing it to Finn.

He studies it, frowning when he lifts his head. "I don't get it."

I sigh. Grant calls him a dumbass. Alyssa just shakes her head.

"I'm afraid you don't have a romantic bone in your body," Alyssa says to Finn, who also happens to be her former boss.

"I have one particular bone that's not romantic." He chuckles. Takes a sip of his drink, rattling the ice in his glass while Alyssa looks on at him with disgust.

Just another day with the Lancasters.

Mother comes storming back into the living room, seemingly out of breath. "Tell your lovely girl to bring a dress with her, Crew. We're going to have a formal dinner tonight."

Aw shit. "Seriously?"

"Yes. Do it right now, young man, before she leaves her house. We're dressing up!" Mother turns to Alyssa. "Did you bring something appropriate to wear for a formal dinner, dear?"

"Actually, I did." Alyssa smiles serenely, calm as can be despite my mother's endless efforts at rattling her. You learn quickly that you always need to be prepared when you're spending time with the Lancaster family. You never know what might happen next.

"Oh. That's fine then." Mother sniffs, seemingly disappointed she didn't cause an issue.

I feel sorry for Alyssa. It's a huge responsibility, getting involved with the oldest Lancaster son. My parents will put her through the motions, and will do their best—especially my mother—to drive her away. If Alyssa stands her ground and doesn't back down, she's golden.

But it's going to take a long time for her to gain their approval.

Those expectations aren't on me and Finn, as unfair as that

sounds. Poor Charlotte had to marry right as well, being the only female. Not that our father particularly cared where she ended up, considering her children would never be Lancasters.

My family is actually pretty fucked-up. Poor Wren.

Knowing her, she'll just kill them with kindness. She's just that sweet.

By the time she actually arrives, I'm anxious, and my palms are sweating. I know I saw her only yesterday, but I'm dying to get my hands on her. And when I receive the notification that she's headed up the penthouse elevator, I go out into the corridor to greet her.

The ding sounds and the elevator doors slide open, revealing Wren standing there in her puffy black coat and the pink Chanel bag I gave her hanging from her shoulder. She's carrying a duffel bag and a shopping bag full of wrapped presents, and there's a giant smile on her face when she walks out.

Straight into my arms.

I hold her close, breathing in her familiar, floral scent. "I missed you."

"You saw me yesterday."

"And it still felt too long." I squeeze her. Kiss her forehead. Savor the feel of her in my arms.

God, Grant was right.

I am pathetic.

Pulling away from her, I take her bags. "You ready to meet my parents?"

Her eyes go wide. "Are they really that bad?"

"Nah." I'm trying to go easy on her.

She stands up taller. "I'm not scared. Let's do this."

"Who are the presents for?"

"You." She smiles. "Your parents. I didn't get anything for your brothers though."

"Those assholes need nothing," I reassure her.

She laughs. "You're always calling them that."

"Because that's what they are."

"They can't be that bad." She wrinkles her nose.

"Just wait and see."

...

My brothers watch their mouths around Wren, which I appreciate. Father doesn't seem that interested in her, but who is he ever interested in? Grant, and that's about it. The rest of us can go to hell.

Alyssa senses an ally and makes plenty of conversation with her, which eases Wren's nerves. I appreciate what Alyssa is doing, and tell her as much as we get ready to open presents.

Grant better marry her soon—no one tolerates his grumpy ass like she does.

Mother loves Wren. I can tell by the way she looks at her. The things she says. The gift she gave my parents—a set of tree ornaments in Tiffany blue crystal from Tiffany's.

The gift she gives me is small. Sentimental. A five by seven framed map with a red dot on the gallery I followed her to in Tribeca.

"These are more for where a couple first met," she says, her cheeks pink as she explains it. "But the gallery is where everything...changed for us."

I stare at the framed map. The red dot that's really in the shape of a heart. Too bad it's not a pair of red lips. "I love it."

"Do you really? You don't think it's cheesy?"

I lean in and press my mouth to hers. "Nothing you give me is cheesy. I love this."

"You two—" Grant starts, but Alyssa slaps her hand over his mouth, muffling whatever else he wanted to say.

"Are very cute," Alyssa finishes for him.

Grant rolls his eyes. Finn snorts.

I say nothing. Just smile at the girl who has my heart.

Shit. That's still a little hard for me to wrap my head around.

Once presents are opened, everyone splits off in a different direction, and I drag Wren back to my bedroom. I'm about to shut the door when she stops me.

"We should leave it open."

I frown. "Why?"

"Isn't it a little...inappropriate?" She makes a face.

Ah, my innocent birdy. Still so sweet.

Leaving the door partially open, I go to her, pulling her in for a kiss. She responds immediately, pressing her lush body to mine, her arms circling my neck and her fingers diving into my hair. I break the kiss first, staring into her eyes.

"Tell me you want that door to remain open."

"I'm not having sex with you on Christmas Day with your family here," she whispers.

"It's not Christmas. It's your birthday."

"Whatever." She shakes her head. "Are we really dressing up for dinner?"

"Oh, get ready. My mom lives for that shit."

"I like her. Do you think she likes me?"

I kiss her again. "Definitely. She liked your gift."

"I'm glad. I really struggled with it." Her gaze goes to her brand-new Chanel bag sitting on the foot of my bed. "I love my gifts from you."

"Oh yeah?" I run my fingers through her silky soft hair, staring at her pretty face. I could look at this face forever and never get tired of it. "I probably went overboard."

"You so went overboard." She grins before kissing me. "I loved it though. That you bought me *A Million Kisses in Your Lifetime*..."

"You loved it."

"So much."

"I meant to send you a blank canvas but forgot," I admit.

She laughs. "We can go buy some."

"You'd remake it for me?"

Her brows shoot up. "You'd want me to?"

I nod. "Definitely. I like the idea of a canvas hanging in my house with your lipstick prints all over it. A million kisses just for me."

She throws herself at me, her body colliding with mine just before she kisses me. I hold her close, my hand clutching the back of her head as I devour her mouth, my tongue sweeping, tangling with hers. I break away to whisper against her lips the three words I never believed I would say to Wren Beaumont.

"I love you."

Her shiny eyes meet mine. "I love you too."

"I meant what I said when I gave you *A Million Kisses in Your Lifetime*." I pause. "I want to give you that in real life too. I want to be the one you always want to kiss. The only one you wear Chanel lipstick for."

Her smile is huge. Blinding. "I don't want to kiss anyone else. Just you, Crew. Only you."

She kisses me again to prove it.

# CHAPTER FIFTY-THREE

## WREN

It's New Year's Eve. My least favorite holiday of the year. I'm at the Lancaster residence with my boyfriend. His parents went to a party and they're staying the night at the hotel where the festivities are being held, and Crew promised we'd be all alone.

Just the two of us.

But the moment I show up at his apartment, I realize he tricked me, and I don't mind at all. There are people from school there. People I know and like, including Maggie. Lara and Brooke. I spot Ezra and Malcolm talking in a corner, the both of them laughing. Balloons crowd the ceiling with long curling ribbons, all of them pink and gold and white. Pink roses cover every available space and there's a tower of champagne glasses on a table, each one full of the bubbly liquid.

I spot a pink and white cake on another table, surrounded by presents.

It's everything I described to him that night. Every single thing.

I glance up at Crew, who's watching me with so much love shining in his eyes.

"You threw me a party," I whisper.

"A New Year's birthday party," he says, grabbing hold of my hand and pulling me in for a kiss. "I hope you don't mind."

I'm so overwhelmed I'm afraid I might cry.

"I don't mind," I croak, grateful he holds me close so I can sniff into his shoulder, closing my eyes tight so the tears don't leak.

"You look beautiful, Birdy," he murmurs when I finally pull away.

I'm wearing a sparkly white dress. The sleeves are poufy and the bodice is deep, showing plenty of cleavage. The skirt is extra short and I leave a trail of iridescent glitter everywhere I go.

"Thank you. So do you."

Crew is in a suit. Black. White shirt underneath, the top buttons undone, no tie necessary. He looks handsome and sexy, and every time his gaze lands on me, my skin goes hot, because I know what he's thinking about.

Me and him, naked. That's happening soon, after the guests leave. But right now, I want to go say hi to everyone.

So I do.

I make the social rounds, Crew by my side, like we're a real couple, which we are. There's a table laden with catered food and plenty to drink, and eventually I get a plate, loading it with food before I grab a glass of champagne from the tower and sit with Maggie, drinking and eating while we catch up with each other.

It feels so good, spending time with my friends and knowing Crew is nearby, always with a steady eye on me. He mentioned to me a few days ago that he and Ezra talked it out, and they're not angry at each other anymore, which makes my heart happy.

Eventually someone starts playing music and it's so loud, people start dancing. The alcohol is flowing.

It's turned into a real party.

"Have a drink, Wren!" Ezra encourages and I shake my head.

"I'll wait until midnight," I tell him, sending a secretive glance in my boyfriend's direction.

"Aw come on—"

"Leave her the fuck alone, Ez," Crew says, effectively shutting his friend up.

I can't help but giggle. He's still so grouchy. But never really toward me.

When it's close to midnight, I end up standing by the Christmas tree, staring out at the city's glittering lights. The heavy scent of pine still lingers, and I glance over at the tree, taken by the white lights. Crew comes up to me, I see his reflection in the window. He wraps his arm around my middle, his hand splayed across my stomach as I lean into his solid weight behind me.

"I want to tear off this dress." He streaks his fingers across my stomach.

"If you tear it, I'll hurt you."

He chuckles near my ear. "So ferocious. You've learned how to step it up, Birdy."

Thanks to him. And my mother. And my own self. I don't need to be scared and worried all the time. I can do things on my own.

I can be my own person. I don't need anyone's help—unless I ask for it.

And it's perfectly okay to ask for it.

"It's eleven-fifty-two," he whispers in my ear. "Want to be naked and in my bed by midnight?"

"No. We have guests," I say primly. "I want to be right here with glasses of champagne and we can toast each other when the clock strikes twelve. What do you think?"

"I think you're trying to reenact your deepest fantasy," he says.

"I think you want to reenact my deepest fantasy, thanks to this party you threw me," I remind him.

I remember how I told him about this not so long ago. How I wanted to have a combination New Year's Eve/birthday party. Yet my birthday is over. The year is almost finished.

A new year is dawning and my life is about to change. It

already has.

In the best possible way.

"How about we toast each other, kiss right at midnight, and then you can take me to your bed and do whatever you want to me," I suggest to him.

"Fuck, are you serious?" I glance up at him to see that hopeful expression on his face and I want to laugh.

"I'm dead serious." It's the least I can do after everything he's given me. Besides, I'll benefit from it no matter what.

"I can get Ez and Malcolm to kick everyone out eventually."

I smile. "Sounds like a plan."

"Let me grab some champagne."

He leaves me standing by the tree and I turn toward it, lightly touching the branches. The delicate ornaments hanging there. They're all white and some look made of spun glass. Delicate snowflakes and trees. Thin glass balls and twisted candy canes.

"Here you go." Crew hands me a champagne glass full of golden, bubbly liquid while keeping one for himself. The music shuts off and the TV is turned on, one of those New Year's Eve countdown shows on. "We've got three minutes till midnight."

"Getting closer." Nerves fizz in my stomach, and for once on this night, they feel good. They feel right. This new year is going to be one full of endless possibilities. Big changes. An exciting future.

People start passing out hats and noise makers, and I take one, blowing it in Crew's face. He grimaces, snatching it out of my hand.

"What color are you wearing tonight?" He's talking about my lips.

"Sensible is the name." I smile, desperate to take a sip of my champagne but wanting to wait for it to hit midnight first. "You like?"

"I love all the colors on your lips so far. Best gift I could've ever given you—and myself."

"You never did tell me how the salesperson reacted when you made your request," I tease him.

"She thought I was joking." He chuckles. "I then launched into a long explanation about the art and the story behind it, and when I was finished, she said she would love to help me." His gaze finds mine. "She told me I must really love this girl and I told her yeah. Actually, I do."

My heart is overflowing with emotion at what he just said. The way he's looking at me. The crowd gathers together around the TV, some of them standing close to us, and Malcolm has a noise maker, which he blows at us, making me laugh.

"The countdown is almost on!" someone announces.

"Less than a minute," Crew whispers, and I realize I don't want to watch it on TV when we could look out the window and witness part of the actual countdown happen outside. We'll be able to see fireworks at least.

"Let's look out at the city," I suggest, and we both turn to stare out the window, our backs to everyone.

He's watching me. And I'm watching him. When everyone else starts to count down, he does too, his voice soft.

Just for me.

"Ten. Nine. Eight. Seven. Six."

I join him.

"Five. Four. Three. Two. One."

"Happy New Year, Birdy." His face is so close, his lips brush mine when he speaks.

"Happy New Year," I murmur just before I kiss him.

Despite the yelling and shouting from our party goers, I also can hear the dull explosions of fireworks shooting into the air. The roar of people welcoming the new year down on the streets. I pull away, to watch the fireworks. Red and white blasts of color fill the sky, and Crew slips his arm around my shoulders, tucking me into him, his glass clinking next to mine.

"To the new year," he says.

"To the new year," I repeat before we both take a drink.

The champagne fizzes in my throat and I take another sip, eventually draining the glass. Crew does the same, taking my glass from me and setting them on a nearby table before he grabs my hand and leads me back to his bedroom.

We forget about everyone else. We're only focused on each other.

It's dark inside, the curtains open to let in the light from the skyscrapers, and when he pulls me to him, I go willingly. A soft moan leaves me when he races his hands up and down my sides, his fingers gathering the fabric of my dress.

"I can't get enough of you," he says just before his mouth is on mine and I open to him completely, my tongue darting out to meet his. The kiss is decadent. His mouth tastes of champagne and when his hands slip beneath the hem of my dress to land on my bare backside, I shiver.

He goes completely still. "You don't have panties on."

"I don't have a bra on either," I tell him.

The hungry gleam in his eyes sends heat rushing between my legs and he quickly turns me around so my back is to him. He drifts his fingers across my exposed skin before tugging on the zipper. Pulling it down until the dress becomes loose on my body, falling forward. He pushes it off of me with impatient hands until it's a heap around my feet and I kick it away, about to slip off my gold stiletto sandals when he stops me, his hand resting on my naked hip.

"Keep them on," he practically growls.

I do as he asks, and when he turns me to face him once more, our mouths meet hungrily, his hands seemingly everywhere at once. On my waist, my hips. My breasts. My nipples. He cups me between my thighs, his fingers teasing, dipping inside, and I relax my thigh muscles as much as I can, wanting more.

"I want to fuck you against the wall."

My entire body lights up at his suggestion.

Hmm. We've never done that before.

Next thing I know I'm against his bedroom wall, close to the windows, the city lit up before us. In the recent past, I would be freaking out, afraid someone might see us. Me. Completely naked.

Now I don't even care. I'm too drunk on desire for him. The need to feel him moving inside my body overpowering everything else.

Slowly, he presses his fully-clothed body into my naked one and I hiss out a breath, my skin coming alive at the brush of his shirt and pants on my skin. He kisses my neck, his hands lightly resting on my hips, his mouth drifting down to my collarbone. My chest. He bends his knees, his lips wrapping around one nipple, and I thrust my hands in his hair, holding him to me.

"Fuck, you're beautiful," he murmurs against my chest, his hand slipping down to stroke between my legs. I'm wet. I can hear his fingers slick through my desire, and I close my eyes, lightly banging the back of my head against the wall. Overcome already by his touch.

When he rises up and takes my mouth once more, his fingers still busy between my thighs, all I can do is let him stroke me, my knees threatening to buckle. He circles and rubs my clit, pleasure spiraling through me, and I know I'm close. I reach for his belt buckle, fumbling with it so badly, he bats my hand away and takes over. Undoes the belt, unzips his trousers and then I'm the one who's slipping my hand into his pants, curling my fingers around his erection.

Next thing I know, I'm being lifted up, my legs going around his waist, his erection free and right where I need him the most. He slams into me so hard I lose my breath, his cock sliding in and out of my body while I cling to him, my mouth open against his neck, my arms wrapped around his broad shoulders. His hips piston against mine, his speed increasing with his every thrust, and I go completely still, already on the verge of an orgasm.

He knows just how to touch me—and where. My whimpers are an indication of what I want, where I want it, and he knows.

Already he understands my body and can give it exactly what I want.

What I need.

My climax comes out of nowhere and is so strong, I struggle to breathe, my mind a complete blank. The only thing I can concentrate on is the intense tremors wracking my body. Radiating throughout my limbs. It goes on and on, like it's never going to stop, and I swear at one point, my heart stops beating.

He comes too, a low groan sounding from deep in his chest, rippling across my skin. When it's over, he presses me into the wall with all of his weight, my sweat-covered skin clinging to his clothes, our bodies still connected. He throbs inside me, his breath harsh, irregular. His mouth close to my ear.

"I like watching you when you come," he whispers, and I duck my head, still shy sometimes, which is silly.

He has seen me naked so many times over the last few weeks, it's not even funny.

I nod, still unable to speak. Too overwhelmed by what he makes me feel.

Everything we do together—especially this—feels so good, so right. I'm connected to him in a way that I don't have with anyone else.

Not my friends. Not my family.

No one.

Just him.

His mouth brushes my ear as he whispers, "I can make that happen again."

"I know you can." I smile. I wonder if he can hear it in my voice.

"I do it all the time," he continues.

A soft laugh leaves me.

"You laugh, but you know it's true." He nips my lobe with

his teeth. "I can make you come again and again. All night, if you'll let me."

A soft sigh escapes me, and when he nuzzles my neck, Crew whispers, "Say something."

"I love you," is what I tell him, and he lifts his head so he can stare into my eyes.

"I love you too." His smile is one of pure satisfaction.

"Take me to bed," I demand.

"Why?" His hands slide over my bare butt, as if he's going to carry me to the bed—with him still inside my body. "Are you tired?"

He's teasing me.

I shake my head. "I want to ring in the new year properly. For the rest of the night." I kiss him, my tongue darting out for a lick. "With you."

Crew pulls out of me and lowers me to my feet. I'm kicking off my sandals when I notice something, and I reach for his jaw, turning his head to the side when I see it.

Lip prints all over his neck.

"I need to take a photo," I start to say, but he grabs hold of me and carries me over to the bed, falling on top of it with me.

"No, you don't. You have a lifetime to do that, remember?" He kisses me, stealing my breath, but not quite stealing all of my thoughts.

I rest my hand on his chest, stopping him. "Do you think this is going to work? Really?"

His smile is slow. Breathtaking. He touches my cheek. Drifts his fingers across my skin. "Yes, I do. No one else tolerates my rude ass like you do."

I burst out laughing, joy making my chest hurt. "And no one else understands me like you do."

He kisses me. "There's one."

I frown. "One what?"

"Kiss. I think I'm going to keep track of how many kisses I

give you from now on."

"That's impossible."

He kisses me again. "You think so? Watch me."

Another kiss.

"That's three."

And another one.

"Four…"

I climb on top of him, silencing his new countdown with my lips.

We don't need to keep count.

I know he's going to give me at least a million more.

# EPILOGUE

## CREW

*TWO YEARS LATER...*

We're at my parents' house in the Hamptons, celebrating Christmas. Why we're out here, I'm not quite sure, but my mother wanted to do something different this year, and she didn't want to spend it with the other Lancasters.

"We have our own family now," she explained. "With Grant and Alyssa, and Perry and Charlotte. Oh, and you and Wren. And soon there will be plenty of grandchildren."

She told me this at Thanksgiving, when she called me. Talk about making my balls shrivel up.

"Yeah, well, don't expect any grandchildren from us yet," I told her with a nervous chuckle.

Wren just shot me a dirty look, though her eyes were dancing, as if she found my sudden pain hilarious.

She's a bad girl.

My bad girl.

Presents were already opened earlier this morning. Brunch had been served hours ago and now we're getting ready for dinner. A formal affair, we've all been notified that the men wear suits and the women wear semi-formal dresses.

This sent Wren into distress.

"I don't know what to wear." She has four dresses hanging on the closet door, contemplating them as she chews on her fingernail.

I come to stand beside her, tilting my head to the side. "I like that one."

It's black and stretchy looking, the fabric shot through with silver sparkly thread. It'll cling to her like a glove and have me lusting for her the entire night.

I'm into torturing myself when it comes to Wren and her unequivocal hotness, so I'm down.

"Really?" She waves a hand at the dress covered with gold sequins. "I like that one better."

I shake my head. "Save that one for New Year's."

She turns to smile at me. "That's a good idea."

Decision made, she grabs the dress and goes inside the walk-in closet to put it on, shutting the door behind her.

"I've seen you naked before," I remind her.

Soft laughter is my answer.

"Why are you getting dressed in there?" I shuck my jeans and slip on a pair of black trousers, realizing I'll only be able to change into half my outfit because my shirt is hanging in the closet, which is currently occupied by Wren.

"I want it to be a surprise," she tells me.

I tear off my sweater and stand there waiting for her shirtless. She takes her sweet time, which I know is how she operates, yet I'm impatient anyway. She fusses over her tits and worries they'll look too big and I have to reassure her that they're perfect. Because they are.

Just like she is.

The past two years we've spent together nonstop, traveling the world. We decided to forego college and get some real-life experience, with Wren adding to her growing art collection during our travels. She came into a small trust fund when she turned eighteen from her mother's side of the family, and she's been investing wisely in unique pieces of art ever since.

I might buy her a piece or two, but she deters more than encourages my indulgence in her. Her parents recent divorce and subsequent division of assets has put worry in her, and I hate that.

The Beaumont art collection is a wondrous thing, and it was recently sold in two separate auctions with Sotheby's. Her parents made an absolute killing. Cecily has already started a new collection.

Wren cried both days of the auction, too overcome at the loss of all that art. She doesn't know about the piece I bought for her at a different auction, a piece her mother spotted in the Sotheby's catalog and called me right away to tell me about it.

She will soon enough though. As in tonight.

We've traveled all over Europe. Spent a month in Japan. A summer in the Canadian mountains. Two weeks in Switzerland. We return to home base because it's necessary, and Wren likes to catch up with Maggie, and Lara and Brooke, who are all going to college in New York City. Plus, she wants to spend time with her mother.

Her relationship with her father still isn't the best, and there was even a period where she didn't talk to him at all, but they're speaking more now. She even went and saw him yesterday for Christmas Eve, which was a huge step. He's living with Veronica, who no longer works for him. She hates art, but she does love spending Harvey's money.

Figures.

It's not trendy, spending the holidays in the Hamptons, but my mother has always wanted to be more of a trendsetter. More like she's adopted that Lancaster trademark *I don't give a shit* attitude the rest of us have.

Wren's mother is here as well, because I asked her to come. I want her to witness what is about to happen tonight, because it's a game changer.

A life changer.

"Okay, ta da!" Wren kicks the door open, and she throws her arms out, that dress clinging to her sexy as fuck body, just like I knew it would.

My gaze roams over her, not sure where to land first. "Holy shit."

"What do you think?" She turns, revealing that the back of the dress is completely open before she whirls back around to face me. "You like? Oh, I can already tell you do."

I lunge for her, my hands on her waist, my mouth on hers. She presses her hands on my chest, holding me off yet again. "Where's your shirt?"

"In the closet where you were."

She slides her hands down, her fingers curling around the waistband of my trousers. "I think you should go to Christmas dinner just like this."

"Fine." I tug on the neckline of her dress, the stretchy material moving freely, until one perfect tit is hanging out. "And you get to go like this."

"I don't think so." She lets go of me and tucks herself back in, mock glaring at me. "You need to finish getting ready."

As I get dressed, I do my best to ignore the nerves growing within me, hoping this too observant girl doesn't figure me out just yet. She's seemingly oblivious, her good mood wearing off on me, until I can't help but smile too.

This is what she does to me. Makes me happy. Lifts me up. Doesn't let me get away with being a total asshole—most of the time. She's sweet and fun and smart and interesting and I enjoy spending every day with her.

And though we're young and she's only just turning twenty fucking years old, I know without a doubt, I don't want to live my life without her. I need to make things official.

Hopefully, she'll say yes.

We eventually leave the guest room we're sharing and head

downstairs to the formal dining room, where everyone is waiting. Drinks in hand and appetizers readily available. Wren's mother is talking with Alyssa, who is very pregnant with Grant's baby—a girl. Just knowing he's going to bring a female into the world has changed my brother completely. He's nicer to all women, and won't let our father say one bad word about the first grandchild being a girl.

Even though he wants to, the misogynistic old bastard.

Finn came to the Hamptons alone—perpetually single and happy about it. Charlotte is with her husband Perry, and though they've been through a lot, they look happy. In love.

Dad is slinging back scotch and Mother is fussing over the flower centerpieces. Wren goes to help her—my girl still loves to fuss too—and while she's distracted, I make sure the piece I had delivered earlier is where I instructed it to be placed. I check my pocket to make sure the ring is still there, and yeah, it hasn't grown legs and ran off.

Fuck, I'm nervous.

"I have an announcement," I call to the room and everyone turns to look at me, questioning expressions on their faces.

Especially Wren's.

Praying like hell I don't fuck up my prepared speech, I launch into it.

"So there was a girl I didn't know who walked onto campus our freshman year, and I thought she was the most beautiful girl I'd ever seen. I hated her on sight."

My brothers laugh. So does my father. My mother just sighs and shakes her head.

Wren smiles at me, already knowing this story.

"There was something about her that I saw in myself, though I never truly believed we had anything in common. How could we? She was the complete opposite of me, or so I thought. Until we had psychology together our senior year. And our teacher paired us up for a project. I learned a lot about her, and she learned a lot about me. And yeah, we were also drawn to each other, so now here we are. Together for the last two years. The best two years of my life." I smile at her, and she smiles in return, her expression suddenly nervous too.

Does she know what I'm about to do?

"I realized that what I saw in her before wasn't what I saw in myself. Not at all. Wren isn't like me. She's an actual part of me. And I can't imagine my life without her in it."

The room has gone completely silent. Wren's eyes shine with unshed tears.

"You might hate me for this, doing this on your birthday and Christmas but…" I go to her and drop to one knee, taking her hand in mine. "Wren, I love you so damn much. Will you marry me?"

I reach inside my pocket and pull out the ring I chose just for her.

A single diamond solitaire, round cut. Simple. Three carats. Large enough, but not over the fucking top like the rings worn by every other Lancaster bride that's ever existed.

And it's dangling off the stick of a cherry Blow Pop.

"Oh my God." She bursts out laughing, her cheeks turning pink, and I smile. "Really, Crew?"

"Answer me, Birdy." I hold the lollipop—and the ring—out to her.

"Yes," Wren whispers, her gaze meeting mine as she nods over and over again. "Yes, yes!"

I pull the ring off the Blow Pop and slip it on her finger, and she splays them out, the diamond winking up at her and nearly blinding me.

Rising to my feet, I pull her into my arms, kissing her senseless. Someone starts to clap and soon the entire room is filled with applause. Even my father is clapping and smiling, and that's quite the accomplishment.

"Oh my God, I love you," Wren says just for me, kissing me

yet again.

"What the hell is up with the Blow Pop?" Finn asks, his gaze dropping to where I still clutch it in my hand.

"Private joke," I tell him.

Wren smacks my chest lightly, smiling.

Her mother approaches us, pulling me in so she can deliver a quick kiss to my cheek. "I am so proud to have you as my future son-in-law."

"Thank you." Cecily and I have always gotten along. We both only want the best for the most important person in our world.

Wren.

"Are you ready to give her the other present?" Cecily asks.

Wren gasps, her wide eyes on me. "There's *another* present? Crew, if you keep this up, you will eventually never be able to top yourself."

I just laugh. "I'm not worried about that. And yes, Cecily. I'll go grab it."

I walk into the small sitting room that's connected to the dining room and grab the canvas before I bring it into the dining room for Wren to see. The moment she spots it, she covers her mouth with her hand, her eyes wide with shock.

Her gaze goes to her mother, and then to me. "Where did you find this?"

"Sotheby's," Cecily answers for me. "There was another auction. One that got overshadowed by ours."

There's sadness in Wren's mother's eyes, and I understand why. Losing her marriage, her art, hasn't been easy for her. But she's strong. She's already doing so much better.

Wren drops her hand to her side and slowly approaches the piece. Another one by the same artist, this one untitled, though it matches *A Million Kisses in Your Lifetime*. Made at the same time but smaller, with those multi-layered Chanel kisses all over the canvas.

"I thought this one went missing," Wren says, her gaze sliding over to me.

"Thank your mom. She found it. I just bought it."

She turns to her mother, smiling at her before she rushes me, wrapping her arms around me so tight I swear she's got me in a stranglehold. She kisses me in front of everyone, pulling away so she can murmur, "You're in trouble now."

I frown. "What do you mean?"

Her mouth finds mine yet again, soft and sweet, and I drown in her taste. Loving that this woman is mine. All mine.

When the kiss is over, Wren smiles, the sight of it stealing all the air from my lungs.

"Now you owe me two million kisses."

# Exclusive Bonus Content

# WREN

'm nervous.

I've never had a real someone to give a Valentine's Day gift to before. Oh, when I was in elementary school, I handed out Valentine's Day cards to my class each year, just like everyone else. I even saved extra-special cards to give to the boys I thought were cute. When I was in the third grade, I helped my mom make heart-shaped sugar cookies, and we frosted them pink so I could hand them out to my classmates.

But that's it. I had no boyfriends, no real crushes. My dad sent me roses when I was thirteen, but I remember thinking they didn't count. I wanted someone other than a family member to send me flowers.

More than anything, I craved a *real* boyfriend—someone who was madly in love with me and wanted to shower me with sweet words and wonderful gifts. My younger, hopeful heart dreamed of a boy who would love me unconditionally and treat me like a queen.

Now I have my dream boy.

Crew Lancaster.

If you'd told me when I first started at Lancaster Prep my freshman year that I would fall in love with Crew and he would fall in love with me, I would've laughed in your face. He seemed so grumpy all the time. Always scowling and glaring at me whenever I walked past him. I ignored him because he scared me. He was too much. Too intense.

Smiling, I shake my head. Maybe we wasted a lot of time, but I have no regrets over how we connected in psychology class. He's a different person now. No more scowls, no more moody glares aimed in my direction. When he looks at me, all I see is love. When he speaks to me, all I hear is the kindness in his voice.

And when he touches me? I want to melt right into him. Want to feel his strong arms wrap around my waist and never let me go—

The knock on my dorm room door startles me, and I suck in a sharp breath.

"Birdy, are you in there?" Crew's deep voice rumbles from the other side of the door.

Scrambling off the bed, I take his Valentine's Day present and stash it in my closet, flipping my hair behind my shoulders before I run my hands down my uniform skirt, smoothing it out. Pasting a smile on my face, I open the door, my heart tripping over itself when I see Crew standing there waiting for me.

I drink him in for a moment. He looks so handsome in his school uniform, his golden-brown hair flopping over his forehead when he tilts his head to the right, that slight smile curving his lips as he contemplates me. "Happy Valentine's Day."

Before I can say anything, I realize he's holding a pink heart-shaped box stuffed full of pink roses in his hands, and he thrusts it toward me.

My heart threatens to burst out of my chest, I swear. "For me?"

"No, they're for Miss Taylor." He rolls his eyes, his mood playful. "Of course they're for you."

Ugh, he's too handsome. I can barely look at him right now. School is going to start in a few minutes, and there are people everywhere, getting ready to walk over to campus.

But all I'm thinking about is when I can next get him alone.

I take the box from him, the scent of the roses hitting me, making me smile. "They're beautiful."

"You're beautiful." He glances to the left, then the right, before returning his gaze to me. "Let me in your room for a minute."

It's my turn to check out who's around us, panic filling me at his suggestion. He loves to push me out of my comfort zone. "Crew..."

"Just do it, Birdy. Only for a few minutes." He takes a step forward, crowding me, and I back up into my dorm room, Crew following me inside. He shuts the door and leans against it, watching me, his hot gaze raking over me from head to toe. "You look good."

I throw my arms out like I'm exasperated, which I sort of am. What if someone catches us in my dorm room alone and with the door closed? We'll get in trouble, even if he is a Lancaster. Or maybe we won't. He does seem to have a lot of pull. "I look the same as I always do."

"Which is gorgeous." He pushes away from the door and heads straight for me, his gaze never straying. "You like your Valentine's gift?"

"I love it," I whisper, a shuddery breath leaving me when he wraps his arms around my waist and pulls me to him. "I love you."

"I love you, too." He kisses me, my lips automatically parting, his tongue sweeping the interior of my mouth. I grab hold of the lapels of his uniform jacket, trying to get as close to him as possible. He finally breaks the kiss first, pressing his forehead to mine.

"Let's ditch school," he whispers.

"We can't."

We're quiet for a moment, the only sound our mingled breaths until he speaks.

"Always my good girl, aren't you."

Crew doesn't say it as a question. This is just how I am, and he accepts me no matter what. "We should go to class."

"But what about my gift?" He lifts his brows.

My smile is secretive. "I'm giving it to you tonight."

"Oh yeah?" He raises his brows.

I nod, slowly extracting myself from his embrace. "Hopefully you'll like it."

"If it's anything like what you gave me before Christmas, I'm going to love it," he says without hesitation.

I burst out laughing. I bought a sexy bra and panty set when we went to Vermont, and I can only assume he thinks I've found more lingerie.

"That wasn't a gift for you," I remind him as he opens my door. "I bought it for myself."

"Pretty sure I'm the one who thoroughly enjoyed that particular gift," he drawls.

My entire body flushes hot. "What I got you for Valentine's Day is even better."

He snags my hand as we exit the dorm room and head down the hall. "I can't wait to see it."

# CREW

All day I'm distracted, thinking about Wren. Though there's nothing really new about that. I'm always thinking about Wren.

When can I talk to her again. Look at her again. Make her laugh again. Kiss her again. Get her naked again.

Pretty sure I'm addicted and not looking to give up this overwhelming need for her anytime soon.

By the time school is over, I'm jonesing like a junkie who

needs his fix, eager to get my hands on my girl. I wait for her outside, grateful for the early spring–like day. The sun is shining, and there's no snow on the ground. The seasons are changing, and we're getting closer to the end of school. Eventually, we'll graduate, and I can't wait.

Once that happens, we'll finally be able to start our lives together.

I spot Wren before she notices me, and I watch her walk, her short skirt swaying. How good her legs look with the white knee-high socks and black Mary Jane shoes on her feet. She's got this sweet-yet-sexy way about her that gets my blood pumping every time I look at her.

I'm a complete sucker for this girl. I can't wait to take her back to my room and have my way with her—

"What are you doing here?"

I blink, realizing it's Wren asking me that question. "Waiting for you."

"I need to go back to my room first and get your present." The pout on her face is so cute I kiss it off.

"I'll go with you," I murmur against her lips.

She takes a step back, shaking her head. "I'll meet you at your room."

No one bothers us there. It's where we spend the most amount of time together, because we're isolated. Alone. Just the two of us.

"You promise?" I ask.

Smiling, Wren nods. "Always."

Twenty minutes later, she's knocking on my door before she walks inside, a giant, bright red gift bag dangling from her fingers. She's also changed out of her uniform and is wearing a pale pink dress with puffy sleeves and a short, flouncy skirt that hits about mid-thigh.

"Birdy, you look good enough to eat," I tell her. Her dress makes me think of a pretty pink cupcake. A sexy pink cupcake.

Is there even such a thing?

"Stop." She's blushing when I go to her and wrap her up in my arms, kissing her before she can say anything else. The bag slips from her fingers and falls to the floor, and she's pulling away from me, a panicked gasp escaping her as she bends down and grabs the bag. "For you."

Wren holds the bag out toward me, and I take it from her. "What is it?"

"Open it up and see," she says almost shyly.

I toss the pale pink tissue paper out of the bag, my fingers curling around the edge of a canvas, and I immediately know what it is. I pull it out of the bag and stare at the canvas for a while, my heart thudding extra fast.

There are kisses all over it in various shades. My own version of *A Million Kisses in Your Lifetime*, made just for me.

"It took me way longer than I thought it would," she says, sounding nervous. "Like...hours. And I made a complete mess of myself. I had lipstick all over my face, especially my nose. I looked ridiculous."

"I love it." My gaze is still on the canvas. On Wren's lip prints. There are so many, layers and layers of them, just like the original. "Did you use the lipsticks I bought you?"

Her laughter sounds nervous. "Of course I did. I have four hundred of them."

"Did you use all of them?" I finally lift my gaze to hers, wondering if she can feel the love I have for her.

It overwhelms me, the depth of my feelings for this girl. Especially with moments like this. I never thought I could love someone as much as I love Wren, but I do. I'm never letting this woman go. I hope she knows that.

I hope she feels the same way about me.

"I didn't use all of them," she admits, her nose wrinkling. "Some of the shades wouldn't go with the color scheme I've got going on."

Chuckling, I take the canvas and set it on top of my desk so it leans against the wall. "I love it."

"I'm so glad."

I snag her hand and pull her into my side, wrapping my arm around her shoulders as we both stare at the canvas. "Thank you. It's the best gift you could've given me."

She tilts her head back when I look down at her, a giant smile on her pretty face. "I'll make another one for you."

"You will?"

Nodding, she reaches up, cupping my cheek. "I'll make you a million of them if you want me to."

"That might be too many." We both laugh, and I sober up quickly. "I feel like I didn't give you enough gifts for Valentine's Day. Only flowers. And dinner."

Her eyes light up. "We're going to dinner?"

"I made reservations at that Italian place downtown." I tug her closer, dropping a kiss on her lips. "We have just enough time to fool around before we go."

"Ha! You wish." She tries to shove at my chest, but I don't budge. "And you've already given me everything I could ever want, Crew. The roses are perfect."

"Yeah?" I kiss her again, like I can't help myself. "I think you're perfect."

She smiles, and I can feel her mouth moving against mine when she speaks. "I love you, Crew."

"I love you, Birdy."

"Happy Valentine's Day."

# ACKNOWLEDGMENTS

I wrote this long ass book in a short amount of time because yet again, I found myself consumed with a Lancaster. I know Sylvie should've been the next book out, but … Crew came to me like Whit did last year. In December, he started whispering in my ear, urging me to create a Pinterest board. A playlist. I was furiously writing in my notes on my phone until I realized, hey. Just write the book.

So I did. And now you're holding it in your hands and hopefully you enjoyed it. Crew is no Whit. I can't duplicate him, he's one of a kind. Crew is nicer than Whit, even though he started out like a jerk. But once he really fell for Wren, he pulled out all the swoony moments. Gah.

The piece *A Million Kisses in Your Lifetime* actually exists. Go look it up. It's cool. There really is a very wealthy couple who got a divorce and split up their massive art collection – I read an article about them in December. What is it about December that is so inspiring for me? Drew Callahan came to me in December 2012 …

Fun fact: I lost 12,000 words on this book in the middle of January. That's … a lot. I was devastated. I CRIED. At one point during this moment of crisis, I was going to put it on the back burner and focus on something else. But they wouldn't let me go. By this point, they literally consumed me. So I rolled up my sleeves and wrote like a woman possessed (I was). I listened to the playlist on repeat while writing. Those songs are them and their story and I've never been more obsessed with a playlist. Some of the songs come from Euphoria (they have such great music).

By the way, Crew is Charlotte Lancaster's little brother and you'll meet her in The Reluctant Bride. She marries Perry Constantine – reluctantly. Oh just wait! I adore them too!

As always, a giant thank you to everyone who reads my books. I cannot do this without you, and you mean so much to me. I also want to thank everyone at Valentine PR for taking care of me – Nina, Kim, Daisy, Kelley – you ladies are the best! Nina, thank you as always for your insight. You made the ending of this book that much better.

Thank you to my editor Rebecca and proofreader Sarah for all that you do. And to Serena for her solid notes. Jan for her love and enthusiasm and edits/graphics. Huge shout out to Emily Wittig for bringing the cover in my head to life. And for being such a sweetheart.

p.s. – If you enjoyed **A MILLION KISSES IN YOUR LIFETIME**, it would mean the world to me if you left a review on the retailer site you bought it from, or on Goodreads. Thank you so much!

*A Million Kisses In Your Lifetime* is an emotional romance that ends in a satisfying happily ever after. However, the story includes elements that might not be suitable for some readers. Reference to drug use and bullying are included in the novel. Readers who may be sensitive to these elements, please take note.

an imprint of Entangled Publishing LLC